Wed...

For better, forever...these marriages were meant to last!

Three passionate novels!

In October 2007 Mills & Boon bring back two of their classic collections, each featuring three favourite romances by our bestselling authors…

WEDDING BELLS

Contract Bride by Susan Fox

The Last-Minute Marriage by Marion Lennox

The Bride Assignment by Leigh Michaels

MISTRESS MATERIAL

The Billionaire's Pregnant Mistress by Lucy Monroe

The Married Mistress by Kate Walker

His Trophy Mistress by Daphne Clair

Wedding Bells

CONTRACT BRIDE
by
Susan Fox

THE LAST-MINUTE MARRIAGE
by
Marion Lennox

THE BRIDE ASSIGNMENT
by
Leigh Michaels

MILLS & BOON
Pure reading pleasure

DID YOU PURCHASE THIS BOOK WITHOUT A COVER?
If you did, you should be aware it is **stolen property** as it was
reported *unsold and destroyed* by a retailer. Neither the author nor
the publisher has received any payment for this book.

*All the characters in this book have no existence outside the
imagination of the author, and have no relation whatsoever to anyone
bearing the same name or names. They are not even distantly inspired
by any individual known or unknown to the author, and all the
incidents are pure invention.*

*All Rights Reserved including the right of reproduction in whole or
in part in any form. This edition is published by arrangement with
Harlequin Enterprises II B.V./S.à.r.l. The text of this publication or
any part thereof may not be reproduced or transmitted in any form
or by any means, electronic or mechanical, including photocopying,
recording, storage in an information retrieval system, or otherwise,
without the written permission of the publisher.*

*This book is sold subject to the condition that it shall not, by way of
trade or otherwise, be lent, resold, hired out or otherwise circulated
without the prior consent of the publisher in any form of binding or
cover other than that in which it is published and without a similar
condition including this condition being imposed on the subsequent
purchaser.*

® and ™ *are trademarks owned and used by the trademark owner
and/or its licensee. Trademarks marked with* ® *are registered with the
United Kingdom Patent Office and/or the Office for Harmonisation
in the Internal Market and in other countries.*

*Harlequin Mills & Boon Limited,
Eton House, 18-24 Paradise Road, Richmond, Surrey TW9 1SR*

WEDDING BELLS
© by Harlequin Enterprises II B.V./S.à.r.l 2007

Contract Bride, The Last-Minute Marriage and *The Bride
Assignment* were first published in Great Britain by Harlequin
Mills & Boon Limited in separate, single volumes.

Contract Bride © Susan Fox 2003
The Last-Minute Marriage © Marion Lennox 2004
The Bride Assignment © Leigh Michaels 2003

ISBN: 978 0 263 85526 5

05-1007

*Printed and bound in Spain
by Litografía Rosés S.A., Barcelona*

CONTRACT BRIDE

by

Susan Fox

Susan Fox figures she's lived enough of her life in the city to consider moving back to the country. Her country dream home would include a few pygmy goats to take care of the lawn, a couple of ponies for granddaughters Arissa and Emma, a horse or two for herself, and whatever stray cats or dogs might happen by looking for a home. Until then, she fears she'll have to make do with a lawn mower, three always-up-to-something cats and two very naughty but adorable stray kittens.

Susan loves to hear from her fans. You can contact her via her website at susanfox.org

PROLOGUE

THEY married that morning in front of a judge at the county courthouse. Because the brief ceremony wasn't so much a celebration as it was a legal technicality, their witnesses were a couple of law clerks the judge had called into his chambers at the last moment.

His Honor didn't comment on the somber stillness of the bride and groom, though he took several moments to study and remark upon the handsome infant boy wrapped snugly in a light blanket, who slumbered peacefully in his father's arms.

The judge had heard gossip about the couple before him. The groom had been widowed nearly four months ago when his wife had suddenly died a handful of days after the baby's birth. The bride had been his dead wife's best friend.

No doubt some, when they heard about this, would consider the hasty marriage a small scandal. Maybe it was, but His Honor was inclined to go easy on them. He knew Reecc Waverly socially and by reputation. Leah Gray had graduated high school in the area and sometimes taught Sunday School.

The judge could tell at a glance that this was no

love match, and that made him hesitate to perform the legalities. Reece's stern face held the haunted traces of a man who'd been poleaxed by tragedy; his bride's face was pale and she had a faintly heartsick look about her. If either of them had consulted him about this ahead of time, he would have strongly advised them against taking such a drastic step so soon.

But since both were legal adults competent to make agreements and bear responsibility for them, he summoned the impartiality of his status as a judicial official and led the couple through the formalities.

CHAPTER ONE

LEAH WAVERLY entered the den, relieved to see that her husband of eleven months was standing at the patio door instead of working at his desk. With one hand braced on the door frame and the fingers of the other wedged in his front jeans' pocket, Reece stared out broodingly at the lengthening shadows on the patio out back.

She knew he'd heard her nearly silent tread on the carpet because she'd seen the subtle ripple of tension in his wide shoulders. Yes, he'd been tense around her lately, but she'd also caught a hint of restlessness and what could only be dissatisfaction. Had he recovered enough from Rachel's death to take a good long look at what they'd done?

The question had eaten at her for weeks and she could no longer bear her dread of the answer. Better to get it into the open, better to know for sure...

However carefully she worded this, Leah already knew that her husband's response would never be the one she'd hoped for. Reece had buried his heart when he'd buried Rachel, and whatever heart he'd had left, he'd dedicated solely to his young son. There was nothing left for the plain woman he'd so suddenly married, and as the months had stretched on, Leah had become more certain of that by the day.

She knew Reece well enough to be sure he'd never ask for a divorce. Because he wouldn't, it was up to her to offer it. She was certain he'd be relieved, and once she assured him she was willing to work out a peaceful arrangement to share custody of little Bobby, he'd be grateful to be able to get on with his life.

Though she'd known from the beginning this time would come, she'd had the foolish hope that Reece might develop some kind of affection for her. Male/female friendships often deepened into love. Maybe not the intensely passionate kind that he'd shared with Rachel, but certainly the low-key, mutually caring kind.

And yet as time had gone on, Leah had been forced to realize there was simply nothing between them. There'd not been a single word of personal caring, never so much as a passing glance to misinterpret. She was certain now there never would be. She'd finally reached the conclusion that she loved Reece enough to want to see him happy again, even if his happiness would never be with her.

What she regretted with all her heart was that Bobby would grow up being shuttled back and forth between a father and adoptive mother who'd made such a foolish bargain. Though Reece had married her to protect the boy if something should unexpectedly happen to him as it had to Rachel, in hindsight it was obvious to Leah—and probably to Reece by now—that it would have been more prudent to wait.

But a man who'd been devastated by the sudden death of the woman he'd been wildly in love with, trusted more in cruel tragedies that struck out of the blue than he did in the more mundane and temporary events in life, at least for a time.

The fact that Leah had essentially taken advantage of Reece's worries for her own selfish reasons was something she'd probably never forgive herself for. That's why she had to do this for him. She wasn't certain how much longer she could live with him anyway, because the heart-numbing distance between them was already too painful.

When Reece lowered his hand from the door frame and turned, Leah felt again the heavy ache of longing and love she'd secretly been tortured by for years.

Reece Waverly was a big man, over six foot tall with wide shoulders, muscle-thick arms and long, powerful legs. He'd showered before supper, and the clean jeans and white shirt he wore were still crisp. Perpetually somber and taciturn, his tanned, weather-creased skin made him look rugged and harsh. His bluntly masculine face was made even more dramatic by his dark eyes, black eyebrows, and the formidable set of his strong jaw. The thin slash of his lips carried a hint of ruthlessness Leah had never seen evidence of.

And yet the look of him now was worlds different in every way from the man he'd been when Rachel had been alive. He'd been a softer, less intimidating man, more given to smiles and teasing glances. He'd been more open, more apt to speak since he was a well-read, thinking man who enjoyed being sociable. He'd had a sense of humor and a masculine charm that was irresistible.

But Reece had been on top of the world then, completely in love with Rachel, and looking forward to the birth of their first child.

Leah so missed the man Reece had been—the man she'd felt such guilt for loving—almost as much as she missed Rachel.

A fresh wisp of heartache went through her, and she almost lost her nerve. She had to force herself to make a start.

"Is it still convenient for a talk?"

The dark eyes that had regarded her almost blindly for months were suddenly sharp on her face, and she felt the pressure of that sharpness as they examined every soft feature. But then his gaze met hers and she felt the probe of it go so deep that she got the alarming sense that he'd read her thoughts.

And maybe he had, because his somber expression appeared to harden.

"You don't ever need an appointment, Leah. I told you that earlier."

Leah brought her hands together primly at her waist, not really surprised that they were trembling. "You did," she said gently, "but you looked deep in thought."

His gaze narrowed the slightest bit. It was clear that he was alert to something in her face and in the way she held herself. Since she was stiff with tension and couldn't stop the faint tremors of dread that passed through her in waves, it was no wonder he was taking a closer look.

His gruff, "Go ahead and have a seat," was a relief, since she'd feel steadier sitting. Leah chose one of the wing chairs on his side of the room, and noted that he stayed standing where he was, his back to the patio doors and the rapidly darkening twilight.

As always, he kept himself remote from her. As always, she was careful not to trespass. Leah sank down and rested her elbows on the chair arms then laced her fingers together to let them dangle over her lap. She tried to collect her thoughts, but it was supremely hard to do.

Oh God, if she thought there could ever be a chance for Reece to care for her, she wouldn't do this. But the utter deadness between them was proof enough that Reece would never feel anything for her. Leah made herself begin with something mild.

"You haven't given your answer yet about going

to Donovan Ranch for the barbecue next Saturday, so I thought I'd tell you that whatever you choose to do, I've decided to go."

Leah saw a glimmer of something shoot through Reece's gaze, and though wary of it, she managed to keep her voice casual and even.

"I've made arrangements for someone to take care of Bobby. Unless you'd like to have a day and an evening alone with him."

Leah finished with, "If you decide to go, we could either use the sitter or take Bobby with us. There'll be other children there, so he'd enjoy that."

"When did you decide this?" The near growl in his low voice gave the clear impression of disapproval.

In all these months, Reece had never once questioned her judgment. He'd often asked her about decisions she'd made regarding the boy, but only to inform himself. He'd never remarked at all on decisions she'd made about her personal activities, so this was unusual.

She nervously tightened her fingers and spoke, careful to make her tone practical rather than critical. "When I reminded you about it last week, you didn't seem interested."

A breathless anxiety made a sweeping pass through her insides, and she took another small step toward the subject she meant to open.

"Since you and I aren't...in the habit of doing

things together, I didn't think you'd mind if I decided to go. As I said, I've made arrangements for Bobby that you can control however you like, whatever you decide to do about Saturday."

Reece's somber expression had gone stony and Leah felt uneasy. She'd irritated him, but couldn't for the life of her imagine why. Though Reece's temper was legendary, he'd never given a single hint of turning it on her or his son. Informing him that she was going to a neighbor's barbecue seemed too small a thing to provoke him.

And yet the strained silence hung between them and built. It helped a little to keep in mind that Reece was a good man and a fair one, who was as naturally decent as the day was long. She had nothing to fear from a man like him, no matter his temper. She couldn't have agreed to their bargain, much less adored him for years, if she hadn't known those things as absolute facts.

The real danger was that he'd somehow find out how much she loved him, and then either reject her feelings outright, or worse, pity her for having them.

"You haven't got much out of our deal, have you?"

Reece's question was jarringly direct and a signal that he might have guessed the real reason she'd wanted this talk. The growl in his voice had softened, though his stony expression hadn't.

Leah sensed something, perhaps regret, perhaps

guilt, but she automatically discounted that impression and considered it nothing more than wishful thinking. A longing heart would always see a banquet in a table crumb. Pride roared up to keep her from revealing even a hint of her true feelings.

"I've gotten exactly what I bargained to get," she told him, then made her stiff lips relax a little into a smile. "And I have Bobby. Being able to love and raise him is more than enough."

Leah tried not to blink at the half-lie in that last part. Though at twenty-four she'd never had more than a hasty kiss on the mouth once by a boy who'd done it to embarrass her, she had the same female longing for affection and intimate tenderness as any other woman, in spite of her inexperience.

"So you're satisfied with the way it's been." Reece's gravelly words were not a question, but a statement.

Leah caught the cynical gleam in his dark eyes and didn't understand it. Or why he'd even think to remark on whether she'd been satisfied or not by the way things between them had gone.

The past eleven months had revolved around the boy, the ranch and the polite day-to-day cooperation between a stay at home wife who cared for a house and child, and a rancher who spent hours a day working outdoors or doing paperwork in the den. The emotional sterility between the two of them had been so heart-numbing that Leah often wondered if they were even friends.

"I'm...satisfied we've both done what we agreed to do." Leah cringed inwardly at the small hesitation, but it was hard to face the relentlessness she suddenly sensed in Reece.

It was even harder to maintain eye contact with the dark eyes that seemed to flicker with perception when she was trying so hard to hide the truth, at least the most dangerous truth: her real feelings.

"I remember we talked about more than just protecting the boy when we started this," he said then.

The reminder completely threw her. She recalled Reece's remarks on that subject with distressing clarity. It had been in this very room at almost the same time of day that he'd made them.

It was the only time either of them had so much as hinted at the possibly of having other children. Or of personal needs, having sex in particular.

"I reckon sex will be part of this deal, since it's a marriage," he'd said, and it hurt to remember the bleak, almost grim look in his eyes, as if he was resigned to the task only because he saw it as a marital obligation.

"Won't be likely for a time," he'd gone on, glancing away from her before he'd added, "but we've both got needs."

His low voice had trailed off and she'd got the impression that the thought of sex with any woman but Rachel was not only vaguely distasteful to him, but that he also couldn't imagine that sex would ever again be something more than a biological function, perhaps to have more children, but mainly as a physical release.

At least he'd not insulted her obvious lack of desirability by rejecting the possibility of ever having sex with her. And because he'd also let her know that he was willing to have other children with her if she wanted them, he apparently hadn't considered her an unworthy recipient of his seed.

Of course, eleven months had gone by and if Reece had ever had a "need", she'd never known about it. Which only confirmed the idea that Reece felt so little for her that he didn't think of her in terms of sex.

Reece's gruff voice brought her back to the present. "You remember that, don't you?"

His dark gaze shifted downward to flash quickly over her body. So quickly it seemed almost mechanical. As if it was expected that a man who'd brought up the subject of sex might at least make a cursory inspection to familiarize himself with the physical attributes of the woman he'd suggested it to.

Leah felt her cheeks go abnormally hot with a mix of feminine shame and very feminine indignation. Without so much as a single nonaccidental touch between them in all these months, and no hint of personal affection from Reece, sex was the last thing she'd consider. Particularly when the look he'd just given her had been so clearly obligatory. Not even she was so hungry for love that she'd allow herself to be so coldly used.

"I think we've moved past the point where the things we talked about that night might have made sense," she said stiffly, just managing not to give in to the fiery hurt she'd sustained. "I think you've realized that too."

Her heart was pounding so hard that she felt a little dizzy. Her refusal had set off sparks in Reece's dark gaze and she felt a corresponding nettle of resentment. It took so, *so* much to keep her voice even and her words reasonable.

"Neither of us was thinking straight after Rachel died," she told him. "Now that we've had these months to put things into a more moderate perspective, I think we both have doubts about going on together."

There. She'd got it said and the world hadn't come to an end. The minor softening of Reece's stony expression had vanished, but he was still silent. She tried not to fidget while his dark eyes bore into hers like twin drills.

There was something in the way he stared over at her that compelled her to go on, something that suggested he needed to hear more to be convinced. Leah made a try at doing just that.

"As I said, we made the decision to marry at a time when we weren't quite ourselves," she said calmly, careful to keep her tone mild, though she couldn't keep the tremor out of it. "Lately you've seemed...unhappy. In a different way than before, so I...thought it was time to discuss what might need to change, even though the change that probably seems most sensible is divorce."

The booming silence that followed was as much a sudden assault on the room as a thunderclap would have been. It had impacted with such power that it was difficult, even in the aftermath, to decide if an actual clap of thunder had sounded around them, or if it had truly been a silent shockwave.

But maybe it had been an actual thunderclap, because the storm was suddenly visible in Reece's harsh face. His dark eyes snapped with angry surprise, and the ruthless line of his mouth now seemed more promise than vague threat.

"Are you asking for a divorce?"

The blunt question wasn't unexpected, but his gravelly tone of voice carried a steeliness that warned how rigidly he controlled himself. Leah felt her heart skip faster, and forced herself to shake her head.

"There's a difference between asking for a divorce and offering one."

The moment the words were out of her mouth she wondered why she'd put it that way. She should have simply answered "yes". The huge tide of hurt and unhappiness that rose up added to her alarm and she mentally scrambled to show none of it.

Oh, God, don't let him see, don't ever let him find out...

"I've made the offer," she said coolly, so relieved that her tone was calm and practical that she blundered into undermining her purpose even more. "What you do with it is up to you."

She'd somehow stood to her feet without being fully aware of it until she felt the back of her knees brush the front of the chair. But whether her body had taken action to help her assert herself or to flee, she didn't know. At least she could see that her more temperate answer to Reece's question had gotten her message across just as clearly as a more definitive one.

Reece's weather-tanned face was like a granite monolith. A ruddy flush she recognized as fury had crept into his lean cheeks, but she knew by his iron silence that he wouldn't inflict it on her.

"I'll look in on Bobby before I go to bed. Goodnight."

Leah turned and moved around the chair to walk as normally as possible to the door then into the hall. Her knees were rubbery and her legs felt heavy and weak, but she managed to make a dignified exit.

She'd got the job done and except for that part near the end, she'd managed it fairly well. Though she might have delivered it all a bit less stiffly, she'd survived and Reece hadn't guessed anything of her real feelings about either the divorce or him.

The need to spend time with Bobby was overwhelming, so she hurried down the hall to the bedroom end of the large, single-story ranch house. The child's room was next to the master bedroom, and both rooms were linked by a connecting door.

Leah had never shared the master bedroom with Reece, much less shared his bed. He hadn't offered and she'd certainly never asked. Given her pick of bedrooms, she'd chosen the one on the other side of Bobby's. Reece had noted her choice and for her convenience, he'd had another connecting door put in the shared wall between her room and the baby's.

As Leah slipped silently into Bobby's room, the arrangement struck her as even more telling. At first, it had been understandable that she and Reece wouldn't share a room or a bed, and she'd completely agreed. Rachel's death had been too fresh and agonizing for them both, and it was scandalous enough that they'd married so soon after.

But as the months had gone by without so much as a hint of real closeness between them, Leah had reminded herself that she couldn't reasonably expect more. Except for the baby, there was nothing between them but a marriage certificate and the same last name.

Reece had bargained for a woman to help raise

his son and he'd wanted to settle a life that had been shattered by death and shock and upheaval. He'd also been determined to prevent his son from ever being raised and exploited by his maternal grandparents, if something should happen to him.

Leah had been a means to get an adoptive mother he trusted for his infant son and to keep his home life in order. He'd meant for Leah to be a fail-safe protection for Bobby if he was no longer around. He apparently hadn't been thinking much about the wife he'd have to live with to get all that. And after what she'd sensed in him these past weeks, he'd surely awakened to the fact that having a wife had created almost as many problems for him as getting one had solved.

Bobby's room was dimly lit, thanks to the ceramic puppy lamp she always left on. The house was so quiet that she could hear the child's soft baby breaths almost from the moment she walked into the room.

She crossed to the baby bed and looked down blurrily into the sweet face of the sleeping child. His dark silky hair lay in charming disarray, and his long, black lashes fanned out thickly on chubby, sleep-flushed cheeks.

Leah put out a hand to tenderly touch his open fingers, marveling at his beauty, her heart breaking with love. She couldn't love this baby more if she'd given birth to him herself. There was nothing she wouldn't do for him. Not even the love she felt for Reece was as powerful as the love she felt for this dark-haired cherub.

Eventually, she eased the light blanket higher on his chest and turned to go to her room. She left the door between her room and his partway open, as always, so she could hear in case he woke up during the night.

As Leah began to get ready for bed a dozen doubts about her talk with Reece began to pick at her sense of accomplishment, but the important thing was that she'd got the subject into the open.

As a successful rancher and businessman, Reece was comfortable making decisions, and he'd learned better than most how to quickly determine and evaluate all the facts of a situation, and then to identify his options. His decision to marry her was probably the only truly bad decision of his adult life. And that had only happened because he'd been blinded by grief over Rachel and worry about his infant son's future.

Deciding to divorce her wouldn't require much thought. For Reece, it wouldn't be a "yes" or "no" answer as much as it would be a "how soon?" one. He'd probably reached his decision before she'd gotten a handful of steps down the hall from the den.

Her obligation had been to put the subject before him and to signal her permission and approval. He'd probably confirm his decision to divorce her first thing in the morning at breakfast. After that, the only wrangling there'd ever be between them—over Bobby—would begin.

And even that was nothing to lie awake and fret about. Leah had been the baby's main caregiver, and she'd naturally be responsible for the majority of his care, at least while he was so young. The rest they could work out as Bobby got older.

She had no fear that Reece would somehow banish her from Bobby's life, particularly since part of protecting Bobby had meant that Leah had had to adopt him. She had as many parental rights as Reece did, and since they were both mindful of Bobby's best interests, they would both play major parts in the boy's life whether they stayed married or not.

As she lay in the dark, her sense of accomplishment and relief slowly gave way to a heavy heart. What she'd done tonight had virtually sealed the death of her fondest, most impossible dream. Though it had taken a secretly agonizing eleven months to finally kill it, what she'd done by offering Reece a divorce was to acknowledge that the dream of openly loving him and being loved by him was well and truly lost.

And it was only right that she would never see that dream fulfilled. She'd fallen in love with Reece years ago, long before he'd ever dated her best friend, but she hadn't been able to stop loving him, not even when he'd married Rachel. She'd suffered tremendous guilt over that, but never enough to overcome her feelings.

Then she'd compounded the wrong of being in love with a married man by grabbing the chance to marry him after he'd been widowed, at perhaps the only time in his life that he'd ever been vulnerable. The guilt and heartache she'd suffered and might continue to suffer over her selfish feelings for her best friend's husband, were fitting punishments that she accepted.

At least Rachel had never suspected. Hopefully Reece would never find out, either.

Leah turned onto her side and stared into the dark for a long time. She must have dropped off to sleep sometime before it got too late, because she never heard Reece's bootsteps as she usually did when he passed her room on the way to his own.

CHAPTER TWO

REECE'S first impulse had been to go after Leah and drag her back to the den to have it out. His second had been to walk over to the liquor cabinet and pour himself a double Scotch. Once he'd done the latter, he tossed it back like a man on fire trying to douse the flames.

But the conflagration of anger and surprise and guilt wasn't so easily put out. The hell of it was, he was overdue to have his meek wife stand up to him. Though she'd used softly polite, tactful words, she'd nonetheless given him a sound thrashing and called him to account.

Leah Gray Waverly had turned out to be the perfect mother, calm and competent, as loving as she was gently patient and wise with the boy. She made certain Bobby saw him in the morning before he left the house, she timed the baby's schedule to his to maximize their time together, and she arranged nightly for him to spend time alone with his son.

She'd also been the ideal wife. After his housekeeper had retired just after their sudden marriage, Leah had cooked his meals, washed his clothes, and single-handedly kept his large, six-bedroom house

25

virtually dust free in the middle of a ranch headquarters where dust hung in the air around the clock. In between all that, she ran his errands, took his phone calls when he was out, and generally made his home life an aggravation-free island of pleasantness and serenity.

But whatever he'd thought about Leah's quiet temperament, what she'd done just now reminded him that the lady had a backbone. Tonight she'd shown a steely pride that was no less formidable than his own.

As Reece poured himself another drink, he did so more thoughtfully this time. He hadn't meant to be so indifferent to her, he hadn't meant to take everything she'd done for him and give her nothing personal in return.

He'd given her his son, the most precious person in his life, but what woman who thought anything of herself would have been content to love and help raise her best friend's child and put up with being an unpaid servant to a husband who, as far as she'd be able to tell, hadn't appreciated any of it?

For weeks his conscience had been dogged by the things he'd neglected with Leah. He'd put her name on his bank accounts, but she'd never spent so much as a dollar of his money on herself. He had yet to take her out to a nice restaurant or a social function. The only time he'd attended church with her had been on the Sunday she'd had Bobby dedicated.

Hell, he hadn't even remembered her birthday until four months after it had passed.

After being married to a near hermit for the past eleven months, it was no wonder she'd informed him that she meant to go to the barbecue, with or without him.

Rachel had told him things about Leah that he hadn't thought about for years. About her nomadic childhood, the many abandonments by both her father and mother, her eventual ordeal in a series of foster homes. According to Rachel, Leah's biggest dream had been to someday have a family and a home.

She had a legal son in Bobby and she lived in one of the finest homes in the area. But his preoccupation with Rachel's loss had cheated her out of the complete family she must have wanted and had probably left her feeling like a slave instead of a marriage partner. Hence her solemn little bombshell tonight.

Yet he felt nothing for her aside from gratitude—gratitude and guilt. The turmoil of that had nettled him for weeks, but he couldn't seem to help that gratitude and guilt were the only things Leah stirred in him.

Losing Rachel had left him empty. Any woman who wasn't *her* was merely female. No one to wonder about, and certainly no one to get excited about. His hormones had come back to life, his lust still fired over the usual sights and thoughts, he still had powerful male urges that craved satisfaction, but the mysterious allure of tenderness and sweet feelings were gone as completely as Rachel.

In his mind and heart, love and sex were associated exclusively with luxurious red hair, freckle-flecked satin skin and exotic emerald eyes that sparkled with passion and a zest for life.

Suddenly the memories were white hot, and he relived the phantom feeling of Rachel's lush body pressed against his. His palms ached to slide over her soft skin to tenderly cup and caress, and his fingers tingled with the unforgettable sensation of what it had felt like to lavish pleasure on her.

Pain and bitterness welled up at the torment, and Reece forced the powerful memories to stop. He determinedly fixed his thoughts on the living woman—*the wife*—he was obligated to crave.

But desire didn't rise very high over long sable hair that was usually pinned up or worn in a French braid; it didn't crave the touch and warm feel of lightly tanned almost dusky skin. Eyes that were a deep, quiet blue didn't suggest anything more enticing or arousing for him than somber mysteries and unhappiness, and his heart was already weighted down by those.

Try as he might, he couldn't picture Leah's pretty eyes going slumberous with lust, and he couldn't imagine her losing her very rigid self-control to clutch at him in the high heat of sexual intimacy. It was as unthinkable of Leah as it would have been of an elderly maiden aunt.

The harsh bite of guilt he felt for the unfair comparison made him finish the second Scotch in another punishing rush.

He didn't want Bobby to be hurt, and divorce would do a masterful job of hurting the boy. Surely his lack of sexual interest in Leah was a remnant of Rachel's loss. That and the fact that he'd barely paid attention to her as a potential lover, and he'd never been curious enough to find out what she might really be like when she wasn't being a mommy or teaching Sunday School.

Rachel and Leah had been closer than sisters. So close that he knew Rachel wouldn't think much of him for cheating Leah out of a loving home. Particularly when Leah had given up her chance of finding a man whose heart could be all hers so she could come to the aid of her best friend's husband and infant son.

Feeling gut sick over what Leah had sacrificed and how poorly he'd repaid her, Reece set the tumbler down with a soft thud then made himself walk over to his desk. He picked up the silver-framed photo of Rachel and turned it to study her face.

The flatness of the image impacted him. He tilted the frame slightly, as if to get a better look at the thickness of it, but the photo paper behind the glass suddenly looked as thin and unsubstantial as any other photograph.

For the first time Reece felt detached from the color image, and his heart grabbed futilely to recapture the sense of connection. It was as if he'd known this achingly beautiful woman a long time ago, too long ago, and something in him flinched with surprise at the feeling of distance. It had only been fifteen months since the wreck, and yet it suddenly felt like another lifetime, one that had belonged to some other Reece Waverly.

In the space of mere moments, the memory of Rachel had gone from white hot and all but tangible to something more like a dimly remembered dream.

Which reminded him of the worst part of these past weeks. Rachel had been fading from his mind. A little here, a little there, he was starting to forget the things he'd been convinced were burned on his heart forever. Except for the soul rocking flashes of sudden memory, the everyday details of how Rachel had moved, how she'd smiled—even how she'd touched and taken care of their son that handful of days—had begin to cloud over until he could only rarely summon them at will.

Would her memory fade completely away? Was he man enough to face the bleakness of that second loss if she did? The loneliness he already felt was brutal.

Reece stood there for several minutes more, wondering if he was drunk, wondering whether these strange feelings and impressions meant anything, but eventually realizing how weary he was. What he did next wasn't so much a decision as it was a necessity.

He didn't want to ever look at a picture of Rachel and feel this disconnected from her. The clarity of the photo was a reminder that the living image in his brain seemed to be growing more fuzzy and indistinct. Better to never see it again than to feel so eerily detached from both the woman and the life they'd had together.

Once he'd switched off the desk lamp, Reece turned and carried the framed picture to the bedroom end of the dark ranch house. He didn't need a light to walk through the big house he'd lived in since birth. He went into the first guest bedroom he came to, and moved across the carpet to the dresser by memory. He fumbled for a drawer catch and opened the drawer just enough to put the picture inside.

It was best to ignore the hollow rattle of the silver frame against the wood bottom of the empty drawer as he pushed it closed. Nevertheless he hesitated, as if he might think of a rational reason to change his mind and put the picture back on his desk. Eventually, he left the drawer closed and walked out of the room and into the hall.

The soft glow of the light Leah always left on in Bobby's room spilled into the hall and drew him, particularly tonight, though it was his usual habit to look in on the child.

Bobby was sleeping peacefully, so he lingered a bit before he backed a step away from the bed then paused to glance toward the partially open door between the baby's room and Leah's. It was too dark in her room to see more than a wedge of carpet, though from this angle he hadn't expected to be able to actually catch a glimpse of her.

The mental picture of what she might look like asleep and his quick curiosity about what she wore to bed came so suddenly that he felt a new kind of jolt. He'd never had a single thought about Leah's preferences or private habits, so this was a new thing.

But then again, he'd either had just enough booze to inspire a faint spark of curiosity about Leah because he'd been trying to summon some kind of desire for her, or he was drunk enough to have lost a few inhibitions so that the idea of sex without love wasn't such an empty one.

Either way, he couldn't take the small spark seriously. It would surely be gone by morning, smothered out by the cold reality of another day.

Reece heard Leah's soft laugh just before he reached the kitchen that next morning.

"No, no, let's not put the toast in your cup. It goes in your mouth, silly boy."

Leah was never late putting a hot breakfast on the table. She might have been up half the night with Bobby or had to deal with the boy waking up earlier than normal, but somehow she handled every complication so competently that Reece could have set his watch by her.

Bobby had awakened early, probably with his usual soaked diaper that required a quick bath, but when Reece stepped into the kitchen his son was clean and dressed and sitting in his high chair with a bib on. He was gnawing on a piece of toast as Leah finished putting food on the table.

Reece felt a nettle of guilt and an equally sharp nettle of resentment. He already owed Leah more than he could repay, yet she just went on being perfect. Relentlessly perfect. Her perfection was a silent indictment of his notable lack of perfection where being a husband was concerned. The mild headache he'd woke up with began to pound.

"Daddeee!"

Bobby's excitement to see him gave Reece a rush of pleasure and love that somehow soothed the rawness he felt.

The baby had his dark coloring, though Bobby's features, particularly his green eyes and the way he set his mouth, fairly shouted testimony that he was Rachel's son. The tender pride Reece felt in the boy might have added to the volatile churn of emotion that was still riding him from last night, but his relief to not only see but also identify the ways Bobby resembled his late mother slowed some of the churn.

Reece crossed to where the high chair sat between his place at the head of the table and Leah's to his right. He ruffled Bobby's dark hair before bending to give him a kiss on the forehead.

"Good morning," Leah said quietly.

"Morning."

Reece sat down just after Leah did, then automatically took hold of Bobby's hand as Leah briefly said grace.

Quick and soft, the small prayer was another unintended reminder that Leah was a wonderful mother to his son. No detail of the child's upbringing was being overlooked by her, while Reece himself had failed to provide him with something as elemental and necessary to a happy childhood as having a daddy and mama who loved each other.

The boy needed to grow up seeing a normal and settled relationship between his parents. How long would it be before he was old enough to note the significance of having a mama and daddy who never touched, who never embraced, and who didn't even sleep in the same bed? His mood going darker, Reece took the meat plate Leah passed to him and silently served himself.

Leah was so tense that she felt awkward and self-conscious. Should she ask Reece what he'd decided or wait for him to tell her? Now that the big moment was almost here, she realized even more sharply how difficult it would be to actually hear that he would take her up on her offer to divorce.

Be careful what you ask for. How fitting that of all the things she'd asked for in her life and hadn't gotten, she would actually get the one thing that would hurt the most.

She put Bobby's plate on his tray and gave him his fork. The thought of what a divorce would mean to this happy child made it nearly impossible to look him full in the face.

"Do you have special plans for today?" Reece asked, and Leah felt her nerves jump. She managed to glance his way briefly, but not to actually make eye contact before she focused on filling her own plate.

"I thought I might go to San Antonio to find something new for Saturday. It could wait till tomorrow if you have something you need done today."

"Wouldn't mind ridin' along," he said, his low voice oddly gruff. "What time?"

The information was a surprise, but then Leah realized that Reece might have planned for them to consult with their lawyer as soon as possible. Or rather, he would consult with his lawyer while she found one to represent her.

"I'd planned to leave you a cold lunch and start

midmorning, but we could go anytime. Just so I have an hour or so to shop.''

At this point, there was no sense in dancing around the subject that had to be dominating his thoughts as strongly as it was hers. And if she had to find a lawyer, she might as well know it now so she could check the Yellow Pages before they set out.

"So you've made your decision?" Leah asked, then made the mistake of taking a bite of fluffy eggs before she realized she probably wouldn't be able to swallow them past the huge lump of dread in her throat.

The charged silence that followed her question increased her self-consciousness. She reached for her coffee cup to try to wash down the eggs.

Reece didn't answer right away, and his silence felt ominous. She set down her coffee cup and glanced at him the tiniest second to find her gaze trapped by the laser intensity of his. As if he'd been waiting for her full attention, he gave her his answer.

"I won't tell my boy that I divorced his mama because I couldn't live up to my end of a commitment. There'll be no divorce."

The growling words were a complete and utter shock. If she hadn't been sitting, her knees would have given out. In the next second she experienced such a stab of panic that it was all she could do to not jump up and flee.

Reece's grim expression was intimidating, and she weathered another wave of panic. The only thing worse than divorce would be for Reece to tough it out and stay married to her. But how long would it be before he regretted—and then bitterly resented—giving up the chance to divorce her early on so he'd be free to find a woman more compatible with his idea of marital satisfaction?

Or would Reece make an effort for a while, but then realize he simply couldn't tolerate going through the motions with a woman he couldn't truly care for? By then, either her hope would be soaring at an all-time high only to be cruelly disappointed, or she'd suffer through all his efforts knowing every moment that it was only because of his iron-willed determination that he stuck it out with her.

Worst of all, how long before Bobby would be old enough to realize his parents didn't love each other? And when he figured out the depth of the personal sacrifice Reece had made for his sake, would he feel gratitude or would he feel guilt? Would he blame Leah for his father's unhappiness? Or would he figure out what Reece seemed oblivious to so far: that Leah had taken advantage of his father at a vulnerable time?

There was literally no way for the three of them to be happy for any length of time, if ever, under any of those circumstances. Because Leah believed so absolutely that Reece would never come to love her, she ignored that possibility altogether. And without even the possibility of love, could there ever be anything certain ahead except a new level of misery for them all?

Leah's gaze shifted from Reece's. She knew she must have telegraphed her distress to Reece when he spoke.

"Wasn't that the answer you wanted to hear?"

Leah dropped her hand to her lap and gripped her napkin. She felt sick suddenly, so any further attempt to eat would be futile. She tried to come up with the right thing to say.

"You're a very good man, Reece. And an honorable one." She made herself look over at him so he could see that she meant those words completely. The hard glitter in his dark eyes didn't make it easy to go on. "I think you'll work very hard to make something of this marriage. I should have expected you to react this way…" She let her voice trail off the moment she saw the spark of temper as he sensed what she would say next. She went determinedly on.

"But I'm certain once you've truly had time to consider it, you'll see things the other way." She gripped her hands together in her lap as she struggled to present a neutral expression. "I won't hold you to anything but shared custody of Bobby when the time comes."

Reece's face went flinty. "Bobby stays on Waverly Ranch, under this roof where he belongs."

It was a declaration of war. Leah knew it and went cold. Though she should have expected this too, it was chilling to hear Reece bluntly state it. Now they'd not only be emotionally and physically aloof from each other, they'd be adversaries, which made the precarious situation between them even more perilous and destined to end badly.

Leah lifted her napkin to the table and calmly eased back her chair to stand. She couldn't keep her composure and stay in the room another moment, but she couldn't allow Reece to get away with his declaration. He'd run over her from here on if she didn't.

"I won't take offense this time, Reece," she managed shakily. She wouldn't remind him of their legal agreement regarding custody of Bobby, but she'd use it if she had to. It was just more prudent to stand up to him without it. This time. "But if you mean to persuade me that this marriage has a chance, declarations like that aren't very convincing."

Leah maintained eye contact with him, though his dark gaze was fiery now. She eased to the side to push her chair closer to the table.

"You didn't finish your food," he growled, and she got the impression that he might have preferred to simply order her to sit down, but was wary of how she'd take that. It was a relief to have fresh proof that he wouldn't bully or boss her, no matter how angry he was.

"I probably nibbled too much while I was cooking and spoiled my appetite," she said quietly. The gleam of perception in his gaze told her he knew she'd stretched the truth to avoid officially pinning the blame for her sudden loss of appetite on him. "Could you look after Bobby while I take care of some laundry?"

Reece's gruff, "Sure thing," was a thin cover for his displeasure and frustration, and they both knew that too.

Leah calmly crossed the kitchen to the short hall to the laundry room though her knees were shaking. Had she just made things worse or better?

The truth was, she no longer knew what to think. She certainly didn't know much about the Reece Waverly she'd actually married. Whatever she'd known about him before, mostly by observation then later from Rachel, didn't seem to quite fit the man she had to deal with now.

At least she'd set some sort of limit and had drawn a line on the kind of verbal exchanges she wanted to avoid, and Reece had essentially backed down. But for a man as naturally dominant as he was, how long would that last?

Rachel had never thought twice about standing up to Reece, and she'd done it as confidently as she'd done everything else in her life. Rachel had tamed a lot of Reece's bluster and his natural tendency to autocratically run everything. But he would have expected that from Rachel. It would have seemed odd to him if Rachel hadn't stood up to him.

But Leah wasn't the woman he'd been so fervently in love with—was *still* in love with—so she had to watch her step. She was very aware that she'd have to depend completely on Reece's sense of fairness as well as her own ability to tactfully and consistently hold her own, because it was imperative that Reece respect her.

She couldn't afford to go to war with him, not when Bobby would be the one who'd suffer most. And though Reece couldn't love her, the last thing she wanted was to somehow make him loathe her. It was hard enough to weather his indifference.

And it was more crucial than ever that Reece never guessed what she felt for him. Until now her feelings had been easy enough to conceal, because a man who barely paid attention missed a lot of things.

Reece would be paying attention now. To everything. He'd be looking for ways to keep their marriage together, at least for a while, and it would be natural for him to exploit any advantage.

Since his greatest advantage would be to discover how much she loved him, she'd have to take special care to keep him from somehow figuring it out.

CHAPTER THREE

WHO the hell was Leah Waverly?

His curiosity last night about what she wore to bed mocked him now. The soft-spoken, compliant woman who'd lived with him all these months had somehow turned prickly and assertive practically overnight.

He'd married her because of her devotion to Rachel and to Bobby, and because he knew she'd fight any claim Rachel's parents might make on the boy if something happened to him. She'd always been meek about her own interests, but the child was another matter.

He'd seen the panic in her eyes and heard the faint tremor in her voice, but the lady had managed to look him straight in the eye and deliver her veiled little ultimatums. Though she'd used mild words, there was an inflexibility behind them that warned she'd meant what she'd said, however difficult it was for her to speak up for herself.

It was also a fresh reminder that where the boy was concerned, she was prepared to fight like a hellcat.

"Daddeee, mo' juice."

Bobby was leaning his way, twisting in his high chair as if to somehow put himself in his daddy's line of sight to get his attention.

Reece felt the mild surprise of realizing the child might have asked him more than once. He covered it with an automatic, "What's the magic word?"

Bobby straightened and reared back against his chair as he declared an eager, "Please!"

Reece reached for the pitcher of orange juice and poured a sensible half inch of liquid into the boy's cup, just like Leah always did, before he handed it over. Bobby seized it with both hands and lifted it too suddenly to his mouth. Reece barely managed to grab the spare napkin to catch the overflow of juice as it spurted from both sides of the cup lip.

"Take it slower next time, pard," he said gruffly, hastily adding his own napkin to catch and blot the rivulets that dribbled down on the bib. He patiently took the cup from Bobby's hands and set it aside. "Ready to get down?"

"Yeah, down. Down."

Reece stood, then belatedly reached for the damp washcloth Leah always had on the table to gently wipe away the stickiness from the baby's face and hands. The bib went off next, then the loosening of the chair tray before he lifted Bobby out and set him on the floor.

By the time he turned back to his own breakfast, Reece realized he was no longer hungry either. As

Bobby toddled over to the cabinet door where Leah kept a few toys, Reece cleared the table. Though he'd never done that before, it seemed important that he demonstrate some kind of usefulness to his wife.

He finished up a few minutes later, then set the dishwasher controls before he wondered what the hell was taking Leah so long in the laundry room.

Leah had folded a basket of clean towels and washcloths in record time, started a load of Reece's work clothes, then stacked a second basket of Bobby's things on top of the towel basket before she carried them through the house to put away.

She went to Bobby's room first and efficiently put his things where they belonged. She'd just finished when she noticed that the small picture of Rachel that usually sat on the dresser top was gone. A quick glance around confirmed it was nowhere in the room.

After she carried the basket of towels to the linen closet and put them away, she took a moment to hurry into Reece's room to make up the bed. She was just fluffing the pillows when she thought to glance toward the tall chest where a picture of Rachel normally sat.

The fact that it was gone was a confirmation that the absence of the one in Bobby's room wasn't a mistake. She wondered if the one in the den had also been put away. The pictures had been there yesterday, so Reece must have taken them away before he'd gone to bed last night or sometime this morning before he'd come to the kitchen for breakfast. He'd apparently taken the step before he'd told her his decision to stay married, so he'd already begun to act in good faith.

How hard had it been for him to put the photos away? She'd not begrudged the fact that they'd been displayed in the house. Even she had taken comfort from having them around because she'd been so close to Rachel.

The sound of Reece's voice from the doorway startled her.

"There's your missing mama."

Leah hastily finished smoothing the bedspread before she glanced toward the hall door.

Reece carried Bobby on his wide shoulders and the boy was giggling while he gripped Reece's hair. The contrast between Bobby's gleeful face and Reece's somber one made her realize he'd seen her staring at the spot where Rachel's picture had been.

"Thanks for looking after him," she said. "If you have things you need to do, go ahead."

"I see you noticed the picture."

Leah nodded. "And the one in Bobby's room."

"They're in the dresser in the first bedroom. When you get time you might wrap 'em up to save for Bobby. I'll put them in the attic over the garage later."

"I can take care of it before we leave."

The awkwardness between them then was distinctly uncomfortable, apparently more so for Reece than for her.

"We could use some new pictures," he added, injecting a brisk quality into the words that gave them the hint of an order.

Leah searched his gaze and felt a pang. This was significant somehow, but she wasn't sure if it was a comfort or a worry to hear him talk in terms of "we" and of acquiring things for a future together. It was too soon to hope for anything, not when they were still so emotionally distant with each other. No number of small plans could begin to make up for that.

"That might be good," she said, careful to sound noncommittal before she changed the subject. "When would you like to leave for San Antonio?"

"How 'bout we leave in time to get to the mall when it opens?"

"All right." Leah was still surprised Reece was going with her, particularly to a mall where he knew she was going to shop for clothes. Rachel had often joked about Reece being allergic to shopping of any kind, and that he'd hated women's shops in particular.

"I think I can take care of the photos and a few other things so we can leave by seven."

Reece nodded and turned with Bobby still riding

high on his shoulders. "I'll keep the boy out from under foot."

Leah watched them go, a little stunned. The overwhelming sense that something between them had changed was unmistakable, but she didn't dare take the impression seriously. Reece was a good man. Of course he'd make a noble attempt at having a real marriage, at least for a while.

Because she knew they'd both feel better later if they could say they'd at least tried, she'd accommodate him, though there were some things she wouldn't allow.

The most important thing to keep in mind was that she couldn't set her hopes on any of this. She couldn't afford to make that mistake.

The long trip to San Antonio was tense and uncomfortable, and it was obvious that they were anything but at ease with each other. Because there seemed to be little more than inane topics of conversation between them from time to time, Leah began to get a headache long before Reece found a parking space near the entrance of the mall.

The well-read man who'd always been able to talk to anyone on any subject apparently couldn't find anything worthwhile to talk about with her. Yes, he'd been largely uncommunicative for months, but he'd also just indicated that morning that he didn't want to divorce. On the other hand, perhaps he was already having second thoughts.

Or, he might have figured he could go on being just as laconic with her as he'd been so far, though she knew for a fact that he'd found plenty of things to talk about with Rachel. That was why she'd left it to Reece to initiate conversation.

It might not be fair to do that, but the last thing she wanted was to be the only one who tried to smooth over the awkwardness between them.

Better for Reece to figure out right away that they'd never have even a minimally satisfying marriage. Eleven months had convinced her it wasn't possible to have that, not without love. Reece needed to understand it too, the sooner the better.

Bobby was thrilled every moment they were in the mall, and he loved touring it all in his stroller. Reece was patient with the child and often stopped so Bobby could get a closer look at the things he seemed interested in. Leah was able to shop for something new without feeling like she was putting Reece through torture.

After she'd paid for her selections, she caught up with them outside the pet shop, where Bobby was chattering excitedly over the antics of a rowdy pair of golden retriever pups in the window.

"D'you think we ought to take him inside?" Reece asked when she arrived to stand next to them.

"Are we sure we want him to know he can go

inside?" she returned with a wry smile. "We'll have a hard enough time getting him away from this window, but..."

She was distracted because Bobby was trying to get out of his stroller to reach the puppies through the glass. She leaned down a little to put a gentle restraining hand on the boy to keep him where he was.

"But?"

"But, I love to watch him discover things," she said, then gave up and set down her shopping bag to lift the boy from the stroller. "I've never taken him inside to see the birds or the fish or any of the creepy crawly things." She turned with Bobby and glanced up at Reece who obligingly took the boy. "Maybe that's something his daddy can show him."

"You aren't going in?"

"Oh, I'll go in, but you're the one who'll have to figure out how to get him to leave peacefully once he's gotten a good look at everything."

Reece grinned, and Leah's heart jumped with pleasure at the unexpectedness of it.

"Perfect way to get him out of the pet store is to tell him we'll look at toys next," he said.

Though it wasn't safe to do, Leah couldn't help trying to cling to this moment, so she did her best to keep things between them light. "Oh my, Daddy. What will you bribe him with to get him out of the toy store?"

Reece's grin widened and again she felt that magic leap of pleasure as he said, "You don't think the two of us grown-ups can manage this baby?"

"Let's just say we haven't faced enough challenges with him to feel reasonably confident of that yet."

"Then it'll be an educational experience for all of us."

Leah raised her brows and gave a noncommittal smile. "I'll bring the stroller."

They went into the pet shop and Bobby's excitement over the variety of animals was a pure joy to watch. Reece was so good with him, so patient, and they actually spent a significant amount of time in the store while Bobby looked over everything to his heart's content.

Reece finally leaned toward her to growl, "The owner's giving us one of those looks that says we either need to buy something or clear out."

Leah whispered back, "How shortsighted of him. We could be grooming a future customer." She sent Reece a sparkling look. "So to speak."

It was one of those electric little moments. Completely unexpected, yet as palpable as a touch, a shared moment that somehow cleared some invisible hurdle and landed them both on the same side.

Leah was the first to look away, terrified she'd somehow conjured up the impression because things between them that day so far had otherwise felt uncomfortable. Despite the fact that this could never work, her heart still yearned for a miracle.

They managed to get Bobby out of the store, and it wasn't difficult at all. When he'd started to protest, Reece had simply informed him that it was time to move on. Bobby had settled right down, and he'd seemed happy to be returned to the stroller.

They left the mall for a family restaurant, and after Bobby got a fresh diaper and they'd all washed up, they were seated at a table near a window so Bobby could watch the traffic while they ate.

Things were a bit more relaxed between them, though nothing like those fleeting moments in the pet store. Bobby grew cranky after lunch, so they decided to save the trip to the toy store for another day and drove back to the ranch.

Bobby slept most of the way home, and he was still asleep when Reece carried him into the house and settled him gently in his bed.

A phone call that Reece had to take lasted long enough that Leah got involved in a few chores until she heard Bobby wake up. Reece stayed in the den the rest of the afternoon, and Leah was impatient with herself for feeling disappointed.

Her foolish heart had already, against her will and common sense, taken far too much encouragement from what could just as easily have been a friendly exchange between any two strangers who'd happened to be standing in front of any display in any mall store in the country. Even comparing it to normal husband/wife interactions made it seem even more dismally common and unremarkable.

Frustrated that she still wasn't able to quell the sense of expectation she felt, Leah went to Bobby's room, discovered he was awake, then set about collecting him and an assortment of toys to take to the kitchen. She had a new dessert recipe that might be good to have after supper. Getting back into her normal routine would go a long way toward putting things in perspective.

Supper was again little more than an opportunity to prove that things were still as awkward between them as they had been on the trip to San Antonio. The only real difference was that Reece was generous with his compliments to her about the meal, particularly the rhubarb dessert.

Afterward he'd taken Bobby and disappeared into the den as he normally did between supper and the time Leah gave the baby his bath, so she finished up in the kitchen, then went out into the living room.

Hoyt Donovan had hired a country-and-western band for the dance that would be held the night of his barbecue, so Leah switched on the television then looked for the dance video she'd bought on her last trip to town.

Her lack of romantic experience included the fact that she'd never learned to dance. The only time she'd been asked, the boy had changed his mind on the way to the dance floor in order to dance with another girl. Leah had avoided dances from then on, though she loved to watch dancers in movies.

Because the dance at Hoyt's would be casual, with a lot of ranch hands from ranches in the area, it was possible she'd be asked to dance. There usually weren't enough female dance partners to go around, so it wasn't conceited of her to think someone might want to dance with her, at least once.

So when she'd seen the dance video on a bargain table at the video store last weekend, she'd bought it. It couldn't hurt to use the video to figure out a few of the steps to some of the more common dances, just in case.

A half hour into the video, she heard the doorbell and switched off the tape to go answer the door. Hoyt Donovan stood on the doorstep. As tall as Reece, Hoyt was built just as powerfully. They both had dark coloring, both were rugged looking, but Hoyt had a streak of deviltry and fun that Reece's more somber nature never permitted these days.

Hoyt was also a flirt whose tastes ran to beautiful women. One after another. But despite his numerous, brief romances, Hoyt was one of Leah's favorite people, though she'd never confessed that to anyone but Rachel.

Hoyt whipped off his black Stetson. "Eve'nin', Miz Leah."

"Hello, Hoyt," she said, then stepped back to

open the door wider. "Reece is with Bobby in the den. Go on in."

Hoyt walked into the foyer. "Has he decided about Saturday?"

"You'll have to ask him," she replied as she closed the door and turned. Hoyt had upended his Stetson on the foyer table.

"You're still comin', aren't you?" He'd lowered his dark brows in a mock threat against changing her mind.

Leah smiled. "Yes. I'm looking forward to it."

"That's no wonder. You probably married the biggest killjoy in all o' Texas. How the heck do you put up with the grouch?"

It was a fairly frequent comment and question. Though Hoyt always joked about it, Leah knew he disapproved of Reece's reclusiveness. She had no idea if Hoyt disapproved of her or not, or her sudden marriage to Reece, because he'd always been very nice to her.

"I get by," she said with a polite smile.

"Well, whether he comes or not Saturday night, I wanted you to know before the stampede starts, that three of those dances are mine."

"Stampede?"

"Yeah. Stampede. The men are going to run over each other to dance with you. But just remember, I get three. The first one, if I can."

Leah gave a bemused smile. "Thank you for the

offer, but the only stampede that will happen is when I step on your toes during that first dance. Once they hear you howl, they'll be running in the other direction."

"Darlin', you could walk on my toes and theirs all night, and there wouldn't be a man among us who wouldn't want to keep dancin'."

She rolled her eyes at the outrageous prediction. "We'll see."

Hoyt's dark gaze grew momentarily serious. "Yeah, we will. And you'll see I'm right."

A little embarrassed that Hoyt was so clearly teasing her about something she knew would never be true, Leah found herself confessing, "I don't even know how to dance."

Hoyt's expression shifted to comical dismay. "What kinda men do we have around these parts if none of 'em's taught you to dance?"

Before she could give a lighthearted answer to that, Hoyt caught her hand.

"We'll remedy that right now," he vowed as he started out of the foyer into the living room, towing her along. Leah couldn't immediately think of a polite way out of it until she belatedly remembered the video.

"You don't have to bother," she rushed out. "I bought a video."

Hoyt stopped and turned to her. "A video?"

"Yes," she said a little breathlessly. "A dance

video. I was watching it just before you got here, so you don't need to—"

The information made him glance around for the TV remote. He located it on the coffee table, then aimed it at the screen and pushed play.

The video began in the middle of a dance instruction for the Cotton-Eyed Joe. Apparently satisfied, he set the remote aside and turned to her. He held out his arms.

"Well, come on. This is one of the fancier dances, but you'll catch on."

Leah put up a hand and eased back a step. "That one's too complicated." Hoyt shook his head and Leah felt a little desperate suddenly. "And, there's not enough room in here."

Hoyt caught her hand and she found herself turned so she was hip to hip with Hoyt with his arm around her.

"There's plenty of room. We'll just walk through the steps on this one, and not worry about keeping up with the beat. Or the video."

It was a very nice feeling to have Hoyt's strong arm around her and to have her hands in his. He patiently instructed her in every move of the complicated steps until they'd worked their way in a wide circle around the coffee table, sofa and armchairs. The video had moved on to another instruction, but they continued in the circle a second time, a little faster, but she bungled it only marginally less.

Leah finally pulled away, laughing. "Let's just say there are plenty of other dance steps I should probably learn first. Easier ones, I hope."

Hoyt had gotten tickled too, and he complied, though he reached for the remote again. Leah thought he'd rewind to another part of the tape, but instead he pushed stop and switched the station to the country music channel. The video for Garth Brooks's latest ballad had just started, and Hoyt set down the remote to turn to her.

"You can't start simpler than this one, darlin'. Come on."

Leah hesitantly reached for the broad-palmed hand he held out to her. This time, Hoyt pulled her fully into his arms. She'd seen this slow dance lots of times, but she'd never realized just how very personal it was until she was in Hoyt's arms, one hand in his and the other resting on his chest, looking up into his handsome face. Knowing that little more than two inches separated them, if that, made her feel self-conscious.

But oh, the feeling of being held in someone's arms was such a rare, rare delight! Would it feel like this with Reece? Leah tried to ignore the question and focus solely on how nice it felt to be held by Hoyt.

He gently led and softly coached her to follow. It

really was such a simple dance that it truly didn't need rehearsing. Leah enjoyed it, more for the novelty of being held in strong arms than because it was a dance so easily mastered.

That's why it was such a surprise when she suddenly felt as if she were doing something wrong. A few more steps only increased that sense of wrongness, so she stopped dancing. Hoyt stopped moving the moment she did.

"Hey there, Leah," he said, his voice so low only she could have heard it. She automatically glanced up. "I think your fool husband's finally comin' this way. A few more steps together oughtta do it."

Before it dawned on her what Hoyt meant by "oughtta do it," he'd got her moving with him again, only this time he'd pulled her closer and bent down so his mouth was almost touching her ear.

"Forgive me, darlin'. I'm on your side."

Shocked by Hoyt's whispered confession, Leah had only a rushed heartbeat or two to consider the consequences.

CHAPTER FOUR

REECE had dimly heard the country music and the odd noises coming from the living room, but another phone call had prevented him from investigating. By the time he'd hung up, the TV was still on, but the odd noises had stopped. It was about time for Leah to give Bobby his bath anyway, so he decided to share the process tonight in hope of engineering a better sense of partnership between them.

He already felt like a fish on a bicycle. It shocked him to realize how hard it was to find some sense of personal companionship with Leah, and that troubled him. The secret had to be in doing things together, though today he'd felt like he was only going through the motions. If he wanted to make this marriage work for the boy's sake, he had to do better, whether his heart was in it or not.

Bobby briefly protested being taken from his toys, but then he rubbed his eyes and Reece knew that in spite of his long nap today, he was ready for bed. He carried the child on his arm and felt a sweet stroke of tenderness when the little one laid his head trustingly on his shoulder.

There was nothing he wouldn't do for his son, not

a thing. Leah was a good-hearted, gentle woman who'd long ago earned a place in his heart because she loved the boy. Surely he could love her the way a man ought to love his wife, if only for the boy's sake.

That was the moment it occurred to him that perhaps Leah felt nothing for him either. He hadn't exactly been at his best these past months, so he couldn't find fault with her for that. It seemed arrogant that he hadn't thought of it before.

The idea only frustrated him more. How did you get a woman to fall for you if you couldn't seem to summon much feeling for her?

The consequences of the hasty marriage they'd made bore down heavily. How had he ever thought there could be a lick of permanence in such an empty-hearted deal? Particularly after the marriage he'd had with Rachel, how could he have considered settling for so much less? At the time he'd been thinking of the baby, but he should have taken at least a little time to think about Leah and himself.

Those questions and their answers did nothing to lift his dark mood or to inspire much confidence in the outcome.

When Reece walked around the corner into the living room, the scene before him gave him a jolt. He came to an abrupt halt as his brain registered the sight.

His wife was dancing in the arms of his oldest

and best friend. The best friend who attracted more women than a sane man would have had time to deal with; the best friend who'd never met a lady he couldn't charm. The best friend who was now dancing far too close to his wife.

And his wife seemed amazingly receptive when Hoyt leaned close to whisper in her ear. Leah turned her head slightly as if to catch what he'd said, and her lips must have come little more than a hairbreadth from Hoyt's jaw.

His wife was not only dancing in the arms of his best friend, she had her hand on his chest. Leah had never so much as touched him in any way beyond accidental, yet there she was, dancing in the close embrace of a man who seemed to have no problem at all getting her to do it.

Reece had always been amused by Hoyt's talent with the ladies, but there was nothing even remotely amusing about it now.

The jealousy that suddenly burst up was so fiery that he was taken completely by surprise. On some level, he knew his feelings were unreasonable. Hoyt had danced with Rachel lots of times, and he'd never felt threatened. But the idea that Leah was slipping away from him stirred up every caveman instinct he had. And the fact that she seemed to be enjoying herself with Hoyt in a way she might never with him, just aggravated him more.

* * *

Hoyt led Leah in a slow turn that enabled her to catch a glimpse of Reece's face. There was no way to mistake his rigid expression or the glitter of anger in his dark eyes.

Leah's first reaction was guilt, but then pride roared up. Why on earth would Reece be angry? She was simply dancing with another man. Even if he didn't trust her for some wild reason, Hoyt was his oldest and closest friend, and Reece must surely trust him completely. She knew for a fact that Reece had never been given to jealousy with Rachel, so she was both mystified and offended by this.

Not quite twenty-four hours ago she'd told Reece she was going to a barbecue either with him or without him, and he'd not given a single indication of whether he'd go with her or not. But now that he'd walked in on a dance lesson, he was suddenly angry about it. From the look on his face, he must have considered it some form of adultery.

Leah tightened her fingers on Hoyt's hand and hoped he didn't stop dancing. When their next steps turned her so she couldn't see Reece's face, she whispered an urgent, "Could we finish this dance?"

She didn't worry about her telling question. Hoyt was close enough to Reece to know or have guessed about their marriage, and also Hoyt had all but volunteered himself as a coconspirator of some kind just now.

Hoyt's rasped, "Sure thing. Let 'im cut in," made her panic a little.

She hadn't thought to do that. She'd only meant to finish the dance. Though only moments ago it had felt a little wrong to be dancing with Hoyt and enjoying the feel of his arms around her, she couldn't let Reece think that she could be cowed by a disapproving look. Dancing with Hoyt was, after all, harmless. If Reece hadn't shown such unreasonable anger, she might have stopped dancing right away.

But now that Hoyt had put the idea in her mind, she realized that this could either be an unexpected opportunity to remove a bit of the touch-me-not barrier between them, or it was another opportunity to reinforce it.

What did she truly want? And would it make any real difference between them either way?

It suddenly mattered very much what Reece did. If he let her finish the dance without cutting in or didn't ask to partner her for another, she would be terribly hurt. And yet what would it be like if he cut in now? Would he glower and fume the whole time, or would they relax a bit and be a little more at ease with each other?

The ballad moved on toward the end and time seemed to slow until it felt like hours between each note. Leah's tension coiled tighter until the song finally ended. In the second or so of silence that followed, Leah felt the hollow pain of deep disappointment. A glance at the TV screen showed the end credits and then the VJ gave the intro to the next music video.

Leah pulled back and Hoyt released her. She was afraid to look up into his face for fear she'd see a look of sympathy, though she pasted a smile on her stiff lips.

"Thank you, Hoyt. You're a fine dancer," she said, unable to defeat the excruciating self-consciousness she felt on top of everything else.

And it was acutely embarrassing that Reece had done nothing. He was still standing in the doorway with Bobby, so it was obvious he didn't plan to ask her to dance, even if the next video had been a slow tune.

"My pleasure, Miz Leah," Hoyt said gallantly.

Leah turned toward Reece. "I'll take Bobby for his bath. Unless either of you would like some iced tea before I go?"

Hoyt didn't allow the silence to stretch longer than a couple of edgy heartbeats. "Nothing for me, thanks. What I stopped by for will only take a minute," he said before he called over to the sleepy boy, "Hey there, Bobby. Those ol' eyelids are lookin' mighty heavy."

Bobby tried for a smile that looked more cranky than friendly, and his resemblance to Reece was unmistakable, as if father and son were on the same wavelength. Leah walked over to take the baby.

She didn't look into Reece's face as Bobby reached eagerly for her then snuggled into her arms. As always, she and Reece managed the exchange without touching. It was probably for the best to have yet another confirmation that the no-touching barrier between them was still so firmly in place. And because it was, it was no wonder Reece hadn't elected to cut in.

"Well, goodnight to you both," she said hastily, then moved past Reece to carry Bobby toward the bedroom end of the house.

Reece led the way to the foyer and the front door, more irritated with himself than ever. He'd known the moment Leah wouldn't look him in the eye that he'd hurt her feelings. Once he and Hoyt stepped outside the house, Reece caught a hint of what was coming. Hoyt rarely kept his opinions to himself.

"You're as hard-hearted as you are stupid, amigo," Hoyt declared. "It's a wonder that gal hasn't packed your son up and moved to town."

Reece felt the set-down like a punch to the gut. "What the hell do you know about it?"

"Observation and common sense. She's too damned skittish with you. A woman who feels secure and liked—or in this case, *loved*—doesn't act like she does." Hoyt elbowed him sharply. "And a man who treats his woman right wouldn't get jealous in the first place."

"Who the hell says I'm jealous?"

"I say so. And a jealous man gets jealous because he knows he's done wrong, so he uses jealousy to cover his guilt. That way, it's the woman's fault, not his."

They'd reached Hoyt's pickup truck as Reece growled, "You're as full of bull as ever."

Hoyt suddenly flashed him a grin as he opened the driver's side door. Though this was a touchier subject than they usually tangled over, they both knew each other well enough to hand out the brutal truth. If one or the other took offense, well, it wouldn't be the first time they'd settled things in a more direct, less complicated manner.

"That might be," Hoyt agreed, knowing his lazy tone would rile Reece even more. "But you've never in your life been this big a jackass. You oughta take a smart pill. Better yet, teach your woman to dance after she puts the boy to bed."

Hoyt watched, satisfied as Reece's face darkened with temper.

"I think you've worn out your welcome for one night," Reece grumbled, then opened the truck door wider to hurry Hoyt on his way.

"Reckon so," Hoyt said his grin stretching. "Just one of the burdens of bein' an expert on the fairer sex." As he'd figured, Reece wouldn't let that one pass without a remark.

"How's the expert doin' these days with Eadie Webb?"

The surprise of the question made mincemeat of Hoyt's amusement and his cocky smile fled. "Eadie Webb is none of your business. And she's not my wife."

Now it was Reece's turn to smile, though it was a grim one. "Leah's not your wife either."

Hoyt narrowed his eyes. "Point taken, though it's an awful weak one."

Reece felt the last of his temper deflate. He released the truck door to shove his fingers through his hair in a rare show of weariness.

"Hell," he growled as he looked out over the front drive to the highway. "I don't have the first idea how to keep her. Not a good first idea anyway."

Hoyt dropped a companionable hand on Reece's shoulder. "So tell her that, knothead. Choke back some of that hellacious pride and be honest. Leah Gray is a sweet little gal. Been poorly treated, so she's probably scared to death you're gonna turn her out." Hoyt paused a moment, then added somberly, "And the minute she thinks you might, she'll be gone."

Reece shot his friend a surly look. "What are you, psychic?"

"So she's mentioned the D-word, huh? Figures."

Hoyt shook his head and gave Reece's shoulder a consoling squeeze. "The last thing she really wants is to be divorced. I'd bet money on that."

He dropped his hand from Reece's shoulder and went serious. "But I wouldn't bet money on what *you* want. You don't love her at all, do you?"

The blunt challenge was another sharp needle to Reece's conscience. "When did I ever say that?"

"When did you ever say you did?"

Reece swore fervently for a moment but Hoyt wasn't intimidated by it. "I'm not sure I could lay next to Leah every night and not fall for her."

Reece glared at him, but admitted nothing. Apparently Hoyt hadn't expected him to because he went on.

"But I figure the two of you haven't so much as stood in the same bedroom in broad daylight yet. Unless it's Bobby's bedroom. That's one of the first things I'd fix, if I were you."

Reece's temper shot back up several degrees. "Well, you aren't me."

"Nope. But if I was, I'd tell her my thoughts, I'd apologize, then I'd turn on the nearest radio and dance with her. Might even kiss her. But tomorrow I'd tell her to move her things into my bedroom. If she didn't, I'd find a way to get her to let me come to her bed." Hoyt grinned. "It's okay to seduce your wife."

"Well hell," Reece groused. "Fancy that. I might have a marriage on the rocks that I haven't really had yet, but I'm lucky enough to have a know-it-all *bachelor* friend to point out my manly shortcomings and give me expert *marriage* advice. All my troubles are solved."

Hoyt chuckled and gave him a hearty thump on the back. "Shoot, think nothin' of it, pard. Just remember, you get what you pay for."

Reece's long missing sense of humor suddenly came back. Hoyt must have seen the glint of its return, because they both laughed. It was Hoyt who wound down first.

"Well, I'd better get down the road and leave you to your wife's tender mercies." Hoyt gave Reece another hearty slap on the back, then turned to step up into the pickup. "But if you don't show up with her Saturday, I'll bring a posse to drag your sorry backside to my place."

He slammed the truck door to punctuate the warning, then grinned over into his friend's surly face. "Good luck."

The big engine rumbled to life and Reece took a step back as Hoyt hit the gas and the truck roared off. He turned back toward the house and for the very first time in his life, Reece wished for a little of Hoyt's gift with the ladies. And maybe a dash of his friend's cocky hubris.

By the time he closed the front door and moved through the big house turning off the last of the lights, he reached the bedroom end of the house. The sound of Bobby's fussing and Leah's soothing voice was a confirmation that the bath was probably over but she hadn't finished putting the boy down for sleep yet.

"Oh my, sweet boy," Leah crooned as Reece stepped through the doorway and stopped. "You're so, so tired. Help me get this last snap, then we'll rock-a-bye baby."

Bobby's response was an out-of-sorts, "Ooohoo, rock-a-baby-bye, Momma," that gave Reece's heart a small pang. It wasn't the first time the child had gotten too tired and then become fussy, but Leah handled it as she always did, with tenderness and unrushed patience.

The small pang became an ache that felt almost like affection. Almost like longing. The crazy yearning to be crooned over and soothed like she was doing with the boy seemed profoundly childish, and yet it uncovered a need for comfort that he'd never admitted, not even to himself.

Reece watched from the doorway as Leah finished with the baby's nightshirt then started to lift him from the bed. Bobby grabbed for her and managed instead to tear one side of her hair from the barrette. Without missing a beat, Leah reached up to pull the barrette free, and her shiny sable hair rippled down to flow past her shoulders then down her back to her narrow waist.

Reece was struck by the elegance of the way it had fallen, and the rich shine as the soft lamplight caught it. It'd been years since he'd seen Leah wear her hair loose, and she'd never worn it this long. Then again, he might have seen her wear it down sometime in the past few months, but it hadn't made much of an impression on him.

It made an impression now, and Reece felt a burst of sensual heat that signaled a reassuring stir of male interest. Leah looked less reserved and aloof with her hair down, less matronly, more…feminine.

Still oblivious to Reece's presence in the doorway, she tossed the barrette in the direction of the dresser, caught a swath of her hair to gently pull it away from Bobby's hand, then picked up the child and the small stuffed pony that was one of Bobby's favorites.

Bobby clung to her neck, crying nearly full-throttle now, but she turned to walk calmly to the rocking chair to sit down. She didn't see Reece until she tried to offer the pony to the fussy boy.

Her gaze dropped back to Bobby as he clutched the pony and then put his head down on her shoulder. Somehow he managed to keep the pony tucked under his arm while he sucked his thumb. Leah started rocking and the fretful howls continued for a few moments, then began to wind down.

Reece crossed the room to crouch down beside the rocking chair and place his hand on the boy's back. Bobby turned his head and focused on him, and quieted even more.

"He feels a little warm tonight," Leah remarked quietly, and Reece could tell by the tiny waver in her voice that she was even more uneasy with him than she'd been before. "There's an ear infection going around. If he has a bad night or he's not feeling better in the morning, I'll call the doctor."

Bobby's howls were now little more than babyish gurgles that were more evidence of growing contentment. He blinked his eyes heavily a time or two as he struggled to keep them open. Leah continued to rock as Bobby finally went silent and his eyelids dropped closed a last time.

Reece shifted his hand down the boy's small back until it hovered a bare inch from Leah's fingers.

"I was out of line earlier," he said, keeping his voice low. "Been out of line for a long time, and I want to apologize. It's a fact that I don't know what to do with you or about you, but I didn't mean to hurt your feelings. Not tonight and not all the other times I must have. I've been selfish and I've been thoughtless."

Leah's blue gaze shifted toward him and he saw

clearly her wary surprise, though it was obvious to him that she thought she'd concealed it.

As apologies went, it was stiff and almost sounded rehearsed, but Leah sensed it was genuine. The wonder of that sent such a swell of emotion through her that she felt a sharp sting of tears. The sting brought with it a thick feeling in her throat that panicked her. She couldn't let Reece see how much this meant, and yet it would be churlish not to be gracious. Surely she could do that much without giving anything away.

"I appreciate that you told me. Thank you." Certain that would be the end of it, Leah glanced away.

But the moment Reece's big hand eased down to warmly cover hers, Leah jumped and her gaze flew to his. The small start roused Bobby, who made a noise of protest and lifted his head slightly before he dropped it back down on her shoulder and relaxed again.

The sudden gleam in Reece's gaze told Leah he'd been surprised by her involuntary reaction to his unexpected touch, but then his face went utterly somber.

The warm feeling of his hard, callused hand made her skin tingle. Just one simple touch from Reece affected her more powerfully than being in Hoyt's arms, and somehow that made everything more tragic. It would have been better to never know.

"I reckon I've left off touching you so long that you're bound to jump when I do it now." The gravelly texture of Reece's low voice seemed to invade her because she felt it low in her middle.

Leah almost couldn't defeat the emotion that had risen higher at his small confession. She tried to give him a small smile without actually looking at his face. Her "I'm probably just…tired," came out as choked as it felt. To cover it, she said a quick, "Would you like to rock him?"

Leah immediately felt guilty for the nervous offer because it would disrupt the baby who'd just settled down. And because she'd offered solely to distract Reece. Her tension shot higher.

"It's my fault you're so uneasy with me that you'd like to run."

Leah's face went hot and she felt painfully transparent. The Reece Waverly of the past several months hadn't been perceptive at all. Even worse, the soft gruffness in his low voice and the way it sent a velvety sensation through her was something she was compelled to resist.

She didn't dare look at him. "As I said, I'm tired. It's been a long day."

Leah's nerves screamed with the tension now. It was a wonder that Bobby hadn't sensed it, but then, judging from the heavy way he laid against her, he was probably long gone.

Her soft, "Is he asleep?" managed to give away a hint of the desperation she felt, but she couldn't seem to help that either. Only a determined act of will helped her to slide her hand from beneath Reece's before he could answer. She almost breathed a sigh of relief when his hand fell away.

Irrationally worried that Reece might somehow counter her move away and touch her again, she gently gathered Bobby and stood to carry him to his bed. Reece followed to look on as she carefully laid the boy on his back. Leah spared a moment to move her hair out of the way before she set the stuffed pony aside.

Reece had gripped the bed rail, so she drew the light blanket up to cover the boy to his chest before she stepped back. Reece silently lifted the side of the bed into place until the catch snapped securely.

Leah was about to turn away when Reece caught her elbow. His hard fingers were gentle, but she felt the steely inflexibility in them. The contrast between Reece's towering height and hard male physique and her own much smaller stature and feminine softness had never impacted her as strongly as in that moment.

Reece was literally big enough to force her to do anything he wanted, yet despite the steel in his gentle grip she was aware every second that all it would take was one word or one move on her part to get him to release her. The impression was powerful.

More powerful still was the near paralysis she felt as sensation after sensation whirled and spiraled through her just because he'd caught her arm and was standing so close. An expectation she'd never felt this acutely in her whole life began to glitter and rise.

What would happen now? What would Reece do? Or was she making too much of this?

CHAPTER FIVE

"I DON'T remember your hair being so long," Reece said gruffly, and Leah felt something like a fist close around her heart to lightly squeeze.

Reece turned her more fully toward him and lifted his free hand.

"I see some stray hairpins," he remarked, his voice going smoky now.

Leah actually quivered when his big fingers plucked gently at her hair. Her knees went weak at the delicate sensations that poured over her scalp and streamed down her body.

The utter magic of Reece's gentle search could overcome her reserve in mere seconds and she had to stop him while she still had the will to try. Leah jerked up a hand to feel for the pins.

"Wh-why don't you check Bobby's bed for others?" she said shakily, somehow managing to turn away and pull her elbow from Reece's grip at the same time. "I always use a certain number, so I'll know if any are lost," she babbled on. "Bobby might put them in his mouth, you know."

Reece caught her hand and she was instantly immobilized.

"So we'll count the ones you have left," he said, as he turned her to face him again. Leah's body ignored the protest of her panicked brain. "No sense disturbing the boy with a search till we know."

The sensation of Reece lightly touching and plucking and sometimes running his fingers through her hair made Leah so breathless that she felt dizzy. She'd never imagined anyone's touch could have this effect on her, not even Reece's.

But he had so much more experience than she did, he knew so much more. Her deep, deep craving to touch and be touched, to love and be loved, made her as vulnerable to this—to Reece—as her inexperience did.

"You have beautiful hair," he rasped, and she felt the warm puffs of his breath feather lightly across the crown of her head. "I never knew it would be this soft."

Leah was completely paralyzed by what he was doing to her, and she stared at his chest in a near hypnotic daze as Reece slipped her hairpins into his shirt pocket. Her eyelids dropped shut helplessly on the sight, and when Reece's big fingers combed lightly into the hair at the sides of her face, she felt like she was sinking into a sweet ocean of sensation.

Reece gently gripped her head to tilt it back, and she didn't have the power to lift her hands to steady herself much less stop him. Leah was dimly aware that she tried to speak, and she must have because she heard herself say the words.

"Don't...please."

"How are you gonna stop me?"

The low question was so muted that it felt as if it had been spoken in a distant room. The magic that radiated through her from Reece's warm hands zoomed low to impact her most feminine places, and she couldn't think of an effective way to answer him. She wasn't sure she wanted to.

The cool touch of his firm mouth on her slightly open lips made her draw in a quick breath. Reece toyed lazily with her lips, then pressed a little more firmly.

Leah felt a feeble stir of self-consciousness, but it evaporated in a heartbeat as Reece's mouth became a little more aggressive. She felt her palms cover the backs of Reece's big hands, but she was only barely conscious of the fact that she'd been able to lift them after all. She was shaking all over but still the nibbling, teasing and periodic demand of his lips went on.

Her insides had melted and now bubbled with a wild heat that demonstrated to her just how complete her prior ignorance of intimate things had been. And how helpless she was to control her reaction to this first introduction.

If Reece's lips hadn't eased away from hers that moment, she might truly have fainted. As it was, she clung weakly to his thick wrists. He lowered his hands to her waist and gripped it firmly. Her hands settled naturally on his hard chest. Her palms felt scorched by the heat of him through the taut cotton of his shirt, and she felt the echo of her own pounding heartbeat beneath her fingers.

As the universe slowly came back into focus, Leah began to feel ashamed of the way she'd responded to Reece. She'd heard about "knee-weakening" kisses, but she'd not taken the idea seriously. And since at twenty-four this had been the first true kiss of her life, she was even more embarrassed over what had surely been an unsophisticated response.

The worst part was that she knew without looking up at Reece's face that he must have guessed that. And that he'd also realized he'd just stumbled on a sure way to manipulate her.

If he chose to use it against her.

"I—I wish you hadn't..."

The surprise of hearing herself speak was more troubling evidence that she'd somehow lost the ability to think circumspectly before she spoke. But then, her response should have already told Reece everything he needed to know. Or *almost* everything.

"We're done living like roommates," he growled and she felt the harsh possessiveness beneath the words. "Tonight's the start. Tomorrow we'll put our things together."

Reece's blunt decree jolted Leah further out of her sensual fog. As if he'd felt her immediate resistance to the idea, he went on.

"I'm not ready for sex either, but we've got a marriage to live up to. Husbands and wives share a bed."

Leah pressed against his chest. Reece loosened his hold to allow her to distance herself, but he caught her hand lightly as she stepped back and prompted her to look up into his face. The moment she did, he released his hold on her fingers.

"You were right about this marriage," he said starkly. "We made it when we shouldn't have, and now we're facing the consequences. But divorce carries its own consequences. Worse ones for Bobby than for us."

Leah felt her resistance weaken at the reminder and she couldn't seem to help that her gaze shifted toward the sleeping boy. Reece's low words brought her attention back to him.

"I won't rush into another mistake, so I mean to give this marriage some effort. Serious effort."

Leah started to glance away evasively when he added, "I reckon you aren't as aloof now as you were."

Male knowledge glittered in his dark eyes. Leah

didn't know how to answer him, much less how to credibly deny what he'd said.

However much she'd tried to squelch it, some part of her had still wanted to know what it would be like to be the focus of Reece's romantic attention. Though common sense predicted how very risky and doomed to fail the actual experience would be, after what had happened moments ago, Reece's near-mandate was not as objectionable as it should have been. In fact, she couldn't seem to summon much objection to it at all.

A feeling of inevitability stole over her. It was already obvious that Reece would never let up until she did what he wanted and tried to save this marriage. And perhaps they should give it serious effort. When they tried and then failed, the foolish hopes that had been stirred up again by that kiss would have long since been pounded out of her heart.

At least she'd never wonder if she could have done something more to spare Bobby the hurt of divorce, though she'd carry that eventual failure with her to the end of her days.

Leah dropped her gaze from Reece's and turned away though she sensed his expectation too strongly to leave the room. It was as if she was tethered to him by some invisible cord.

"Leah?"

The smoky gruffness of his low voice pulled at something in her and she felt her heart break a little.

When Reece decided he couldn't be happy with her, she'd be devastated, and yet the obligation she felt to Bobby was keen.

"Tomorrow, Leah. I can help you move your things or I can look after Bobby while you do."

Leah's back was to Reece, so she lifted her hands to press her fingers over her still sensitive lips. She could still feel that long, deliciously long, kiss. She mentally reviewed all her objections, then squeezed her eyes closed as she accepted what lay ahead. She lowered her hands and straightened a bit.

"There's something I want you to do first," she said quietly, then turned to face him. It took an incredible amount of nerve to get the words out, but it was suddenly imperative that she do so. Since Reece was insisting on this, she wanted something in return for agreeing to do what, in essence, was guaranteed to become the most devastating heartbreak of her life.

"I'd like you to switch the bed you've been sleeping in with one of the guest room beds. Or even the one in my room," she said, then hesitated when she saw the faint surprise in Reece's dark gaze before she went on.

"I'm not sure I want to explain why I don't want to share that one with you, but I don't. I'd also appreciate any other changes you might...make."

Specifically, she meant the few things of Rachel's that were still in his room—Rachel's jewelry box on the dresser for one—and in his closet. And, as far as she knew, there might even be something of Rachel's left in the drawers. Reece had packed up most of her things and either stored them or given them away months ago.

Leah didn't believe either of them needed to have daily reminders of Rachel—not in that bedroom—and when she moved her things into the drawers Rachel had used, she didn't want to happen across anything she'd have to remove. It was better for them both if Reece did that himself.

And it might be prudent for Reece to at least go through one final ritual of removing Rachel's things. It would be a last chance for him to change his mind because it would be a graphic reminder that he was replacing the woman he'd deeply loved with one he might never love.

Though she'd loved Rachel and knew she'd live in her shadow for as long as this marriage lasted, Leah needed to feel as if she had as full an opportunity as possible to make her own small place with Reece, however pessimistic she was about actually being able to do that.

She was married to Rachel's husband and she was raising Rachel's son. Though Leah didn't imagine anything she could ever do or be to Reece would ever eclipse Rachel, she at least wanted something that was "Leah's," even if it was only a bed. Besides which, Leah wasn't certain if she could bring herself to sleep in the bed Reece had shared with Rachel, since it represented the most intimate part of their lives together.

Reece's expression slowly grew solemn as the understanding of what she was asking sunk in.

"I'll take care of it."

The words were brusque, and Leah wondered if he realized how forced they sounded, as if he was making himself agree to do something he loathed.

"Well then," she said stiffly after a moment, "I need to get to bed."

"How many hairpins?" Reece's question stopped her and she gave a quick, "Eight. How many did you find?"

"Eight."

He reached into his shirt pocket to get them out. Leah walked to him and held out her hand. Reece dropped them into her palm, and his fingers lightly brushed her skin. As recently as an hour ago that might not have happened. Leah closed her fingers on the pins.

"Thank you." She couldn't fully make eye contact as she murmured a soft, "Goodnight."

"Night."

Leah turned and walked to Bobby's dresser for her discarded barrette then moved as calmly as she could into the room that would be her sanctuary only one night more. She was relieved beyond words when she was able to close the door and lean back wearily against it.

She'd been afraid Reece would kiss her again, but she'd sensed his upset with her over the bed and Rachel's things, so she shouldn't have worried.

The suddenness of everything tonight sent a fresh shock through her that was followed by a huge wave of fatigue. When she summoned the energy to straighten and cross to her private bathroom, she had to practically drag herself through the motions of undressing and taking her shower.

By the time she'd finished getting ready for bed and opened the door to Bobby's room a few inches, she was too worn out to do anything more than crawl into her bed and fall instantly asleep.

Early that next morning, Reece announced that they were going to San Antonio to shop for new bedroom furniture. Though Leah had protested the unnecessary expense, Reece rejected the notion.

"You can either help me pick it out or suffer my choice," he'd told her, and she felt a little sick that her demand last night had led to this.

"Please, Reece. I don't want to do this. If this is your way to make me back down, then I will. Replacing everything will be an incredible expense, even if we don't match the quality of what you already have. And there are four other beds in this house, so it's a foolish waste of money."

"It's Waverly money," he'd said tersely. "It's about time the Waverlys got some new things around here."

His stern expression seemed to soften fractionally. "You can pick one of the guest bedroom sets to donate to charity and set up my old one in that room. Maybe some family in the church could use the one you pick to give away. It's all good quality."

The suggestion was a fine one that muted some of her objection. She thought right away of a family who might benefit.

"That's a very generous idea," she said, but Reece cut across what she was saying, bluntly ignoring her praise.

"The men'll be here in a half hour to move everything out."

Leah immediately thought of the things that should be done before they arrived and rushed through her breakfast. She left Bobby in Reece's care while she hurried in to strip the bed and move the lamps and the things on top of the chests and dresser to one of the guest rooms.

The fact that Rachel's jewelry box was missing made her realize Reece must have cleared her things away last night or done it before he'd come out to breakfast. She was touched by his quick action, particularly since she knew it must have been difficult for him.

Leah barely finished her preparations before the

ranch hands arrived. She took charge of Bobby while everything was moved out and divided between the three guest bedrooms. The clothing in the drawers could stay where it was until the replacement furniture was delivered. All that was left was for Leah to run the vacuum in the now empty bedroom, which took more time than usual because there was so much more exposed carpet and she also took time to use the edger attachment along the baseboards.

Though Leah was skeptical they could find replacements and have them all delivered that day, Reece seemed confident that it could be done. Nevertheless, they packed up Bobby and left for San Antonio in time to arrive when the furniture store opened.

Leah was appalled at the prices for the fine quality solid wood furniture Reece insisted upon and told him so when the saleswoman stepped out of earshot to check on the availability of a chest they'd been looking at. For the first time that morning, Reece slid his arm around her waist and leaned down.

"We could replace every stick of furniture in the house and not feel the slightest ripple in Waverly net worth." Now his rugged face went more stern. "So if you pick something just because you think it's cheaper, I'll pick the most expensive set in the place and you'll be stuck with it."

Leah squirmed inwardly at the small threat. "If I'd known you'd do this, I wouldn't ha—"

"If you hadn't, I would have. If we'd done this right from the beginning, we would have come here before we made the trip to the courthouse."

The saleswoman came bustling back, all smiles. She took a moment to say something playful to Bobby who was becoming impatient because the stroller was sitting still, before she told them the chest could be ordered. Because they needed the furniture that day, they moved on to another room setting.

Leah managed to get Reece to make the actual selection, and he picked the impressive four-poster bed with matching pieces that she'd secretly admired. Reece took care of the payment and delivery arrangements while Leah got Bobby a drink of water and a fresh diaper.

Though she'd been skeptical of Reece's ability to have the furniture delivered that day, he'd got it done. A new bedspread and bedding came next, since the window treatment in the master bedroom was a neutral one she liked. Leah selected drawer liners and they took those things with them, along with a tired and hungry little boy who could no longer be put off with crackers.

They had lunch before they left town, then settled Bobby in his car seat for the long ride home. There was a pleasant sense of ease between them. Reece had touched her casually, but often enough to maintain the growing sense of connection between them. Now the long silences between them didn't feel so empty and Leah began to grow more comfortable with them.

They arrived home an hour ahead of the furniture truck and that gave Leah time to launder the new bedding. She kept Bobby out of the way while the furniture was carried into the house. Reece had her direct the placement of the pieces, and she let Bobby watch as the big bed was assembled and the new mattress and box springs were set into place.

When the delivery men finished, Leah left Bobby with Reece to go collect the new bedding from the dryer. Bobby was crawling under the big bed when she came back. To her surprise, Reece helped her fit the bed ruffle and mattress pad, then helped her put the sheets on the bed. He even tucked in the bottom of the top sheet at the foot of the bed on his side, doing an impressive imitation of her crisp folds as he did.

The bed pillows got new cases, then the bedspread went on. Bobby chortled from beneath the bed and stuck his head out from under the dust ruffle to get Leah's attention. She bent down to respond and he giggled through a lighthearted game of peek-aboo.

The warm sense of family and shared tasks might have been overlooked by most other people, but for

Leah those simple moments were precious. Something inside her began to relax and feel warm and satisfied. A faint sense of permanence slipped through her but then was gone before she had little more than a scant second to recognize it.

Leah straightened and glanced over automatically at Reece, who stood on the other side of the big bed. His dark eyes were somber, and his rugged face gave nothing more away. She realized he'd been staring at her for a time, including those moments she'd crouched down to play peekaboo.

What had she done to make him stare? Had what they'd done that day just dawned on him and now seemed extreme? Was he having second thoughts?

Leah knew she could torture herself indefinitely with those questions. Overall, the day had been a pleasant one that made her feel a little more optimistic about the future. She hadn't expected that, but even if she was making too much of the day, she didn't want to lose the feeling yet.

"You look...thoughtful," she said, then made herself give him a small smile. "Did you just realize how big a dent we made in the Waverly net worth?"

Something shot through his dark gaze and he tipped his head back the smallest fraction as if to study her from a slightly different perspective.

"I was thinking that you're beautiful. I was wondering why I never saw it so clearly until now."

He paused, and it was just as well he did because

what he'd said was such a shock that Leah needed to remember how to breathe.

"Like last night with your hair," he said almost absently. "I've been looking at you for months. Years maybe. I don't know who I thought I was looking at, but it wasn't you."

Leah couldn't maintain eye contact with Reece. She didn't know what to think of the stunning things he'd just said, much less think of a way to answer them or to even acknowledge them. The excruciating shame of a lifetime crept up.

Beautiful was the last thing she was, and she couldn't imagine why Reece would say that. She knew he wasn't a cruel man, so she knew he'd not said it because he'd meant it as some kind of sarcasm.

Was he trying to convince himself that she had the look of a woman he should have married? Rachel had been an uncommon beauty, and it was a fact that Leah was not.

"I think maybe the lighting in here needs to be turned up," she said, trying to make a joke of it before she rushed on. "I need to cut the drawer liners so we can get your clothes switched. I can move my things in after supper."

She hesitated a moment, still unnerved by what he'd said and even more jangled by his silence now. "If you're still certain you want me to. Last chance to change your mind."

Bobby chose that moment to crawl from under the bed on his daddy's side.

"Daddeee, gimme up."

Reece ignored the baby. He was still staring over at her and she went breathless again waiting for him to say something about her offer.

"Daddeee, gimme up. Please!"

The high little voice seemed to break Reece's concentration, so he picked Bobby up.

"Gimme up, huh?" he growled, and the sparkle of humor and love in his eyes as he gave the boy a tickle was as gently affectionate as Leah had ever seen. "I'll 'gimme up.'"

With that, he pretended to toss the boy through the air to the center of the big mattress, managing to catch Bobby to slow his descent and have him land with a soft bounce.

Reece pressed his big fists on the mattress to bounce the boy several times, and Bobby giggled with delight. Leah couldn't help but smile, though she was aware that Reece still hadn't commented on what she'd said. And the longer he took to do it, the more she began to believe that what he had to say wasn't good.

Reece stopped bouncing the child, who was still giggling, then picked him up and swung him to the floor.

Bobby protested that immediately. "Daddeee, gimme up!"

"It's your mama's turn to 'gimme up,' son." The little boy grinned over expectantly at her.

Reece put one knee on the mattress and stretched out his hand to her.

"Come on, Mama, let's see if this bed was worth the price." The sparkle of humor and affection that lingered in his gaze now had a glint of challenge mixed in.

Leah put out her hand, then thought better of it and started to pull back. Reece caught it anyway and in seconds he had them both on the bed, with Leah lying in his arms while he leaned over her. His voice was a warm growl.

"The last thing I'm gonna do is change my mind, Leah."

And then his head descended and his lips settled forcefully on hers. Almost immediately, he deepened the kiss. The shock of the small invasion made her gasp.

Though she was too vastly inexperienced to be sure, Reece made this kiss feel as if he was staking claim to her, and she was helpless to keep from putting her arms around him. The carnal mating his mouth gave hers was beyond anything she'd expected, but then he mellowed the kiss and somehow drew her into matching his aggression.

His big hand began a sensual exploration of its own that made her shiver with new surprise before she melted every place he touched. She suddenly couldn't get enough of the wild tumble of sensation though she was nearly drowning in it.

Somewhere in the distance, she heard Bobby's voice, but it wasn't until Reece reluctantly lifted his mouth from hers and his hand moved away that she began to realize Bobby had managed to pull himself onto the bed and was climbing on Reece's back.

It was remarkably painful to have the kiss stop so suddenly, and she lay there in the aftermath trembling as she slowly became aware that Reece's big body was also trembling. She saw the harshness of frustration on his rugged face though his dark eyes sparkled with amusement at the boy's antics.

He was gentle with Bobby and shifted himself away slightly as he reached back to pull the boy around and tuck him between them. Bobby was delighted.

"Daddeee, gimme up."

Reece chuckled, though it sounded a little strained. "You mean bounce. But we might be done bouncin' baby boys for one day."

"Bouws, Daddee, bouws!"

Leah smiled a little, still dazed as she waited for the world to stop spinning. Bobby grabbed a handful of Reece's shirt to pull himself into a sitting position between them.

"I think you started something," she told Reece.

"Are you talkin' about the boy or you?"

Leah looked over into the smoldering lights in

Reece's dark eyes. "I'd meant Bobby, but yes. I didn't expect that."

"Neither did I, but it was a fine taste."

Bobby reclaimed Reece's attention, and Leah took the opportunity to roll away and slide to the edge of the bed. She sat there a moment, waiting to feel a little less weak before she stood up. Reece had rolled to his back to lift Bobby into the air. It was a game they called "airplane" and it was clear that Bobby was wound up.

"If you wouldn't mind keeping him occupied, I'll get the drawers lined," she said.

"Go on ahead," he said as he took Bobby and rolled off the bed. "I'll see what I can do to get this one calmed down."

Leah was on her way out of the bedroom to find a pair of scissors, when the distant chime of the doorbell sounded.

"I'll get it," Reece said, then carried the squealing baby under his arm like a football and followed Leah out into the hall. Leah opened the linen closet after Reece and Bobby passed her, then found the scissors and returned to the bedroom.

She'd just started unrolling the drawer liner when she heard Reece call out for her. Leah checked her hair in the dresser mirror, surprised that she hadn't thought of that right away.

And she should have, because her barrette was askew and her hair was about to tumble free. She ended up rushing through Bobby's room to hers, then took a hasty few moments to brush out the length and rapidly put it back up.

In the stronger light of her bathroom, she could see that her face was flushed and her lips were puffy. She looked as if she'd just been given the kiss of her life. Although she had been and she'd loved every moment of it, Leah was more than a little appalled that she'd now have to face company.

She turned off the bright light, then hurried through her bedroom to the hall.

CHAPTER SIX

LEAH heard Margo Addison's voice just as she neared the end of the hall nearest the living room. Margo was Rachel's mother, but other than coloring, mother and daughter had had precious little in common.

"The boy always does that, Reece. It's not good that he's picked up her shyness."

Leah stopped, fully aware of who *her* was. Though Rachel and Leah had been best friends since their sophomore year of high school, Margo had objected relentlessly. The glamorous snob had been appalled that her beautiful, popular daughter had made a friend of a homely nobody who'd had the added notoriety of being a foster child from a white trash background.

Rachel, of course, had defied her mother and continued their friendship anyway, inviting Leah to parties or picking Leah up in her own car so she could either participate in school-related extracurricular activities or do things with other friends. They'd even studied together, because Leah got better grades. Leah had been happy to tutor her friend, who wasn't particularly attentive in class, because it was a way she could repay Rachel's friendship.

Though Leah had often suspected that Rachel had initially chosen to befriend her because she knew her snobbish mother would have a fit, Rachel soon proved herself to be a loyal and genuine friend.

Reece's low voice made Leah refocus on the conversation. "Leah does a fine job with the boy, Margo. He's just not used to you." Margo's Southern belle tone was saccharine.

"Why, of course she's doing a wonderful job with the boy."

Leah grimaced because she'd had years to know Margo would make a token agreement but then make her point anyway.

"It's just that children pick up the oddest things. Have you reconsidered hiring a nanny? The exposure would be so beneficial to the boy. And I've managed to hear of two very fine candidates. Both have such well-rounded, educated upbringings, so either of them could make certain Robbie's exposed to a variety of educational and cultural experiences that he might not otherwise have."

Reece's voice went lower. "My son is exposed to everything his parents mean for him to be exposed to." Leah picked up the faint warning in that and felt herself relax a little.

She'd weathered Margo's often hateful private comments to her from the beginning of this marriage, but she'd never before overheard anything Margo might have said to Reece when she was out of the room. She'd assumed it was going on, because Margo regarded Leah as a stain on her otherwise pristine life.

It touched her to have this proof that Reece defended her, whether she was present to know about it or not. She'd rarely worried that he'd be influenced against her by the things Margo might say to him in private, because she already knew what he thought of his former in-laws. He'd felt so strongly about them in fact, that he'd been willing to do anything to prevent his son from ever being raised by Margo, and to ensure that the boy's ranching inheritance was secure. It was the main reason he'd married Leah.

"Why, of course, dear," Margo went on, "I thought I'd mention it in case you—*and* Leah— change your minds. I'll continue to keep an eye out as Robbie gets older."

Robbie. Margo's persistent use of that name always set Leah's teeth on edge. Margo had made clear to her daughter before the boy was born that she not only disapproved of the name Robert but also disliked the nickname Bobby because it was so common. Referring to Bobby as Robbie better satisfied her sensibilities.

Leah felt guilty for hovering out of sight in the hall and silently moved back a few steps before she started forward, knowing her footsteps would now be heard. She steeled herself as she stepped out of the hall and walked into the big living room. As if Bobby hadn't seen her all day, he scrambled off his father's lap and toddled over to her.

Leah automatically bent down to pick him up, then carried him over to hand him back to Reece.

"Hello," she said, making herself smile pleasantly at Margo and her equally elitist husband Neville. Neville usually let Margo do most of the talking, but only because she spoke for both of them. "Can I get the two of you something cool to drink? We have iced tea and soft drinks."

Margo's green eyes sliced over her critically. Leah knew her cotton shirt and jeans were another indication to Margo of her low class background. Margo wore her perfectly tinted red hair styled to within an inch of its life and her white designer dress was the very height of summer fashion.

"I think I'd prefer something stronger...dear." The fractional hesitation was deliberate.

Leah glanced at Reece. "Would you mind?" She didn't serve liquor to anyone. Her family and her childhood had been destroyed by alcohol, and her personal bias was so strong that she'd have nothing to do with it.

Yes she knew Reece kept liquor in the house and that he sometimes had a drink, but she merely dusted the cabinet and the bottles and kept the glassware clean. The fact that Margo knew all about Leah's bias and the reason for it accounted for her request. And she made that particular one every time she and Neville stopped by. Because Leah had never discussed it with Reece, she had no idea whether he realized what was really going on or not.

Until she saw the perceptive glimmer in his dark gaze before he looked over at Margo.

"What would you like, Margo? Neville?" Reece got to his feet and automatically passed Bobby back to Leah.

"A vodka for me. What would you like, Neville?" she said to her husband. Before Neville could answer, she looked back at Reece. "Make that two."

Reece started for the den, and Leah went to one of the armchairs and sat down with Bobby. Instead of keeping the boy on her lap, she set him on the floor.

"Why don't you find your blocks? Maybe your grandmother and grandfather would like to see you build something."

Bobby stuck a finger in his mouth and thought about that. Leah pointed to the lamp table nearby that had a basket beneath that was half full of alphabet blocks. Bobby looked toward them, then cast a shy gaze at Margo and Neville.

Leah's soft, "Go on," prompted him walk partway there before he turned around and trotted back to climb into her lap.

"The boy's what? Fifteen months?"

Because Reece was no longer present to hear it, Margo's voice had lost its too sweet tone. Leah knew something was on its way.

She glanced over at Margo and smiled though it felt as fake as it probably looked. "Yes. Last week in fact."

"Have you taken him for his regular checkup?"

"He has an appointment next week," Leah answered, prepared for yet another small grilling session. Margo so bitterly resented that Leah had adopted her grandson that she never missed an opportunity to question Leah's competence.

The silence stretched and Leah let her gaze stray from the now silent, disapproving pair who sat on the sofa opposite her chair. She couldn't account for Margo's sudden silence, except she was probably saving up for Reece's return.

Nevertheless, it was a relief to hear Reece walk back down the hall and step into the living room with the drinks.

Margo took hers and thanked him profusely. Reece had just handed Neville his drink when Margo went on.

"It should be time for his measles-mumps-rubella. I hope someone's educated you about those."

Leah kept her smile firmly in place as Reece sat down. "I've read—"

"Have you quizzed the doctor about the wisdom of having each of those shots given separately? My physician tells me there's some concern about the usual practice of administering all three at once."

"As I said, I've read about them," Leah repeated calmly. "I also discussed the alternative with our doctor."

Margo's brow went up. "When was this?"

"At Bobby's last checkup."

"Well, I wouldn't mind going along to this next appointment," Margo said briskly. "I'd like to see for myself that this new young doctor is the person I want taking care of my grandson's medical needs."

Leah somehow maintained her polite expression. Margo's motive for doing that would be more to somehow harass or embarrass her than it would be for the good of the child, though neither of them would ever acknowledge that in front of Reece.

Reece spoke up. "Leah and I are satisfied with both the doctor's expertise and Bobby's care, Margo. There's no reason to concern yourself."

Reece's words had a finality that warned Margo that she was trespassing. He changed the subject.

"We're leaving in a few minutes to go to town for an early supper," he said. "Nothing fancy, just hamburgers and malts at the Lasso, but you're welcome to come along.''

Though this was the first she'd heard of it, Leah was both relieved and amused by Reece's announcement. Margo and Neville had, in the past, dropped by just as Leah was about to put supper on the table. And since it wouldn't be polite not to invite them for the meal, she'd had to scramble to come up with impromptu vegetarian dishes.

Then, of course, she'd had to sit by and conceal her irritation when neither Margo nor Neville did more than push the food around on their plates.

Those times were always uncomfortable and aggravating for Leah, mainly because Margo was so adept at subtle digs and minor disagreements. Whatever the subject, she made a point of pressing Leah for her opinion, then immediately took the opposite view. She fussed over Bobby, but only to usurp Leah's care or to give condescending advice.

Leah had long since tired of such juvenile tactics, but she weathered them to keep the peace. She was aware of the fact that losing Rachel had devastated both Margo and Neville, but because they were such remarkably cold people, it was easier for them to channel their grief into added resentment of her.

A small part of her had hoped that some of Margo's subtle digs might eventually penetrate Reece's distraction and provoke him as much as Leah was provoked. Apparently that time had come.

The Lasso was a small family-owned restaurant that neither Margo nor Neville would be caught dead in, so it was certain they'd decline the invitation. The fact that Reece had never taken Leah out to eat anywhere before yesterday made the sudden suggestion another nice surprise.

Margo recovered quickly from her shock and rallied. "Ah, so our Leah is taking cook's night off. Good for you, dear. Preparing the same meals day in and day out would be wearing, I imagine. I've never understood why Reece didn't hire a new cook and housekeeper after the last one retired, but I imagine you enjoy keeping up your best skills."

Margo barely took a breath before she glanced over at Bobby and coaxed brightly, "Come here, Robbie. Give Grandmum a kiss before she goes home." She held out her manicured hands to the boy, then gave a little pout when Bobby turned his face shyly into Leah's shirtfront.

"It might help, Margo," Leah dared softly, "if you called him Bobby." She saw the flash of surprise in Margo's eyes. One red-penciled brow arched high.

"Well, dear, that almost sounds like a...a criticism."

Leah's calm, "It's a suggestion," was the prelude to a brief silence. And then Neville stood up. That was apparently a signal to Margo who also stood.

"Well, we'll be going." Now she gave Bobby a

wide smile and wiggled her fingers playfully. "Bye-bye, shy boy. Maybe next time you'll give your Grandmummy a nice welcome," she said before she added a singsong, "She'll bring you a present."

Thank heavens it was all over quickly then as Reece escorted them to the foyer then walked with them out to their car. Bobby immediately scrambled off Leah's lap and trotted over to the basket of blocks to drag it out from under the table.

When he had, he dug one out and held it up to declare, "Block!"

Leah leaned her head on the chair back and smiled. The child was himself again. "That's right. Would you like to bring them into the bedroom while Mommy finishes the drawers?"

She got up and helped Bobby carry the basket of blocks through the house to the master bedroom. He decided to line the blocks up along the edge of the new bed, so she got busy with the drawer liners and quickly finished. She'd gotten a laundry basket out of the linen closet to begin the transfer of clothing from Reece's old drawers into the new ones when Reece found her in the hall.

Leah was wary of his harsh expression, but she knew right away she wasn't the cause of whatever he was irritated about. No doubt Margo had made a parting shot.

"You aren't doing laundry now are you?" he asked gruffly.

"No. I was going to start moving your clothes."

"Put the basket away. I'll bring the drawers in. No sense handling everything twice."

In short order, Reece had carried in the drawers and Bobby toddled over to inspect the neatly stacked folded clothing. She and Reece worked together in silence to quickly make the transfers before Reece carried the drawers back to the guest rooms.

Leah took a few moments to change Bobby's diaper, then led him back to the bedroom and encouraged him to put his blocks back in the basket.

"How about we get to town? We'll move your things later."

Leah smiled. "Good idea. I was waiting for you-know-who to begin asking for you-know-what. By the time we get there and order, he'll be more than ready to...you know."

Reece's stony expression cracked. "You-know-who and you-know-what. Wonder how long those'll last?"

"Not too long," she said her dark brows going up. "In case you missed it, he perked up the moment I said 'you-know-who,' so I think he's figured out more than we realize. We'll soon have to brush up on our spelling skills, no doubt."

Reece was smiling over at Bobby as the little boy dropped another block into the basket. His love and pride was evident and the harshness had completely smoothed from his face. He looked relaxed and he looked ruggedly handsome. Leah couldn't help that her heart gave a little leap of attraction.

They gathered up the baby then drove into town for supper. After the busy day, it was a treat to not have to cook and clean up. Bobby enjoyed the outing, and it was another minor event that gave Leah a pleasant feeling of family.

Few people had ever seen the three of them together in public, and it was clear when other restaurant patrons either waved or stopped by their table for a quick hello that Reece seemed slightly uncomfortable with the sudden attention, though he didn't remark on it.

Later, they drove home and Reece helped her move her things into the master bedroom. He participated when she gave Bobby his bath and helped dress the boy for bed and tuck him in. Afterward Leah collected her toiletries from her bathroom and found places for them in Reece's.

When she was finished, she unpinned her hair then unclipped her barrette. The activity that day had mostly distracted her from tonight, but her tension had been rising steadily for the past two hours. Though they'd spent the entire day preparing to share the same bed, it still seemed too soon.

It didn't help a lot to remind herself that they should have passed this point months ago. The fact that they were doing this now—and only because

Reece had insisted—still seemed as radical and ill-advised as marrying him in the first place.

And then she remembered that kiss last night and the one this afternoon and felt herself tremble with a potent mix of fear and feminine excitement. Would he go slowly and wait for feelings to develop between them or would that matter to him? The moment she'd brought up the subject of divorce, he'd gone out of his way to oppose the notion.

Would he rush things in the bedroom in order to consummate the marriage? He could probably guess that taking that step might make it even more difficult for Leah to leave him.

And a man didn't necessarily have to be in love with a woman to have sex. Though Leah couldn't imagine it with a man she didn't love, she was inexperienced enough, and yes, she loved Reece enough, that she didn't know if she could resist if he decided to seduce her.

How could she raise the subject of delaying intimacy without sounding like a nervous virgin? How could you tell your husband that a few kisses were fine, but no more? Or that you were wearing a long nightgown to bed so you hoped he owned pajamas?

Would he really understand that her inexperience and natural shyness was particularly inhibiting when she thought of actual lovemaking?

Leah put the barrette and hairpins out of the way on the counter.

Be careful what you wish for...

The old saying made another taunting pass through her mind. She suddenly couldn't bear to completely move into Reece's space. Because she had a deep need to maintain whatever sense of privacy and autonomy she could, she picked up her soap and her shampoo then got her blow-dryer and one of her brushes out of the drawer to carry them back to her old room. She'd shower in there, at least tonight. After taking a moment to collect her long nightgown and robe from the new dresser drawer, she made a quick dash through Bobby's room.

The boy was fast asleep, and she knew Reece must be busy finishing up some of the paperwork he hadn't gotten to that day. If she hurried, he'd never know the difference.

It felt good to go through her nightly routine in the place that was so familiar. She'd loved the beautiful room she'd lived in all these months. The master bedroom was larger than this one and the new furniture was gorgeous, but Leah had already felt like a princess in the room she'd had.

She'd never lived in such luxury, not when she was growing up and not as an independent adult with a tiny apartment down on the town square, so it was hard not to feel nostalgic about this, however silly that was.

Leah finished with her shower, dried her hair, then put on her nightgown and robe. The soft yellow cotton gown with narrow straps was completely opaque and covered her down to her ankles, as did the lightweight matching robe that went over it. She belted the robe loosely at her waist, then collected her towels and put them in the hamper.

As she slipped back through Bobby's room to go to the master bedroom, the last thing she expected was to find Reece already there waiting for her.

She faltered to an uncertain halt when she saw him sitting in an armchair he must have carried in from one of the guest rooms. He'd slouched down in the big chair, his head leaned back against it, his long length supremely at ease. His dark gaze sparkled with male interest as it made a leisurely sweep down the front of her belted robe to linger on her bare feet.

Her own wide gaze made a tour of its own. He'd obviously just showered, probably while she'd been using the hair dryer. His dark hair was still a bit damp and he was wearing jeans that were zipped but not buttoned, and because he wore no shirt, she could see the superb muscle definition of his chest and that it was lightly dusted with dark hair. The sheer masculinity of him in the dimly lit, quiet room reached out and wrapped around her.

"Is using the shower in here a problem for you?"

Leah cringed inwardly at the question. "I'm...a little nervous. Kind of a...last time thing. Maybe. I don't think so."

The babbling answer made her face go hot, and she felt ridiculously adolescent. She couldn't take her eyes off Reece, and they felt as big as dinner plates.

She couldn't seem to recover from the sight of him sitting there slouched down, his muscled arms resting on the chair arms, his long, denim-clad legs bent at the knees. His feet were bare, too. The unbuttoned jeans gave her the sudden idea that he'd only put them on because he didn't own a pair of pajamas.

So then, of course, he wouldn't be wearing them to bed—either the jeans or pajamas. The fact that there was no telltale peep of underwear behind the open button made her heart race.

CHAPTER SEVEN

IT WAS stunning to remember that little more than forty-eight hours ago they'd been so estranged from each other that she'd felt compelled to approach Reece with an offer to divorce.

Since then, they'd gone through a series of small changes that felt like little earthquakes compared to the deadness of the nonrelationship they'd had before. All day today those small changes had been evolving into ever larger ones, but this last one—sharing a bed with him—now seemed far too dangerous and potentially disastrous to allow.

It was too soon, far too soon. Leah felt completely unable to cope with this, though she'd dreamed of Reece for years. Romantic fantasies and nebulous desires bore no resemblance to the blatant sexual reality of a half-dressed Reece Waverly. And when you added the unbuttoned jeans and the strong sense of sensual peril, she felt every bit the untouched virgin she was.

Leah put her hands together in front of her waist, lacing her fingers together tightly to still their tremors as the silence between them began to feel heavy.

She felt so self-conscious and awkward. At least she could still think of something to say.

"I hope my alarm clock won't disturb you. I often wake up before it goes off, so you might not hear it at all."

Leah pressed her lips closed on the nervous babble she'd been on the verge of and prayed for Reece to end the suspense.

"You're nervous," he remarked calmly.

"And you're not," she said back. "I'm sorry. This isn't such a big adjustment for you since you were...married before." The small smile she forced had a sickly curve that she wasn't aware of. "I'll try to be more adult about it."

With that, she turned toward to the bed then hesitated. "Which side do you prefer?"

"Either's fine. Take your pick."

Leah walked to the side nearest the bathroom, since she'd put her alarm clock on that bedside table. She pulled down the bedspread and top sheet then untied the belt of her robe with fingers that felt hopelessly uncoordinated.

Taking off the robe to drape it across the foot of the bed felt even more awkward, and instead of laying it neatly as she'd meant, it landed in a twisted heap. She snatched it up and had another try with roughly the same result. A quick glance toward Reece told her he'd watched her every move with interest.

An edgy feeling of embarrassment and frustration made her suddenly irritable.

"For my next trick, I'll get into bed, then roll over and fall out onto the floor."

This time, she managed to lay the robe tidily across the foot of the bedspread. Reece chuckled, and she heard him get up.

"Are you always so obsessively neat?"

Leah glanced warily in his direction as he walked to his side of the bed. She was aware that there were no pajamas in sight and that he might be about to shuck his jeans. It was difficult to keep his question in mind.

"I appreciate order. It doesn't always take so much time to be neat," she said, referring to the robe. "Keeping order allows you to be lazy, actually. Small messes take small moments of time and effort to straighten, as opposed to big messes that can take hours. Not to mention the ambition it takes to face them. A little preparation makes up for itself in time saved."

Oh Lord! The nervous little lecture made her sound like a persnickety spinster who starched her underwear and gave her furniture the white glove treatment.

Now Reece grinned over at her flushed face. "Will you fold me away in a drawer somewhere if I get too messy?"

Her flushed face grew painfully hot. "I'm sorry. I sound obnoxious, don't I?"

"You sound scared to death."

Her swift, "I am," came out involuntarily and her pride took another solid hit. "Why did we do this, Reece? And the expense today..." She turned away and sat down on the edge of the mattress, feeling guilty and bitterly disappointed in everything, particularly in herself.

She felt the bed move slightly and went so tense that her body ached with it. Reece's big hand closed warmly on her shoulder as she felt him settle on his side behind her.

"You're wound up tight, darlin'. Lay down here and I'll work out the knots."

Leah reflexively started to rise, but his strong hand kept her where she was.

"No better way for you to relax than to let me prove I can be trusted."

"You don't need to prove anything to me," she said, glancing back over her shoulder to see his skeptical look. "I can relax on my own. I'll be fine."

"Not tonight," he said grimly. "I'm not gonna lay down next to a coiled spring and wonder when it's gonna snap."

The no-nonsense look on his face shamed her. She felt like a complete ninny, and she knew Reece didn't suffer fools gladly.

Only because she was certain her nervousness had offended and aggravated him did she submit, and she reluctantly lay down on her stomach. She'd been careful to make certain the nightgown still covered her all the way to her ankles, so she turned her face away from Reece and squeezed her eyes closed.

Reece rose and set his knees on either side of her thighs before he gently drew the pillow from beneath her head. Leah couldn't suppress the delicate shiver when he gathered her long hair.

"Your hair is like silk," he said gruffly, and she somehow endured the sweet sensation of feeling him handle it. "You ought to wear it down more."

When he laid it aside and his hands finally settled warmly on her upper back, they felt big enough to span the width of her shoulders.

"Ever had someone work out the kinks before?" he asked as his fingers began to gently search out and probe the small areas of tension.

Her soft, "No," didn't sound at all definitive, though it was.

Leah couldn't remember not craving to be touched. Because the craving was so strong and because she knew she was particularly vulnerable to it, she'd kept herself so rigidly aloof from the mere opportunity that Bobby was almost the only person who'd ever been allowed to cross that line. Dancing with Hoyt Donovan had been a huge, huge thing for her, and now that seemed like nothing compared to this.

With Reece there was an entirely new and deeper dimension of touch, not only because of the sexual element but because she loved him so very much.

As his hands began their careful labors, Leah felt the full horror of that discovery. She'd loved him for years, yes, but she'd tried very hard these past weeks to numb herself to her feelings until loving him was an idea that she'd become slightly detached from.

Yet the intensity of it must have been creeping back over her the past two days, particularly with that kiss last night. The horror she felt suddenly was because it had just dawned on her that she'd never loved Reece as much as she did now.

"You're fightin' me, darlin'," he murmured, and she felt the dampness beneath her closed eyelids. The person she was really fighting was herself, though he'd never guess that.

She'd never considered herself self-destructive, but she wondered about it tonight. If she'd still possessed the strong will to survive that had taken her this far, she would have found the strength to throw Reece's hands off and fled to barricade herself behind a locked door. Or to have at least refused him and made it stick.

But the hard-palmed, callused hands and fingers that moved with such devastating authority on her body slowly spread an intoxicating magic that radiated everywhere. And then the diabolical gathering of heat in her most feminine places began and Leah knew this was the beginning of the end for her.

What Reece was doing would ensure that he could have whatever level of physical intimacy he wanted, whenever he chose for it to start, for however often and long he wanted it to go on. What amazed her now was how many years she'd managed to live without having the simple basic human need to be touched satisfied. Surviving so long without it was surely her own personal eighth wonder of the world. What Reece was doing to her now easily comprised the first seven.

As she entered that sensual twilight that wasn't quite sleep, Leah wondered dimly if Reece's heart was at least minimally involved in this. Or had everything these past forty-eight hours, particularly what he was doing now, simply been the practical action of a savvy, experienced man who wanted to keep his marriage intact?

Then again, maybe it wasn't so hard to decide what he was thinking about this or what he might really feel about doing it. Perhaps he'd given his answer long before she'd thought of the question.

I'm not gonna lay down next to a coiled spring and wonder when it's gonna snap.

Spoken, no doubt, by a tired man who'd much

rather take a few moments to ensure a good night's sleep than a caring husband whose only motive was to give comfort to his wife.

And yet his unrushed hands conveyed anything but a lack of care. Leah was literally lulled to sleep by the sweet pleasure of his touch.

She awakened that next morning a dozen minutes before her alarm clock went off. The male warmth that pressed against her back from her head to her heels and the arm that rested heavily around her waist, created a sense of security and belonging that she'd rarely felt.

Loathe to move away, she lay quietly to savor it. Leah shifted her arm and cautiously laid it on top of Reece's. Though his arm was much longer than hers, she fitted her small hand over the hair-roughened back of his for a few moments. The hunger to explore while he wasn't awake to know it, made her lightly trace the veins and scars on the back of his hand.

Did she dare lace her fingers with his? Reece's slow, steady breath assured her he was still sleeping, so she gently slid her fingers between his and curled her fingertips into his hard palm.

Doing such silly, trivial things suddenly seemed tantamount to a mouse braiding the ruff of a sleeping lion. Lions didn't appreciate braids, particularly when they woke up to find prey within reach. Playing finger-patty with a virile man who'd been celibate for nearly year and a half might be appreciated in a way she wasn't ready for if her exploration woke him up and he realized the opportunity to end his celibacy lay trapped beneath the weight of his arm.

Better to stop the foolishness and slip out of harm's way. An experimental move made her aware that her nightgown had crept up in the night. The simultaneous realization—that Reece had worn neither jeans nor pajamas to bed—made it even more prudent to slip away.

Leah might have made it if Reece's arm hadn't flexed to drag her back solidly against him.

His voice was rusty from sleep. "You've still got four minutes."

Her soft, "But I'm awake now," made him chuckle.

"So am I."

With that, he rolled her to her back, then rose up on an elbow to loom over her. His dark eyes studied her face and she went breathless as his head descended.

His lips pressed so gently against hers that she felt the warmth of them wash through her in a sensual wave. The scratchy burr of his beard stubble added a rough texture she hadn't felt before, but the kiss was over too soon for her to decide if she liked it or not.

He drew back to growl, "Good morning," and she got out a shy "Good morning" to him.

He reached over to slide the switch on her alarm, probably the moment before it was due to go off. "Now you can go," he said and Leah couldn't miss the sparkle of humor in his dark eyes.

She rolled away from him to the edge of the bed then walked to the dresser for a bra and jeans before she went to the closet to collect a shirt to carry with her into the bathroom. When she'd finished with everything and come out, Reece had dressed and was waiting his turn.

Bobby was still sleeping soundly, so she rushed quietly to the kitchen to start breakfast. The world seemed to have shifted. Now as she went about meal preparations, there was a level of satisfaction and permanence that hadn't existed before, perhaps because she felt a little more like a wife than a cook and housekeeper this morning.

What about Reece? Did he feel a little more like a husband? Or did he merely feel relief because last night had helped put the question of divorce a little farther out of the picture?

Determined to keep her hope to a sensible level, Leah went about making breakfast to distract herself.

Reece went back to working outside, and Leah followed her normal morning routine. He'd not only reminded her of the bedroom set he'd given permission to donate, but he'd asked her to try to make arrangements today so he could have some of the men move it out and get it delivered.

A call to the pastor set everything else in motion, and he agreed to receive the furniture at the church in order to facilitate the anonymous donation Leah considered proper. The set would be delivered later that afternoon to the family who'd recently lost their possessions in a house fire.

The men came to move out the furniture after midmorning, and Leah was grateful to get that taken care of. Once they were gone, she took Bobby and hurried into the empty bedroom to give it the same thorough vacuuming as she had Reece's room. Since the men would stop back when they returned from town, she wanted things ready for them to move Reece's old set in.

By the time everything was done and she served lunch, Bobby was cranky enough for a nap. Leah finally gave up trying to get him to eat the little sandwich she'd cut into fancy shapes and let him have the cookie she'd meant to save for his dessert.

Reece had been silent through most of the meal and Leah wondered at that. At least at breakfast they'd talked over the arrangements for the furniture. Just a bit ago, Reece had come in, washed up and taken a moment to kiss his son, but once he'd sat down for grace and started eating, he'd seemed preoccupied. Not even Bobby's fussiness had done more than draw his gaze briefly.

Leah couldn't help wondering if they were back to business as usual. He'd kissed her that morning before she'd gotten out of bed, but there'd been nothing after that. Yes, he'd made eye contact with her, but there'd been no glimmer of interest and not so much as a shared touch between them.

It was suddenly hard to reconcile Reece's cool distance now with the profoundly sexy male who'd sat in that armchair last night and let his warm gaze wander lazily over her.

The emotional abandonment of her childhood and a lifetime of insecurity made it impossible to ignore the significance of this.

Leah got Bobby to drink the last of his milk, then reached for the damp washcloth to gently wash the cookie crumbs from his face and hands. When she finished, she set the cloth on the chair tray, then stood to unlatch it and lift the boy out.

"Tell Daddy you'll see him later," she said softly and Bobbie's fussing turned to tears.

"No nap, Mama, no!"

"Oh yes, sweet boy," she said with a soft chuckle of sympathy as she cradled him tenderly.

Reece glanced at her but his dark gaze slid so quickly from her to the baby that she couldn't miss the small rebuff. He reached over to give Bobby a soft pat on the back.

"Go on with your mama, do what she says."

Leah moved away from the table and carried the boy through the house to his room. She heard the soft chime of the doorbell, but ignored it since Reece was in the house.

After removing Bobby's shoes and changing his diaper, she put up the side of the bed. She lingered only long enough for Bobby to rub his eyes and turn onto his side. He was good about going right to sleep, so she moved out of the room.

Since she hadn't heard the doorbell a second time and Reece hadn't called her, she assumed whoever it was had either come to see Reece or was already gone.

Though she wasn't up to facing Reece's remoteness again, she needed to get things done in the kitchen. If they had a guest, it wouldn't be proper not to offer something to drink on a hot day. A quick pass by the kitchen and the living room showed her they were empty, so she went down the hall in the opposite wing of the house to the den to check there.

She heard Reece say something but didn't see Hoyt Donovan until she'd walked into the room.

"Well, amigo," Hoyt was saying, "now that we've got that outta the way, how'd you do with my advice about Leah the other night?"

The question impacted her like a slap and Leah came to a breathless halt. Hurt blossomed, followed quickly by a flash of anger so intense that she felt the heat of it scorch her face all the way to her hairline.

It was just after Hoyt had gone home that Reece had given her that soul-shattering, out-of-the-blue kiss in Bobby's room, followed by his insistence on sharing a bed. Too angry over the insight to be thinking straight, Leah spoke up.

"What advice was this, Mr. Donovan?" she asked, and had the satisfaction of seeing both men give guilty starts. "By the way, would you like something to drink? Iced tea?"

Hoyt seemed to fumble a bit, and that was unusual for a man who'd never been known to be a loss for words. He couldn't have confirmed her suspicion more emphatically had he made a full confession.

"Ah, well…"

Hoyt glanced toward Reece, then back to Leah. It was clear to her that Hoyt was trying to come up with a tactful way to word his answer that would be truthful and yet not completely accurate.

Leah made herself smile, though it probably looked as strained as it felt. "You don't have to answer that, Hoyt. I'm sure you meant well. Would you like the tea?"

"No. No thanks, Miz Leah. Don't wanna cause you the extra work."

"The tea is the least of the extra work I've done the past two days," she said, unable to keep her gaze from straying to Reece's stony expression. She was bursting with the need to say something to him, but the harsh reserve of lifetime was reasserting itself.

"If you change your mind about the tea, let me know."

With that, she turned away and walked from the room, her back rigid with angry pride. She stalked to the kitchen where she cleared away the lunch dishes with a ferocity that finished the task in record time.

In truth, she was more angry with herself than she was with Reece. He'd genuinely adored Rachel, and Leah couldn't fault him for not being able to find something in his heart for her, but it was excruciating to wonder how hard it had been for him to go through the motions.

Leah finished wiping the counter before she draped the dishcloth over the faucet and washed her hands. When she finished, the muddle she'd made of everything crowded in and she leaned dispiritedly against the counter.

Perhaps something had been accomplished after all. Perhaps now Reece understood in a way that he hadn't before that kissing a woman and sharing a bed with her, along with all the other inconsequential things they'd done the past two days, weren't things that he could continue putting himself through indefinitely.

After all, he'd lived the real thing. He, more than

she, ought to be particularly repelled by the idea of forcing himself to go through the motions with her after the passionate romance he'd had with Rachel.

Because he'd been as remote from her today as before, he must have realized that already. Her heart seized the idea and she felt bitterly certain. And it hurt to know how quickly he'd come to that conclusion.

A prickling at the back of her neck got her attention and she lifted her head to glance over her shoulder.

The surprise of seeing Reece standing a few feet away with his feet braced apart and his arms crossed over his chest, startled her badly. She let go of the counter edge and turned jerkily to face him.

CHAPTER EIGHT

HOYT was nowhere in sight, so he must have hightailed it for home. Leah couldn't blame him. One look at the stormy expression on Reece's face and Leah suddenly wished she had someplace safe to escape to herself. No sense pulling any punches.

"This won't work, Reece. You know it already, don't you?" Her voice was remarkably steady considering her heart had jumped into her throat.

"The hell it won't," he groused.

Leah's gaze shied from his. "I'm clearly not the right woman for you. If I were, things between us the past two days would have happened naturally. You wouldn't have needed someone to list things for you to do, and you wouldn't have had to...force them."

"You're wrong."

His gruff words were a pronouncement that she was compelled to challenge.

"How am I wrong? Hoyt gave you advice, you decided to take it. We had a couple of kisses and we've slept in the same bed. I think you realize you can't go on like this."

Reece's gaze wavered from hers momentarily and

he let out a harsh sigh. When his gaze came back to hers it had softened. So had his voice.

"I know what you heard and it's plain your feelings were hurt. I admit Hoyt hands out plenty of advice to folks who don't ask for it, but if you think I had to force myself to do a damned thing I've done with you, then you're blind. As a bat."

She shook her head, not believing him. "Oh, Reece." She paused when she saw the flare of anger in his eyes. "I'll stay with you as long as you want me here, but please don't force things because you think I'll leave if you don't."

"You think I forced myself to kiss you?" Reece unfolded his arms and looked faintly amused.

Leah studied him warily. "I don't know, but I can't stand to think you might have. And you've been distant again today—and unhappy—like before. It's not that I expected grand romantic gestures, but I do know when you've put up no trespassing signs."

Reece gave her a narrow look. "You wanna know why I've been standoffish today, or would you rather keep jumping to conclusions?"

Leah couldn't maintain eye contact with the harsh probe of his gaze and looked away. She leaned back against the counter and crossed her arms, resigned. "I suppose."

Reece started her way and she looked up. He reached her just as she straightened from the counter. Just that fast, his hands spanned her waist. Before she realized what he was doing, he lifted her to the counter next to the sink. She'd grabbed his shoulders reflexively and now she kept her hands there. She felt a fierceness in him and her instinct was to keep him at a distance if need be.

His rugged face was stern and his gaze was turbulent. "You sure you wanna hear this?"

Leah gave a hesitant nod.

"I want you to stay, and I'm getting what I want," he said, then added tersely, "so far."

He paused, his grip easing only a bit on her waist though he didn't release her.

"Because I'm getting that much, all I've been able to think about today is how long it's been since I've had sex."

Her gaze shied from his at the stark declaration, and she felt her face go hotter. Reece flexed his fingers on her waist to prompt her to look at him. When she did, she saw that his gaze was smoldering now. His low voice went gravelly.

"I don't trust myself not to take you to bed while the boy's taking his nap." The harshness on his face seemed to amplify his utter bluntness as he added, "You deserve more than to be rushed just because I'm burning up."

Leah was so shocked she couldn't move.

"That explain it for you?" His tone was just short of belligerent.

Her soft "yes" did little to temper the fiery lights in his dark eyes. She wanted to do more than just rest her hands on his wide shoulders, but Reece was so tense that the cotton-covered flesh beneath her palms felt like iron. His dark brows lowered in a surly frown.

"Now what's wrong?"

Leah couldn't help the nervous giggle that came gurgling up. "I'm afraid to move."

She felt some of Reece's tension ease away as he made a sound that was part growl and part chuckle. He leaned close, hovering a scant inch from her mouth before his lips seized hers and he pulled her to the edge of the counter.

When she felt him fit his hips snugly between her thighs, Leah's shock was quickly swept away beneath the aggressive possession of his mouth. She clutched at him, and the sharp desire she felt wrung a soft moan from her.

Just when she thought she might not survive the dizzying wonder of his mouth and now his hands, Reece began to temper the kiss. Far too soon, his mouth shifted off hers and his arms closed even more tightly around her.

He was trembling, and Leah felt a stir of feminine power. Reece's heart was beating even harder than hers, and it pounded them both. He pressed his lips fervently into her hair then nuzzled her neck for several breath-stealing moments more before he started to pull away.

"Ease up on me, lady," he said hoarsely. "At least while it's daylight."

He studied her flushed face then his gaze lifted to her hair before dropping back down to her kiss-swollen lips.

"Find something quiet to do. Let me go back to paperwork and forget you're in the house."

Leah stared, still a little dizzy. Reece had never looked harsher, he'd never looked more masculine and powerful. Everything feminine in her was completely overwhelmed and thoroughly attuned to him. There was nothing faked or insincere about any of this, and she doubted she'd ever think so again.

Reece lifted her down then pulled away to turn and stalk from the kitchen without a backward glance. Leah sagged against the counter because her legs barely held her up.

It was much later, probably late afternoon, before it dawned on Leah that there was a world of difference between the kind of love she so craved and what Reece had been talking about. It distressed her to realize that for all that time, the difference hadn't mattered to her at all.

And he hadn't mentioned waiting until he felt something for her, only that all he could think about was sex and that she didn't deserve to be rushed.

Once again, the emotional consequences of what she'd gotten herself into seemed endless.

The moment Reece saw his wife at supper, he knew he'd confessed too much that afternoon. She was the standoffish one now. He sensed her unease and it made him feel like a sex-crazed animal.

Leah was more sensitive than Rachel and so much more fragile and vulnerable. He'd automatically compared Leah to Rachel out of habit, and in the past he'd done it in a way that made Leah seem second best, if that. But there was a depth to Leah that intrigued and drew him, an untouched naïveté and wary innocence that seemed both sweet and sad.

He felt almost as tender toward her now as he did toward Bobby, and that got his attention. Any notion of second best was gone and he wasn't sure when it had happened.

Like noticing how long her hair was the other night and how pretty her eyes were, and yesterday, how subtly beautiful she was. Subtly beautiful, because Leah's wasn't the kind of beauty that struck you at first sight as Rachel's had, but the kind of beauty that dawned more slowly then repeatedly drew and held the eye. The kind of beauty that went deeper and far outlasted the kind that spanned a handful of years then began to fade.

And this was the woman who'd taken such fine care of him and his son all these months. The goodness and generosity in the countless things she'd done had conferred a beauty all their own.

Leah deserved so much more than she'd gotten so far. As he cut himself another piece of steak, he decided to do something about the silence between them.

"What do you do when Bobby's with me in the evenings?"

Leah looked his way. "I read or watch a movie. Or there's some little chore to take care of. Sometimes I go for a walk."

"You can go anywhere on this ranch, you know," he said as he caught the piece of steak on his fork tine. "Take one of the pickups if you want. Just tell someone where you're going. Same thing if you want to go riding."

She looked down at her plate and pushed at a lima bean. "It's been a long time since I've gone riding. I'm probably not very good at it anymore."

"It'll come back to you fast enough. I'll take you with me some morning while it's cool."

Her quiet blue gaze came up to meet his and he could tell she liked that idea. "I'd have to find someone who'd take Bobby that early."

"Maggie'd be a good one for early mornings," he said, referring to his foreman's wife. "Why not call her after supper? We'll go the first morning she can do it."

Leah nodded, feeling a little more at ease. Bobby

tried to shift his plate off his chair tray, but she calmly reached over to take it. Reece went on.

"I reckon we're overdue to find someone to help out around here anyway," he said. "If you had more time to yourself, going out early with me wouldn't be complicated. We can hire whoever you like."

Leah set Bobby's plate out of harm's way on the table but didn't comment. She'd loved having a home to take care of, and she'd taken enormous pride in that. She knew she wasn't very modern that way, but she'd never been very sophisticated or particularly obsessed with the notion of a career, particularly when having a home and a family was something she'd hungered for her whole life.

"I never meant for you to handle everything single-handedly after Ina retired," he went on. "I think I brought that up a couple times over the months, but Bobby's getting older. And things are changing between us."

Leah searched his face as he looked down and finally took the bite of steak he'd just cut. His was a common sense suggestion, but another adjustment. A big one, since one of the things that Leah had been grateful for the past eleven months was that everything between them had been completely private. Without a live-in housekeeper, there'd been no one around to witness the stark emotional and physical distance between them, much less discover they'd slept in separate beds all this time.

She wasn't certain yet how much things would actually change between them, so the last thing she wanted was to bring a stranger in. The potential for gossip was something she was leery of.

"I'll think about it," she said at last, passing Bobby his cup.

Reece frowned and finished with the bite of steak. She looked down at her plate but felt his scrutiny and knew he was impatient with her answer.

"I've got people who can handle things for me, Leah," he persisted. "It's only fair for you to have people who can handle things for you. To free up your time."

Leah looked over at him, compelled to point out the critical difference. "But your people don't sleep under this roof, and they aren't in the house all day and night like a housekeeper would be."

She was thinking of that afternoon when Reece had come to the kitchen. The idea that a housekeeper might have accidentally walked in on that made her queasy. After all, she'd walked into the den at an awkward moment herself when Hoyt had been here.

She saw a flicker of something in Reece's gaze that suggested he'd just thought of the same thing.

"So find someone to work part-time," he told her. "No law says we have to have a live-in like Ina. Truth to tell, now that I've done without live-in help all these months, I'm not sure I'm as fond of the idea anymore.''

Leah relaxed a little at the compromise, pleased that Reece had proposed it. "I didn't grow up with housekeepers and cooks, so having them isn't important to me. But you're right about Bobby. He's becoming more and more active, so it might be nice to have someone come in for a day or two a week. I'll ask around and see who might be available."

"Good. Do the things you like and leave the rest to whoever you hire. Later on, if you decide you want more than a day or two of help, add more days. Add a whole week. Move them into the house. It's up to you, since this house is your territory."

It was a typically chauvinist remark and Leah suppressed a sudden smile, amused by it rather than insulted. And because she'd thoroughly enjoyed taking care of this house and was proud of how well she'd done with it, the remark was as much an acknowledgment of that as it was a declaration that she had a place of authority on Waverly Ranch, however modest others might consider that.

Even Rachel might have laughed at how unliberated that was, but Rachel had never known anything but privilege and security, and she'd managed to always get her way wherever she went. For someone who'd never really had a home of her own other than her small apartment, much less any sort of authority over it, being in charge of the Waverly ranch house was akin to ruling a small kingdom.

Reece finished with his steak and reached for his glass of iced tea. Leah noted that and set down her fork.

"I made dessert. Nothing fancy, just a no-icing corn cake sprinkled with powdered sugar. Unless you'd rather have it with coffee later."

"How much did you make?"

"Just a small pan."

Reece grinned over at her and she felt the warmth of it to her toes. "Enough for now and later on?"

Leah smiled, flattered. Now that Reece was paying attention, he wasn't shy about expressing his appreciation. "Both if you like."

"Both, then. I can get it. Where's it at?"

"In the top oven," she said, amazed at the sense of closeness his offer gave, though she knew it was silly to confer so much on such a small thing.

Reece got up and walked to the double ovens to get out the small cake plate and carry it to the table. He stopped by the counter where she'd set out the dessert plates and a serving spatula. By the time he sat down, Leah had refilled their tea glasses and added a small measure of milk to Bobby's cup.

Bobby had been fairly quiet at supper that night, but he lit up when he saw the cake. "Kay, kay!"

Reece served them all, then had a taste of the

modest dessert. After he had, he fixed her with a faintly cranky look.

"Is cooking and baking one of the things you'll be sharing with hired help?"

Leah had just taken a sip of her tea and now set the glass down. "Probably not, but would you like me to?"

"Hell, no."

Leah smiled, but then discretely pointed at Bobby who was putting a pinch of cake into his mouth. "Oops, Daddy."

Reece immediately assumed a penitent expression though his dark eyes were laughing. "Thanks much, Mommy. I'll watch my language. Good cake."

"I'm glad you like it," she said, then had a taste of her own.

Their table conversation hadn't been scintillating or witty or brilliant, but the deep down happiness it caused felt sweet. The two people she loved most in the world were with her. One she knew loved her completely because she was the woman he'd grow up thinking of as his mother. The other at least liked her as a friend again, and he'd made it clear he wanted her to remain in his life. And he desired her. There had to be at least some caring in those things, something that might grow into a bit more.

After dessert, Reece took care of washing Bobby's face and hands while Leah cleared the table and loaded the dishwasher. He whisked Bobby away for a fresh diaper, then brought him back just as she finished.

"How 'bout that walk?" he asked, and Leah was again struck by the pleasure of having him ask.

They took a leisurely walk down to the stables in the warm evening. Bobby toddled along with them, and they paused whenever he stopped to look at something. Reece caught her hand and Leah felt the dizzying thrill of his warm grip.

They looked at some of the horses in the stable, and Reece led his sorrel gelding out of a stall. He put Bobby on the big horse's bare back, and then put a cautious hand on the boy's leg as he walked the horse down the stable aisle and back. Bobby clung to a hank of red mane and enjoyed every moment of the ride.

When it was over, Reece lifted him off and set him on the ground. Bobby immediately howled his protest.

"Gimme up, gimme up!" Huge tears shot down his pink cheeks and he stamped his little feet in a truly impressive temper tantrum.

Leah and Reece exchanged shocked looks, then tried not to laugh. Reece straightened to his full height and forced himself to glare down sternly at his small son.

"Bobby, that's enough."

The snap of authority in Reece's low voice got Bobby's attention, and Leah felt her heart squeeze at the sight as the tiny boy abruptly went silent and looked up, round-eyed, at his towering father.

"That's better. Come here." Reece reached out to guide the child closer to the horse. "Tell Boss goodnight."

Bobby lifted his little hand and waggled his small fingers. "Ni-night."

The massive horse stretched his nose toward the boy to blow his warm breath against him. Bobby giggled and reached eagerly for the horse's big head.

"Gimme up!"

Reece held him back and gave a low, "Not now. Give him a pat and we'll let him go night-night."

Leah couldn't help her grin at the sound of Reece's gruff voice as he repeated Bobby's babyish "night-night." In the next moment the swift stab of love she felt made her eyes sting.

She looked on blurrily as Reece patiently guided the little boy's hand to the horse's nose for a few gentle strokes.

"Ni-night, hose," Bobby said solemnly, and Reece shot Leah a grin.

She wondered if the reason the little one was so somber with his goodnight might be because he was thinking about how near his own bedtime was. She looked on as Reece set the boy on the other side of the stable aisle.

"Stand right there," he said with gentle sternness

before he turned back to the big horse and led him into the stall.

Leah watched to make certain Bobby stayed where he was until the horse was put away and Reece walked out to shut the stall gate. Bobby rushed over to him and Reece plucked him off the floor to lift him to his shoulders.

They walked together toward the ranch house, and Bobby chattered, still wound up over his ride. Reece set him on his feet when they got to the back patio. He and Leah sat together on the wide bench swing out back while Bobby played with his small collection of outdoor trucks.

Reece dropped his arm across her shoulders and pulled her tighter against his side. After a moment, he reached over and caught her left hand to gently examine her fingers.

"I didn't even get you a ring."

The remark was unexpected and Leah was instantly uncomfortable. She couldn't look at him.

"There were so many other things on your mind. On both our minds."

"Don't make excuses for me, Leah."

She lifted her free hand to put it over the back of his, unable to stop the gesture of fondness. She looked into his dark eyes.

"I'll do what I want," she dared softly. "And what would a ring have meant eleven months ago?

It was difficult enough to cope with everything else."

His face went utterly grim and he looked down at their clasped hands. He gave hers a gentle squeeze, and his words came out in a low rumble.

"We're done skipping over things. We'll take care of the rings tomorrow."

She sensed his guilt and felt bad about it. "Please, Reece. We don't know—"

"*I* know, Leah," he said sternly, and looked at her. "This is for life. Unless you can tell me you don't feel anything for me and you doubt you ever will."

The sudden silence in the wake of his demand put her squarely on the spot and she mentally scrambled for words.

"I couldn't say either of those things," she said at last, unable to look away. She'd meant to be more evasive than that, but instead she'd revealed more than she'd meant to. She held her breath, hoping Reece hadn't realized that, but his steady scrutiny told her he had. Her gaze shied from his.

"Then we'll get those rings tomorrow." The subject was closed.

"It's time for Bobby's bath," she said as she pulled her hand from Reece's and quickly stood.

She felt him watch her every move as she helped Bobby stow his trucks under a patio bench. When Bobby trotted away from her toward the end of the patio opposite the house, Reece intercepted him. He tucked the wiggly little boy under his arm like a football and carried him into the house after Leah opened the door to the kitchen.

Though neither of them had mentioned the word "bath" or "bedtime" to the baby, by the time they walked into the hall to the bedrooms, Bobby started his usual protest.

"No baff, Mama. No ni-night."

Reece chuckled. "Can't put dirty boys to bed without a bath."

"No ni-night!"

Reece swung the boy upright to carry him on his arm as they reached Bobby's room. Leah followed the pair as they crossed the carpet to the bathroom.

Once they'd got the baby's clothes and diaper off and Leah carried his little sneakers to empty them of the dirt he'd picked up on their walk, Reece took over Bobby's bath. She'd put the child's soiled clothes in the hamper and was standing by with a fluffy towel when Reece lifted him out of the tub onto the bath mat.

In no time at all, Bobby was dry and dressed for bed. Though he was now fighting sleepiness, he offered them both a round of kisses and sweet hugs before they put him to bed and retreated to the hall.

Reece's amused gaze met hers. "You'd best call Maggie before it gets late," he reminded her. "I've got a couple of things to finish up in the den, then I'll be ready to turn in."

There was another message beneath the words and Leah felt the sultry whisper of it. She thought immediately of what he'd said that afternoon about sex and burning up, and felt her cheeks heat.

Reece hadn't shown a single sign of the masculine fierceness he'd had in the kitchen that day, so her tension had ebbed completely away. Now it came rolling back and brought with it a feminine anticipation that was part dread and part excitement.

It was too soon for that level of intimacy and yet she felt the potent lure. For a woman who'd come to believe she'd never have even a few of the things they'd shared the past few days, she couldn't help craving more. Surely Reece couldn't be intimate with her and keep his heart completely remote?

"Something wrong?"

Leah automatically shook her head and forced herself to smile.

"Maybe just shy about calling Maggie," she said, relieved to think of something truthful. "I haven't talked to her for a few days, and I've never asked her to keep an eye on Bobby. I usually hire Marie, since she does day care in town."

Though she could see the watchfulness in Reece's gaze, he seemed to accept her explanation.

"Might want to see if Maggie'd like to do it on a regular basis for pay here at the house."

"That's a good idea."

They went their separate ways after that, and Leah was grateful for the time alone. Maggie agreed to come to the house and watch Bobby any morning Leah liked, since she was always up as early as Leah was to cook her husband's breakfast. And she was very interested in watching Bobby on a regular basis for pay, though she'd wanted to think about it.

Maggie often hired on as an extra ranch hand at different times of the year, particularly foaling time. She was a quilter, and donated a lot of her time to local 4H groups. She and Jim had two grown sons who were living on their own, so she'd had vast experience with little boys. It would be a wonderful match.

Leah checked on Bobby to make certain he'd gone to sleep, then crossed to the connecting door to step into the silent master bedroom. She switched on a lamp, unable to keep from glancing toward the huge bed as her tension jerked up a few extra notches.

CHAPTER NINE

LEAH brushed her teeth and took her first shower in the master bath before she dressed in her nightgown and dried her long hair. Though she'd made too much noise to hear whether Reece had come into the bedroom or not, she assumed he had. He'd showered before supper tonight as he most often did, and it was getting late. Since they got up just after four in the morning, a nine p.m. bedtime was the norm.

By the time she turned off the bathroom light and came out, Reece was sitting up in bed with a pillow wedged between his back and the headboard. He'd brought in a stock magazine and was thumbing through it, but his dark gaze shifted to her and went somber as it fixed on her face, then her hair before it made a lingering sweep of the rest of her.

"I should have come in when you did earlier. I haven't had the pleasure yet of takin' your hair down." He leaned his head back against the big headboard to give her a lazy look. "I reckon I will soon enough though."

Leah couldn't help that her face felt warm. It was hard to keep from staring at Reece's wide, masculine chest and lean middle. He set his magazine on the bedside table then reached over to flip down her side of the bedspread and top sheet in a wordless invitation. She fumbled with the belt of her robe then slipped it off to drape it over the foot of the bed.

The quiet room was heavy with a low-level charge of expectation. It went without saying that there'd be no sexless massage tonight, not when Reece's dark gaze was virtually eating her up. Last night, she'd fallen asleep so quickly that she hadn't truly faced lying awake next to him at a time with the most potential for lovemaking.

Tonight she'd be awake, and her insides were knotting tighter with every wary beat of her heart. She got into bed and pulled the covers up. Reece slid down and turned onto his side to prop his jaw on a fist and look down at her. His other hand curled around her waist and his voice lowered to a rasp.

"I can feel your heart going a million beats a minute, Leah."

Her gaze shied from the gentle probe of his. She felt stiff, and she kept her hands folded primly on her middle because as idiotic as it was, she didn't know whether she should touch him or not. "I don't mean to be so nervous." An awkward smile burst up from the self-consciousness she felt. "I'm not very good at knowing what to do."

"What do you want to do?"

The question somehow pierced deep, landing someplace so lonely and lost and afraid that the words were out of her mouth before her brain could catch them. "I'd like to feel free but be safe, not so tied up inside." Once that much had come out, she took a shaky breath and let herself say the rest. "I don't want to make the wrong choices, Reece. I'm...terrified this is all a big disaster in the making."

It probably qualified as one of the biggest confessions of her life, and she laid there a little in shock to realize how easily it had slipped out in the beginning, and yet how easy it had been to decide to include the rest of it. A huge wave of emotion surged up from the turmoil of nerves and longing she felt.

Reece lifted his hand from her waist and caressed her flushed cheek. The light touch sent a shower of tingles through her.

"We're done with disasters, you and I." The solemnity in his dark eyes was powerfully persuasive, and Leah couldn't seem to help falling prey to it. "We've gone too long without being close. Time to change that."

And then his dark head descended and his cool lips eased gently onto hers. He retreated a hairbreadth as if waiting for some signal from her. She lifted her hands to tentatively touch his bare chest with her palms and fingertips.

Leah felt the shudder that went through him before his lips seized hers and his arms slid around her. The kiss was long and lavish and so carnal and hungry that Leah felt as if she was being devoured. She couldn't help her wild response, or that she trembled when his big hand closed warmly on her breast. When his lips moved off hers, she still had enough presence of mind to stifle her moan of disappointment. They were clinging to each other almost painfully tight.

His mouth pressed fiercely into her hair before his hot breath gusted into her ear.

"Tell me no, Leah," he rasped. "Do it now, baby."

Leah opened her mouth to speak, then couldn't. Terror, desire, and the unmet needs of a lifetime had just coalesced and focused themselves exclusively on this one man, the man she'd loved for years. Lingering worries about the future seemed to stand at a distance, and she was so unutterably weary of carrying them that all she could feel was relief.

The craving she'd had to love Reece openly and to be loved by him seemed so close now that she could almost reach out and touch them. At least the first part of them, because being loved by Reece—really loved—still seemed as impossible as ever.

And there'd been no declarations of love from either of them. It was too soon for those too. Would they ever come?

"Tell me no, Leah," he repeated hoarsely.

The sudden thought—that there was a time limit on all this in spite of Reece's declaration about their marriage being for life—sent sharp anxiety through her. So many of the good things that had come her way seemed to have time limits. Quick ones.

So many other good things, the biggest ones, were meant to last a lifetime. Parenthood and marriage were the main ones. And yet her parents hadn't wanted the responsibility of raising her or of keeping in contact with her.

Marriages, even some good, seemingly stable ones, ended with alarming frequency. Reece's own good marriage to Rachel had been tragically cut short. Life itself was so easily cut short.

The primal need for more, for everything she might be able to get and everything she was driven to somehow make up for, made it impossible to tell Reece no. The sense that these special days with Reece couldn't last was strong and increased her need.

Not even the terror of being vulnerable to him in the most intimate way possible, was strong enough suddenly to save her from herself. If it all ended tomorrow, next week, next month, or somehow lasted as long as a year, she wanted at least this much. Reece pressed a warm, rough kiss on her shoulder and she felt the prickle of tears.

She turned her face to kiss the side of his neck.

His skin was so amazingly smooth there. She couldn't seem to help that her hands moved restlessly on him. He lifted his head from her shoulder only enough to grind out her name.

"Leah?"

It was a last chance she didn't heed, and she was too far gone to answer with anything but an urgently whispered, "Love me, Reece. Please."

Little more punctured the thundering silence that followed than the sound of callused hands on soft fabric, the whisper of bodies on fine percale, and their jagged breaths and quiet sighs. The excruciating magic of touch was given and received.

A nightgown was smoothed away, rich sable hair was tangled and stroked. Silky skin was tenderly chafed by hair-rough flesh. Small hands moved with growing confidence as instinct took over and her body learned what gave him pleasure.

And when the many fevered kisses and expert touches brought them together in the deepest and most elemental way, they soared to some lofty, breathless place, a place of sparkling light and sweetness that was nearly unbearable. They hovered there a precious scattering of heartbeats and then began the rippling descent that took them back to earth and landed them softly in the quiet, dimly lit hush of the big bedroom.

They lingered over a last, lazy kiss then lay together skin to skin, overcome by a satisfying lethargy. Leah fell instantly and deeply asleep, so immune to second thoughts and regret that she forgot she'd ever felt such things.

Reece awakened in the night and realized neither of them had turned off the lamp. He didn't bother with it now either.

He'd all but wrapped Leah's small body in his, and he eased back a bit to watch her sleep. Her cheeks were flushed and her beautiful hair was everywhere. He took a lock of it between his thumb and forefinger and rolled it gently, savoring the silky feel of it.

He'd gone too fast with her, and it made him feel like a selfish brute. But the feel of her small body felt good against his. Right. And he wanted her again, though he could wait this time.

It shocked him a little to realize that his desire for Leah last night had banished any thought of Rachel from his mind. Until now. A mental search for Rachel's red-haired, green-eyed image brought nothing. A cold feeling of loss went through him and he felt it collect in his chest.

And yet the crushing sorrow he expected next didn't come. There was no sense of guilt or disloyalty. Instead, his brain conjured the memory of Leah's beautiful eyes going heavy-lidded with pleasure. The sound of her soft breathing made him remember the other night when she'd spoken soothingly to a fussy and overtired little boy. He'd heard her do that before, but it had never affected him like it had that night.

Leah's natural gentleness and sweetness of soul warmed him and gave him solace. The moment he felt it he sensed something deep inside him shift. Just that quickly he knew his grief for Rachel had tucked itself away somewhere, and he felt the coldness in his chest recede.

Leah stirred then, and though she was still deeply asleep, she frowned and made a restless move. He relaxed his hold on her and waited as she rolled over away from him. She'd flung her arm across what was left of her side of the bed and her wrist and hand dangled limply off the edge of the mattress.

Reece smiled at the lovely sight of her soft nudity. If she'd been awake to know she'd shown him so much at once, she'd be head to toe with a fiery blush. He liked that his wife had been untouched until last night. It humbled him to remember that he was the only man she'd ever been with, and to know that every attitude she'd ever have about lovemaking had gotten its start last night with him.

It suddenly mattered very much that he'd treated her with utmost care despite the overwhelming need to have her. It might have been too soon, but he didn't completely regret that. He knew instinctively that Leah could never easily walk away from him now, not when she'd responded to him with such a helpless lack of reserve. And a woman like Leah wouldn't have allowed last night to happen at all unless she'd had her own hope for their marriage to be permanent.

Love me, Reece. Please.

Had she said it that way because she'd meant to use the word love, or because she was more comfortable referring to sex as lovemaking? Leah had probably never spoken a crude or harsh word in her life, so she might automatically choose the word love over sex. She'd no doubt prefer that what they'd done had been love rather than merely sex.

And although she'd been on guard with him for as long as he could remember, she hadn't been on guard when she'd said that.

A settled feeling spread through him and urged him close to her back. He slid his arm across her waist and lifted his head to press a lingering kiss on her bare shoulder. He lowered his cheek to her pillow and closed his eyes. He must have fallen deeply asleep because he didn't know it when Leah managed to slip from beneath his arm long before the alarm clock went off.

They'd forgotten to have the second serving of corn cake last night, and Leah had completely forgotten to tell Reece that Maggie was available to watch Bobby that morning so they could go riding together.

She'd managed to get out of bed without waking Reece and taken a quick shower before she'd gotten dressed. Her hands were trembling as she braided her hair. If she wore it like she normally did, her old Stetson might not fit, and her hair was too long to wear loose while they were riding.

Leah fretted with her hair, then took more pains than usual making sure the light makeup she'd put on was just so. When she finished and tucked in the tail of the long-sleeved blue blouse she'd chosen for that morning, she managed to make a twisted mess of it and had to start over.

No number of other trivial thoughts or obsessive little tasks could truly calm her. She'd been trying not to dwell on how worried she was about facing Reece this morning, but she'd failed miserably. She finally went still and gripped the edge of the bathroom counter before she looked up to closely study herself in the big mirror over the sink.

No one in the world had ever seen her behave as she had with Reece last night. Most people would never have suspected she was capable of that kind of wildness. She hadn't come close to imagining it of herself. Even now, she searched her face for a hint of what might remain, though she couldn't see anything. She closed her eyes and remembered the feeling of it, the almost shameless aggression, the complete lack of self-control.

Whatever secrets she'd thought intimacy might

uncover, she'd never expected to have every careful bit of her reserve and self-control stripped away to reveal things even she'd not suspected she was capable of. And she'd never imagined how very vulnerable it was possible to be until Reece had demonstrated it to her. Thoroughly.

What would he think of her this morning?

It was a fact that he'd not seemed to have a single complaint last night. On the other hand, he'd lived without sex for many months, so she doubted he'd have too many complaints about the sudden end of his celibacy.

But it was true that many men lost interest in a woman once they'd had sex. And a woman who allowed sex too soon and too easily was often not taken seriously.

Nearly everything they'd done in this marriage had been out of the natural order. Now they'd had sex before they'd truly developed the nonsexual part of a good relationship. Her reasons for grabbing for every bit of closeness she could have with Reece last night now seemed the height of foolishness. She'd probably doomed the tiny chance she'd had to make this marriage work.

And she'd been such a novice. It was completely possible that he'd been far less carried away by it all than she had.

The moment her mind moved on from that torture to the worry over birth control—in their case, the lack of it—Leah decided she couldn't stand another second of worry and suspense.

Reece was just pulling on his second boot when she stepped out of the bathroom. The moment he glanced at her, his dark gaze warmed and she felt herself relax the tiniest bit. He straightened and walked right to her.

"I take it Maggie can watch the baby this morning," he said as he gripped her waist and bent to give her a gentle kiss.

Her heart quivered with joy at the welcome, and her hands automatically came up to his chest. She felt foolish for being so worried.

"How did you know?"

"You braided your hair. I've seen you do that on the days you take care of the flowers because you always wear a hat. Since those flowers can't possibly need another second of attention this week, I figure you're going riding with me." He smiled. "At least I hope you are."

Reece slid his arms around her as if it was the most natural thing in the world. Leah pushed her hands up his chest and rested them on his wide hard shoulders.

"I didn't know you paid attention to things like that," she said quietly.

"I've been paying attention the last few weeks...but I've been memorizing things the past few days."

He leaned down to kiss her again and his hands moved low to pull her snugly against him. The kiss went carnal then and Leah felt the wildness come crashing back. It took so much to temper her response, but she'd tormented herself with enough worry about it that it was important to demonstrate, at least to herself, that she had some self-control. Even then, she found herself beginning to slip over the line.

The pressure of Reece's mouth eased away just enough for him to growl against her lips, "Oh, darlin', how 'bout I just have you for breakfast?"

It was hard to cling to at least a bit of common sense. When his lips skimmed across her jaw to lightly nibble her neck just below her ear, she could barely form a coherent thought.

"M-Maggie said she could be here at six," she managed to get out.

It felt so, so wonderful to be pressed up against his hard masculine body and remember what it had felt like last night skin to skin. When his warm breath feathered over her ear she gasped raggedly at the stark pleasure it caused.

"I think we need a honeymoon someplace," he rasped. "No work, no people, nothing but the two of us."

"What about...Bobby?" she said breathlessly, staggered by the touch of his tongue on a sensitive spot even as her heart leaped with joy at Reece's suggestion and what it meant.

As if on cue, they both heard a happy, good-natured "Mommee" from the partially opened door to the next room.

Reece's low chuckle sounded strained. "We've got an early bird."

He gave her a lingering kiss on the cheek then resolutely eased away a space. His dark gaze was heavy-lidded. Leah let her hands slide down his chest and she eased back a little more. He caught her fingers and gripped them a few seconds before they heard Bobby call out again, impatiently this time.

"Mommeeee."

"Maybe you could see to the boy, Mommy. I'd better shave." He leaned down for a swift, hard kiss then released her hands, though he seemed reluctant to do so. When he did, Leah moved away from him to the connecting door on legs that still felt deliciously weak.

But she could have danced on air! She'd never imagined a man could look at her the way Reece just had. *As if he loved her.*

Excitement, expectation and happiness whirled so strongly inside her that she felt like she was floating as she got Bobby dressed for the day. Reece joined her in time to carry the child as they went to the kitchen.

By the time they finished breakfast and the dishes were cleared away, Maggie arrived. Bobby didn't protest being left behind because Maggie had brought along an oversize inflatable ball that he'd immediately wanted to play with.

The early morning was already warm but perfect. Reece chose a pretty black mare for her and took his big sorrel. They planned to ride to one of the creeks not far from the headquarters. It was to be a relaxed ride, and not as long as it could have been since Leah wasn't used to riding.

"Don't want to cripple you up," Reece declared after he explained what he had in mind. She agreed but had insisted on saddling the horse herself, though it had been so long since she'd done it that she was slow. Reece waited while she worked and he'd shown no sign of impatience, though he checked to make sure the cinch was tight enough when she finished. To her consternation, he'd taken up a good six inches of slack in the cinch strap with one expert pull before he secured the excess and let down the stirrup.

Once they were mounted and riding down one of the alleys that cut through the network of corrals, Leah glanced his way.

"Have you decided about going to Hoyt's tomorrow?"

Reece sent her a sparkling glance. "It'll be my

pleasure to take you, Leah. I apologize for making you wonder.''

Leah smiled. It was as if she'd stepped into an alternative universe that morning. One so beautiful and perfect that it was suddenly everything she'd dreamed of.

They were on their way back to the house from the creek before the perfection began to worry her. The first dark tendrils of guilt began their insidious rise. The worst of that concerned Rachel, but she couldn't let herself face that one yet. The guilt that seemed most immediate—and most in need of confessing—was about birth control.

It was something they should have discussed, something she should have thought about long before last night. But when you were married to a man who never touched you, being on the pill wasn't necessary. And the notion of becoming pregnant with Reece's child was anything but undesirable. She loved Bobby so much that she'd love to have a little brother or sister for him. At least one of each. Bobby shouldn't grow up an only child as she and Reece had.

Though Reece had once told her he was willing to have other children with her, she needed to know if that was still all right with him. And like so many other things in their marriage, a pregnancy now would be too soon so they'd need to do something about birth control. She waited until he glanced her way then made a nervous start.

"You told me months ago that you didn't object to having other children with me," she said, then added, "Has that changed?" She couldn't help that she held her breath as she waited for what he would say.

A gleam of humor sparkled in his dark eyes. "Did we make a baby last night?"

Leah relaxed and shook her head.

"The time wasn't right, but we'll need to use something until I can get a prescription."

Reece's rugged face went somber. "You'll marry me, won't you, if I wind up pregnant?"

The outrageous question startled a giggle out of her. Reece grinned. "I don't mind living dangerously, Leah, but you're the one who has carry for nine months. You decide when."

He reached over and caught her hand to give it a squeeze. "So yes, I do want more kids." His fingers tightened.

His horse crowded against the mare and he tugged her closer as he leaned toward her for a quick kiss. His lips touched hers and sent a bolt of feeling through her, but then a massive wave of emotion surged up. As Reece pulled away and released her hand, that massive wave was still strong enough to make her eyes smart.

She truly had stepped into a beautiful alternative

universe that morning. The relief and gratitude and joy of it all was almost unbearable.

And yet neither of them had spoken love words. Though she'd couldn't have done the things she'd done for Reece and with him without being deeply in love with him, she knew very well that Reece might be able to do and say everything he had without being "in love" with her. He could out of gratitude and friendship and certainly affection, but unless he told her what his exact feelings were, she had no real way to be certain.

Then again, perhaps she needed to let the whole notion go. Reece was showing her in so many ways that she mattered to him, that he cared about her. When she thought about how grateful she was to finally have the man she loved care about her and respond to her, she realized she'd gotten greedy.

Reece was bending over backward to demonstrate his desire to stay married to her. Why should she expect him to jump through one more hoop?

Just a handful of days ago things had been so lifeless between them that the only chance of happiness for either of them had seemed to be divorce. Since then, the earth had not only shifted on its axis, it had reversed the poles. Night had exchanged places with day, and the chill of near-estrangement had been banished by the balmy temperature of mutual desire and companionship.

Besides, Reece still loved Rachel. She couldn't

expect him to simply switch off a love that had been that deep and powerful, or to suddenly decide he was in love with someone else. After all, she'd never been able to stop loving him, not even when he'd married Rachel.

What she did believe was that he'd made a little space in his heart that was completely hers. As long as she remembered that and allowed herself to be content, she could live without extravagant declarations.

But how long would she be able to keep from making an extravagant declaration of her own?

CHAPTER TEN

ONCE they returned to the house and Maggie had gone home, Reece was so doggedly determined to get the rings that he whisked her away to San Antonio. Marie had been able to keep Bobby in town, so they were able to take the trip by themselves.

Leah only barely thwarted Reece's enthusiasm for buying the most spectacular—and no doubt, the most expensive—rings they found. She neatly distracted him by insisting on a wedding ring for him.

"I don't wear rings," he'd said gruffly, and she'd had to insist.

His next try, "I'd lose a finger out working," brought her quick, "You could put it in your pocket."

He'd finally agreed and tried on a few handsome choices when Leah remembered that Rachel had never been able to persuade him to wear a wedding ring. The fact that he was indulging Leah now was a pleasant surprise.

In the meantime, she found the perfect rings. They were beautiful and elegant, but not as flashy as Rachel's had been. The only real disagreement between them happened when it came time to pay and Leah insisted on paying for Reece's ring.

She'd always lived frugally and still had savings, though the ring would put a hefty dent in them. Her reminder that this was a ring exchange ended his protest.

They had lunch at a wonderful San Antonio restaurant, then started home. Bobby had finished his nap and was ready to go by the time they got to Marie's to pick him up.

Leah's heart was full, and the quiet joy she felt was easily the best of her life. Each moment they spent together was profoundly sweet, and she reveled in their growing closeness. The sense that they were truly connected made her feel relaxed and optimistic, and that she could confide anything to him.

The craving to tell Reece how much she loved him was so intense that it took everything she had not to do it. Only the fact that she could never be the one to say it first deterred her, though it was already hard to guard her words.

Ironically, it was thinking about how hard it would be to keep from telling Reece she loved him that brought her guilt about Rachel roaring up.

In view of how much she loved Reece and her complete loss of control and common sense last night, she suddenly had real worries about what she might say in the heat of the moment.

A simple, "I love you," might easily come out as a helplessly candid, "I've loved you so long." And now that Reece seemed to miss nothing, it would be natural for him to wonder—or to even ask—how long that had been.

She'd been in love with Reece since the summer before her senior year of high school. The foster parents she'd lived with back then used to own a small ranch in the area, so she'd seen Reece often enough.

He'd been seven years older than she, and he'd taken charge of Waverly interests after his father's death the year before. She'd been nothing but a teenage kid to him, but he'd always taken time to say something kind to the homely nobody most people overlooked.

Perpetually starved for attention, Leah had been completely smitten, though she'd only confessed that to Rachel one time in the beginning. Leery of being teased, she'd not mentioned it again. She'd tried very hard to appear aloof to Reece, though she'd lived for even a glimpse of him.

Leah and Rachel had been twenty when Reece had started dating Rachel, and their instant love affair became a sudden marriage that had devastated Leah. Somehow she'd made peace with that.

After all, it wasn't as if Reece would ever fall for her, much less marry her. She'd chosen to be glad that the two people she loved most were in love with each other, though she'd never been able to stop her feelings for Reece. She'd felt tremendous guilt for that because she'd seen it as a betrayal of her best friend.

Though she doubted her feelings fit into the traditional definition of adultery, her conscience had been so tender about it that it might as well have been the primary one.

Particularly after Rachel had died, and Leah had jumped at the chance to marry Reece when he'd asked. The weight of that knowledge, and the guilt she still felt for taking advantage of him at a vulnerable time, suddenly made her deeply uneasy.

Should she confess it all to Reece or not? The question nagged at her the rest of the afternoon and evening.

That night, she was so quickly and completely swept away by Reece's lovemaking that she forgot all about her guilt and her worries about love words slipping out.

The sleeveless sundress Leah had bought for the barbecue had a fitted bodice with a deep V and a gathered waistline that flared to a full skirt. The bright red, orange, gold and blue vertical stripes flattered her and looked festive.

While Bobby played nearby late Saturday afternoon, Leah surveyed herself in the full length mirror in the master bedroom, smoothing the bodice into place.

Reece walked into the closet behind her and she glanced toward his reflection. He'd chosen to wear a pair of dark blue jeans and his usual white shirt, but this one featured scrolling white embroidery on the Western-cut yoke that gave the shirt a faint glow, and emphasized his weathered tan. The glowing white and dark blue next to her colorful dress was complimentary, and the contrasts made them stand out.

Reece slid his hands around her waist from behind and nuzzled the side of her neck. He'd folded back the long sleeves of his shirt as he normally did, and she lifted her hands to rest them on his bare wrists, loving the hard feel of his hair-roughened skin and the thick muscles beneath.

"You look beautiful, Leah," he breathed, then glanced into the mirror to make eye contact with her reflection. "It's gonna be hard to share you with a crowd tonight."

The sexy look in his eyes was a promise for later, and she felt her body react.

"By the way, the baby-sitter's here," he said, then pressed his lips against her hair. A tingling weakness went through her and she felt herself melt. Since she was watching in the mirror she saw the way he closed his eyes on the kiss, as if he was savoring it.

"Did you show her the list I made?" she asked a little breathlessly. She'd made a list of emergency numbers, including Reece's cell phone and the number for Donovan ranch, along with a list of where to find things for Bobby. She'd also prepared a casserole the sitter could pop in the oven, and she'd made certain there were selections of soft drinks and snacks.

"Not yet. We probably ought to show her around the house."

He loosened his arms and Leah stepped away to get her handbag. Reece picked up Bobby and they all went out to show Marie's sister Melody around, then Leah waited while the teenager read through the list she'd made in case she had questions.

Bobby protested briefly when they kissed him goodbye, but he was acquainted with Melody from his visits to Marie's day care, so the girl easily calmed him.

Once they were on the highway for the fairly short drive to Donovan ranch, there were no distractions from Leah's feelings of guilt. Although nothing she'd done that day had helped her to truly escape them, they seemed to grow worse with each mile they traveled. By the time they arrived at the Donovan Ranch and Reece parked the SUV under a tree in the front yard, she realized worry was tainting everything.

It was becoming increasingly clear that her conscience wouldn't let up. The part of her that remembered in excruciating detail how it had felt to be rejected and abandoned by her mother and father, was terrified that history would repeat itself with Reece.

Though she'd not deserved what had happened to her as a child, her disloyalty to Rachel and her eagerness to take advantage of Reece's marriage proposal were certainly worthy of comeuppance.

And yet there was another part of her that assured her it was safe to confide in Reece. The man who'd been sensitive enough to be kind to a lonely teenager would surely understand.

What he wouldn't understand was her betrayal of her best friend and the fact that she'd essentially taken advantage of him at a vulnerable time. After all, she could have tried to reason with him about his worries and perhaps helped him find a solution for protecting Bobby that wasn't as drastic as marrying her. But she'd kept silent, hardly daring to believe her good luck.

Until the day they'd stood in front of the judge and she began to realize exactly what it was that she'd been about to do. And by then it had been too late.

Hoyt had seen them drive in and met them on the lawn.

"Too bad you brought the killjoy, darlin'," he said as he took her hand and gave it a squeeze.

Leah couldn't help her startled laugh. Reece reached over to gently remove Leah's hand from Hoyt's and give him a reproving look.

"Where's Eadie hidin' out?"

Hoyt's grin fell a bit. "Eadie's hidin' out where she always does. At home."

"Probably tired of handling your social calendar. Which new Saturday night gal did you invite? The blonde with the ratty hair or the brunette who can't figure out how to button her blouses?" Reece aimed a sparkling glance at Leah who only barely managed not to laugh at the apt description of the women Hoyt usually dated. "Pardon the blunt talk, darlin'."

"I didn't invite either of them," Hoyt grumbled. "I asked Eadie to come over, even told her she didn't have to dress up if she didn't want to. I offered to teach her to dance—again—but she said she's not interested in dancing."

"She's not interested in men," Reece commented.

Hoyt's expression went a little grim. "Reckon not."

His obvious disappointment over Eadie's absence made Leah curious. It almost sounded as if he had feelings for Eadie, which was surprising since Eadie was nothing like the glamorous beauties Hoyt usually dated.

Leah actually knew very little about Eadie Webb, since she'd been a couple years ahead of Leah in school. And Eadie didn't socialize much at all.

The three of them walked to the huge, heavily shaded backyard and mixed with the crowd. The food tables were crammed with various hot weather dishes and Hoyt left them to help take up the last of the beef and carry the large platters of meat to the tables. After everyone started through the buffet lines, they filled their plates and the three of them sat together at one of the tables.

The food was excellent, and the crowd virtually picked the buffet tables clean. The desserts on the dessert table went next. As the early evening air began to cool, the country band began to tune up. Hoyt had had the wooden dance floor set up on the section of lawn that was most protected from the evening sun.

He managed to persuade Reece to let him have the first dance with Leah, but only because Reece made him forfeit the other two dances he'd planned with her. The first dance was a rollicking one, and Leah was laughing by the time the number ended and Hoyt passed her into Reece's arms.

Reece was also a fine dancer, and patient enough

to give her a few lessons at the edge of the dance floor. Later, when some of the couples started dancing the Cotton-Eyed Joe, Reece coaxed her to give it a whirl and they took their place in the large circle. By the time the music stopped, Leah had managed to get at least a small part of the dance right.

They sat out the next few dances to visit with other guests, before Reece led her to the dance floor for a couple of the ballads.

"Looks like Hoyt's finally given up on Eadie," Reece remarked to her during the second dance. Leah glanced in Hoyt's direction to see him leaning against a tree trunk, solemnly watching the dancers.

"I didn't know Hoyt was interested in her."

"He's not, he only thinks he is. She's one of the rare unmarried females he's ever been around who doesn't fall all over herself to get his attention, so she's the rare unmarried female he takes seriously."

Reece grinned down at her. "Might be a case of wanting what he knows he can't have. The fact that Eadie doesn't date and doesn't seem interested in men—him in particular—just adds to the fascination."

Leah had never dated either, mostly because she'd never been asked. She'd refused Rachel's matchmaking schemes, and she'd stayed home or done things with friends when she wasn't working. The fact that Eadie didn't try to get Hoyt's attention was also telling, and she suspected Eadie's no-show was far more significant than either Reece or Hoyt had guessed.

It was the perfect description of Leah's life, both before and after Reece had married Rachel. Leah, of all people, knew what it was like to secretly be in love with someone you were certain would never love you. She'd gone out of her way to hide her feelings, particularly after Reece and Rachel had started dating.

In Hoyt's case, he was something of a womanizer, which would probably make Eadie doubly wary of taking any sign of interest from him seriously. And she probably thought he'd only invited her tonight to be polite. There was nothing worse than a token invitation. If Eadie had feelings for Hoyt that she thought were hopeless, she'd avoid being around him, particularly at a social event at his home.

The whole issue of one-sided, secret feelings, whether they were Hoyt's or Eadie's, suddenly brought back the guilt she'd been able to set aside the past couple of hours. She didn't realize her upset had shown until Reece's low voice penetrated her worried thoughts.

"Something wrong?"

Leah glanced up hesitantly, then away. It was probably the most perfect opening she'd ever have, but the risk she was taking was so monumental that she wasn't sure she had the courage. And the dance was no place for confessions.

"I'd...like to talk about it. Later," she said, then glanced up at him again. His rugged face went a little somber and she could tell by the way he searched her face that she'd passed the point of no return. She had to tell him now.

It was nearing eleven by the time they'd had their fill of dancing. Leah had promised Melody's mother that they'd make sure the teenager had time to get home by midnight, so they needed to leave.

After they made their way along the edge of the crowd, saying goodnight to neighbors and friends, they found Hoyt and thanked him for the fine evening. The ride home was increasingly tense, and neither of them spoke.

Melody reported that Bobby had needed to be rocked to sleep, but that the evening went well. Reece saw her off. Leah took a few moments to call Melody's mother to let her know the girl had just started the drive back to town.

Reece had walked through the house turning off lights, so he was waiting when she hung up the phone in the kitchen.

She turned toward him. "Would you like something to drink?"

"Nothing for me, thanks," he said, his low voice quiet. "What was it you wanted to talk about?"

Leah was too restless to sit down. She felt awkward and edgy, and gripped her hands in front of her waist while she fumbled for a start.

"I was thinking tonight while you were talking about Hoyt, that maybe it was Eadie who might...have feelings for him."

Her theory seemed to amuse him and he smiled. "Honey, if she's got feelings for Hoyt, she's got a funny way of showing it."

Leah tried to force herself to smile, but it probably looked as flat as it felt. "She might not, but thinking about it made me realize that I needed to tell you about something I did. Something very wrong. More than one thing, actually, and you need to know."

Reece gave her a skeptical look. "What could you have done that was so bad?"

She took a breath, but was too tense to get in much air. And then she wasn't sure how to make a start. Her heart was suddenly pounding and she felt her eyes sting.

"I had feelings for a married man," she said quietly, and felt the sting intensify at her cowardly wording.

"I never did anything about those feelings," she went on, "not a single thing. And no one knew, not even Rachel. Until now."

Reece moved closer and she stared at his chest, willing herself not to cry or lose her nerve.

"Are you still in love with him?" She could tell by the grim tone in Reece's voice that he was suddenly taking this seriously.

"I was seventeen when I first met him." She glanced up at him briefly but couldn't make eye contact before her gaze dropped. "I had a terrible crush on him. He was handsome and gallant, and I'm absolutely certain he never suspected."

It took her a moment to regain control of the emotion that was roaring higher. There was no sense keeping either of them in suspense, so she took another shallow breath that didn't feel like nearly enough.

"And when he fell in love with my best friend then later married her, I couldn't seem to stop loving him."

She felt Reece's surprise and turned to walk a few shaky steps away. She pressed a fist against her lips, her heart pounding sickly in the silence. She eased her fist away to go on.

"Loving you was disloyal to Rachel and a betrayal of her friendship." The words tumbled out then, along with the tears he couldn't see. "I took advantage of you at a vulnerable time. Over these past few weeks I realized I couldn't stand for you to go on being unhappy, so I offered you the divorce. I thought it might make up for the wrong of everything else."

It was so hard to keep her voice steady. "But then everything happened so quick this week. I started thinking we might have a chance to be happy and you'd never have to know."

Now that she'd got most of it out, she felt some of the pressure ebb slightly. "But I know. And now, you know too."

The tears that had been streaking silently down her cheeks were blinding now, and she tried to wipe them away with her hands as she waited for Reece to react. She couldn't hear anything over the loud roar of blood in her ears.

When Reece's big hands settled warmly on her waist, she flinched a little. And then his arms slid around her and tightened as he bent to press his lean cheek against hers.

"Oh, darlin'," he rasped, "darlin'."

Leah's felt her heart quiver at his tender tone. He kissed her cheek then pressed his jaw even tighter against hers. "I never, never guessed, but it was me who took advantage. You loved Bobby and I used your devotion to get what I wanted. I deprived you of a husband who'd love only you, and it didn't help any more to remind myself that I'd married you to protect the boy. But then you walked into the den the other night and dropped that little bombshell."

He lifted his head and loosened his hold. Leah's

fist was still pressed against her lip. She was stiff, balanced on the razor edge of dread.

I deprived you of a husband who'd love only you. It sounded like a confirmation that Rachel would always have the lion's share of his heart.

She didn't resist when he turned her toward him. He gently pulled her hand down and she looked up into his eyes. Her voice was hoarse. "The worst is that I betra—"

Reece's finger came up to her lips to gently silence her. "You never said a single word, you never gave me so much as a look, Leah, whatever it was you felt." He gave her a faint smile. "Fact is, I thought for the longest time you didn't like me at all."

Leah felt the first trickle of real relief, and she went weak with it as her tension began to ease away.

"I tried so hard to stop caring for you," she said shakily. "So very hard."

"Caring about someone, loving them, isn't something you can turn on and off like a faucet," he said gruffly. "It's either there or it isn't. You act on it or you don't. You didn't act, you didn't do a single thing to hurt or hinder Rachel's marriage to me. I reckon that proves you were more loyal to Rachel and her happiness than to whatever it was you felt for me."

He paused and a faint smile eased across his

mouth. "As far as you taking advantage of me in a weak moment, I reckon we're even. And the way it's working out, it looks like getting married was something we would have come to in time anyway. You still would have been coming around to see Bobby, and I was bound to look at you like I did the other day and finally see you. One way or the other, we woulda ended up in this kitchen some night."

He lifted his hands to her damp cheeks to tenderly cradle her face. She lifted her hands to his lean waist.

"So I damned sure hope you still love me, Mrs. Waverly," he growled, "because I'm in love with you now."

Elation shot through her, and Reece's lips settled on hers for a long, sweetly gentle kiss.

He eased away only far enough away to whisper, "Never figured to ever feel like this again, like I'm whole." He pulled her into his arms to tightly hold her. "You did that for me, Leah. I love you, baby."

Her heart went wild with happiness, and she held on to Reece for dear life. "I love you so much," she got out, "always. Always."

Reece loosened his arms and bent to pick her up, taking a moment to kiss her again before he started across the big kitchen. He switched off the kitchen light with his elbow, then strode through the dark house to the hall and the bedrooms.

They made a brief detour through Bobby's room to look in on him, then Reece carried her on into their room. He nudged the connecting door almost closed then carried her to the bed.

Their lovemaking that night was both a sweet celebration and the glorious prelude to a long, contented life together. There were other children. Three more. The girls came next, but Bobby had to wait for a kid brother.

The memory of a lost lover and best friend was kept fondly close, but the hurt of the past mellowed to a dimly felt, bittersweet ache, soothed away by a love and tender devotion that regularly lit their contented hearts with bursts of glittering joy.

THE LAST-MINUTE MARRIAGE

by

Marion Lennox

Marion Lennox is a country girl, born on an Australian dairy farm. She moved on – mostly because the cows just weren't interested in her stories! Married to a 'very special doctor', Marion writes Medical™ romances as well as Mills & Boon® Romance (she used a different name for each category for a while – if you're looking for her past Mills & Boon Romances, search for author Trisha David as well).

In her non-writing life Marion cares for kids, cats, dogs, chooks and goldfish. She travels, she fights her rampant garden (she's losing) and her house dust (she's lost).

Having spun in circles for the first part of her life, she's now stepped back from her 'other' career, which was teaching statistics at her local university. Finally she's reprioritised her life, figured what's important and discovered the joys of deep baths, romance and chocolate. Preferably all at the same time!

Don't miss Marion Lennox's exciting new novel, *Their Lost-and-Found Family*, out in November 2007 from Mills & Boon® Medical™.

CHAPTER ONE

MARCUS BENSON shoved open the fire-escape door—and ran straight into Cinderella.

Marcus running into anyone was unusual in itself. The influence of the Benson Corporation reached throughout the international business community, and Marcus, at its head, was a man held in awe. Bumping into people was unheard of. A path usually cleared before him.

It wasn't just power, wealth and intellect contributing to the aura surrounding him. He was in his mid-thirties, tall and superbly fit, with jet-black hair and striking, hawklike features. His charisma and influence were such that women's magazines were unanimous in declaring him to be America's most eligible bachelor.

And Marcus was likely to stay that way.

Well, why not? His experience of family life had been a disaster. His time in the armed forces had taught him loyalty and friendship, but loyalty and friendship had ended in tragedy. So Marcus Benson was a man who walked alone.

But that was before he met Peta O'Shannassy.

And Peta's kids, dogs, cows and catastrophe.

He didn't see that now, though. All he saw was a kid who reminded him oddly of Cinderella.

But Cinderella should be in her castle kitchen, tending the fire. Hungry. Wasn't that how the story went? Surely she shouldn't be eating her lunch on the landing of a New York fire-escape.

Maybe Marcus was making a few assumptions. He assumed this was Cinderella. He assumed it was lunch. In reality, all Marcus saw was a spilled yellow drink, a flying bagel, and, underneath, a tattered kid with bright chestnut curls and skimpy clothes.

So maybe she wasn't Cinderella.

Who, then? A street kid? She was wearing shorts, a frayed T-shirt and battered sandals. His first impression was of a waif.

His second sensation was horror as waif—and lunch— fought for balance, lost, and tumbled to the next landing.

What had he done?

He'd been in too much of a hurry. There weren't enough hours in the day for Marcus Benson. He had people waiting.

They'd have to wait. He'd just knocked a kid down half a flight of stairs. She was crumpled in a heap on the next landing, looking as if she wasn't going anywhere.

It seemed an eternity while she slid, but in fact it was two or three seconds at most. The next moment, Marcus was brushing the bright curls away from her face. Trying to see the damage.

Again he had to do a rethink. She wasn't a street kid—or not the type that he recognised.

She was clean. Sure, she was covered in what remained of her bagel and her milkshake, but her mop of curls were soft to touch. Her shorts and her T-shirt were freshly laundered under the mess he'd made, and she was...

Cute?

Definitely cute.

She wasn't a kid.

Maybe she was about twenty, he thought. Her eyes were closed but he had the impression that it wasn't unconsciousness that was causing her eyelids to stay shuttered. There was a sense of exhaustion about her, as if she was closing her eyes to shut out more than the pain and shock of the moment. Dark shadows smudged deeply under her eyes. She was thin. Far too thin.

His first impression solidified. Cinderella.

Her eyes fluttered open. They were wide green eyes, deep and questioning. Pain-filled.

'Don't move,' he said urgently and she focused on his face, questioning.

'Ouch,' she whispered.

'Ouch?'

She appeared to consider.

'Definitely ouch,' she said at last, and the strain in her voice said she was trying hard to make light of something that was worse than just ouch. She didn't move; just lay on the steel-plated landing as if she was trying to come to terms with a catastrophe that was just one of a series. 'I guess I spilled my milkshake, huh.'

'Um...' He looked down to the next flight of steps. 'Yeah. Definitely.'

'And my bagel?' Her accent was Australian, he thought. It was warm and resonant, with a tremor behind it. From shock? From pain?

But she was worried about her bagel. He smiled at that, albeit weakly. If she was worried about her bagel, chances were that she wasn't suffering injuries that were life-threatening.

'I'd imagine your bagel is at ground level,' he told her. 'It'll have turned into a lethal missile by now.'

'Oh, great.' She closed her eyes again and his impression of exhaustion deepened. 'I can see the headlines. Australian drops New Yorker with jelly-loaded bagel. I'll probably get sent to prison-for-terrorists on the first flight out of here.'

'Hey.' It was too much. Marcus Benson, who seldom—well, *never*, in fact—let himself get involved, put his hand on her cheek in a gesture of comfort. Good grief. He'd blasted her down a flight of stairs. He'd ruined her lunch. He'd hurt her—and she was trying to turn it into a joke.

'Australian Braining New Yorker with Bagel is the least of our legal worries,' he told her. 'How about Corporate Idiot Shoves Australian Downstairs?'

She opened one eye and looked up at him. Cautiously. 'You mean I can sue?'

'For at least the cost of a bagel,' he told her, and his words produced a smile.

It was a great smile. A killer smile. Her eyes were deeply green and they twinkled, as if it was their permanent state. Maybe she wasn't twenty, he thought. Maybe she was older. With a smile like that... Well, a smile like that took practice.

He'd never seen a smile like it.

But he couldn't stop and think about a woman's smile. Or he shouldn't. He was in a rush. The reason he'd used the fire stairs was that he was in a hurry. The lift had jammed at just the wrong time. His assistant would be waiting at street level, checking her watch. He had a deal to close.

But he couldn't just leave this kid here.

He lifted his cellphone. 'Ruby?' he snapped as his assistant answered.

'Marcus.' This was a busy day, even for the super-efficient Ruby, and his assistant sounded worried. 'Where are you?'

'I'm on the fire-escape. Can you come up, please? I have a situation.'

As he tucked his phone back into his jacket he found himself suppressing a grin. A situation on the fire-escape. That'd have Ruby having kittens all the way up. Ruby was efficient but things like...well, situations on fire-escapes were unusual, even for Ruby.

She'd cope, he thought. Ruby always coped. But until the cavalry arrived he needed to focus on the girl.

'Are you hurt?' he asked, and found she was staring straight up at him now, both her eyes fully open. She'd rolled over on to her back. There was a dollop of jelly wedged under her curls near one ear, and he had the weirdest desire to wipe it away...

Heck, cut it out, Benson, he told himself. This was getting personal. He didn't do personal. That was what Ruby was for.

But apparently the waif didn't want his attention just as much as he didn't wish to offer it. 'Thank you for asking,' she said politely. 'But I'm fine. You can go away now.'

He blinked. 'I can go away?'

'You're in a rush. I sat in your way. You've squashed my bagel, you've spilled my milkshake and you've hurt my ankle, but hey, it's my fault. I'm—'

'You've hurt your ankle?'

'It appears,' she said with cautious dignity, 'to be hurt.'

He checked her out. Her legs were long and tanned and smooth. Really long, in fact, and really tanned, and really smooth. They were great legs. It was incongruous that they ended up with shabby leather sandals that looked as if they came from a welfare shop.

The shoes weren't the only jarring note. One ankle was puffing while he watched.

'Hell.'

'Hey! It's me who's supposed to swear. Why don't you just go away so that I can?'

'Don't let me stop you.'

'A lady doesn't swear in front of a gentleman,' she told him, lifting her ankle so she could see it. Mistake. She winced and let it drop. Cautiously. But still the determination was there to move on. Ignoring pain. 'While I might not be a lady, by the look of the suit you're wearing, you must be a gentleman,' she managed. 'That's about the most gentlemanly suit I've ever seen.'

Here they were again. Talking about him. He found himself glancing down at his Armani suit and thinking, Yeah, that's all it took. Wear a suit that cost a few thou' and bang, you're a gentleman.

Even if he did toss kids downstairs.

'I'm really sorry,' he told her, and she nodded as if she'd been waiting for it.

'I wondered when we'd get around to that.'

She took him aback. It wasn't just her accent that was

unusual, he decided. It was everything about her. She was hurting—hurting badly. He could see it behind her eyes. But she wasn't letting on. She was sassy and smart, and she wanted him to disappear so she could swear in private. Or do whatever she had to do in private.

'Is it only your ankle that's hurting?' he asked.

'Isn't that enough?'

'I guess it is.' He touched her foot, lightly probing, and saw that it hurt. A lot. 'That was quite a fall.'

'You thumped out of there hard.'

'I guess I did.'

'I'm fine,' she said, and he knew that, though she was trying to keep things light, there was a load of bitterness behind the words. 'Leave me be.'

'That ankle might be broken.'

'Yeah, with my luck...' She broke off and seemed to try to haul herself together. She even managed to produce that smile again. Almost. 'No. Don't worry. It'd be hurting more if it was broken.'

'Can I help you inside?' He motioned to the door he'd just come from.

'To the offices of Charles Higgins?' Her eyebrows hiked up in mock incredulity. 'Attila in there wouldn't let me sit on her settee and eat my bagel. You think she'll let me sit on her settee now I'm covered with banana milkshake?'

'I guess she wouldn't,' he said, his voice a trifle unsteady. Attila... He knew exactly who she was talking about. Charles Higgins's secretary.

'You were waiting to see Charles?'

'Yeah.'

Marcus knew Charles Higgins. The man was sleaze. A king-sized ego with the morals of a sewer rat. Because of renovations—the same renovations that were causing problems with the lifts now—Marcus had been forced to share a corporate washroom with Charles Higgins for the last few weeks. But that was as far as their relationship went. The man's brains were in his balls. He had a reputation for dealing dishonestly with dishonest money.

Marcus owned this building. He might lease part of it to Higgins but it didn't mean he had to like the man.

He couldn't understand for a minute what business this girl would have with a slime-ball of a lawyer like Higgins.

'You had an appointment?'

'At ten this morning. Three hours ago.' She was still lying on the landing, her fingers tentatively probing her ankle. 'Attila keeps fobbing me off. Finally I was so hungry I dived out and got lunch and Attila told me I'd have to eat out here. Enter you.'

That made sense. Higgins's secretary, a woman of indeterminate years and with a bosom like plate armour, had a reputation for being nastier than Higgins himself. If that was possible.

'You know...' It was a crazy conversation. Any minute now Ruby would arrive and rescue him, but meanwhile maybe he could give her a bit of advice. It couldn't hurt. 'You know, maybe if you want to talk to high-powered New York lawyers, then maybe shorts and T-shirt and scruffy sandals aren't going to cut it.'

'Scruffy...' She probed her ankle and winced yet again but she was able to focus on what he was saying. 'You're saying my sandals are scruffy?'

'Yes,' he said firmly, and he almost got that smile again. Not quite. She was in real pain, he thought. Where on earth was Ruby? 'Scruffy is a polite way of describing them, really.'

'They're my aunty's.'

'Um...good?'

'She's dead,' the girl said as if that explained all. It didn't. But he had to say something.

'Oh,' he said and this time he definitely got the smile.

It was worth working for. It was a *great* smile.

'I brought corporate clothes,' she told him. 'I'm not silly.

But I've come from Australia. I came in a hurry because my aunt was dying, but I did pack decent clothes. Unfortunately the airline is playing keepings-off with them.'

'Keepings-off?'

'I put my clothes on the plane in Sydney. I put me on the plane in Sydney. I got off the plane here, but clearly my suitcase fell out somewhere around Hawaii. So now someone in Hawaii's wearing my good, Charles-facing suit while I'm forced to wear the only clothes I have. I had one pair of decent shoes but I was stupid enough to use the same pavement as a New York mutt with poor choice in toilet placement. With ten minutes to make it here, Aunt Hattie's sandals were all I had.'

'You didn't think of buying something else?' he asked, and that was a mistake. He'd shoved her down the stairs, he'd hurt her, and she'd reacted with humour. Now, though, he got a blaze of anger that made him take a step back.

'Yeah. Toss a little money at the problem and it'll go away. Of course. What's money for? Just like Charles. You leave your mother with Peta until it looks like you'll inherit; then you haul her over to the other side of the world. Economy class. When she's dying! Even when you can afford all this! Only you don't really want her. You dump her in some appalling nursing home to die alone, making sure you get her to change her will first...' She bit her lip and the wash of pain across her face was dreadful.

'Um... I don't have a mother,' he said cautiously and the anger exploded even more.

'Of course you don't. I wasn't talking about you. I was just grouping you.'

'Categorising me?'

'Yes.'

'I see.' He didn't. In fact, he didn't have a clue what was going on. Her anger was palpable and he needed to break through it in order to get some... Well, some order.

'Who's Peta?' he asked.

'Me.' She glowered.

'You're Peta? Hi. I'm Marcus.'

She wasn't about to be distracted.

'I can do without the introductions. I haven't finished being angry yet.'

His eyebrows hiked. 'I'm sorry. But... Peta?'

'My dad wanted a boy,' she snapped, recovering momentum. 'And will you be quiet when I'm letting off steam? You and Charles and Attila the Hun in there, you judge. You think just because I'm not wearing an Armani suit—yeah, I can tell it's Armani, I'm not stupid, no matter how patronising you sound—that I don't matter. I'll never get to see Charles. I've used the last of my money to care for and bury Hattie, and if I don't get to see him...' She gave a deep, raspy breath, the pain and the shock of the last few minutes finally surfacing to the point where they couldn't be hidden.

She'd been using her anger as a barrier, Marcus realised, and it wasn't working. Whatever was behind was breaking through.

'This is stupid,' she whispered. 'You don't give a toss, and anyway, you'll have a secretary like Attila in there, and even if I threaten to sue the pants off you, you'll just turn to your secretary and say fix it. Keep her away from me...'

'I wouldn't...'

But of course he would.

'Mr Benson?' a voice said behind them and it was Ruby. His cool, unflappable assistant to whom he handed life's problems. Life's hiccups. The personal stuff. 'Is there a problem, Mr Benson?' Ruby said smoothly. 'How can I help?'

Ruby was wonderful. She was the answer to Marcus Benson's prayers.

Somewhere in her indeterminate post forties, a stout and sensibly dressed Afro-American, Ruby gave off the aura of someone's mother or someone's aunt. She was neither.

Nor did she have any secretarial qualifications. She had

been an obscure, unnoticed clerk in Marcus's vast financial empire when he'd found her almost by accident seven or eight years back. Marcus had been trying to juggle a Japanese delegation, a team of lawyers after his blood, and a posse of journalists and photographers from *Celebrity-Plus Magazine*. His highly qualified secretary had wilted under pressure.

In desperation he'd gone to the outer office and called for anyone—anyone!—who could speak even a little Japanese.

To his astonishment Ruby had risen ponderously to her feet. She'd studied a little Japanese at night school, she'd told him, and he'd expected nothing. But what he'd got... In twenty minutes she'd charmed the Japanese businessmen and organised an on-site lunch, she'd diverted the reporters with vouchers to a nearby exclusive wine bar, and she was calmly taking notes while Marcus coped with the lawyers. And when he appeared flummoxed she even suggested priorities.

Her priorities were always right. Marcus had never looked for another assistant. Ruby didn't move fast. She was unflappable, and she was worth diamonds. More than diamonds. Now she assessed the situation at a glance, she figured what Marcus wanted and she proceeded to provide it.

'If Mr Benson has hurt you, we'll do everything in our power to rectify it,' she told the girl. 'Mr Benson has an appointment right now which must be kept, but I can help.' She gave Marcus an enquiring look—a look they both knew—which asked whether she should be sympathetic. She got a nod. A distinct nod and a smile. The combination of nod and smile was Marcus's sign language for go all out to be nice.

And Marcus meant it. He was feeling really guilty here. If Ruby could make things better for this chit of a girl, then it'd be worth losing his precious assistant for half a day.

'I'll take you to the local medical facility and let someone see that ankle,' Ruby was saying as Marcus backed away a little. Letting her take charge. 'We'll replace your damaged clothes. I'll buy you a decent meal and I'll organise a cab to take you home. Is that okay?'

Marcus's face cleared. It sounded good to him. Generosity would definitely help here. There was still the niggle of guilt, but Ruby would assuage it.

But it seemed they were not to be let off so easily. Or maybe they were being let off too easily.

'Thank you.' Peta pushed herself into a sitting position. She glanced from Ruby to Marcus and back again. Her face had shuttered, showing no pain, no anger...just nothing. It was a defence, Marcus realised. A shield.

'Thank you but I don't need help,' she told Ruby, with another half glance at Marcus that said, Yeah, hadn't she been right all along? Here was his secretary ready to sweep his problems under the carpet. Peta's look said she knew exactly the type Marcus was—the type who decreed when life got too difficult, pay someone.

Her look also said the sooner she was shot of him the better she'd like it.

'I'm not going to sue, and my problems are not your problems,' she told them both. 'I have an appointment to see Mr Higgins. He's running hours late as it is. If I leave now he'll say I missed my appointment and I can't afford to do that. So thank you, but I'll stay here. Filthy or not. I can't afford to lose this chance.'

'Mr Higgins won't see you like that,' Ruby told her, blunt as ever, and Marcus's face tightened.

'I've already told her that. I doubt if he'll see her at all.'

Ruby's lips pursed, acknowledging that he might be right. 'But if she has an appointment...'

'You know Charles, Ruby. He's not about to let Peta anywhere near his corporate offices looking like this.'

'Hey, excuse me,' Peta said cautiously, looking up at the two heads talking over her. 'Can I join in this conversation?'

'Of course.' Marcus's brows snapped together as Ruby's eyes widened. The waif wasn't a victim, then.

'He has to see me,' Peta was saying. 'I have an appointment.'

'An appointment with Charles means nothing if he figures there's the least chance you might not be able to pay,' Marcus told her. 'And pay well.'

'He has to see me,' she repeated. 'He's my cousin.'

Silence while they took that on board.

'Charles Higgins is your cousin?' Ruby asked, and Peta nodded. She didn't look too pleased about it, though. In fact, she looked as if she'd prefer the relationship didn't exist.

'He is. Worse luck.'

'But you have to make an appointment to see him?' Marcus didn't understand.

'Yes.'

'You're running really late, Mr Benson,' Ruby said warningly, but Marcus had heard enough.

To say he disliked Charles Higgins would be an understatement. He detested the man. The word around town was that the man was utterly unscrupulous. He and his equally unscrupulous associates had rented office space here when Marcus had been in Europe; Marcus had been really annoyed that the man had been granted a twelve-month lease, and given the least excuse Higgins was out of here. He was trying to manoeuvre it now. But meanwhile... This girl would get nowhere with him. He knew that.

So did Ruby. He could read it in her face.

So, the best thing they could do for this girl was to clean her, feed her and give her a ride back to whatever cheap accommodation she was using.

But...

But.

He'd hurt her. He'd made her life difficult when it was already impossible. He could see that. There was real desperation in her eyes.

He knew enough of Charles Higgins to guess that the girl would be being screwed. He had no idea how—all he knew was that it was true. She was alone and bereft and he'd hurt her.

She expected him to throw his assistant at her and leave her to face the wolves alone.

Damn, he couldn't do it. He couldn't.

'Ruby, can you reorganise my afternoon?' he said, and he said it as though every word was being dragged out of him. As if he couldn't believe what he was saying.

Not seeing this deal through this afternoon might well cost him thousands. But it couldn't be helped. When Marcus made a decision the decision was made—and his decision was made right now.

'If you'll set everything back a few hours, I'll take Peta over,' he told Ruby. And then, as his assistant's eyebrows hit her hairline, he clinched it.

'I'll face Charles Higgins with her.'

'You...'

Marcus was left in no doubt of what she thought of him. She was still seated, with Marcus and Ruby speaking over the top of her. She was still—waif-like? Her mop of chestnut curls was tousled and wild, her freckled nose was completely free of make-up and that dollop of jelly was still there. And so was her antagonism towards him. Peta stared up at him and he thought ruefully that he might as well be Charles Higgins himself. Was it the suit? he wondered. Or the presence of his assistant? Tokens of power... Whatever, there was no doubting that she was looking at him with contempt, as if such an action as he proposed was just a figment of his imagination.

'Why not?' he demanded. He looked from Peta to Ruby and found their expressions matched. Both women were looking at him as if he'd lost his mind.

'The project is important,' Ruby murmured, but he thought he detected a trace of a smile behind her normally expressionless eyes.

'I know. I'm trusting you to keep things on ice until I can take over again.'

'And when will that be?'

'A couple of hours.'

'Let's keep you clear until tomorrow,' Ruby suggested and there was no mistaking the laughter now. 'You might find ankle-fixing and clothes-shopping and lawyer-facing takes a bit longer than you think.'

'Um... Maybe you can do the ankle fixing and the shopping,' he said, suddenly uneasy. 'Then I can take her in to see Charles.'

'No!' Astonishingly, Ruby shook her head in definite disagreement. 'No, Mr Benson, I shouldn't do that. This is a fine gesture on your part and it'd be unfair of me to take over.'

'Ruby...'

'Hey.' Still seated beneath them, Peta was catching her breath. Catching her dignity. Sort of. 'There's no need for any of this. I told you. I don't need help.'

'If you need to face Charles then you need help,' Marcus told her and Ruby nodded.

'Take his advice, miss,' she said gently. 'You're Australian?'

'Yes, but...'

'If I was in Australia, then I'd take your advice on your territory,' she said. 'But this is corporate America. There's no one more at home in this territory than Marcus Benson. You put yourself in his hands and you're putting yourself in the hands of an expert.'

'I don't want to be in anyone's hands.'

'You truly think you can get what you want without me?' Marcus demanded and she faltered.

'To be honest...'

'To be honest, what?'

'To be honest, I don't think I can get what I want anyway,' she admitted. 'I was a fool to come. But I need to try.'

'So if you've come all this way,' Marcus said, his tone becoming gentler, 'why not give yourself the best chance you could possibly have? Take my advice.'

'Put myself in your hands?'

'That's right.'

She stared up at him, bemused, and he gazed back down. Astonishingly, her eyes were bright and challenging. Her chin tilted upward, somehow defiant. She might look bereft but she certainly didn't act bereft. She had spirit, Marcus thought appreciatively. And courage.

It seemed she also had the sense to know when to concede. 'Okay.' She swallowed. 'Okay.'

Ruby beamed. Marcus Benson's assistant, it seemed, was enjoying this. Enjoying this a lot. 'You do exactly what Mr Benson says,' Ruby told her, and Peta gave her a rueful smile.

'I'm not much good at doing what anyone tells me.'

'Then be tactful,' Ruby told her and his assistant even had the temerity to chuckle. 'Maybe it'll be good for both of you. Okay. I'm off to save the world—or your deal, Marcus—while you two front the awful Charles. I know which I'd rather. Good luck.'

'Um...do you employ her?' Peta asked as Ruby disappeared down the fire-escape with an airy wave. Ruby had come to work this morning looking tired, but now she was practically bouncing down the fire-escape.

'I acquired Ruby,' he said, watching her disappear. 'By accident. Sort of like getting hit by a bus.'

'You really like her.' Peta's face had focused. All at once she seemed really interested. Her distrust backed off a pace.

'I don't do like,' he told her. 'I'm a businessman.'

'So if Ruby threatened to quit...'

'I'd raise heaven and earth to keep her,' he admitted. 'Of course I would. As I said, I'm a businessman.'

* * *

First the ankle. Which she intended to ignore.

'My ankle's just a bit bruised. It's no problem.'

'Your ankle's puffing while we watch.'

'I've done worse than this and lived without a doctor. I've come too far and time's too important to waste any in a doctor's waiting room.'

'You won't have to wait. Put your hands around my neck and I'll carry you…'

'You? Carry me? What, are you crazy? I'll be sorry for myself with a strained ankle; you'll be a cripple for life.'

'I can carry you.'

'No one carries me. Ever.' She hauled herself up against the stair rail and took two tentative hops.

It clearly hurt. A lot.

'Peta…'

'No.'

Enough. 'Yes,' he told her. And, although he'd never done such a thing in his life, he stepped forward and hoisted her into his arms.

She weighed nothing.

'Do you ever eat?' he demanded, stunned, and she gave an indignant wriggle.

'Eat? Are you kidding? Of course I do. Except when corporate businessmen throw my lunch downstairs. Put me down.'

'No.' Maybe she wasn't too thin, he decided, tightening his grip. Maybe there were curves—just where there should be curves. She smelled good. She felt…good.

Inane. It was a stupid response but he couldn't help it.

'Are we catching the lift?' she demanded and he stared down into her overbright eyes.

'No. We'll take the stairs.'

'You'll drop me.'

'I won't drop you.'

'I'll do more damage than a bagel if I hit anyone below.'

'I won't drop you.'

'No one's ever carried me before,' she said, and to his astonishment she stopped her indignant wriggle and suddenly relaxed. 'Good grief.' Her green eyes twinkled. 'Okay. Let's do it. Maybe I'll even like it.'

'Maybe.'

'And if you burst a blood vessel we're going to an emergency department after all.'

'So we are,' he said faintly and held her a little tighter. 'So we are.'

She had him intrigued. Her reaction when she saw his car intrigued him as well. Robert, his chauffeur, was waiting at street level. He must have been pre-warned by Ruby. He didn't blink an eyelid when he saw his boss approach with his strange burden and by the time Marcus reached the car the back door was already open.

Peta, however, was less than ready to enter a black limousine with tinted windows.

'Holy cow. I'm not getting in that thing.'

'You're sounding like a country hick,' Marcus told her and she glared at him.

'Yeah, well, you sound—or look—like a mafia boss. I know which I'd rather be. Chauffeurs. Limousines. Tinted windows, for heaven's sake.'

'I need them tinted. I work in this car.'

'Right.' She hesitated, removing her arms from around his neck, and as she did he was aware of a sharp jab of loss. She'd put her arms around him for security but it had felt...good. But she wasn't thinking about the sensations he was feeling. She was doing some forward projections. 'No one can see in. How do I know if I get in this car I won't end up in concrete shoes?'

Enough. 'Robert, help me put her in the car—with force, if necessary,' he told his bemused chauffeur. 'And open the blasted windows! Mafia... Good grief!'

* * *

Then there was the medical clinic—a personalised service only available to New York's mega-rich. Peta was almost hornswoggled.

'You just roll in here and someone sees you?' They were waiting for X-rays and the chairs they were sitting in were luxurious leather. Gorgeous!

'Of course.'

'There's no of course about it,' she snapped. 'If I'd had this when Hattie...' She took an angry breath. 'Could Charles Higgins afford this sort of place?'

'If the rent he pays is any indication, of course he can.'

'I'll kill him,' she muttered and sat back and glowered the entire time her leg was bandaged.

'You're lucky. It's not broken but it's still badly bruised,' she was told by the attendant doctor. 'Stay off it. The nurses will fit you with crutches.'

Fine. Obviously still angry and with Marcus silent by her side, she hobbled her way to reception. And grew angrier still when Marcus paid.

'I can pay.'

'I'm very sure you can't,' Marcus told her gently. 'It was my fault. Let me.'

'Money,' she whispered. 'It solves everything. As long as you can screw the world to get more of it.'

Then there was the little matter of her clothes. With Peta safely resettled in his mafia car, Marcus directed Robert to Fifth Avenue.

'I just need a wash and I'll be fine,' she told him, but he shook his head.

'No. Charles is never going to admit you into his office looking like this.'

'But—'

'But nothing. It's stupid going back there now to wait for a reception you're not going to get. Let me help.'

Let him help more. He couldn't believe he was doing this. Was he crazy?

He didn't get involved—he never got involved—and for him to make this offer...

She had no expectations of him, he thought. He could back away right now. There'd be no repercussions. He'd never hear from this woman again.

But he couldn't. He stared down at the defiance in her face, and he saw the trace of desperation behind the defiance. There was no way he could walk.

He wanted to help. Come what may. For the very first time in many, many years, Marcus Benson wanted to be involved.

CHAPTER TWO

MARCUS thought he knew women. Marcus was wrong. And so was the shop where he took Peta.

One of the women he'd dated had told him once that the shop stocked fabulous business clothes but Peta hobbled in and looked around in suspicion. The shop assistants reacted the same way.

They smiled at Marcus. They were cautiously and patronisingly polite to the waif he had in tow.

Still, they were here for clothes. Not for pleasantries. Marcus didn't have time to mess around.

'Can you fit Peta out in something corporate?' he asked the assistant and Peta flashed him a look of annoyance.

'That makes me sound like a Barbie doll. Let's dress her in Corporate today.'

'Don't you want me to help you?'

'No.'

'Peta...'

'All right.' As the assistant searched the racks for something suitable she flashed him a look that was half apology but the defiance was still there. 'I know. You're being really nice. I'm being really stupid. But this feels...wrong.'

'It's sensible. Just do it.'

'Try this,' the assistant said, with a bright smile at Marcus. Peta was ignored. She held the suit up against Peta, but it was Marcus who was clearly expected to make the decision.

He might have, but he never got the chance. As the girl smiled across at Marcus, Peta lifted the price tag.

She yelped.

Marcus doubted if he'd ever heard a woman yelp before.

but she yelped. She pushed the suit away and stared at him as if he'd lost his mind.

'What, are you crazy?'

'What do you mean?'

'Look at the price. I can't afford this.'

'I'm paying. I told you. I ruined your clothes.'

'Yeah, you spilled my drink over my five-buck shirt and you're intending to replace it with stuff that costs three thousand dollars?' She fended off the suit some more. 'Three thousand dollars! Look, this seemed a really nice idea, and I'm delighted to have a bandage on my ankle and these neat crutches, but suddenly it's out of hand. You've done enough. I can't take any more. Can I leave? Now?'

She was backing towards the door.

'You won't get in to see Charles,' Marcus warned. He watched the conflicting emotions play over her face and felt the same conflict himself. He'd been enjoying himself, he decided. It wasn't half bad—millionaire playing benefactor to very attractive waif. But the waif was supposed to be grateful. She was supposed to smile sweetly and acquiesce.

This was like Cinderella saying the glass slipper didn't fit. Or didn't look right.

She was still backing, no mean feat on brand-new crutches, and the conflicting emotions were giving way to overriding distress. 'I just have to deal with Charles my own way,' she muttered.

'You agreed to do this.'

'I was stupid. I must have hit my head on the way down the stairs. So now, somehow, I'm standing in a swish store with a guy who has more money than I'll ever dream about—and he's offering to spend enough money on a suit to feed my family for a year.'

'Your family?'

Her face shuttered even more, and the pain intensified. 'I don't need to talk about my family. I'm out of my depth. I need to leave. I'm sorry.' She backed a bit more until she was balancing in the doorway. 'I'm sorry. Thank you very much for all you've done.'

'Peta…'

'I can't do this. I can't.'

He caught her three doors down. She'd tried to move fast but she was on crutches.

He'd followed. Of course he'd followed, even though he was unsure why he was still intent on helping. But he let her have a little space until she cooled down.

She was forced to cool down. Her anger could only carry her so far before the pain in her ankle caught up with her. He watched her slow. He saw her steps falter as if she was unsure where to go from here.

He saw her shoulders slump. Saw the despair catch up.

And when he caught her… As he put a hand on her shoulder and turned her around to face him, he wasn't surprised to see tears welling behind those lovely eyes.

The tears stopped the moment he touched her. She swiped her cheek and pulled back. Swaying dangerously. He put out his hands to steady her but she backed some more.

'Leave me alone.'

'I'm sorry.'

'You shouldn't be sorry. You were trying to be nice.'

He carefully pushed away the urge to play fairy godfather some more. He tried to put himself in her place. It was hard, but maybe he could manage it.

Once upon a time he'd been dependant, too, and he knew how much harder it was to take than give. It was just… In the last few years there had been so many takers.

Peta was a novelty. But he could adjust.

'I was a bit insensitive,' he managed. 'I had this idea that I could help. And I'd like to.'

'You can't.'

'I can, you know,' he said softly. 'It would be my privilege. If you let me.'

'Yeah, toss money.' Another angry swipe at tears she clearly despised and an angry sniff. 'It's all you know how to do.'

'I'm sorry.' He was stymied. He didn't have a clue what was happening. How had he got himself in this situation?

He could just stop. He had no reason to persist.

Why did he?

He had no idea what this woman wanted with Charles Higgins. He had no idea whether he could help her.

All he knew was that he wanted to know more.

'Can we start again, please?' he asked, and she sniffed once more and stared up at him, her face loaded with suspicion.

'Start again?'

'I've driven into this like a blunderbuss,' he admitted. 'I have no idea what's going on. I want to help. I don't even know why I want to help but I do.' He reached out and touched her hand. He didn't hold. He simply touched.

He knew that she still had the urge to run. He had it himself.

'Tell me what you need,' he told her. 'What can I do to help? Right now.'

She took a deep breath. Regrouped. Around them were a bustle of Fifth Avenue shoppers—smartly dressed women, suited businessmen. Marcus fitted right in.

Peta didn't fit in at all. But she obviously wasn't thinking of her appearance. She stared at him for a while longer and then made a confession—as if she was forced to admit something she was ashamed of.

'I need something to eat,' she told him.

'You're hungry?'

'I lost my bagel—remember? I didn't have breakfast and that was my lunch. And then I need a ticket on the subway to the backpacker's where I have my things. I need to stay until tomorrow—for Aunt Hattie's funeral. But that's it. I was stupid to try to see Charles. I just want... I think now that I just want to go home.'

'Right.' He nodded, aware all the time that she was poised for flight. 'Okay. I'll organise you transport. But let me feed you first. No.' He shook his head as she backed again and he gave a rueful smile. He knew what she was thinking. At long last he was getting the idea. Money didn't impress this woman. Money made her want to run. 'There's a great deli nearby and it's not expensive. It's simple food but it's good. Concede at least that I owe you a meal. Can you cope with me for a little while longer?'

She stared up at him, seemingly bemused. She balanced on her crutches while she surveyed him. Her green eyes were suddenly thoughtful.

It wasn't the sort of look he was accustomed to receiving from the women he moved with. To say it disconcerted him was putting it mildly.

'You must think I'm really ungrateful,' she said at last, and it was so far from what he was really thinking that he blinked.

'I don't. Let me feed you.'

'Like something in a cage at the zoo?'

He smiled. 'I'm sorry. That was badly phrased. Share a meal with me. Please.'

'Out of charity?'

'Out of my need to give you recompense.'

She stared at him for a long moment—and in that moment something shifted. The Cinderella image receded still further. There was a strength here, he realised. A latent force.

She was out of her depth. She wasn't sure what was happening to her right now, but this was a woman who would normally be in charge of her world.

Things were out of control but she was still fighting.

He'd be lucky if she'd agree to have a meal with him.

But she did, and he was aware of an absurd surge of gratitude as she did the thanking. 'Thank you,' she told him. 'I'd like that.'

'So would I.' And he meant it.

The deli he took her to was one he hadn't eaten at for years, but still he knew it. The proprietor, a big man in his late sixties, greeted him with pleasure.

'Well. If it isn't the great Marcus come to patronise this humble establishment...'

'Cut it out, Sam,' Marcus growled and Sam grinned.

'Yeah, right. To what do we owe this honour?' He glanced at Peta and his wide smile was a welcome all by itself. 'A lady. Of course. And a lady of taste. I can sense that already. I bet you could wrap yourself around one of my specials and not even think about counting calories.'

'I bet I could.' In the face of Sam's friendliness she seemed to finally relax—just a smidgeon. 'Tell me what's good.'

'What's good? In this establishment everything's good. Tell you what...' He cast a sideways glance at Marcus and got an almost imperceptible nod for his pains. Sam's deli was famous in this city and his reputation was richly deserved. He sensed what people needed and he provided it. You came to Sam's for comfort food and friendliness and good humour. Sam provided it in bucketloads. 'Why don't I bring you my specials?' he told them. 'My lunch works. You sit back, think of nothing except what you need to talk about and let me worry about your meal. It's what I do best.'

Think of nothing except what they needed to talk about...

It seemed there was nothing to talk about. Or Peta didn't seem to think there was. The food that Sam brought them was wonderful: a vast, steaming bowl of clam chowder—Sam's speciality, handed down from his grandma, who'd invented clams herself, he told them—and some sort of corn flapjacks that were truly spectacular.

It was good food. No. It was great food, Marcus conceded,

and he found himself wondering why it had been so long since he'd been here. He sat back, enjoying the food but also enjoying the buzz. The place was full of students and young mothers and academics and artists who looked as if they didn't have a buck to their name. All of them were attacking their food the same way Peta was. This was food to be relished at every mouthful.

And while she ate, he found himself thinking of the date he'd been on last night. Elizabeth was a corporate lawyer—a good one. She was smart and sophisticated and beautiful. But she'd toyed with her salad, she'd drunk half a glass of wine and refused dessert.

Her beautiful waistline came at a cost, Marcus had thought, and though she'd invited him up to her magnificent apartment afterwards for coffee, coffee was all they'd had. He'd felt no desire to take things further.

But now...sitting on the far side of the table and watching Peta devour her chowder and relish every mouthful of her flapjacks, he thought he'd rather have this contented silence than smart conversation. Genuine enjoyment.

'What?' she demanded suddenly, and he looked a question.

'I beg your pardon?'

'You're looking at me like I'm an interesting kind of bug. I don't like it.'

'You're Australian,' he told her. 'What do you expect?'

'You've never met an Australian?'

'Not one who likes clam chowder as much as you do.'

'It's the best.' She smiled up at him and he blinked. Whew! That smile was enough to knock a man sideways.

Where had it come from? It was a killer smile. Wide and white and there was a dimple right at the corner of her mouth...

Yeah, right. Get a grip, Benson, he told himself. You need involvement here like a hole in the head.

He needed any involvement like a hole in the head.

'You want to tell me why you need to see Charles

Higgins?' he asked and her smile faded. He was aware of a sharp stab of regret. Damn, he shouldn't have mentioned it.

But it was why they were here. It was important. And, to tell the truth, he was intrigued.

This girl had just knocked back a gift of a three-thousand dollar suit. Just like that. Would any other woman he knew do that? It wasn't as if it had come with strings. It would have been a gift, pure and simple.

'You might have knocked me down, but it was partly my fault,' she told him, and it was as if she'd read his thoughts. 'I don't want to be beholden. To anyone. You spend three thousand bucks on a suit for me and I'll feel sick about it for the rest of my life. And Charles will know it's a front.'

'Charles knows you?'

'I told you. He's my cousin.'

'Then why…?'

She could see where his thoughts were heading and she was way ahead of him.

'You think because I'm family I should have an entrée with him.'

'Something like that.'

'I'm over here because my aunt died,' she told him. 'Charles's mother. I spent the last few days sitting by Aunt Hattie's bedside. I haven't seen Charles. Hattie is due to be buried tomorrow. Charles may or may not come to the funeral. He's certainly not paying for it.'

'So…' He took a wild guess. 'You're not a close family?'

'I'm a very close family,' she told him, and took another mouthful of her flapjack. Difficult conversation or not, she wasn't forgetting that she was truly enjoying this food. But her voice, when she spoke again, held more than a trace of bitterness. 'I'm so close I'm practically glue,' she added. 'Good old Peta. She'll do the right thing. The family thing. But not Charles.'

'So why do you need to see him?'

She took a deep breath. She seemed to brace herself. Her

fork was set down and her chin tilted in a gesture he was starting to recognise.

'Aunt Hattie and my father owned half our family farm each,' she told him. 'My father left us his half when he died ten years back, and the agreement was always that Hattie would do the same. She hasn't. She's left her half to Charles. So I need him...' Her voice faltered then, as if accepting the sheer impossibility of what she was about to suggest. 'I need him to agree not to sell it. To let me farm it until...until I'm free.'

'Free?'

She looked up at him and her eyes were blind with a pain he couldn't begin to understand. 'The farm is all I have,' she told him. 'It can't mean anything to Charles. It's just money. He must see that to do anything but let me live there would be desperately unfair.' She bit her lip and then picked up her soda, trying desperately to move past a pain that seemed well nigh unbearable. 'But that's nothing to do with you. Charles is my cousin. My problem. You've given me a feed. Now I'll clean myself as best I can, go back and try to face him one more time—and if I can't I'll go home. But at least I'll have tried.'

He couldn't bear it. The look of pain. The defiance. David and Goliath, and Goliath was Charles Higgins... She had to let him take the next step with her. 'You can't face him alone,' he told her.

'Of course I can.'

'There's no of course about it,' he growled. 'Charles is a slime-ball. Maybe he's different with family but he's still a slime-ball. Okay, I might be off the track with my offer of three-thousand-dollar suits but my instincts are right. We'll get you something neat to wear and I'm coming in with you. I might not get you more than an interview but I can get you that.'

'How?'

'For a start, I own the building he rents office space in.'

She stared. 'You're kidding.'

'I'm not. Regrettably. I've already decided not to renew his lease when it expires but he doesn't know that. I can apply pressure.'

'But...'

'Finish your soda,' he told her, aware at the back of his mind of his total amazement that he was doing this. That he was getting more and more involved. 'We mustn't keep Charles waiting now, must we?'

They did the dress thing again, but this time Marcus had the sense to keep it simple. They headed to a moderately priced department store and Marcus stood back while Peta chose a neat skirt and blouse and strappy sandals. She looked great, Marcus decided, and then wondered: Why do women wear three-thousand-dollar suits when they can look just as good in far cheaper clothes?

But maybe that wasn't fair. Maybe Peta wasn't any woman. She'd look great in anything, he thought, as Robert drove them back to Higgins's office.

The only problem was that she was a bit pale. Her hands were clenched so tightly that he could see the white in her knuckles. But she was still determinedly keeping up conversation as they made their way past Central Park.

'It's Central Park I most wanted to see,' she told him. 'Ever since I was a little girl I dreamed of riding around Central Park.'

'You're a country girl?'

'I told you—we live on a farm. I milk cows for a living.'

We? Who?

It didn't matter. Did it?

She was expecting a courteous, impersonal reply. He had to fight to find one. Somehow. 'So...you live on a farm yet you dream of coming to New York to ride a horse?'

'It's a different kind of riding.' She gave a hesitant smile and he saw that her hands were still clenched. He had to fight back the urge to lift them—to forcibly unclench them. 'John Lennon loved this park,' she was saying. 'Jackie Kennedy loved this park. All these people that I've only read about.'

'You admired Jackie O?'

'The lady had class.'

'And John Lennon?'

'Oooh, those glasses were sexy.'

'Really?' he said faintly and was rewarded by a chuckle. Her hands, he noticed with satisfaction, were finally starting to relax. 'So who else do you think of as sexy?' he asked. 'Just John? Paul? George? How about Ringo?'

'Ringo was sexy,' she agreed. 'Really sexy. When I see the old clips I think he's cuteness personified. But now every time I hear him I think of Thomas the Tank Engine. It's a bit disconcerting.'

'I imagine it might be.'

She was so different. How had his day been hijacked? he wondered. How had this happened? Instead of making plans and signing million-dollar deals, he was discussing the sexiness of Thomas the Tank Engine.

And enjoying it.

But then they were pulling up outside the offices where Charles presumably lay waiting, and her hands clenched white again.

'Don't sweat it,' Marcus told her and he surprised himself by placing a hand over her much smaller one. The touch surprised them both. It was as if a *frisson* of electricity ran between them, warm, intimate and somehow immeasurably comforting. 'I'm right behind you,' he heard himself saying. 'Every step of the way.'

Miss Pritchard—alias Attila the Hun, Charles's secretary—was her normal appalling self. Peta stepped out of the lift and she saw her coming and sighed. She didn't even pretend to be courteous.

'What do you want?'

'I'm here for my appointment,' Peta said, trying to keep her voice steady. 'It was for ten this morning.'

'Mr Higgins had a moment free at two,' the woman said, her disdain obvious in her intonation. 'But you weren't here. He has no more appointments available until late next week.'

'Then could you ask Mr Higgins if he'll make an appointment free for me,' Marcus said, his lazy drawl making the woman's face jerk from Peta to the man following behind. The man who, until now, had stood in the background and had not been noticed. Marcus. 'I believe the lease for this office space is soon up for renegotiation,' Marcus drawled. 'As landlord I expect a certain professional standard of my tenants. Peta had an appointment at ten this morning and she's still waiting. To have disgruntled clients hanging around my office space is not what I wish in my buildings.'

He motioned to a chair. 'Peta, if you'd like to sit down…' He gave the secretary a glimmer of a mockery of his smile—the sort of smile that had made many a business opponent come close to bursting a blood vessel in entirely appropriate anxiety. 'We'll wait,' he told the woman. 'Tell Mr Higgins that we're here and we'll wait for as long as it takes.'

Attila's eyes had been flat and cold before. Now, suddenly, they looked like those of a goldfish. A goldfish that was swimming over an unplugged hole. There were very few people in this city who weren't aware of Marcus's power. It was legendary. 'But…'

'Just tell him,' Marcus said wearily. 'I'd like to get this over quickly. I hope Mr Higgins feels the same.'

It appeared Mr Higgins did. Five minutes later they were ushered apologetically into the great man's presence.

To say Peta was tense was an understatement. This interview was overwhelmingly important to her, Marcus thought. The look on her face as she walked into Charles's office said she intended to be calm, practical and efficient.

She obviously hadn't counted on the store of anger that

must have been walled up for so long that the moment she saw her cousin it could do nothing but burst.

Charles was seated behind a vast mahogany desk. Before he could stand, Peta had stalked across and slammed her hands palm downward on the gleaming surface, so hard she made the in-tray jump.

'You uncaring toad,' she spat, and Marcus blinked in astonishment. But Peta was obviously past caring.

'You brought Hattie over here and she came because she thought you loved her. She hoped you loved her. But you didn't. You abandoned her.' Peta's voice was loaded with contempt and with icy rage. 'She could have died at home. With me. With Harry. With people who loved her. But you told her you wanted her here. You conned her into coming where she knew no one. How could you?'

'My relationship with my mother has nothing to do with you,' Charles snapped. The man was in his late thirties, florid, wearing a three-piece suit that was as sleazy as it was expensive, and he was obviously deeply disdainful of the woman before him. 'I have no idea what you want from me, Peta, or why you've bothered with this appointment.' He cast an uneasy glance at Marcus and then looked back at Peta. It was apparent that Marcus was the only reason he'd agreed to see her—the only reason he didn't get up now and push her out the door. 'Or how you've dragged Mr Benson into this.'

'No one drags me anywhere,' Marcus said softly. He hauled up a chair and sat, with the air of a man who was here for the entertainment.

'This is family business,' Charles told him, and Marcus gave him his very nicest smile.

'Consider me Peta's family. I've just elected myself. Peta, I hate to mention it but I don't think haranguing Charles on his mistreatment of his mother—justified as it may be—is going to achieve a lot. Let's just cut to the chase and get out of here. This place makes me nervous.'

Charles flushed. 'You don't have to stay.'

'I'm with the lady. Peta, say what you need to.'

Peta bit her lip. She half turned towards him and Marcus was waiting for her. He met her look and he sent her a silent message.

Settle. Anger's not going to achieve anything. What's important?

Peta caught it. She fought for control, taking a deep breath. Moving forward.

'The will...' she began.

'Ah, yes.' Charles had had time to do a regroup, too. 'The will.' With another nervous glance at Marcus, Charles settled deeper into his leather chair. His huge desk was guaranteed to intimidate the most influential of clients, and he clearly had no intention of moving from behind its protective distance. 'What on earth do you have to say about my mother's will?'

'Hattie meant to leave her half of the farm to me.'

'Not so, cousin.' Charles even smirked.

Why do I want to hit him? Marcus thought, and he had to force himself to stay still. To stay an uninvolved bystander.

'Hattie lived at the farm for all her life,' Peta was saying. 'We all have. Everyone except you. You left twenty years ago. But the farm paid for your education. For your travel.' She gazed around the opulent office. 'I bet it subsidised this. Your costs have already bled us dry. You've taken half our profits for ever. It's crazy that she left her half of the farm to you.'

'I'm her son.'

'But we've subsidised you with so much already and she knew I can't afford to buy you out. That it'd force me to sell.'

'That's not my problem.'

'No.' She took a deep breath, obviously forcing herself to stay calm. 'No, it's not. And it shouldn't be. All I'm asking... All I'm asking is that you'll hold on to your half of the farm—let me keep farming it—until Harry's of age.'

'Harry being...' He almost sneered but then appeared to remember that Marcus was watching and turned it somehow into a vaguely supercilious smile. 'Harry being how old?'

'Twelve.'

Twelve. In the background Marcus frowned, absorbing the information. It didn't fit—did it? Surely Peta wasn't old enough to have a twelve-year-old son?

Maybe he should have asked more questions.

'We need to stay on the farm until Harry's eighteen,' Peta was saying, almost pleading. 'Charles, you know how important the farm is to us all.'

'It was never important to me.'

'It paid for your education. It let you be what you wanted and I want Harry to have that choice, too. And it's a really good investment,' she told him. 'I'm more than happy for you to keep taking half the profits, and the land is growing more valuable all the time.'

'I've checked,' he told her. 'It'd sell for a fortune now. Because it's near the sea it can be cut up into hobby farm allotments. You own half. We both stand to make a killing.'

'We love the farm.'

'Get over it. I'm selling.'

'Charles—'

'Look, if that's all you have to say...' He eyed Marcus with disquiet, obviously still wondering how on earth Marcus came to be involved. 'You're wasting my time.'

Peta swallowed. Her hands clenched and unclenched. But, looking on, Marcus saw the moment she realised the futility of pleading. He saw her shoulders sag.

He saw her accept defeat.

And it hurt. It hurt him as well as the girl he was watching. Why did he want to hit someone? Not just someone. Charles. The urge was almost overwhelming.

But Peta had moved on. To the next important thing. 'Will you come to Hattie's funeral tomorrow?' she whispered.

'Funerals aren't my scene.'

'Hattie was your mother.'

'Yeah.' Another sneer. 'And she's dead. I'm over it, just like you should be. And, as soon as the funeral's over, the farm's on the market. It'd be on the market today if it wasn't for that clause.'

'Clause?' Marcus queried.

This was the sort of negotiation he was good at. He'd learned from long practice that it was better not to jump in early—to simply sit back, listen and absorb. Focus on essentials. And probe everything.

Charles flashed him an annoyed glance. 'My mother put a stupid codicil in her will. I left before the lawyer finished, and she did it...'

'Tell me about it,' Marcus said gently and Charles glowered.

'It's none of your business.'

'Tell me about it.'

'If I'm married then I inherit,' Peta said, obviously distressed. 'It makes no sense. Just before Hattie left to come here, I went out with one of the local farmers. Twice. It was enough to make Hattie think about me getting married. As if I could. But she thought... Well, she worried about me, my Auntie Hattie. She thought I'd spend my life caring for the family and not myself. So she must have thought she'd push. By putting in a stupid clause at the end. If I'm married then I'll inherit. But it's not an option.'

'What—never?'

'In a week?' She gave a bitter laugh. 'Hattie... Well, she was terminally ill. She was a bit muddled, even before she left Australia. That was probably how Charles persuaded her to come. She'd have worried about me, but she was here in New York, alone, and Charles would have pushed her hard to leave him the farm. So she wrote a will leaving everything to Charles, but apparently, after Charles left her alone with the lawyer, she added a codicil. The codicil says if I'm married within a week of her dying then the farm reverts to me. But... A week? Maybe she meant a year. Maybe... Well, who knows what she meant, but she said a week. That's by Wednesday.' She turned to her cousin again, her eyes dulled with the knowledge of what he would say. She already knew.

'Charles, please.'

'Just leave. You're wasting my time.' Charles rose, smoothed his already too smooth waistcoat and walked around to the door. He was really overweight, Marcus noticed. Short. Pompous. A slime-ball. It was as much as he could do not to flinch as the little man stalked past him to open the door.

'I'm sorry she's wasted your time, Mr Benson,' Charles told him. 'I'm sorry she's wasted mine. Go back to the farm, Peta, where you belong. Enjoy it for the last few weeks before it's sold. But get used to it. It's on the market the moment the week is up.'

'I'm sorry I wasted your time.'

They'd been silent as they rode the lift to ground level. They emerged on to the street to brilliant sunshine and Peta blinked as if she couldn't believe sun could exist in a place such as this.

'I assume the farm is worth a lot,' Marcus said mildly, and she blinked again.

'What? Oh, yes. You heard what he said. It is.'

'So you'll be well off?'

'Split...no. I won't be well off.'

'Do you have any professional training?'

'Sorry?'

'Do you have a career?'

'Yes. I'm a farmer.'

A farmer. He might have known. Of course. 'Can you get a job somewhere? Farming?'

'Are you kidding? With four kids? Who's going to take me on?'

'Four kids?' he said cautiously, and she shrugged as if it was none of his business. As indeed it wasn't.

Or it shouldn't be.

'Look, I said I'm sorry.' She took a deep breath. 'Okay. Enough. You've been really nice to me. Much nicer than I possibly could have hoped for. I've come over here and I've been with Hattie while she died. Thanks to you, I've seen Charles and I've asked him what I had to ask. I knew it was hopeless but I had to try. For the boys. Now I'm planning to bury my Auntie Hattie with all the love that I can, and then I'll get on an aeroplane and return to Australia. There's an end to it.'

'You have four kids?' He was stuck in a groove, he thought, but had to know. How old was she? Twenty-five? Twenty-six?

Four kids.

His eyes moved involuntarily to her waistline and he thought, no. No way.

She saw his gaze shift. 'What are you staring at?'

'Your figure,' he admitted with a rueful smile. 'You've held up pretty well for four kids.'

Her eyes widened. She looked stunned. And then her face, which had looked strained to the point of breaking, suddenly creased into laughter. A gorgeous chuckle rang out, making others on the pavement turn and stare.

She had the loveliest smile. The loveliest laugh.

'You're thinking I'm a single mum with four kids?'

'Well...'

'They're my brothers,' she told him. 'Daniel, Christopher, William and Harry. Twenty, eighteen, fifteen and twelve in that order. All students. The farm supports them all.' She caught herself. 'Or, I guess, I support them all. They help. They're great kids but it's mostly over to me. Until now. Now I guess the capital will pay for their education but heaven knows where we'll live. The university vacations are four months long. That's when we're a family. And Harry loves the farm so much. It'll break his heart if we have to leave.'

Silence. Marcus stared at her in disbelief.

Four brothers? She was supporting four brothers?

Good grief! So great a load on such slim shoulders. He winced and she managed a smile. Her laughter had gone again. The burden was back in place.

'I've said it before. It's my problem. Not yours.'

'You could always marry.' His voice was still faint with shock and she gave a rueful smile.

'By Wednesday? I don't think so. It was a crazy codicil made by a confused old woman who would have been desperate to make things right for everyone. Which was always going to be impossible.' She took his hand in hers and shook—a warm, firm handshake that was a shake of dismissal. 'Thank you very much for helping me, Mr Benson. You've done more than enough and I'm really grateful. Goodbye.'

And that was that. She turned and manoeuvred her crutches away from him, limping down the pavement, which was crowded with late afternoon shoppers.

She stood out, he thought, and it wasn't just her crutches. In truth, it wasn't her crutches at all. It was her flame hair. Her figure. The lovely curve of her slender neck. And her strength. The way she braced her shoulders, as if expecting to be struck.

It was so like David and Goliath, he thought again, but she had no slingshot. She had no weapon of any kind.

He stood and watched her go. He'd been dismissed. She was asking nothing of him.

She was on her own.

He couldn't bear it. He didn't have a clue what he was doing—what he was saying—but he knew only that he had to do it.

'Peta, stop,' he called, and she paused and half turned towards him.

'Yes?' She had the air of someone who'd already moved on. She looked slight and pale and somehow almost ethereal. As if any moment she'd vanish.

She could, he realised. He had this one moment to prevent it or she'd be gone and he need never see her again.

Which was what he wanted—wasn't it? He didn't get involved. He never got involved. He'd made a vow a long time ago and he'd never been tempted to break that vow.

Until now. Until the choice was to break the vow or to watch Peta take the next few steps and take her burden back to Australia.

He didn't even know what her burden was. He hardly knew her. He had a corporate deal to stitch up; he had a date tonight with a woman most men would kill to be seen with; he had a life in New York...

Peta was watching him, her pixie face questioning. Waiting. Waiting for release so she could disappear.

He couldn't give her that release. And there was only one way to stop her disappearing.

'There is a way you can be married by Wednesday,' he called, and the shoppers around them paused in astonishment.

Peta paused in astonishment.

'How?' she called, but maybe she hadn't called it. Maybe her voice was a whisper. They were twenty yards apart and there were people between. He saw her lips move. He saw the thought in her eyes that he was holding her up for nothing.

But he wasn't. He knew what he had to say and when he said it, it sounded right. Even inevitable.

'You can marry me.'

CHAPTER THREE

SHE couldn't believe what she'd heard. One minute she was looking defeat and despair in the face. This was the end of the world as she knew it. Tomorrow she'd have to bury Aunt Hattie with all the love and honour she deserved, trying to block out the hurt caused by this appalling last will. Then she'd climb on to an aeroplane and go home to face the boys and tell them that she didn't have a clue what their future held.

As opposed to...what?

As opposed to facing the man twenty yards away from her and trying to make sense of his crazy statement.

'I beg your pardon?' she said at last and there was general laughter among the passers-by. Marcus's words hadn't just shocked Peta. More than one person had stilled to listen—to hear her response to this fascinating question.

'He's asking you to marry him, love,' an elderly woman told her. 'He looks a good sort of catch. I'd think about it if I were you.'

'She's young,' someone else proffered. 'Plus she's pretty. She's got plenty of time to play the field.'

'No, but look at that suit,' the older woman retorted. 'The guy's obviously loaded. You do it, love, but don't go signing one of them pre-nup agreements. You take him for all he's worth.'

'Pretty funny proposal, if you ask me,' someone else said. 'You think she's got leprosy or something, that he has to stay two shops away from her to ask her to marry him?'

'Your girl got leprosy?' someone else demanded. 'Is that why the crutches?'

Even Marcus smiled at that.

So did Peta. It's a joke, she thought. It's a joke in appalling taste, but it's a joke for all that.

'Thanks,' she called, with what she hoped was a vestige of dignity. 'It's a very nice proposal but I have a funeral to go to, and then a trip home to Australia. I can't fit you in.'

'I'm serious, Peta.'

She flinched. Stop it, she thought. She'd been through enough. It was time for the sick jokes to subside. It was time for everything to subside. For now, all she wanted to do was to crawl away into a dark cupboard somewhere and mourn her aunt as she deserved.

But Marcus was striding towards her through the throng of entranced passers-by. She felt an almost overwhelming urge to turn and run—fast—but of course she couldn't. Her ankle wouldn't let her. She had to stand and be polite. It was the only thing she could think of to do.

But she wanted to run.

Or did she?

'Marcus...'

'I'm serious.' He reached her and his hands came out and caught hers. They were much bigger than her hands—much stronger. She could feel their strength and she could feel the urgency behind the strength.

She'd been holding her crutches. As he caught her hands, the crutches fell away—which made her feel even more helpless than ever.

'Peta, we can do this.'

'What...what?' She could scarcely muster a whisper.

'We can marry. As you turned away just now I saw it. Your aunt's will has an out. You need to marry before Wednesday and you can. You can marry me.'

'But...you don't want to marry me.'

'Of course I don't. I don't want to marry anyone. But that's just it. Because I don't want to marry anyone then I can marry you.'

'That's stupid.'

'No. It's sensible.'

'Why is it sensible? How can it be sensible?' She didn't know whether to laugh or to cry. Or simply to run. This big man with the smiling eyes was looking down at her with an expression that said he had all the answers to her problems right here. She just had to trust him.

Trust him? She didn't know him. She pulled on her hands but his hold tightened.

'Peta, it can work.'

'How can it work? How can it possibly work?'

But fifteen minutes later, when he'd calmed her down sufficiently to listen, she was starting to concede that it just might.

'I'll have my lawyers sift the will this afternoon,' Marcus told her. 'But if that's all you need—to be married—then I'm happy to oblige.'

She sat across the table from him. They'd found the first coffee shop they could; they'd sank into two deep armchairs and they hadn't moved. Peta felt as if she'd been hit by a sledgehammer.

'But...you only spilled my lunch,' she managed. She felt as if all the wind had been sucked out of her. 'You hardly ravished me. You hardly destroyed my honour or my marriage prospects. And here you are offering to marry me. Why?'

'I don't like Charles Higgins.'

'Then kick him out of your building. Put salt in his water cooler. Cut off his supplies of waistcoats. Whatever. But not this. You're offering to get involved up to your neck.'

But he was shaking his head, smiling. 'No, I'm not. I'm simply offering to get married. That's all. A simple ceremony. We do the deed. Despite what the lady on the street says, we draw up a pre-nuptial agreement saying we have no recourse to each other's property after divorce, and then we go our separate ways. After your estate has been settled, we'll divorce. My lawyers can take care of that. Apart from the one simple ceremony, we need never have anything to do with each other.'

'But—I still don't understand.' She looked up from the mug of coffee she was cradling and met his look head-on. His smile just deepened her sense of confusion. 'Okay, you don't like Charles Higgins,' she said. 'That's not a reason for doing this. Not for you. It'd solve my problems, and that's so important to me that I'm almost tempted to fall in with your crazy plan. But there has to be a catch. There must be. What do you want in return?'

He hesitated.

She watched his face. It was a good face, she thought, somehow forcing herself to be dispassionate. It held strength and warmth and humour. A girl could do a lot worse than marry a man like this. Especially as the marriage would last a whole five minutes.

But it was crazy. It was!

It seemed, though, that it hadn't been a spur-of-the-moment offer. He was really thinking.

'It'd be something good to do,' he said at last. 'I don't know whether you can understand that, but it's important to me.'

'No. I don't understand. Explain it to me.'

'I'd like to help.'

'By playing King Cophetua to my beggar maid?' She flushed and stared down into her coffee dregs. 'I'm sorry. That was ungracious of me.'

'But it's how my proposition makes you feel?'

Her chin jerked up at that and she met his gaze, startled. 'Yes. It does. You understand.'

'That it's a lot harder to take than to give? Yes. I know that.'

'And I know nothing about you.'

'Peta, I come from a background where there was nothing to do but take,' he told her. His eyes held hers, steady and strong. Telling her he was speaking a truth that was important to him. 'We had no choice. My mother was a welfare recipient and I had to fight anyone and everyone to get where I was—and accept help from all sorts of people I'd rather not be indebted to. So... I've spent a lifetime getting to the other side of that divide and now I'm in a position to give. It doesn't mean, though, that I'll expect gratitude or undying devotion. Just a simple thank you and then we'll get on with our lives. And one day when you're on the other side of the divide you might be able to do the same for someone else.'

'Like...take a good deed and pass it on?'

'Something like that, yes.'

'It's some good deed!' She was sounding a bit hysterical, she decided, but then she thought, why shouldn't she sound hysterical? Maybe she was hysterical.

'Peta...'

'Mmm?'

'Let's just marry and move on.'

'How on earth can I marry you?'

'Easy. We get ourselves a licence and we marry. There are formalities we need to go through but I'd imagine if I throw a bit of money and power at those formalities they'll disappear. I don't have the best legal team in New York for nothing. You said we have until Wednesday.'

'Yes, but...'

'That's the day after tomorrow. No sweat. We can do the thing easily.'

'You sound like you do it once a week.'

'I haven't. I've never married.'

'And if you meet the bride of your dreams next week?'

'That won't happen.'

'Why ever not? Are you gay?'

That stopped him in his tracks. He very nearly dropped his coffee and, when he recovered, his mouth quirked upward in a grin.

'No, Peta, I'm not gay.'

'You needn't sound so patronising,' she told him crossly.

'I can't tell. You hardly wear a sign or something. What other reason can you have for not marrying?'

He hesitated. Considering. He was about to indulge in confidences, Peta thought, and she also thought: that's something this man seldom does. What was it about him that made her know that he kept himself to himself? Entirely.

But he was breaking his rules now and his voice, when he spoke, had a reluctance that told her he didn't have a clue why he was doing it.

'My mother married four times,' he told her. 'Four times! And for every ceremony she was your traditional bride. She dressed me up as a pageboy, she glowed with excitement and she told me it'd be a happy-ever-after ending. But she chose losers. Every wedding threw us deeper into trouble. So I stood at the last of those ceremonies and I told myself it would never happen to me. I'd never take those vows. Some things are ingrained, Peta. I'm not about to change my mind now.'

She thought about that but it didn't make sense. 'So your mother wasn't very good at getting married,' she said gently. 'I'm sorry. But there's still a whole bunch of people in the world who think marriage is a very good idea.'

'There were other things. Getting attached... I learned early that independence is better.'

'Easier?'

'Probably easier,' he admitted, and she stared into his face and saw he really meant what he said.

Maybe it was the truth. Independence had a lot going for it. She'd heard. She'd never, ever had it.

But now wasn't the time to be thinking regretfully about an independence she'd never had and was hardly likely to have. Now she had a man sitting in front of her offering her a possible way out of the difficulties that were threatening to overwhelm her.

She didn't know anything about this man. His offer was ludicrous.

Marry him?

He was watching, waiting for an answer. Where on earth was an answer when you needed one?

'I don't even know you.'

'You don't need to know me.'

'You might be a con artist.'

'Yeah. About to scam you out of half your farm. That gives you a choice. It seems that you either trust me and risk losing half your farm or you definitely lose half your farm to Charles.'

'You can't be serious?'

'I am serious.'

'But... I can't.'

'Why not? Is there anyone else that you want to marry?'

She thought about that for a whole two seconds. The concept was crazy. 'No, but—'

'But there you are. Take it or leave it. I'm offering. I'm not really sure why I'm offering but it seems sensible. Will you marry me, Peta? For better or worse. Until distance does us part? Until at least Friday?'

She looked blankly at him—stunned.

'You really are serious.'

'I really am serious.'

Her mind was going in a thousand different directions. A million. But overriding all... Overriding all was the thought that maybe somehow she could keep the farm.

Her head was spinning. Her ankle was throbbing. She felt so near the edge that any minute now she'd topple over. To make such a momentous decision...

'Peta.' His hand gripped hers and held, hard. 'Peta, you don't need to understand. You can't, because I hardly understand myself. All you have to do is trust. Just say yes.'

Just say yes...

Easy to say. Will you marry me?

Maybe it wasn't momentous at all, she thought wildly. People were divorced every day. What was the marriage? A simple document that could be annulled at any time. And the boys would be safe.

She bit her lip. She stared into Marcus's calm grey eyes and he stared back. Still Marcus held her hand. Still Marcus watched her, waiting.

And in the end it was easy. There was nothing else to say.

'Okay,' she whispered. 'Okay, Marcus. Thank you very much. I have no idea why you're wanting to do this but I'm very grateful. So yes, I'll marry you. As soon as possible.'

Marcus Benson, in organisational mode, was a man to be reckoned with. Peta was put into Robert's care and taken back to her hotel with instructions to rest her ankle. Marcus moved on to the wedding.

He'd told Peta he could organise this by Wednesday. In truth it was a guess. He had no idea if it was possible.

A man with no idea turned naturally to his assistant. In crisis, find Ruby. Fast.

Ruby was summoned peremptorily from the boardroom where she'd been putting things on hold because of Marcus's absence. The unflappable Ruby was already feeling under pressure. By the time she reached his office she was almost ruffled, and when Marcus told her he wanted her to organise his wedding she was surprised into the unthinkable response of choking.

It took a glass of water before she could make herself understood.

'You? Married?'

'What's wrong with me getting married?'

She thought about it. Marcus was behind his desk. He watched her with patience, seeing her eyes grow round in response to this extraordinary request. Seeing her think it through.

'To the waif?' she asked cautiously and he nodded.

'To Peta. That's right.'

And Ruby—who had never in Marcus's lifetime been

known to show surprise at anything—proceeded to drop her jaw almost to her ankles.

'I don't believe it.'

'It doesn't matter whether you believe it or not,' he told her, annoyed. 'Just tell me what I need to do it.'

She thought some more. She sipped water and took a visible grip. 'Um… Weddings. I've never done weddings. But… Okay. I can do this.' A bit more thinking. Then, 'Do you have any preferences?'

'Preferences?'

'Like church, civil, white, rose petals, bridesmaids…'

'No preferences. Just a fast wedding.'

'How fast?'

'Tomorrow.'

'Tomorrow!' Ruby's voice came out practically a squeak. She regrouped—sort of. 'Uh, did you say tomorrow?'

'That's right. Wednesday at the latest.'

'There are things like licences. I'm sure there are. Formalities. Queues.'

'Throw as much money as you need at the problem. Just fix it.'

'Gee, how romantic.'

'Ruby,' he said warningly and her eyebrows hiked.

'Yes, sir?'

'Just fix it.'

'Certainly, Mr Benson. Very good, Mr Benson.' She took a deep breath and he could see she was fighting laughter. 'Do we know the bride's name?'

'Peta.'

The eyebrows hiked again. 'I know her first name's Peta,' she said with exaggerated patience. 'We're going to need a bit more information. Just a bit.'

'Right.' He handed a sheet of paper across the desk. 'I had her write down her details. I'm not stupid.'

'So.' Ruby looked down at the sheet. 'Peta O'Shannassy. Aged twenty-six. Australian.'

'That's right.' He hadn't known. He frowned suddenly. Hell, what was he getting himself into? Peta O'Shannassy. She'd written down her name but this was the first time he'd heard it.

'She needs me to do this,' he told Ruby, and she paused from reading the sheet and looked at him. Really looked at him.

'She's in trouble?'

'Yes.'

'You want to tell me?'

He sighed. But Ruby on side was a force to be reckoned with and he'd learned a long time ago it was better just to give in and tell. Briefly he outlined what was happening and, when he had finished, her face had changed. The laughter had gone. The determination he felt was strangely mirrored in his assistant's eyes.

Ruby had met Peta. She knew Charles. Marcus's dislike wasn't purely personal.

But Ruby was moving on again, on to business. Her speciality. 'You'll need a decent pre-nuptial agreement. One that will hold water.'

'Can you get that underway?'

'Sure.' She hesitated. 'You know, Charles won't take this lying down. Not if there's money involved.'

'I suppose he won't.'

'Let me run this past our lawyers,' she told him. 'I'll organise a copy of the will to be faxed here this afternoon. You don't want to go into this blind. Or...' She paused and a glimmer of laughter appeared again behind her eyes. 'Or any more blind than you appear to be.'

'Right.'

Then she hesitated. 'Marcus...'

'Yes.'

'You know... Peta has her contact address here.'

'I told her to put it down in case you need her to fill in forms.'

'Mmm.' She looked again at the piece of paper and cast a cautious glance at him. 'Do you know where she's staying?'

'It doesn't matter. This wedding is a formality. Where she lives is her business.'

'Right.' There was another thoughtful glance. 'It's just… I know this hotel. A neighbour had a friend from Canada who stayed there one night. It's the cheapest place in town. But he came out of it robbed blind.'

Silence.

It was entirely Peta's business where she stayed, he told himself.

But of course it was no such thing. Marcus took the written sheet from Ruby and stared down at the address. His…his bride?

'Can you fix it?' he asked Ruby.

'What—turn up there and tell her Marcus says move?'

'I guess not.' He'd seen enough of Peta to figure that wasn't the best way to go about things. But… He didn't get involved. He didn't!

He was involved. He was involved up to his neck. 'I need to go,' he said finally, and Ruby nodded.

'Of course you do,' she agreed. 'Marcus Benson to the rescue. Good grief!'

But Marcus was no longer listening.

Marcus had already gone.

By the time Robert dropped her at the door of her hotel Peta was past exhaustion. She lay back on the hard mattress and tried for sleep. She'd hardly slept since she'd arrived in this country. The doctors had given her pain-killers and warned her they'd make her sleep. She should be out for the count.

But sleep was nowhere.

It wasn't the noise that prevented her from sleeping. She'd stayed in this place for over a week and she'd learned to turn off from the drunken cacophony that surrounded her.

Nor was she disturbed about her own security. There was

something distinctly comforting about having nothing left to steal. Her passport and her airline ticket were in a money-belt next to her skin and there was nothing else.

The throb in her ankle had even eased.

She should sleep.

But how could she? Marcus was with her. Every time she closed her eyes he was right there, filling her head, his gentle eyes probing...

He was marrying her?

The thought was unbelievable. The concept was unbelievable. Marcus Benson was marrying Peta O'Shannassy.

Who was Marcus Benson? She didn't know. But what could she do about it?

The sensible thing would be to hire a private detective and find out at least a little of the man she intended to marry. She didn't have enough funds to consider it.

But... Her hand rested on her money belt and the same comforting thought arose.

She had nothing worth stealing. He could hardly cheat her. What did she have? Half a farm, split five ways. She had so many encumbrances she felt weighed down with concrete.

If Marcus was marrying her for anything other than altruism then he had a big surprise coming, she decided.

He could have Harry.

The thought came out of left field and, surprisingly, it was good. Marcus would like Harry. Harry might even like Marcus. Harry was the smallest of her responsibilities but sometimes he felt the heaviest.

Yep. She might love Harry to bits but if Marcus wanted him... She was definitely ready to share.

Sharing. It was a good concept. A great concept. Even if it was pure fantasy.

But it was enough to distract her. Her mind stopped spinning just a little. Exhaustion took its toll.

Finally she slept.

* * *

She woke to shouting.

So what was new? People shouted in this place all the time. Half the inhabitants of this boarding house were drunk or stoned or both. But this time it was closer than usual.

Her dormitory held eight beds and the last four beds in the row were covered with fighting bodies. Someone was yelling; there were people punching, clawing, rolling.

There was the sound of broken glass and a woman screamed.

She opened her eyes and someone was grabbing her. Lifting.

'Put me down!' It was an instinctive scream of terror.

'Don't draw attention to yourself,' her intended husband told her. 'Is this your bag? Shut up and let me get you out of here.'

Marcus took her back to his apartment. He brooked no argument, hardly speaking until Robert had deposited them at the entrance to his apartment building, until they'd ridden the lift to the penthouse and he had her behind his closed door.

Even then he wouldn't listen to protests.

'I'm marrying you. That involves keeping you alive until at least tomorrow. So have the sense to obey orders.'

She was still dazed, doped with the pain-killers the doctors had given her. Three quarters asleep. But not so far gone that she couldn't protest. She was balanced precariously on crutches. He'd carried her out of the seedy backpackers' but that had been the end of his carrying role. She'd emerged to face the doorman of this luxury apartment block on her own two feet—just. 'I'm not good at following orders,' she managed.

'How did I guess that?' His severe mouth quirked upward into a wry smile. They were standing in the entrance to his apartment and all she could see was black marble and mirrors. If she wasn't so dopey she'd panic, she thought. She should at least try.

'I can't stay here with you.'

'I guessed you'd say that, too,' he told her. He pointed to three doors. 'Bathroom, bedroom, kitchen. I'm staying at my club. I'll see you in the morning.'

'But...'

She gazed at him, confused beyond belief. This day had got away from her. All she knew was that somehow a day that had started as a disaster had somehow been salvaged, and it had been salvaged because of this man in his lovely suit, with his lovely eyes, with his lovely smile.

Yeah, she was getting maudlin, but he made her feel... He made her feel...

Not maudlin. Something very different from maudlin.

'Thank you,' she whispered.

'It's okay.'

'I mean it.' She reached forward and took his hand. Then, before he could guess what she intended, she raised her face and kissed him softly on the lips. It was a token kiss—a touch—a kiss of gratitude and weariness and need for human comfort. It shouldn't have caused confusion but, as she stepped back, confusion was what she saw in his eyes.

'Marcus...'

'I'd better leave.' His voice was strange. Husky. Unsure.

'You don't need to.' She could sleep on the settee, she meant to say. She meant to add...something. But tiredness and the drugs she'd been given had the better of her and she couldn't think of anything more to add.

What had she said? He didn't need to leave? No. She was right. More than that; she very much wanted him to stay. She was so alone.

What a wimp. She caught herself, fighting for her dignity. Fighting through the haze of pain-killers for any sort of sense at all.

'I meant...'

'I know what you meant,' he told her and he smiled. It

was his smile that was her undoing, she thought desperately. It was a smile that twisted, distorted, changed her world.

'But I still think I'd better go,' he told her. He touched her, a feather-light fingertip tracing of her cheek. Was she imagining things—or was there reluctance to leave?

She couldn't tell. She was in no fit state to tell anything at all.

He knew it. He swore softly. 'Lock the door after me,' he told her. 'And stay safe until morning. No arguments.'

And that was that. He walked out and slammed the door behind him.

No arguments? She stared at the closed door. How could she argue when he was gone?

She was so befuddled she was past thinking. She gathered her crutches and limped forward, stunned. The first door led to the bedroom. To the bed. It was vast, piled high with a mountain of white pillows.

It looked wonderful.

There was silence all around her. There was silence for the first time since she'd reached this city.

No argument?

She had no argument at all. She hobbled to the bed, let her crutches fall—and let herself fall.

Wise or not, five minutes later she was asleep. But as she slept her fingers rested on her cheek—where Marcus's fingers had touched.

And Marcus?

He lay in his bed at his club and he swore into the night. One ceremony and he was finished with her, he thought. One ceremony.

But when he'd walked into that place—had seen the louts fighting—men in a women's dorm—crazy with drink—broken glass...

And Peta, sleeping as if she was so exhausted she couldn't face waking, even to protect herself.

And then she'd kissed him. Her kiss... It had been so defenceless. So—

So he didn't know what. All he knew was that when she'd asked that he stay it had taken all his self-possession not to gather her into his arms and sweep her into his bed.

I'll look after her until she leaves New York, he told himself. That's all I'll do. And then I'll forget her.

Yeah, right.

When Peta had arrived all she'd seen was the bed. And Marcus. When she woke she finally took in her surroundings and they weren't to her taste at all.

She stretched in the vast, luxurious bed and gazed around her. And winced.

Lat night she'd been stunned, exhausted and doped with pain-killers. This morning...

This place might be comfortable, silent and safe but it was also sterile.

It was like something out of *Vogue*, she thought, and then thought, Nope. Not ordinary *Vogue*. Maybe a *Gentleman's Hygienic Vogue*, if such a magazine existed.

At a guess it had been decorated by a professional whose brief was clinical, modern and masculine. The place was cool grey and black. Lots of glass and chrome. Nothing out of place.

Ultra expensive.

She tossed back the covers and hobbled the few steps to the window. Not everything met with her disapproval. Below was Central Park. There were horse-drawn carriages driving right by.

The view was lovely.

She turned around to the apartment and winced again. This wasn't lovely. Not a photograph. Not a personal thing. The place looked as sterile as a hotel.

More so.

Who on earth was this man she was marrying? What was she doing in his apartment?

She didn't have time for questions. She glanced at her watch and practically yelped.

The only time the funeral director had been able to fit Hattie's funeral in was really early.

Like...in half an hour?

She had to go. Marcus had grabbed her meagre bag of possessions and it was still in the hall. She'd wear the suit Marcus had given her yesterday and feel grateful for it. She pressed out the worst of the creases with her hands, showered and dressed in minutes and then she paused at the door, ready to go.

She glanced around the apartment and thought that she wasn't really sorry to leave. The backpacker hotel was awful but if this was home... She'd hate it almost as much.

It was Marcus's home.

So what? Marcus was nothing to her. Nothing at all.

CHAPTER FOUR

'MARCUS...'

Ruby's phone call woke Marcus from sleep—which was unusual. He was usually awake at dawn, checking the international markets. But he'd lain awake long into the night, deeply disturbed by the events of the day.

Peta had got to him. His intended bride. He didn't know how but she'd somehow wriggled her way through his defences and made him concerned. More than concerned. Deeply involved.

He hoped she was sleeping. He hoped her bed didn't seem too big and too strange.

The thought of her alone in his barren apartment was hugely unsettling and for the first time ever he found himself wishing he'd spent a bit more time making the place welcoming. Maybe he should indulge in a few cushions or something. It hardly mattered to him. Home was a place to sleep and dump clothes for cleaning. Strangers organised by Ruby came and magically made the place tidy; fixed his gear; left dinners in the refrigerator on the off-chance that he'd get home hungry.

He hardly noticed.

But he wished his apartment was better now, and by the time he finally slept he'd almost decided to call in another decorator. Which would be a real waste. As soon as Peta left he wouldn't be interested in the place again.

So why was he fussed now?

Why was she getting to him?

He'd slept fitfully and when Ruby woke him his voice was still slow with sleep.

'You got her out of there?' she demanded.

'What?'

'The backpackers' place.' Ruby sounded anxious. 'You shifted her?'

'Yeah. She's at my place.'

'Your place?' He could hear the quickening of interest and he almost smiled.

'I'm at the club.'

'Right.' She thought that through. 'The club. On the other side of town. That's cosy.'

'What is it you want, Ruby?'

'A marriage.'

It was his turn to pause. 'There's a problem?'

'Not with getting you married. I found a judge who's prepared to fit you in, and the legal team have fixed everything up.'

'Then what's wrong?'

'It's the bit about Peta leaving the country that I don't like.'

'What don't you like?'

'She goes home tomorrow?'

'I'd imagine so.'

'And you're staying here.'

'What else would I do?'

'A real husband,' Ruby said thoughtfully, 'would go with her.'

Marcus had been lying back on his pillows. Almost relaxed. Now he stirred himself. He focused.

He knew this tone.

'Ruby, this is not a serious marriage.'

'That's not what the legal eagles are going to say,' Ruby told him. 'I had Adam and Gloria run through the ramifications of this thing. They say that if any legal gain hinges on a marriage then the marriage has to be seen to be serious. A simple ceremony and wedding certificate isn't going to cut it. Charles will have it tossed out on the first hearing. Not all your power and influence will make it work unless you're prepared to spend time together. If you marry the girl, you're going to have to do it properly.'

'Do it properly? What are you suggesting?'

'Well.' He heard her take a deep breath, as though to launch into something she was unsure of. 'Adam and Gloria and I have been thinking.'

Adam and Gloria—the firm's top legal minds. And Ruby. Combined they were his three top people. 'Adam and Gloria and you,' he said cautiously, 'have been thinking what?'

'That you should take a holiday.'

It was his turn to think.

'Are you still there?' she asked.

'I might be.' His tone was cautious.

'You ever had a holiday?'

'I don't need—'

'Marcus, you've been making money ever since your mama abandoned you when you were twelve years old,' she told him and Marcus almost dropped the phone.

'What the hell?'

'You think I don't know? You think none of us know? You've fought every inch of your life. Every inch. All you know is how to make money, Marcus.'

'Ruby...'

'I know.' He could almost hear her holding up her hands, backing off a bit. They didn't intrude into each other's personal lives. They never had.

They liked it that way.

But it seemed Ruby was intent on breaking the rules in more ways than one.

'Marcus, I started out in this financial business because my man and my baby were killed in a car crash,' she told him, her normally matter-of-fact voice becoming gentler. 'I fill my life with my job now because I've done loving and I have nothing left. But you... You haven't even started.'

Her man and her baby. Ruby had had a man and a baby? They'd been killed?

He hadn't known that. Hell, why hadn't he known that?

He'd never asked. He'd understood that there was something in her history but he'd never asked. It hadn't been his business.

And she'd never intruded into his space, either.

So why now? 'You're telling me I need to fall in love?' he ventured, and he was rewarded by Ruby's rich chuckle. She laughed so rarely. It made him think…

What did it make him think? How little he knew this woman? How crazy was the suggestion she was making?

'We're not expecting miracles here,' Ruby told him. 'But Adam and Gloria and I, we figured you've just tied up the e-commerce deal for Forde and there's nothing happening over the next few weeks we can't handle. We figure if you're serious about validating this marriage, then you need to take a holiday. You need to see Australia.'

'A few days won't make a difference,' he told her and she had all the answers.

'A few days won't. Two weeks will. We've checked. The Amerson v. Amerson case sets the precedent. The Amersons married, had a two-week honeymoon, and then separated to work in different countries. They rang each other once a week and e-mailed lots. He was killed, his wife inherited, but his brother sued for his estate, claiming the marriage wasn't valid. The judge decreed it was fine. So that's the precedent you're planning to use. Two weeks in Australia, Marcus, followed by the odd phone call and e-mail. It's that or forget it.'

'Two weeks?'

'At least.'

'I can't.'

'You can.' He heard the smile in her voice. 'You know you can. She's a nice kid.'

'She's a what?'

'No? You tell me what else she is, Marcus,' Ruby said gently—and replaced the receiver without another word.

Leaving him stunned.

Leaving him totally bemused.

He should pull out of this right now, he thought grimly. He stared up at the gilt ceiling of the ornate club bedroom and he thought things through. Or he tried to. Things were getting really muddled.

He thought of where he'd found Peta last night.

He thought of where he'd been—how hard he'd fought to get where he was.

He thought of Ruby, not telling him all these years about her baby and her man. And he thought about why he'd never asked.

He thought of Peta, taking his hands, kissing him...

A holiday. What harm would two weeks do?

What harm indeed?

'Ashes to ashes. Dust to dust.'

Peta stood in the garishly decorated funeral chapel and listened to the priest intone words of farewell to her beloved Hattie.

There was no one else. Charles hadn't come. Of course he hadn't. She'd disliked Charles for a long time, but now... She gazed at the plain wooden coffin and tried hard not to think about how distressed Hattie would be if she knew her son wasn't here to say goodbye.

She tried instead to think of the good times. Of the Hattie she'd known and loved—the Hattie who'd been a mother figure to her for so long.

The good times refused to surface. It distressed her immeasurably that Hattie was being farewelled here, instead of in Hattie's own beloved church back in Australia. She hated the whole thing. That she was being forced to marry a stranger to protect her legacy—a man whose motives she couldn't begin to understand.

Marriage. The idea seemed crazy. It was a figment of her imagination—part of the nightmare that was yesterday. Her feelings for Marcus must have been induced by pain and by drugs, she decided. Today he was a hazy memory.

Today all she could focus on was Hattie.

The coffin was right before her. It was the only real and tangible thing in this whole mess. The priest was murmuring the last blessing, casting Peta an apologetic glance as he did so. He was a kindly man. He could tell she was distressed at this curt service, but he had three more of these to do this morning.

The curtain swung closed in front of the coffin—and it was over.

'She'll have been really glad that you were here.'

The sound of the familiar voice made her jump, and when Marcus's hand came lightly down on her shoulder he had no idea how close she came to turning into his broad shoulder to weep. Marcus a hazy memory? It seemed she was mistaken. He was very, very real.

'M-Marcus.'

'I went back to my apartment and found you were already gone. Then Ruby rang and said the service was now. I'm sorry I didn't make it earlier.'

'But… Why?'

'I thought you might need a bit of support,' he told her. 'And I also figured that's what husbands are for.' He smiled, a gentle smile that was close to being her undoing. 'You loved her.'

It was a statement—not a question—and Peta nodded.

'I've been doing a little research.' He cast an uncertain look at the curtained end of the room—they both did. There was the sound of wheels—one coffin making way for the next. Peta tried really hard to concentrate on what he was saying. 'Your aunt only came back to the States when she became ill,' Marcus told her, apparently seeking confirmation of someone's research. 'At Charles's insistence.'

'Australia was her home,' Peta said drearily. 'But Charles wanted his mother to die here.'

'Why?'

'Can't you guess?' Peta shrugged. 'He made a flying visit to Australia when the doctors told her she had very little time, and he insisted she come back with him. Hattie... I think at that stage Hattie was so grateful he was taking an interest that she'd agree to anything. She came. Then, whenever I rang, she said things were fine. She was even getting better, she said. Only suddenly she stopped ringing and Charles wouldn't answer my calls. I worried and worried and finally it was too much. I got on a plane and came.'

She didn't add that she'd spent all her savings. Everything.

Marcus was calmly watching her, obviously seeing her distress. 'And Charles wasn't doing the right thing by her?'

'What do you think? Of course he wasn't. There was...nothing. She was Australian. She had no health insurance. She wasn't being treated. She was so much worse and he'd put her in a really horrid nursing home and abandoned her. She was so glad to see me. So glad. She was really confused. I found a doctor to see her but by then it was far too late to have any effect. The cancer had done something to her calcium levels, the doctor told me, so she was only having glimpses of reality but at least she knew I was here. She died a week after I arrived.'

'Having changed her will in favour of her son.'

She shook her head, bleakness threatening to overwhelm her. 'It was her right.'

'I think I'm going to enjoy this wedding,' Marcus said grimly and then he glanced at Peta's pale face and obviously decided against pushing his anger further. There was another funeral waiting to happen. This wasn't the time—or the place.

'Let me buy you something to eat.'

'No.' She hauled herself together. 'No, thank you.'

The undertaker was approaching now, an anxious little man, clearly wanting to clear the room so that the next sad little ceremony could take place. He looked at Marcus with obvious curiosity. And then his eyes widened in recognition. 'Marcus—*Marcus Benson*?'

'Yes.' Marcus held out his hand in greeting and the man's slightly impatient expression slipped away.

'Don't hurry,' he told them. 'There's another funeral due but take your time.'

'We will. Thank you.' Marcus's glance was dismissive but Peta edged towards the door.

'I need to go.'

'Stay.'

'N-No.'

'Are you afraid of me?' he asked, his tone softening. 'You know, fear's no basis for a marriage.'

'I'm not afraid of you. I don't even know you. And that's no basis for a marriage, either.'

'No.' He paused. 'No, it's not. And therein lies the problem.'

'There's a problem?'

'There is.'

'Well, then…' She cast another uncertain glance at the curtains, as if unsure whether she should move on. But outside there was a group of mourners gathered, and the funeral director had moved back to wait respectfully by the door. He wouldn't hurry a man of Marcus's stature, but he was still anxious.

Hattie wasn't behind the velvet curtain, Peta told herself. Hattie had gone.

Her future had probably gone as well. This man had offered her a solution which was as crazy as it was unworkable. What was he saying? That there was a problem?

'Well, then.' She did an almost visible regroup. 'Well, then. There's no need even to tell me what the problem is. This whole marriage idea was a crazy, unworkable plan. I need to catch a plane tomorrow and you, I'm sure, have work to do. Thank you for coming this morning. Thank you for your accommodation last night.' Her voice faltered just a little. 'I... I'm very grateful. I sort of needed someone.'

'Anyone,' he agreed, and she smiled.

'You were a very nice anyone.'

'Gee, thanks.'

'Well, it's not every day that a girl gets an offer of marriage from someone as neat as you.' She looked over to the funeral director and gave him a reassuring smile. 'It's okay. We're leaving.' She put her hand out and shook Marcus's, a firm shake of farewell. Moving on. Fast. Before she broke down. She didn't know whether it was Hattie's death or the fact that she was so far from home—or that she'd just allowed herself a glimmer of crazy hope with this mad marriage scheme...

She had to get out of there. Fast.

'Goodbye,' she muttered and turned away before he could see her face—but he wasn't letting go. He held her hand and turned her back to face him.

'No.'

'No?'

'It's still on,' he told her. 'The marriage.' He smiled, a funny lopsided smile that was amazingly endearing. 'Ruby says I can marry you.'

'Well, bully for Ruby.' She paused. 'Your assistant gave you permission to marry?'

'No.' Marcus cast an uncertain glance across at the undertaker. The man's ears were practically flapping. 'Um... Well, yes. Ruby does the busy work. She's figured out the things we need. The formalities. As well as that, I asked her to run the will past a couple of my lawyers. It'd be a waste if we were to marry and not be able to overturn the will.'

'A waste,' she said blankly.

'Well, it would.' He held out a placating hand to the undertaker. 'Five more minutes.' Then back to Peta. 'You see, the lawyers are of the opinion that if you married me and got on the plane tomorrow and I stayed here, then Charles could argue that the marriage was a farce.'

'So what are you saying?' Her eyes widened. 'Are you saying we have to consummate the marriage?'

The undertaker gave a start. The little man choked, met Marcus's eye and carefully backed out of the door. A little. Not out of earshot.

Marcus grinned. 'No, we don't have to consummate the marriage.'

'Well, that's a relief.'

'I thought you might say that.'

She smiled. It was a weak sort of smile but it was a smile for all that. It was the first time she'd smiled that day and it felt okay. More. It felt good.

She was so grateful to this man, she realised. Even if his crazy plan didn't come to fruition—as it surely couldn't— his presence over these two days had lightened her load immeasurably.

He'd made her smile. He'd made her feel as if somebody cared.

She forced herself to focus on practicalities. Somehow.

'So we don't consummate the marriage. What do we do?'

'Ruby says we need a honeymoon,' he told her. 'It seems, legally, we need to spend some time together if we're to be seen as truly married. I've just finished stitching together a deal which has taken nearly three years to pull off. Ruby tells me I haven't taken a holiday in ten years and I guess she's right. She's just read me the riot act and told me that if I don't take some time off I'll drop dead from overwork. Anyway...' He gave a grin that was half amused, half embarrassed. 'Anyway, if you'd like a honeymoon... If you'd like...I could come back to Australia with you for a couple of weeks.'

She stared at him. Stunned. 'You're kidding.'

'I never kid.'

'You want to come home with me?'

He grinned again. 'There's no need to say it like I'm a stray dog.'

'I don't want you.'

'There's gratitude.'

She tried taking a breath. It didn't quite come off. 'I'm sorry.' She shook her head. 'No. I'm not sorry. I don't want a husband.'

'That's good, because I don't want a wife.' He shrugged, still smiling. 'But Ruby says I offered and I ought to go through with it. I've never been to Australia.'

'This is crazy. You can't just take two weeks off—for a stranger.'

'I can—for a holiday.'

'You mean... You'd go off on a tour or something?'

'Ruby says I'd need to stay at your farm.'

'Do you *want* to stay at my farm?'

'No.'

'Then...'

'But I'm prepared to.'

She shook her head. 'Marcus, I don't think I can cope with that level of obligation.'

'I can understand that. But maybe—if you want the farm badly enough, you need to swallow your pride and accept my help. Accept that I can afford to give it and accept that I'll ask nothing in return.' He smiled. 'Except a small glow of virtue which I promise I'll keep under my smug little hat.' He caught her hands and held them, and he looked down at her, his gaze strong and sure. Compelling. 'Are you strong enough to accept this? Taking's hard, Peta. I know that. But—maybe you have no choice.'

His smile faded. He might be as confused as she was but he didn't seem to be showing it. His gaze said *trust me*. His gaze told her he knew the direction she should take; she just had to let him take the lead. Do what he said.

To let a stranger help her in such a way... It seemed crazy.

Impossible. But his eyes said *trust me*. His eyes said *let me take the lead*.

And for Peta, who'd never had anyone take the lead in her life, the concept was suddenly almost overpoweringly appealing.

'No strings?'

'No strings.'

'I'll knit you a pair of socks for Christmas.'

'That would be very nice,' he told her and she choked.

'You haven't seen my knitting.'

'But you'll accept?'

'I don't have a choice,' she said simply. 'I'm very grateful. I hate that I need to be grateful, so I guess... You're just going to have to get used to my socks!'

He ushered her next door to a coffee shop, he ordered pastries and coffee and she didn't argue. She even ate something.

They ate in silence. She was achingly aware that he was watching her—that she was being somehow measured—but there was nothing she could do about it.

She wasn't even sure that she minded.

'What happened to your parents?' he asked at last, and Peta felt her insides twist. It was as if this man could really read her mind. The sensation was incredibly unnerving.

'My mother died having Harry,' she told him. 'Eclampsia. My father was killed when his tractor rolled ten years ago.'

'And you've been it ever since.'

'It?'

'Provider.'

'There was Hattie,' she told him.

'So Hattie looked after you?'

'I was sixteen.'

'So Hattie didn't look after you?'

'I was strong. I could run the farm. I loved Hattie and I couldn't have coped without her, but she had crippling arthritis.'

'So let me get this straight,' he said, obviously thinking it through. 'You were sixteen when you were left on a farm with four other children. The oldest was how old?'

'Daniel was eleven.'

'And your cousin? Charles?'

'He's a lot older than me. He left before my father died. Hattie sent her share of the farm profits to him, and we only saw him when he wanted more money.' She bit her lip. 'She didn't know... Hattie didn't understand how successful Charles was. He kept needing more.'

But Marcus wasn't interested in how successful Charles was. He was focused on Peta. 'So you'd have been sixteen. You were still at school?'

'It didn't hurt me to leave. I loved farming.'

'You mean you had to leave.'

'Yes,' she admitted honestly. 'I had to.'

'And what about now?'

'I run a really successful farm.'

'Do the boys help?'

'Of course they do. Only Daniel and Christopher are at university now and William is at a special school in the city.' She smiled, thinking of her high-achieving brothers. 'Daniel will be a vet and Christopher is in first year law. And William is brilliant. He won a scholarship to a special school for gifted kids.'

'But—you support them all?' He sounded appalled and she shook her head.

'No. They all help. During the holidays.'

'But the rest of the time there's just you?'

'And Harry.' Her smile widened, thinking with real affection of the baby of the family. 'Harry's great. You'll love...' She caught herself and changed the tense. 'You'd like Harry.'

'When I meet him.'

'There's no need for you to meet him.'

'There's every need,' he said brusquely. 'I thought I explained it to you. Where's Harry now?'

'Stowing away in Daniel's university college.' She hesitated. 'He was unhappy about me being away. He's only twelve. So we thought that if he could stay with the boys he'd be happier. The kids are great. They're looking after him. But I need to get back.'

'I can see that you do.' He was staring at her as if she'd grown two heads. 'You carry all this load on your shoulders...'

'Hey, they're my family,' she said, not liking his tone of absolute astonishment. 'What would you do?'

What would he do? They stared at each other and she thought that he really didn't have a clue. He knew nothing of what she had. Of the benefits as well as the responsibilities.

He'd turn away, she thought. He'd run. What man would willingly come within a thousand miles of the sort of responsibility she carried?

But he didn't turn away. Instead, he glanced across her shoulder and smiled and she turned to the coffee shop window to see Ruby waving from the pavement.

'What will I do?' Marcus asked, his voice suddenly almost teasing. Almost laughing. He waved back to Ruby, beckoning her in. 'I'll tell you what to do. I'll hand you over to Ruby to turn you into a bride. I have a deal to stitch up and then I'm free. I'll marry you and carry you back to Australia. For two weeks. On two conditions.'

'What are they?'

'That you don't make me milk a cow! And you don't put me in charge of a twelve-year-old.'

If Marcus was forceful, Ruby was worse. She shooed Marcus back to work and outlined her plans. Which left Peta stunned. Ruby had a vision of a white wedding and nothing was going to deflect her—and the wedding was scheduled in four hours' time.

'I can get married in what I'm wearing,' Peta said, totally confounded, but Ruby would have none of it.

'Marcus Benson has half the women of the world wanting to marry him—and you're going to wear a day dress?' Ruby smiled, somehow managing to rob her words of offence. 'Peta, he's doing you a favour. The least you can do is accept in the manner it's intended.'

It sounded reasonable—sort of. There was only one thing for it, Peta decided. She needed to swallow her pride. 'I'm broke,' she confessed.

Ruby hesitated, but only for a moment. 'Yeah. You are. But Mr Benson has given me a fat cheque to outfit you for the wedding. He told me to do it subtly but I don't know how. Except by telling you that you'd be doing all of us a favour by accepting.'

A fat cheque. Peta drew in her breath. 'I thought I told him—'

'Yeah, you told him. He said yesterday that he'd offended you. He said he tried to dress you as a socialite and you tossed it back in his face.'

'I didn't...'

'Well, I would have, too,' Ruby said honestly—unexpectedly. 'And I think more of you for doing it. But throwing back corporate suits and refusing wedding gowns are different things.'

'He's not... I don't see...'

'You are marrying him,' Ruby said gently. 'You know you are. And you needn't feel guilty that you're doing so. There's no way Marcus will marry anyone else.'

'But I can't accept his money,' Peta said with distress, and Ruby reached out and gave her hand a squeeze.

'Yes, you can. You'd be doing Marcus a real favour.'

'How am I supposed to accept that?' Peta demanded. 'This is ridiculous. I know nothing about Marcus—and here he is, threatening to take over my life.'

'He's not, you know. He's simply involving himself. For the first time ever.'

'I have no idea what you mean.'

'You know nothing about him?'

'No. Apart from his awful mother. But just because his mother stuffed her life doesn't mean he should stay isolated for ever.'

'You know he fought in the Gulf War,' Ruby told her, and the statement was so far out of left field that Peta blinked. Marcus had disappeared in the car that had brought Ruby here, but his presence still lingered. His coffee mug was still on the table before them and Peta found herself glancing at it as if it held some answers. Which was plainly ridiculous.

'You know Marcus came from a poor background?' Ruby probed.

What did this have to do with her? 'He told me.'

'Did he tell you he invested the first dime he ever made?' Ruby gave a cautious sideways look. 'He's good at making money. Seriously good. And he's smart. One of his stepdads introduced him to computers and the man's never looked back. He had investments in the Internet before most people had ever heard of it. But he couldn't escape his background—or lack of it. He was one seriously deprived kid. His mother disappeared when he was twelve and from then he was truly alone. He fought tooth and nail and he got a bit behind him. When the last of his foster families threw him out, he joined the army. Heaven knows why. I'd imagine… He'd never belonged anywhere. Maybe the army promised a sense of family. Or maybe it was that he wasn't all that interested in living.'

'Ruby, that's awful.'

'So was his stint with the armed forces,' Ruby said bluntly. 'I'm not supposed to know this, you understand, but a sergeant in his regiment came to see him one day when Marcus was out of town. Darrell's had a hard time—he was pretty badly scarred and down on his luck and on impulse I invited him to share lunch. So I did and I got the full story of what Marcus went through. Okay, we were on the winning side, but Darrell... He said they saw so much death. Darrell said at the start of the campaign Marcus was an outgoing guy who could share a joke but the more killing they saw the quieter he grew. And then his battalion was caught in an ambush. Most of them were killed. And for Marcus... It was the end. At least that's the way I see it. He's internalised it; he's never talked about it and he's just shrivelled. He came back and he concentrated on building an empire that's stunned the world. But there's nothing else. And then along comes you.'

Peta stared at her across the table, at this big kindly woman with trouble in her eyes.

'Along came me? What have I got to do with it?'

'He cares,' Ruby told her. 'For the first time. He cares what happens to you. He really cares. He's thinking about your welfare and he's offered to marry you. With pride. Even if the marriage will only last for two weeks, you're the only bride he'll ever have. Think about that, Peta. Do you really want to knock back his offer to make you a bride? You don't think you could possibly bring yourself to play the part?'

'But... How? Why?'

Ruby smiled, reaching across the table and taking Peta's work-worn hands in hers. 'All I know is that he's agreed to stop making money for two weeks. He's agreed to care for you a little. I think... If you were to pay him back by making it fun...'

'Fun?'

'I suspect,' Ruby said slowly, 'that it's a concept both of you have trouble with.' She smiled some more, and there was a tinge of real regret in her eyes. 'You know, it's not illegal. And, as for me... You know, Marcus has just given me a cheque for an obscene amount of money to organise a wedding.' She hesitated. And the look on her face changed. 'You know, I had a daughter once,' she whispered. 'If Amy had lived she'd be just about your age. I could be buying her a wedding dress.'

Peta stared at her. Dumbfounded. There were needs all over the place here. Not just hers. Not just her brothers. There was Marcus. And now there was Ruby. 'So it's not just me and Marcus who need to have fun?' she ventured.

'Is it ever just the two of you?' Ruby's eyes held lingering pain. 'I've learned the hard way to keep to myself and no, it's not much fun. But today... Maybe today and for the next two weeks, we could all let our barriers down.' Her smile returned, and there was a hint of pleading behind the tired eyes. 'If you'd like, if you'd let me, what I'd really like to do is make you the most beautiful bride the world has ever seen. Show the world what a bride should look like—see how much we can achieve in a few short hours. And then...' A hint of mischief appeared behind her smile. 'I'd like to write up the most beautiful gilt invitation and have it hand delivered to Charles Higgins—marked urgent.'

Charles. At least Charles was neutral territory. 'You don't like Charles, either?'

'I can't stand the man.' Ruby rose and stood, smiling down at Peta and her smile was a challenge. 'Well. What do you think? Are you prepared to put aside a few scruples and have fun?'

'You mean, do the full bridal bit?'

'It would be great,' Ruby admitted and there was a real trace of wistfulness in her voice. 'Marcus can afford it. The man's so wealthy this is less than pin money. And a wedding—a real wedding—in four hours. It would be fun. Wouldn't it?'

Peta stared up at her. More and more she didn't understand what was happening—more and more she felt as if she was right out of control. But if she was so far out of control why not go the whole way? Why clutch at traces of dignity that were impossible to maintain?

Why not have...fun?

'A white bride,' she whispered.

'The whole works.' Ruby was beaming. 'I know just the place.'

'It's crazy.'

'But wonderful?'

'Marcus would run a mile.'

'Marcus is committed. He goes through with his promises.' Ruby's smile deepened. 'Let's do the whole thing. I know where his sergeant lives—it's half an hour from here. Can you cope with me as a matron of honour and Darrell as best man? And I'll bet Charles will come. He'll arrive expecting to see a farce and what he'll see is the works.'

'The works?'

'Let's do it.' Ruby held out her hand to pull her to her feet. 'Why not?'

'I can think of a thousand reasons why not.'

'Do any of them matter more than enjoying yourself?' Ruby glanced across the street to the funeral parlour and winced. 'Life's for living. Come on. I dare you.'

CHAPTER FIVE

MARCUS was running late. Once he'd got back to his office there were a thousand things that needed to be sorted. To leave for Australia at this short notice seemed impossible.

But Ruby had been there before him, making the impossible somehow inevitable. Every one of his staff seemed intent on pushing him out of the place!

So somehow he'd done it. He'd pushed himself to the limit, but even Robert's skilled driving hadn't been able to get him across town right on time.

He was ten minutes late...

'I hope your bride hasn't beaten you,' Robert said, and when Marcus glanced at his chauffeur's face in the rear-view mirror he found he was grinning.

'Just how many people know I'm getting married this afternoon?' he demanded, and Robert chuckled.

'I'm thinking just about the whole world. The phone in the outer office has been running hot. I gather you haven't been exactly quiet with your wedding plans.'

No. No, he hadn't.

What would happen if there were photographers there? he thought suddenly. What if the press had heard about it? He hoped to heaven that Ruby had been able to persuade Peta to buy a dress.

Something pretty.

Peta stood in the outer office of the Justice's offices and felt absurd. But strangely...good. Light. Free.

Ruby had been right. It had been the best fun. They'd gone to the biggest bridal emporium in New York and when Ruby had explained that it was a rush job, that the wedding was this afternoon, that Peta was marrying Marcus Benson and that money was no object, they'd fallen over themselves to help.

And Peta, who'd lived in a nightmare for so long, had simply acquiesced. Or more than acquiesced, she admitted. She'd tried on one exquisite creation after another. The dress they chose was, in the end, comparatively simple—deceptively so. Of magnificent ivory silk, it had tiny shoestring shoulder-straps and a scooped sweetheart neckline. It looked as if it had been made for her. It clung like a second skin to her tiny waist and then floated out in diaphanous folds, falling softly to her ankles.

She'd stood before the mirror and Ruby had gazed at her, her eyes had misted and she'd breathed, 'Yes!'

The thing had been decided.

They'd found her strappy white sandals, and an urgently called beautician had threaded white ribbons through her auburn hair and applied make-up. Just a little. 'With that tan and that complexion you need to cover nothing. Oh, my dear, you look so beautiful.'

And she did. The Peta who stared back at herself from the long mirror in the bridal parlour seemed unrecognisable.

Then, at Peta's insistence, the bridal team had turned their attention to Ruby because, 'If I'm doing this, then so are you!' Protesting but laughing, Ruby had allowed herself to be talked into a pale blue suit of the finest shantung. The sales-girls had found the dearest little hat and matching shoes; the beautician had decided there was time to give Ruby's curls the most modish of cuts, and Ruby had ended up almost as dazed as Peta.

The team in the bridal parlour had arranged a car to bring them here—a white limousine!—they'd organised white orchids, and at the last minute they'd thrust champagne glasses into their hands and they'd poured champagne for themselves as the limousine departed towards their date with Marcus.

'And I bet they put that on Marcus's bill,' Ruby whispered.

They sipped their champagne; they looked at themselves in stunned awe—and then they did what any sane, mature women would have done in the same position.

They giggled.

On arrival, they'd learned that Marcus wasn't there yet but Darrell was—Marcus's sergeant. He'd done them proud as well, dressed in full military regalia, looking so gorgeous that Peta hardly noticed the scars on his burned face.

'I'm real happy for you,' Darrell told her. 'Marcus deserves someone to make him happy. He was so damned good to me...'

He broke off, choked, and Peta knew how he felt.

She was pretty choked herself.

'You're sure he'll come?' she whispered to Ruby and Ruby gave a smile that said she was as nervous as Peta. The giggles had disappeared.

'I surely hope so. Or you're just going to have to marry Darrell.'

Great. Peta glanced nervously out the window at the street. There were a cluster of photographers in the doorway—obviously waiting for someone important. They'd been here when she arrived. They'd ignored Peta—there'd been three brides arrive since Peta had—but they were obviously intent on someone else.

'This is crazy,' Peta whispered. She looked down at her beautiful bouquet of white orchids and she couldn't believe what she was seeing. 'The whole thing... It's a crazy dream. I can't...'

But then she paused. A car she recognised pulled up out the front. Robert emerged, and then Marcus.

Marcus, looking impossibly handsome. Marcus in a dark suit with, for heaven's sake, a tiny white orchid twisted in his lapel.

Her...husband?

It was all she could do not to turn and run. Run for her life. But Ruby was taking her arm and beaming as if she'd won the lottery, and Darrell was between Peta and the door and there was nothing to do but wait. Wait until he'd run the gamut of photographers.

Wait until he reached his bride.

The door opened and he saw her.

For a moment he thought he must be in the wrong place. He'd been expecting a bureaucrat's office. An official behind the desk. Peta in some sort of more respectable outfit that Ruby had persuaded her to buy.

Instead...

Instead he had a bride.

He froze. For one awful moment he was transported back to the nightmare of his childhood. To the glitz and glitter of his mother's dreadful weddings.

But the momentary impression was just that. Momentary. This was no nightmare. This was Peta. She'd been speaking to Ruby but she turned as he entered and she looked up at him.

She smiled.

Until this minute he'd thought that all white weddings were a nightmare. All his life he'd remembered the gaudy, tinselly creations his mother had worn and he'd felt ill.

But this was different. It had to be. Peta's dress was simple but breathtakingly beautiful.

Peta was beautiful. Her smile widened. Her eyes locked with his.

And in that instant something inside Marcus that he'd hardly known existed shattered and evaporated as if it had never been. The thought that nothing or no one could ever move him.

He'd never thought any woman could be so lovely.

Maybe she wasn't lovely in the way that the tabloids described loveliness, he thought, dazed. Her hair was still a mop of tousled curls—no amount of brushing could hide that. Her nose was snub and she had freckles from a lifetime in the sun. But her dress... Her dress clung to her perfect figure in a soft cloud of white silk. The white ribbons through her beautiful hair were more beautiful than any veil.

No. It wasn't her dress. It wasn't the bride thing. It was her eyes...her smile...the way she looked at him, half apologetic, half daring, wanting him to share this moment, wanting him to laugh, to smile, to simply share her pleasure.

She was smiling and smiling, and it was enough to make his heart lurch. Marcus Benson's heart. Immutable. Untouchable.

She'd ditched her crutches and she looked...perfect.

No. How could she be perfect? Perfection was an illusion. It was crazy. Concentrate on something other than that smile.

Peta's wasn't the only smile. Ruby was there as well—a Ruby he hardly recognised, in a soft blue suit that made her look...well, softer somehow. As if that awful shell she'd built around her had somehow cracked.

Ruby had spoken of a man and a child in her past, but Ruby had worked for him for years and had said nothing before about her private life. How on earth had the advent of Peta into their lives allowed her to lift herself out of her past?

Because that was what had happened. Ruby was smiling from Marcus and back to Peta and the look she directed at Peta was one of pure pride.

And then there was Darrell. How had Darrell got to know about this? Darrell was normally a dour, middle-aged man to whom life had not been kind. His wife had left him during the agonies of skin grafts; he was still deeply traumatised by the events in the Gulf and the ex-serviceman had little to smile about. But now... Now Darrell was dressed in full military regalia and he, too, was smiling, as if this was a true wedding—a true happy ever after.

Which it wasn't. The idea was ridiculous.

Totally ridiculous.

But Peta was still smiling at him and, as he walked towards

her, she slipped her hand in his arm and held it as if he was already hers. It was a purely proprietorial gesture.

It should have made him run a mile.

But there were three people smiling at him—four, if you counted the man behind the desk. And outside was the press. The world was waiting to see if he could make this commitment.

It wasn't a commitment, he told himself, and there was more than a trace of desperation in his inner monologue. It was a piece of paper. Nothing more.

He should hold himself stiffly. He shouldn't smile. He should get this over with fast and move on.

But not to smile would be stupid. Maybe it'd even be cruel when everyone else was waiting.

He stared at Peta once more and it was too much. The corners of his mouth curved. His eyes lit. He smiled…

He smiled just for her.

He took her hand in his—firmly, with no hesitation in the world. And they turned to the man who was waiting to marry them. They made their vows.

Man and wife.

'I now pronounce you man and wife…'

For two weeks?

They'd forgotten Charles.

Ruby had organised his invitation but no one had thought of him again. But as the official words faded and Marcus stared down at his bride, stunned by the enormity of what had just happened, the door burst open and in walked Peta's cousin.

To say he was angry would be an understatement. The man was nearly apoplectic. Charles stood in the doorway, his eyes almost starting from their sockets. His expensive three-piece suit denoted him as an executive, but the uncontrolled fury on his face was more that of a petty criminal. A thug. When Peta turned to see who it was, he lunged straight at her.

He would have hit her. He'd hit her before. Marcus saw that at a glance. He saw Peta flinch and he saw her body brace.

This man had lived with Peta, he thought grimly. There'd been enough violence in Marcus's past for him to recognise the pattern.

There'd also been enough violence in Marcus's past for him to react, and to react fast. In one swift movement, Peta was thrust behind him, and his body was protecting her from her cousin's angry rush.

'You little...' Charles moved sideways as if to grab her but Marcus was faster. He had him by the shoulders, holding him in a grip of steel.

'What the hell do you think you're doing?'

'That...slut!' Charles was beyond logic. He'd come here at a run; he was out of breath and he was out of control. He shoved against Marcus's hold but he was going nowhere.

Foiled, he was forced to explain. To try to voice his fury.

'I got to the office after lunch to receive this.' He hauled back from Marcus's grasp and pulled the invitation from his top pocket. 'This! I don't know how she conned you—'

'No one conned me.' Marcus's voice was flint-hard, cold as ice.

'She must have. That slut, that—'

'Stop. Right now. You're talking about my wife!'

Wife.

The word acted like a wall of ice water. Charles flinched. And stared.

'It's not possible. Peta... Your wife? Why would you want to marry *her*?'

Somehow Marcus managed to hold himself in check. Just. 'You're being offensive.'

'It's she who's being offensive,' Charles spat. 'She's just doing this to rob me of what rightfully belongs to me. The farm's mine. I went to all the trouble to drag the old lady back here—'

Enough.

'Get out.' Marcus turned to the official who was standing, mouth agape, staring in stunned amazement. 'Do you have security guards in the building?'

'I was invited,' Charles hissed.

'The invitation is rescinded.'

'So's your marriage. Marriage? This marriage is a mockery. It's illegal. You can't just marry her and walk away with my property. I'll have it annulled.'

'I have no intention of marrying Peta and walking away,' Marcus said, deliberately misunderstanding him. 'I'm taking Peta back to Australia.' Then, as Peta pushed her way out from behind him, Marcus put his arm around her and pulled her in to him. They stood arm in arm. Man and wife.

'I'm taking Peta home,' he said gently, his eyes on Charles's face. 'In all honour.'

'You've never... You'll never...'

'I am. Get used to it.' He looked across at Darrell. 'Darrell, if there aren't security guards to deal with *this*...'—he said the word *this* as if it referred to some lower form of pond scum—'then could you help me evict him?'

'With pleasure,' Darrell told him.

'I'll help,' Ruby added.

'Hey, me, too,' Peta put in. 'He's my cousin. I should get to slug him.'

'Brides don't slug,' Marcus told her and she managed a smile. Albeit a shaky one.

'Not?'

'Definitely not.'

'Rats.'

'You have something else to do,' Ruby reminded her. 'Something important.' Marcus's assistant glanced at Charles as if he was of no significance at all. 'If you've quite finished?'

'I haven't.' Charles backed to the door as Darrell took a measured step towards him. 'You'll hear from my lawyers.'

'I hope they have better party manners than you do,' Marcus told him. Then he deliberately turned away from the man and faced Ruby. 'What has my bride forgotten to do?'

My bride... It sounded strange. It was a declaration of intention—a declaration that, come what may, Charles's lawyers couldn't hurt her.

It was a gesture of pure protection and, as he made it, Marcus thought, whoa, where am I going? But he couldn't unsay it. He couldn't unfeel it.

He looked down into her face and, as Darrell slammed the door behind her obnoxious cousin, he could see that she was as confused as he was. He was offering protection, but to Peta protection seemed an unknown sensation. She'd fought her own battles, he thought, and somehow, he knew her battles had been just as hard as his own.

The knowledge intensified the sensation. It made him feel even more at sea. More...helpless?

This was an illusion, he told himself. The way he felt about her. The way he held her, pulling her in to his body. It was a façade put on to convince Charles that here was a real marriage.

But Charles had gone now. There was no one here they had to fool, yet Marcus was still holding her and there was no way he was releasing her. No way!

'What's she forgotten to do?' Marcus asked again, and it was Ruby who pulled them all together, Ruby who collected herself. She looked to the official who was still standing in astonishment that the wedding could be so rudely interrupted. But this was a senior official who'd obviously overseen some very strange marriages in his time. He rose to the occasion as a good official should.

'Can we continue?' Ruby prodded, and the man stopped staring at the closed door and managed a smile.

'Right. Where was I? Goodness me. I know. I now pronounce you man and wife.' He took a deep breath and beamed at the pair of them, from Marcus to Peta and back again. The interruption might have been strange and unsettling, but standing before him were a couple whose body language said they belonged. Someone else may have tried to ruin this occasion but Henry Richard Waterhouse, officiating for the City of New York, was here to marry these people and marry them he would.

'That's it, folks,' he said. He closed his book. 'Except for the last bit. The best bit. My favourite part of the day. And here it comes.' His beam widened. 'You may now kiss the bride.'

No.

The word rose unbidden. No. But he didn't say it. Somehow he managed to cut it off. Somehow...

Marcus stared down at Peta and, for heaven's sake, he saw panic there. It was the same panic he felt himself.

They were staring at each other, stunned, as if neither could believe it had come to this. That this wild planning had suddenly landed them in this place, where there was nothing to do but for Marcus to lift his hand, to tilt her chin, for his eyes to lock with hers.

And for his mouth to lower on to hers.

He didn't want to do it. He didn't...

He lied. He wanted to do it more than anything in the world.

And it was only a kiss, he told himself fiercely. It meant no more than their signatures on a piece of paper.

It was only a kiss.

But then his lips touched hers and it was much, much more.

His world changed, right there.

It was as if some sort of short circuit had shut down his brain. Cool, calm Marcus Benson who did nothing without thinking it out, whose world was a series of well planned, carefully orchestrated moves, who never let himself be shifted outside his zone of complete control...

Suddenly he was no longer in control. No. He hadn't been in control since he'd met her, he thought desperately, but he was much more out of control now. His lips met his bride's, and the electricity surging between them felt as if it could slam him into the far wall.

But only if she came, too, he thought, stunned, because there was no way he was letting her go.

He'd put his hands on her waist to draw her close to him—just a little—not to pull him hard in against her. But the warmth of her body was suddenly a fierce, molten link. The fire that surged in that link between them was unbelievable. His hands felt as though they belonged exactly where they were. They were forged into position. As if they'd found their home.

And her mouth… His mouth…

She tasted…

She tasted of Peta, he thought, with the tiny part of his brain that was left available to do any analysis at all. She tasted of nothing he had ever experienced before. She was so soft and yielding, and yet there was such strength.

He could taste the woman of her. He could feel the part of her that yielded to him and yet did not. That found her home in him and yet… And yet… And yet stayed her own sweet self.

She was curving in to him and he knew she was as bewildered as he was at this feeling. This feeling he could hardly begin to analyse. He had nothing to compare it to.

Peta…

It was too much. He was past thinking. He was oblivious to the small group of onlookers—to Ruby and Darrell and the city official, all looking on with bemusement. All he knew was how her lips tasted. How his heart lurched.

How the barren wasteland of his heart suddenly seemed a far-off memory.

Peta…

'I'm sure you'll be very, very happy.'

The official's words broke in to the moment. Somehow. The man was beaming and waiting to grip Marcus's hand, to claim the privilege of kissing the bride, of moving on to the next ceremony…

He didn't hurry them. But this kiss had lasted a long time.

Marcus moved back. A little. Not much. His hands remained on Peta's waist. He stared at her, dazed. She gazed back and his confusion was mirrored in her eyes.

'I didn't…'

'I'm sorry…' They spoke over each other and the moment somehow broke.

'There's no need to apologise to each other.' The official was still beaming, his hand out to take Marcus's and there was nothing for it but to release Peta. To let the moment go. 'A man need never apologise for kissing his wife, and vice versa, and you have a lifetime ahead to do just that.' He gripped Marcus's hand and shook while Marcus fought desperately for normality. For sanity. Then the official turned and kissed Peta, breaking the contact even more. Giving Marcus room.

Letting reality in.

Then, the formalities over, the official stepped back and smiled some more. 'There. All done. I'm sorry for the interruption to the ceremony but it doesn't seem to have spoiled the moment. Congratulations.' He glanced at his watch—surreptitiously, but it was a message for all that. 'There's some papers for you both to sign in the outer office, but that's it. Congratulations, Mr and Mrs Benson. Welcome to your new life.'

The world took over. Of course it did.

Over the next hour Marcus moved on automatic pilot. He signed the register. He accepted congratulations. He faced the press. He shielded his bride as best he could and he smiled. He ate a meal—heaven knew what it was—in the restaurant

Ruby had booked to celebrate the occasion. He listened to Darrell's shy speech and he smiled.

He smiled.

By his side, Peta smiled as well, and her smile seemed just as forced as his.

Finally the formalities were over. 'Darrell and I will take a cab home,' Ruby told her boss. She reached into her handbag and hauled out a pouch. 'These are your air tickets, your passport and all the documentation you'll need for the next few weeks. Your plane leaves tomorrow morning at nine a.m.'

'Mine goes tomorrow night.' Peta had chatted during the meal but she'd sounded strained and the strain was still evident in her voice.

'We took the liberty of changing your flights,' Ruby told her. 'You had a small taste of publicity today. With the short notice, the press contingent was limited. But Marcus's wedding is going to hit the headlines tomorrow morning, and you'll hardly want to be around for the fuss. The society tabloids have been trying to matchmake for Marcus since he made his first million.'

'And now he's hooked.' Darrell's smile matched Ruby's. 'That's great.'

But it wasn't great. 'I didn't hook anyone.' Peta glowered. 'He climbed on the line all by himself.'

'And he can climb off again in two weeks,' Ruby told her. She gathered her handbag and looked to Darrell. 'Shall we leave these two—fishermen?—together?'

'Sounds good to me.' Darrell grinned. He took Marcus's hand and shook—hard—and then he grasped Peta's hands and pulled her in for a kiss to both cheeks.

'You keep wiggling that hook,' he said gently. 'Marcus is the best mate in the world and he needs you more than he knows. So wiggle until he's firmly caught. All the love in the world to you both.'

* * *

Then they were alone. The restaurant had alcoves that were separate rooms, giving absolute privacy. Ruby and Darrell had disappeared and Marcus was left with his bride.

The sensation was...unbelievable.

If only she wasn't so lovely, he thought, a little bit desperately. Or a lot desperately. If only she wasn't so vulnerable. So helpless. So—

'I need to get this gear off. I feel like something that's climbed off the top of a cake.'

Maybe vulnerable wasn't the right word. Maybe vulnerable was a façade that went with the dress.

And she was right. This was silly. They needed to get back to normal. Remove the traces of bridal. But Marcus was aware of a faint tinge of regret in her voice—maybe because it struck an exact chord with what he was feeling. They were moving back into the real world and it hurt.

Maybe he could delay things.

'Even Cinderella had until midnight,' he told her. 'Would you like to extend the fairytale?'

She stilled. 'To do what?'

'You're leaving New York tomorrow,' he told her. 'You haven't ridden around Central Park. Would you like to?'

She stared at him as if he'd lost his mind. Then she grinned and gestured to her dress. 'In this?'

'The best fairytales end in full glamour,' he said cautiously, still unsure of what he was doing. 'Do you trust me?'

'I don't trust anyone offering fairytales,' she told him but the smile that went with her words was suddenly almost cheeky. 'Prince Charming always seemed a bit of a pansy to me.'

And suddenly he found he could smile, too. Properly. He could drop the mask of indifference. She was asking nothing of him in the long term. She wouldn't cling. He could stay with her and then walk away, his good deed done for life.

'If I promise not to be a pansy...'

'I doubt if you could be a pansy if you tried.'

'Gee, thanks.'

'Don't mention it.'

'So what about it? Do you want to have fun?'

Fun. The word hung between them. He stared down at her and he knew instinctively that the word was as foreign to Peta as it was to him.

Fun. Ha! But she was looking up at him and her head was cocked as if listening to an echo that was so far away she could hardly hear.

'You want us to have fun?'

Did he? What was he getting himself into? he wondered wildly. If only she wasn't wearing that dress.

But she was and there was no choice.

'Yes,' he told her. 'Yes, I do. I want us to forget all about the Benson financial empire and the O'Shannassy farm and the likes of cousin Charles. For this afternoon you're wearing a fairytale dress and I've never been married in my life. Can we wave our wand and make it last a bit longer?'

And then a decision—and that smile that could heat places in a man's heart that he hadn't known existed.

'Okay.' His beautiful bride tucked her hand confidingly in his arm and held. Claiming the proprietorship that he'd claimed when he'd given her his name.

'Okay, Mr Benson,' she told him. 'For this afternoon I'll stick with the fairytale. Me and my non-pansy Prince Charming. You and your lopsided Cinderella with the fat foot. Imperfect but game. Let's take ourselves out into New York and have fun.'

CHAPTER SIX

HE TOOK her to Central Park.

Robert dropped them at the Grand Army Plaza as a carriage drew up, a magnificent horse-drawn coach with wonderful greys snorting in their traces. The driver raised his hand in salute to the bridal couple and Marcus beckoned the man closer.

'You looking for a fare?'

The man beamed. 'Do you and your lady want a ride?'

'We surely do.'

'How far?'

'We'd like to see the whole of Central Park—as long as it takes.'

'Well now.' The driver grinned some more and scratched his head. A crowd was gathering, taking in the sight of this lovely bridal couple.

'Well now,' the driver said again. 'Step aboard.' He turned to his horses. 'Come on, boys. Let's give these folks an afternoon to remember. And, seeing as they're just married, we might even give them a rate!'

For Peta the next few hours passed in a whirl. She'd been transported into a make-believe world where anything was possible. Where she was beautiful, desirable, loved. Where the sheer slog of daily grind was replaced by magical clothes, a matched pair of greys, the sights of Central Park, people waving at the bridal pair. The sights...

They climbed down occasionally so Marcus could show her things he enjoyed. When her ankle held her back he simply lifted and carried her, to the delight of the bystanders and ignoring her indignant squeaks. She stood on the mosaic that said *Imagine* while a hundred tourists took photographs. She checked the animals in the children's zoo and more cameras clicked. She stood on the little bridges and the rocks in the Rambles and Marcus laughed and said why didn't he have shares in digital cameras?

And then he grinned and remembered that he did.

Through all, their patient coachman waited, smiling benignly. They'd told Robert to leave them for two hours but it was almost three before Marcus was sure his bride had had her fill. Marcus phoned Robert and told him not to wait. At the end he had their coachman drop them off near a little place he knew...

The little place was a restaurant with food to die for. Still in their wedding regalia, they were ushered to the best table in the house. Peta drank wine and ate food that she'd never imagined existed.

She was tired, but wonderfully so. She hardly spoke. All afternoon she'd hardly spoken. She simply soaked it in, as if this was happening to someone else. Not to her.

This couldn't possibly be happening to her.

But it was. She ate her food, dazed, while Marcus watched her with a tiny smile playing at the corners of his mouth. He was playing fantasy, too, she decided and she could hardly object.

She didn't want to object.

And then, as the waiter poured coffee and she thought this surely must end, a four-piece band started up. Soft music. Simple. Lovely. And Marcus was rising, still with that queer half smile, quizzing her with his eyes. He knew her secret. He was sharing this make-believe.

'Would you like to dance?'

Would she like to dance? The prospect was almost overwhelming. Would she?

'I don't... I can't... My ankle.'

'Trust me,' he said. 'You can. I'll take your weight. Lean on me. Tonight we can do anything.'

She rose. There was nothing else for it. Her lovely skirts

swished against the floor, swirling around her. Marcus pulled her into his arms, lifting the weight from her ankle so she could hardly feel it. The band took one look at this lone couple on the dance floor and struck up the bridal waltz.

It needed only that. Peta choked on laughter and buried her face in Marcus's shoulder.

'Laughter?' He swung her expertly around the dance floor and somehow her feet followed. As if they knew the way all by themselves. Peta, who'd never had the time or the opportunity to be on a dance floor before this night, seemed to know how without any teaching.

Of course she did. On this night anything was possible.

'We're such frauds,' she whispered into his shoulder and she felt him stiffen. Just a little. And then she felt him chuckle in return, a low, lovely rumble.

'As long as we both know it.'

'What time does Robert turn into a mouse?'

He looked startled at that—but he caught the analogy and grinned.

'He's fine until at least midnight. But can I just ask if you'll leave a forwarding address if you do any casting of slippers.'

'My address is Rosella Farm, Yooralaa, Australia.' She smiled. 'Just so you don't have to do any unnecessary fitting. There's a lot of women between Yooralaa and New York to be trying on glass slippers on all of them.'

'And maybe the fairytale wouldn't hold. Maybe someone would have a smaller foot.'

She stilled and looked down to where her right foot peeked out from under her dress. Her ankle was bandaged. The bridal salon had solved her problem by giving her a right sandal three sizes larger than the left.

'I must remember to drop the left one,' she murmured. 'Otherwise I'm doomed. Or you're doomed. You might end up with a bride who's two hundred pounds.'

He grinned. 'But maybe we need to rewrite the fairytale,' he suggested. 'In fact, I'm sure we do. We need to rein up a few more mice and order a bigger pumpkin. Because, instead of fleeing alone, you get to take your Prince Charming along. I'm coming home with you.'

For heaven's sake. As he swung her once more around the dance floor she thought she detected the faintest trace of satisfaction in his voice. What had she got herself into?

'Hey!' She pulled back. 'Let's not get carried away here.' She focused then. Really focused, hauling the fairydust out of her head. 'This isn't real. I mean, even after midnight, after the two weeks. None of this is real.'

'No.' But he didn't stop dancing. Another turn. He was holding her tight to take her weight, half dancing, half carrying. His head was resting on her curls. Which was sensible. Wasn't it? He had to hold her to take the weight of her injured ankle. There was no other reason for it, though, she thought wildly. No other reason she was curved into him, her body moving as one with him.

'Maybe we should go home,' she whispered.

'Home?'

'I mean, to your apartment. I mean... You to your club.' That was the sensible thing to do. Wasn't it?

'I don't think we can do it tonight,' he told her. 'We're married.'

'So?'

'So we have the society pages watching. Do we want them to know we slept apart on the night of our wedding?'

'Yes!'

'I'm sure you don't mean that.'

She thought about it for a bit. Which was really hard. The way her body was feeling... All she was doing was feeling. She had no room for anything else.

'You mean...because of Charles?'

'What else could I mean?'

Of course. What else could he mean? Silly girl.

If only she could think straight. If only he wasn't so near.

'So...' She caught herself. 'You're saying we need to...to stay in the same place?'

'We need to stay in the same place.'

'But...'

'I have a settee in the sitting room that turns into a bed. You needn't worry.'

'I'm not worried.' It was true. It was impossible to be worried when she was feeling as she was feeling. As if she was floating.

'So...you think we should go home?'

'One more turn around the dance floor,' she whispered and he held her closer and she felt him smile.

'How about six?'

The fairytale ended at the front door.

Robert brought them home. Marcus helped his bride alight from the car; she stumbled on her bad ankle and he refused to listen to her protests. He swept her into his arms and carried her into his apartment and the door slammed behind them.

They were left alone. The lights were dim. He was standing in the hallway holding a girl in his arms—his bride—and she was gazing up at him with eyes that were luminescent, trembling, sweetly innocent.

She was so desirable. And she was his wife! He could kiss her right now...

'Cut it out,' she told him, jerking her face back from his and jiggling in his arms. 'Marcus Benson, put me down. Right now.'

'I thought—'

'I know what you thought. I can read it in your eyes.'

'Peta...'

'I knew you'd want something.' She bounced and wriggled some more and he was forced to set her down.

'I don't want anything.'

She fixed him with an old-fashioned look. 'You're saying you don't want to take me to bed?'

There was nothing he'd like better. She read his expression and he couldn't get his face under control fast enough. 'Ha!'

'I didn't marry you,' he said softly, 'to get you into my bed.'

'No. You married me as a favour. But now we're married...'

'It'd be a bonus,' he admitted, and smiled. 'You're saying you don't think so?'

'I don't want to go to bed with you.'

'No?'

'No!'

'There's a definite physical attraction...'

'Between man and woman,' she snapped. 'And tom cats and lady cats. And ducks and drakes and pigs and sows. You dress up in that gorgeous suit and you treat me like you have today and of course there'd be an attraction. But there's no way in the wide world I'm going to bed with you.'

'Why not?'

It was a reasonable question, he thought, but Peta had other ideas on what was reasonable.

'If I fall in love with you I'm stuffed.'

'Why?'

'Work it out, smart boy,' she said and kicked off her bridal sandals. 'Cinderella had no life at all. I'm going to bed. Do I sleep on the settee or do you?'

'You can take the bed.'

'Right, then,' she told him and walked into the bedroom with scarcely a limp. And closed the door behind her. Leaving him...flabbergasted.

What followed was a night of no sleep.

How could she sleep? Peta lay in Marcus's too-big bed and watched the moonlight play over her bridal gown, which was draped carefully over the bedside chair. The dress seemed to shimmer in the moonlight, as if it had a life of its own.

A bridal gown. She'd had a wedding.

There'd be photographs, she thought. There'd been so many cameras pointed at her this day. Maybe one day years from now she'd leaf through an ancient magazine and see this picture.

The picture of a fairytale. With Marcus. Her Prince Charming.

Did Prince Charming milk cows?

Maybe not. In fact, he'd made that a condition of marriage. The thought made her chuckle. She should sleep, she thought. Tomorrow was another huge day.

But Marcus was just through the wall. And he'd wanted to take her to his bed. It had been so hard to bounce herself out of the fantasy, she thought, and wondered how she'd ever done it.

He married me, she told herself. I'm his wife.

What, so you'd go to bed with him to repay the debt?

No, but...

You'd go to bed with him because he makes your toes curl. She winced and wriggled her toes, making them uncurl in the dark.

It'd be a disaster, she told the other part of her brain—the part that was screaming at her to swallow her principles, forget her sensible self and...and do what good girls didn't do. We're worlds apart. You owe him a lot but you don't owe him your heart.

I have his bed, she told the dark. His bed and his name, without the man. Best of both worlds.

Maybe having a man in her bed would be no bad thing. Maybe having Marcus...

Go home, Peta, she told herself. Get yourself back to your dogs if you want company. Settle for reality.

Reality was good, she told herself. Reality was her future.

But for now... She lay in the moonlight and looked at her wedding dress. And thought about Marcus.

Reality seemed a long way away.

He wanted the fantasy.

Marcus lay in the dark and stared up at the ceiling. It was flat. Uninteresting. Boring.

He was flat, uninteresting, boring.

Today had been so different. Today he'd felt transformed. As if life somehow could be something of worth.

Stupid thought.

He lay back on his pillows and made himself remember all those weddings he'd been to as a child. His mother, starry-eyed in white, promising him the world.

'This time he's going to take us away from all this. We're starting on a new life, Marcus,' she'd said, over and over again.

Yeah, right. Pure fantasy. Each time, the new life had begun before the wedding cake was finished and it had been invariably bleak and dreadful.

So here he was, caught up in the same fantasy his mother had used to make life bearable. White weddings. The fairytale.

It was just as well Peta had sense for the both of them, he told himself. Otherwise he'd have her in his arms right now!

Which was a truly crazy thought. To marry her was fine. But to make love to her as his wife... No!

How on earth had he ever become caught up in this? A wife? Australia? The immediate future seemed ridiculous. He'd been caught by a pair of twinkling green eyes, hauled in as surely as his mother had, sucked in by promises.

But it had been Marcus who'd made the promises.

'And I'm surely not dreaming of any happy ever after,' he told the ceiling. 'My life's here.'

Alone with a ceiling?

Whatever.

He'd upgraded her ticket.

Peta wriggled down into the cocoon of her first-class seat-cum-bed and tried really hard to think indignant thoughts. How had he found out her flight was economy? How had he managed to change it, and what right did he have to do so?

But her knees weren't under her chin. She was nestled into a full-length bed. There were fluffy blankets tucking her in soft pillows under her head, soft music playing on her personal entertainment system.

She was on her way back to reality. Back to cows and hard grind. Maybe she could indulge in a little fantasy for now, she thought. And that was exactly what she was doing. Especially as her husband—her husband!—was lying right beside her. If she just reached out...

She didn't want to reach out. Of course she didn't. Peta O'Shannassy had a very tight grip on reality.

Sort of.

He could have used his own jet. But: 'You know how she reacted with the clothes,' Ruby had told him. 'She'll react exactly the same to a private jet.'

'She agreed to your plans for a wedding dress.'

'That was fantasy. A private jet, in Peta's eyes, would be ridiculous.'

'But hell—sitting round airports...'

'Join the human race.'

'I've been part of the human race,' Marcus had said grimly. 'I've moved on.'

'Well, pretend for two weeks,' Ruby had said bluntly, so here he was, on a commercial flight with the prospect of a five-hour stopover in Tokyo.

It was comfortable enough.

Who was he kidding? He was really comfortable. And Peta's round-eyed astonishment had been a delight, even if he did have the feeling she was controlling indignation at his perceived waste of money.

Peta. His bride.

Fantasy... Reality.

The lines were becoming more blurred by the minute.

CHAPTER SEVEN

THE moment she landed she transformed.

For the last few hours of the flight Peta had withdrawn into herself. Finally, at the announcement to fasten seatbelts for landing, she turned to Marcus, her face resolute.

'Thank you very much,' she told him. 'You can stop pretending now.'

'Stop pretending?'

'I mean…' She flushed a little but her face became more resolute. 'The whole wedding thing. Letting me travel with you first class. Buying me clothes. Treating me as your wife. It's been great but you don't need to do it any more. No one here cares.'

'I beg your pardon?'

She smiled at that but it was an uncomfortable little smile.

'I'm sorry. Maybe I put that really badly. It's just… Well, hardly anyone here will have heard of you, and they surely won't be fussed whether we're married or not.'

'You mean… Are you telling me to go away?'

'You really think that Charles will check that we're together?'

'Charles will check.'

'How can he?'

'Private investigators are relatively cheap when there's a lot of money at stake.'

'He wouldn't.'

'He would.'

She thought about it and then nodded, her face decisive. 'Okay. Maybe you're right. But no one can come further than our farm gate without the dogs barking their heads off. You can have Hattie's house. My aunt lived separately from us but her house is on the farm, too.'

He thought about it. 'You don't want me to stay with you?'

'I don't have a guest bedroom.'

'You have four brothers.'

'So?'

'So, if three of them aren't living at home, why isn't there a spare bedroom?'

She paused. She opened her mouth to speak but then appeared to think better of it. And then she smiled.

'You can have Hattie's house,' she told him again. 'Let's leave everything else for now. I wonder who's going to meet us?'

Everybody met them. The plane touched down in Melbourne; they walked through the doors from Customs and Peta disappeared in the midst of a mêlée of large, male redheads. Marcus saw Peta's brothers as a group, their family likeness unmistakeable as they leaned forward over the barrier in their eagerness to see their sister, and then Peta was through and they merged. Peta was enfolded into a group hug, and the hug went on for so long he thought he'd lost her.

But finally she was released. Tousled and laughing, she gazed at them all with affection. Four boys, three of whom were well over six feet, and the fourth a smaller, freckled one with the promise of at least a foot of growth to come.

'I've missed you all so much,' she told them. 'Come and meet Marcus.'

The oldest broke away from the group at that. Lean and gangly, just out of adolescence, the boy's smile died and his face grew serious. Red-headed, freckled like his brothers and all of about twenty, the kid had the same look on his face as the one Peta had worn when Marcus first met her. Defiance, and a vulnerability he was trying to hide. He stepped forward and took Marcus's hand in a grip that was surprisingly strong for one so young.

'I'm Daniel,' he said simply. 'Peta rang. She told us what you'd done for us. We're all so grateful.'

And Marcus, man of the world, world-weary and sophisticated, found himself almost blushing. For heaven's sake. The gratitude of a stripling...

The gratitude of them all. They were all looking at him as if he was their very own personal genie. Peta was smiling, and...

And heck. Enough was enough.

'I only married your sister,' he growled. 'That's hardly a huge sacrifice on my part.'

Daniel managed a shy grin. 'I don't know about that, sir. She's very bossy.'

'Hey!' Peta said.

'She's messy, too,' the littlest one volunteered. 'And she can't cook for nuts.'

'She's pretty good at animal obstetrics, though,' the second one—Christopher?—volunteered. 'Daniel's doing vet science but he still reckons there's no one he'd rather have around during a messy birth than Peta.'

'Meet my brothers,' Peta said faintly. 'Daniel, Christopher, William and Harry. It's just as well you didn't meet them before taking the matrimonial plunge, hey? A list of all my faults and virtues—including delivering cows. Good grief!' She reached out and grabbed the littlest again, hugging him close. 'Did you miss me?'

'Yeah.' Harry sounded embarrassed but he let himself be hugged and even managed a swift hug back before masculine pride tugged him backward. 'Can we go home now?'

'Hey, how grateful is that?' Daniel demanded. 'Harry's been really well looked after in university college.'

'You weren't found out?'

'Everyone knew he was there,' Daniel told her. 'Even the masters. But they didn't say a word.'

'I was really good,' Harry said with virtue. 'I was so good I'm good up to my neck. Peta, I'm really glad you're home.

'So you can be bad again?'

'Yep,' he said and everyone laughed.

But the laughter was a little strained. Marcus was aware that he was being carefully appraised and the sensation was definitely unnerving.

'I don't suppose you guys have any free time to come back to the farm?' Peta asked, and had three head shakes.

'It's end of term,' Daniel told her. 'Exams. In three weeks we'll all be home to do the hay. Unless you need us.' He cast a sideways glance at Marcus and his message was unmistakeable. Unless you need help with this strange guy you've brought home. Unless he's not really the benefactor he's supposed to be. 'But meanwhile...' He glanced at his watch. 'I've got lectures this afternoon and so have the others. Can we leave the brat with you?'

The brat. Peta had her arm around Harry's shoulders and the three older boys were looking at him with expressions that said not one of them thought he was a brat. This family exuded affection, Marcus thought, and the sensation was so...well, warm that it made his gut twist in a sudden surge of longing. But that wasn't what he was here for. He was involved enough with Peta. He had no intention of becoming more involved with her family.

'I brought your truck into the car park,' Daniel was telling his sister. 'But you can't all drive home in it. You won't fit.'

'I assume Marcus will hire a car. I doubt he'll want to be stuck on the farm at my beck and call.'

'Isn't that what marriage is all about?' William asked.

'William...' Peta's tone was warning but the kid was grinning.

'Hey, what would we know?' he asked, spreading his hands. 'But you guys have been married—what—two days? You must be old hands by now. Becking and calling all over the place.'

There was general laughter. It was still strained—this was

a situation that must surely lend itself to awkwardness—but they were nice kids, Marcus thought.

They were a nice family. Of course. How could they not be when Peta was...

No. He needed to stick with practicalities here. A car. He glanced down at his travel documents and, sure enough, there was a docket for car hire. But...

'Maybe this isn't big enough for all of us, either,' he told them. 'It's a sports car from a specialist firm. Ruby knows what I like.'

'What sort of sports car?' Harry demanded, releasing his sister's hand in an instant.

'A Morgan 4/4.'

'A Morgan?' Harry's eyes practically popped out on stalks. 'You've hired a Morgan 4/4? Peta, you've married a guy who hires *Morgans*?'

'Pretty cool, hey?' Peta's eyes twinkled at the bemused Marcus, and the strain eased. 'I guess that settles that. Can we have a quick meal with you guys here to catch up with news? Then we'll go. I'll drive the truck and Marcus and Harry can follow behind in the...what did you say? The Morgan. Right. Let's move.'

Which was why an hour later Marcus found himself travelling south along the New South Wales coast road, not with his fantasy bride—his Cinderella—but with a scrubby schoolboy who asked questions at a mile a minute and who was clearly entranced by this new personage his sister had brought home specifically for his enjoyment.

The farther south he and Harry drove, the more disconcerted he grew. Harry appeared to have accepted Peta's explanation of this marriage as a great piece of good fortune—that good fortune appeared to have been capped off by Marcus's taste in gorgeous blue Morgans—and Harry enveloped Marcus as if he'd been courting Peta for years. The little boy seemed totally, gloriously happy.

'It's not just because of the Morgan,' he told Marcus. 'It's because I'm going home. You'll love it.'

He was more and more out of his ken.

By the time Marcus arrived he'd driven through some of the loveliest country in the world—with a schoolboy by his side chattering thirteen to the dozen. He didn't have a clue what he was letting himself in for.

Peta had reached the farm before them. When he pulled to a stop she was crouched on the veranda steps of a dilapidated cottage, surrounded by a gaggle of misbegotten dogs. The dogs came barking furiously down the steps to the car and Peta followed.

She was still limping, Marcus noticed. She was still the Peta he'd left two hours ago. She was wearing the clothes she'd worn on the aeroplane—the skirt and top they'd bought in New York to face Charles.

But she looked indefinably different. The haunted air had gone, he thought. She was smiling and there was something about that smile...

It was happiness. Her smile was a glow from inside, impossible to turn off. And why? Because she'd just arrived back at this godforsaken place...

No. That wasn't fair, he decided. The country was beautiful. Charles had fought for this place and for good reason. The farm land was softly undulating coastline, dotted by magnificent eucalypts and backed by mountains. In the afternoon sun it looked magic.

But not so the house. The veranda looked as if it'd topple at any minute, and the house attached to it was worse.

'Welcome to Rosella Farm,' Peta was saying through dog barks. 'Down. Down, guys.' But there was no way the dogs were obeying. They were almost turning inside out as they realised it was Harry in the car. Harry did a mighty leap, and dogs and kid ended up rolling joyously in the dust.

But Marcus was still staring at the tumbledown house. 'Is this really your home?'

'Yes.' Peta's smile faded a little. 'But don't worry. Aunt Hattie's house is better. It's a couple of hundred yards further on, behind the dairy. I'll take you there now.'

'Right.' He climbed out of the car, looked around him and made a decision. He needed to ground himself here. This was unfamiliar territory and Marcus dealt in facts. Knowledge was power. Or, at least, knowledge was being just a little less disoriented than he was feeling right now. 'I need a guided tour,' he told her.

Was it his imagination, or did she back off a bit? 'Harry can show you over the farm after school tomorrow.'

Harry's cheerful face emerged from his pile of assorted dogs. 'Sure. But it'll take ages. I'll stay home from school tomorrow and show Marcus everything. You'll need me to entertain Marcus. Girls never know what to do with guys.'

His grin was infectious but Peta was obviously immune. But at least she could look at Harry now instead of Marcus. He was right. She had backed off. 'Not likely,' she told her brother. 'You've missed enough school already. But you can take Marcus down to Hattie's now.'

Thus he was summarily dismissed. Marcus frowned. It was a neat plan. Harry could take him to her aunt's house and therefore let her get on with her life.

So? That was what he wanted, wasn't it?

Maybe not.

'I'll bring your bag in first,' Marcus told her. He'd taken their combined luggage.

Peta shook her head and held out her hand for the bag he'd pulled out of the car. 'I'll take it.'

'Your ankle...'

'Is fine. Leave it here.'

'Don't you want me to see your house?'

'There's nothing to see.'

'You don't want me to carry it to your room?'

'Peta sleeps on the veranda,' Harry volunteered. 'Out the back, out of the wind.' He pushed the dogs aside, rose and turned to playing host. 'There's only one bedroom and Peta makes me sleep in that.'

'Peta sleeps on the veranda?'

'It's...cool,' Peta said.

'I bet it is,' he said, stunned. 'In winter I bet it's really cool. You sleep out all year round?'

'We all had to sleep on the veranda until Dad died,' Harry told him. 'Us boys had a really big bed, and Peta had a littler one at the other end. When Dad died the big ones made William and me move inside so I can hardly remember. But I think I liked it.'

'It's unbelievable.'

'It's none of your business,' Peta told him. Her face shut him out as best she could as she attempted to move on. 'But if you're thinking Harry wasn't looked after, he was. When he was a baby he slept with me. Now... There's basic groceries at Hattie's. There's food in the freezer and long-life milk and juice in the pantry. I'll go shopping tomorrow for whatever else you need. But meanwhile...'

'What are we eating for dinner?' Marcus asked.

We.

The 'we' hung in the air, halting conversation. It was a push in the direction of sharing.

Was that wise? Probably not, Marcus thought, but the idea of calmly driving to another house and foraging in the freezer alone was really unappealing.

'We'll be eating sausages,' Harry volunteered. 'Peta always cooks sausages. She burns them, too.'

'Will there be sausages in my...in Hattie's freezer?'

'Sure,' Harry said expansively. 'Peta buys millions of sausages.'

'Okay.' Marcus smiled down into his bride's confused face. 'Then I'm cooking. Dinner's on at my place. In, say, an hour?'

'You don't even know what's there,' Peta said faintly.

'How far away are the shops?'

'Fifteen minutes by car.'

'No worries, then. Job's done.'

'You can't cook!'

'Who said I can't cook?'

'Can you really?' Harry demanded, suspicion and hope warring on his adolescent face. 'Really?'

'Really.'

'Not stuff like...sushi.'

Marcus grinned. 'I doubt even *my* ability to whip up sushi given a core ingredient of sausage.'

'Ace,' said Harry, deeply satisfied. 'Isn't it ace, Peta?'

Her face said it was anything but ace. 'I need to milk the cows.'

'What, tonight?'

'I'm not paying anyone to milk tonight. If I don't milk there's no income.'

'Can I help?'

'I like milking alone,' she said stolidly. 'You concentrate on your sausages.'

'Your ankle...'

'Is fine. You've done enough,' she told him. 'I don't want you to help.'

The joy had faded. It was still there, he thought, but there was discomfort, too. As though she'd realised that the joy had to be paid for.

And the price was...him.

The second farmhouse was like a doll's house. In much better condition than the first, it had obviously been built for one very fussy woman.

It was pink. Very pink. The outside was a demure brick but the moment Marcus walked inside he was assaulted by pinkness. Pink walls, pink paintings, pink doilies...

'Auntie Hattie liked pink,' Harry said by his side. Peta had abandoned them, leaving Harry to do the honours.

'I can see that she did,' Marcus said cautiously and then he looked down at Harry's bland face. 'It's horrible.'

'It is,' Harry said, blandness making way for mischief. 'Our place is better, even if it's falling down.'

'I don't understand.' Marcus stared around him. 'How come this place is so much better than yours?'

'Better?'

'Well, if you ignore the pink...'

'Oh, you mean money,' Harry said with just a trace of scorn. 'Aunt Hattie always had more than us.'

'Can you tell me why?'

'Easy. My grandpa was fair.'

'Fair?'

And Harry was off, all too ready to tell a story of an injustice he obviously felt strongly about. 'My grandpa had two kids, my Dad and Auntie Hattie. Auntie Hattie had a baby when she was a teenager—that was Charles—but she stayed living here. Grandpa built her this little house. My Dad married my Mum and had five kids. When Grandpa died, he left the farm half to Dad and half to Hattie, even though our family did all the work. Peta says Dad was really angry. She says that's another reason why Dad hated women.'

'So...'

'So all the income from the farm had to be split into two. Half to Hattie and half to us.'

'Who works the farm?'

'Peta, mostly. We help.'

'Did Hattie help?'

'Hattie never worked.' Harry gazed around the little house and grimaced. 'Except to paint things.'

'That seems unfair on Peta,' Marcus said thoughtfully and Harry nodded.

'Yeah, it is, really unfair, but Charles always said we had

a choice—do it like that or we could leave the farm. My Dad never wanted to leave the farm—he couldn't be bothered and as long as there was enough money for his drink...' He bit his lip at that, and suddenly looked very young. 'I guess I shouldn't have told you about Dad drinking. It's what Daniel told me. But Peta would growl.'

'I won't tell her.' Marcus frowned. 'So... Peta stayed and worked the farm. Why did your brothers leave?'

'Peta made them.'

'Why?'

'She said there was never going to be enough money for us all to be farmers and they were going to have careers if she had to drive them off with sticks.' His grin returned. 'When Peta gets bossy no one can argue with her.'

'I guess you're right at that.'

'Are you really going to make sausages?'

'Not if I can help it. Where's the freezer?'

'I'll show you. Hattie used to go to the city sometimes and buy gourmet stuff. There might be something interesting. But...not too interesting.'

'Let's go look,' Marcus told him. 'Can you cook?'

'No!' Harry told him, startled.

'Then you're about to learn.'

By the time Peta came in from the dairy she was tired. Good tired, she thought though, as she showered. Great tired. The cows—her girls—were all fit and healthy. They'd swivelled their great bovine heads as she'd appeared at the gate to lead them up to the dairy; there'd been gentle moos and, moving among them, she felt she'd come home.

Home.

No one could take it from her, she'd thought over and over as she'd washed teats, adjusted cups, released one cow after the other and given each an affectionate pat as they ambled off towards an evening of grazing the lush pasture on the cliffs around the house. Home. At long last the threats to her security—her father and her cousin—were gone.

Marcus had given this to her. It was a huge gift. Vast.

She stared down at the plain band of gold on her finger. Marcus had insisted they each wear one for a year—'Let's do this right.'

He'd done it right.

And she'd sent him off to Aunt Hattie's.

Maybe he'll like pink, she told herself, and grinned to herself as the cool water streamed over her. And at least he'll be comfortable.

And he'd be away. Separate. Life could get back to normal. From this day…

'Peta?' Harry was yelling for her and she poked her head out of the shower.

'Mmm?'

'Marcus and me have made dinner. It's ace. You gotta hurry before it gets cold. Marcus says hurry.'

He waited for her, jigging up and down with impatience as she hauled on clean jeans and a T-shirt. 'Come on. Come on.'

So much for eating toast on the veranda and getting her head together. 'Didn't you want to have dinner just with me tonight?' she asked.

'Are you kidding?' Harry demanded, amazed. 'Marcus is ace.'

'Yeah, but…'

'And you should see what we've cooked.'

Curry.

Peta walked in the back door of Aunt Hattie's little house and stopped in astonishment. Curry! She'd never smelled such a thing in this house. It'd take three cans of air-freshener for Hattie to lose it. Hattie would never tolerate it.

Then Marcus appeared in the doorway and she stopped thinking about Aunt Hattie.

She'd never seen him like this.

The first time she'd met him, Marcus had been dressed formally. He'd been wearing a business suit. For the wedding he'd gone even more formal, and he'd worn a suit on the way out here on the plane. He'd looked an experienced business traveller and Peta had been vaguely self-conscious beside him.

No. Peta had been *incredibly* self-conscious beside him.

But now... He'd changed. Transformed. He was wearing jeans that were almost as faded as hers, with a plain T-shirt that stretched tight across his chest and showed the muscles rippling down his arms. His deep black hair was tousled as if he'd run his fingers through it often and often. There was a smudge of something orange on his cheek.

He was wearing a pinny.

It was one of Aunt Hattie's pinnies, she thought. Pink. Frilly. With a bow attached.

She stared. She'd come prepared to be stiff and formal and polite—welcoming to a guest but here to have a fast meal and then say a formal good night and get away.

Stiff, formal and polite didn't get a look in. One glance and she was lost. Laughter bubbled up and exploded.

'What?' he demanded, mock offended as she whooped. 'What? Don't you like my apron?'

'It's...' She fought gamely for control but lost. Another whoop or two and then she tried again. 'It's a very nice pinny. Did you tie the bow?'

'I tied it for him,' Harry said behind her. 'He had his hands all covered in yuck stuff and said "find an apron" and that's all Auntie Hattie had.'

'It's a very nice apron,' she managed. 'It's a very nice bow. Well...well done, boys.' She fought a bit more for control. 'Um... Is that curry I can smell?'

'It is.' Marcus beamed at her as if a protégée had just proven herself incredibly clever. 'Harry said he liked curry.'

'How... Did Auntie Hattie have curry powder?' She was fascinated.

'You don't make curry out of curry powder,' he told her.

'No?'

'No. You really don't cook, do you, Mrs Benson.'

Mrs Benson...

The label came out unexpectedly and hung. She bit her lip and tried desperately to ignore it.

'When I was eight years old, I had a very sensible grade teacher,' she told him. Somehow. 'Mrs Canterbury was Yooralaa's answer to Emily Pankhurst. One day she took us girls aside and said if we were ever to amount to anything we should never learn to type, never learn to sew and never learn to cook. I followed her advice to the letter.'

'Well done, you,' he said faintly, obviously bemused. 'And here you are, amounting to lots. But hungry. Curry powder, huh?'

'So how do you make curry without curry powder?'

'You take the little bottles of herbs Hattie has in a collection labelled Gourmet Delight. It looks as if it was bought for decoration rather than use but she has everything. Coriander, cumin, turmeric, cardamom, you name it. Nothing's ever been opened so it's still good. Then you lift the cute little ornamental chilli plant off the veranda where it's obviously been placed because it clashes with pink. You pick two chillis. You take a hunk of frozen lamb, a can of tomatoes, a few lemons from the tree outside, and *voilà*.'

'*Voilà*? Is that Indian for delicious?'

'Of course it's Indian. And absolutely it's for delicious. Hungry?'

Was she hungry? She smelled again and the smell did things to her insides she found extraordinary.

No. It wasn't just the smell, she thought. It was the whole experience.

A man in Hattie's house.

A man in her life!

There were enough men in her life, she told herself desperately. She had four brothers whom she loved. She'd coped with a neglectful father and a violent cousin. Six men. She didn't need any more. Ever.

But Marcus was holding the chair for her to sit. No one had ever held a chair for her. Marcus was smiling at her. No one had ever smiled at her...

Was she crazy? Of course people had smiled at her. All the time!

No one had ever smiled at her like Marcus.

She was home, she told herself. Life had to get back to normal. This was some crazy two-week aberration—a man cooking for her—a man acting as if he cared. It'd go away. He'd go away and then her life could go on as normal.

Could it?

They sat across the table from him, Peta and her little brother, and they ate his curry as if they'd never eaten such food. They savoured every mouthful.

Marcus's cooking was his secret pleasure. His mother had never cooked. For the first few years of his life he'd lived on hamburgers and Coke. Then one of his mother's boyfriends had wooed her by hiring a chef for the night. Marcus had been sent to bed while the two had a romantic *tête à tête*, but the smells had been tantalising. The next day the leftover ingredients filled the kitchen. He'd investigated, then had a long discussion with the lady in the next door apartment.

The result had left him delighted. It had been the start of a skill that until now had never been shared. But sharing...

It was great, he thought. His food was being consumed with total enjoyment and it added to his satisfaction tenfold. Peta and Harry discussed the curry with absolute fascination; they ate every scrap and the three dogs under the table were left to eye each other disconsolately.

'Where did you learn to do this?' Peta demanded and he

told her. That felt odd, too—talking about the past to a woman who looked as if she was really interested. Who looked as if she really cared.

She didn't. She couldn't, he told himself. This farm was her life and she had no part in his. He knew that, but as the last of the curry was finished and she rose to go, he was aware of a sharp stab of loss.

'I'll make coffee,' he told her but she shook her head.

'I have milking in the morning. Five a.m. I need to go to bed. And it's back to routine for Harry. He has school.'

'Aw...'

'Come on, Harry.' Peta hauled Harry to his feet and whistled the dogs. 'Come on, guys. We need to go home and let Mr Benson get his sleep.'

'It's just after eight o'clock,' Marcus said, startled. 'Even Prince Charming got a better look-in than that.'

'You left Cinderella in New York,' Peta said firmly. 'And she's staying there.'

CHAPTER EIGHT

THE silence was deafening.

Peta and Harry left, the dogs followed, and Marcus was left in his little pink house with his thoughts.

His thoughts weren't exactly little and pink. They were large and black. He cleaned the kitchen and polished the pink bench-tops. He unpacked, put his clothes on the pink clothes hangers, stared at the pink walls, thought about how many hours there were in two weeks and how much pink a man could stand.

Not much more than this.

He set up his laptop and logged into his work space. It was nine at night, which meant it was five in the morning in New York. No one was online.

He'd expected a sheaf of correspondence from Ruby. There was nothing.

A man could go crazy.

Where was everyone? He stared at his cellphone. He could ring. There were plenty of things he could discuss.

He'd wake everyone up.

They worked for him. They'd get over it.

But...

'Have a holiday,' Ruby had told him. 'I mean it, Marcus. No work. Take two weeks. We don't want to hear from you. See if you can do it.'

She'd said it as a challenge and he'd reacted as if she'd been stupid. But now, staring at his cellphone and at his idle computer, he knew Ruby wasn't stupid. Ruby knew him better than he knew himself.

Maybe because she'd walked the same lonely road.

Tonight had been good, he thought. Tonight had been...excellent. Teaching a twelve-year-old to cook a curry.

It was more than that, he conceded. His pleasure had come from watching a twelve-year-old enjoy himself. And more than that. Watching a twelve-year-old's big sister enjoy her little brother's pleasure. Giving his Cinderella more.

Tonight Peta had been happy and it had felt good. It was a strange sensation but it had felt right. Making Peta happy.

Caring.

Whoa! He caught himself and gave himself a mental swipe to the side of the head. He was getting soppy here. This whole situation was for two weeks, he told himself. Only two weeks. Two weeks, Benson, and you're out of here.

He was going nuts.

But what the heck was a man to do? He flicked on the television and watched an inane American sitcom. What on earth was this country doing, importing this stuff? Was it funny?

How the heck would he know when he couldn't concentrate?

How had he ever got himself into this mess? he demanded of himself. The world seemed to be going to bed, but how could he go to bed? His head said it was six a.m. New York time and every single part of him was awake.

Peta had adjusted to New York time, he thought, so maybe she'd be feeling like he was. How could Peta be calmly going home to bed?

On her veranda?

That was another thing to think about. To chew over. To make a girl sleep on the veranda...

This set-up was dreadful, he thought. Appalling. She must have had the pits of a childhood. He thought of her lying in a bed—probably with broken springs—probably with threadbare blankets—setting the alarm for the crack of dawn or earlier, so she could get up to milk her cows.

She was a real Cinderella, he decided, whether she admitted it or not. And he... He'd volunteered to rescue her.

No, he hadn't. Offering to marry someone for two weeks out of practicality hardly turned him into Prince Charming.

There must be more he could do.

She couldn't be asleep. Not if the bedsprings were sticking into her. And...what was that fairy story about the pea? The princess sleeping on a hundred feather mattresses, yet still disturbed by one pea underneath the bottom layer.

Fairytales! He was losing his mind.

But the image refused to go away and he found himself opening the back door and staring outside. *You're going to rescue her from a pea?*

I'm not going anywhere.

But he was. He refused to stay one minute longer in this little pink room in this little pink house.

He'd just wander by her veranda, he told himself. Just to make sure. And if there were any peas that needed removing...

Well, maybe he was just the man to do it.

Don't do it, he told himself. *Just go for a walk. And if you end up close...*

Sleep was nowhere. Peta lay and stared into the dark and tried to conjure up the pure contentment she'd always felt in this bed. In this place.

When their father had died the boys had conducted a vote and had decreed the inside bedroom was Peta's. She'd refused. For as long as she remembered she'd lain in this little bed at the far end of the veranda while the boys lay in the bigger bed at the other end. They were not too far away, but not too near. This was her private place. Here she could haul the bedclothes up to her nose and disappear into her thoughts, while out in the wide world cows chewed their cuds, trees rustled in the wind, the sea did its thing, owls hooted, frogs croaked...

This farm was alive at night and it was her company. She'd missed it so much while she was in New York.

She should be revelling in it now.

She should be sleeping. She should. Instead she lay and stared out into the starlit sky and all she could see was Marcus.

Marcus did a circuit of his little house and decided to extend his tour. The moon was full. He could see the shapes of the cows in the paddocks, the shadowy trees and the mountains in the background. He could hear the soft hush-hushing of the surf below the house. He could smell the eucalypts and the salt of the sea.

All of which should make Marcus, a city boy born and bred, scurry back to his little house and close the door against the elements. Instead he found himself wandering in a wider arc from the house. Just walking. Following the tracks made by generations of Peta's family as they went about their business on the farm.

Getting closer to Peta?

He'd already discovered from Harry that Peta had visited Hattie—often. He'd learned that Hattie's presence had meant that the children were allowed to stay on the farm when their father died. But apparently Hattie had been a weak woman who'd cared for Peta but hadn't been able to stand up for her against her own son.

'I can't remember much about Charles,' Harry had told him. 'I was too little when he went away. But Daniel says Charles was a real creep. He hit everyone who got in his way. Auntie Hattie had to stay here when Charles was a kid because there was nowhere else to go, but Charles hated it. He hated us. Everyone was really pleased when he went away and it was awful when he came home. Dan says he just came home looking for money and he made Auntie Hattie cry. There was never enough money for him. That made Peta angry; she wouldn't let him hit Auntie Hattie so he used to hit Peta. A lot.'

The bleak little outline fitted exactly with what Marcus knew of Charles, but it made him see red just to think of the creep hitting Peta.

Of anyone hitting Peta.

Marcus had never really thought about it but, if forced, maybe he would have said he'd had an appalling childhood. But apparently there were others who'd had appalling childhoods. More appalling childhoods than his.

So? Other people had got over it. So why couldn't he?

The image of his mother and her series of boyfriends still made him cringe, but it was more than just his childhood holding him apart from the human race, he thought. He knew what happened when he got attached to people. Dreadful things. It was so much better to stay apart...

His feet kept walking. The moonlight played on his face. He wasn't in the least tired.

He walked closer. Closer to Peta's sad little house. Closer to the veranda. She'd be solidly asleep, he told himself. No one would wake.

The dogs were his undoing.

They came out of nowhere, not vicious, not snapping, but ecstatic to see a human being awake. Harry—informative Harry, whom Marcus had pumped unashamedly during curry-making—had told him that the dogs had stayed here while Peta was away, fed by the businesslike neighbour who did things for money. To have Peta and Harry home was obviously wonderful in the dogs' eyes, but Peta and Harry had gone to bed, which was really boring, and here was the friend who'd fed them scraps from his curry.

Marcus's plan on walking unnoticed round the farm counted for nothing. As an ex-soldier he should have known better. The dogs were yapping and yelping and bounding, and then a voice called out of the night.

'Tip. Bryson. Who's out there? Come here, boys.'

Peta. He'd scared her, Marcus thought, dismayed. He hadn't meant...

'If that's you, Marcus, watch your feet for cow pats. We've let the cows graze in the home yard.'

Cow pats. So much for terror!

What was a man to say to that? It seemed the lady wasn't scared at all. 'I'm watching,' he managed, stunned.

'Good for you,' she called and, astonishingly, there was laughter in her voice. 'Come here, boys.'

She meant the dogs, he thought. Only the dogs.

'Are you in bed?' he called.

'I surely am.' This was really strange, like speaking to a disembodied head. 'Which is where you should be.'

'I'm not tired. Why aren't you asleep?'

'Maybe I would be but strange men keep wandering around in my cow pats.'

'You don't sound as if you're even near sleep,' he complained. 'Are you saying it's my fault you're awake?'

'I wouldn't say that,' she said cautiously. 'Not exactly.'

'What would you say?'

'That I'm really happy to be home.'

'Even if it means you're sleeping on the veranda?'

'I like sleeping on the veranda.'

'Seriously...'

'Seriously.' There was a moment's hesitation and then obviously a decision. 'Come on up and see.'

'You're inviting me into your bedroom?'

'I'm inviting you onto my veranda. There's a difference.'

'And the dogs get to play chaperon.'

'Hey, I'm hardly about to get swept away on a tide of girlish passion here,' she said with some asperity. 'And if you're thinking of indulging in the same...'

'Girlish passion?'

'That's the one. I have a pitcher full of cold water and I'm prepared to use it.'

He choked. 'It's a great invitation.'

'And it's only made once. Are you coming up or not?'

Was he? His feet were already moving.

She looked about twelve years old.

Marcus reached the end of the veranda and stopped in astonishment. He wasn't sure what he had thought he'd find but it wasn't this.

Her bed was a single bed pressed hard against the far wall. So far so good. That was what he'd thought she'd have. But he'd expected a barren little cot. What he found were...

Cushions. Pillows. Quilts. A vast mound of glorious bedclothes in semi-ordered chaos. In the dim moonlight he could scarcely make out colours but he could see enough to know that this was a mad and vibrant mix, an eclectic scattering of whatever Peta fancied. There must be a dozen huge pillows mounded up beside her, spilling over onto the floor. The oldest of the farm dogs, a greying old collie called Ted-dog, was curled up beside the bed. As Marcus approached he gave his tail a faint wag as if to say, I'm very pleased to see you and I'll be even more pleased if you don't expect me to get up.

Marcus could see where he was coming from. If he was curled up on a mound like this...

So much for his pea.

'It's great, isn't it?' Peta said. She wiggled farther down under her bedclothes so only her nose emerged from the gorgeous quilts.

'I thought you were deprived,' Marcus said before he could stop himself and she pushed the quilt down a fraction.

'Deprived?'

'Abusive father. Dead mother. Made to sleep outdoors...'

'My dad wasn't abusive. He never liked girls but he didn't take it out on me. He simply didn't have time for me.'

'And your mother?'

'She wasn't much interested, either. I have really scant memories of her. She stayed inside and had babies.'

'Something you would never do?'

'If I had babies I might make a push to make sure they were happy,' she told him. 'Our mother really liked babies but as soon as we started being messy it was outside and get on with our lives.' She pushed herself up on her cushions and looked past him out to where the moon hung over the sea. 'It was just as well it was a great outside. How lucky were we?'

'Lucky?'

'We had this.' She put a hand down and fondled Ted-dog's ears. 'We had the dogs. We had each other. We had a great childhood.'

'You didn't have any money.'

'I don't see you happy,' she said softly. 'Because you have money. Where would you prefer to sleep? In that sterile, awful Manhattan apartment, or here? This is the best bedroom in the world.'

'And if it rains?'

'I hang plastic from the veranda rails. And if it gets really, really cold I might even let a dog or two in for company. It's great.'

'I'm sure.'

'You don't sound convinced.'

'I think I like central heating.'

'Turn around,' she said. Her voice was suddenly urgent. She was sitting bolt upright now in her amazing bed. She was wearing a T-shirt, he thought. A T-shirt. How many women of his acquaintance slept in anything other than sexy negligées?

But, 'Look,' she said again and he was forced to turn and look.

And he was caught.

It was lovely, he had to concede. In fact, in truth, it was breathtakingly beautiful. The moon was casting a ribbon of silver over the sea. Below the house, the waves were breaking in long, low lines. The foam from their breaking was caught in the moonlight, a soft white pattern of hushed time.

The sand was wide—the tide must be full out as the beach seemed to spread for miles. The house was only about two or three hundred yards from the beach. The soft breaking of wave after wave was a lullaby all by itself.

Between here and the beach stood four or five vast gums, their canopies almost another roof. There was a huddle of cows under one. Sleeping. Settled on the lush pasture for the night. He couldn't see from here but he could imagine their jaws contentedly chewing, conjuring flavours of the grasses they'd eaten during the day.

'This is why I married you,' Peta said softly. 'Not for money.'

'Not for love?'

She turned and grinned at him. 'You're looking for romance?'

'Um…no.'

'I've had a very nice wedding,' she told him. 'Thank you very much. But isn't that how the story goes? A white wedding and then the princess gets to live happily ever after?'

'With her prince.'

'Who needs a prince? I have this. I have my dogs. I have security for the boys.'

'You're telling me I can go back to New York?'

'Oh, no, I need you here,' she told him quite kindly. 'You said that yourself. Two weeks to make the marriage valid.'

'And then I can clear off?'

'That's what you want to do—isn't it?'

'Of course.'

'But I did decide I'd invite you up onto my veranda,' she told him, as if granting some huge concession. 'Just once. So you can see what you've given me.'

'So you can point out that you don't need me after two weeks?'

'That, too. I keep getting the feeling that you see me as some sort of charity. Well, I was,' she admitted with sudden candour. 'You've saved me. I just wish I could save you back.'

'Save me?'

'You don't have a very satisfactory life,' she told him.

Good grief.

Marcus stared down at her in the moonlight. She was hugging her knees, looking at him in consideration. As if he was some sort of interesting bug...

The sensation was indescribable. He'd be less uncomfortable if the story of his life was splashed across the front page of the *New Yorker*.

'Will you cut it out?' he demanded.

'Cut what out?'

'Butting into what's none of your business.'

'If you don't want me to,' she said, obliging. She ducked down under her covers and disappeared up to her nose again. 'Good night.'

He'd been dismissed. He should turn around and head down those rickety steps again. But...

But. It was a simple word and he couldn't get over it. But. But what? He didn't have a clue.

'Aren't you suffering from jet lag?' he asked.

'Jet lag? After the aeroplane bed I had? You have to be kidding.' Her voice was muffled by bedclothes, almost indistinct.

'I mean time zones,' he said, a little bit desperately. 'I feel as if it's morning.'

'I do, too, a bit,' she agreed, still muffled. 'But the cows will be awake at five o'clock. I have to get up then, so I need to sleep.'

'You want me to go away.'

She put the sheet down a smidgeon and stared up at him, only her eyes above the sheet.

'You're lonely!'

'No, I...'

'Hattie's house is creepy,' she told him. 'All that pink. I wouldn't wonder if you're lonely.'

'And you're not?'

'I do miss the boys,' she admitted. 'Harry sleeps inside now. He has a computer and he reckons the cables get wet out here. So he ended up in the bedroom. But I liked it when they slept out here.' She motioned to the other end of the veranda. 'It's a great place to sleep. If you like you could try it.'

'What...share your veranda?'

'It's a very long veranda.'

'Do you always ask strange men...'

'You're not a strange man. You're my husband.'

Yes. Yes, he was. The thought was incredible.

'And if I tell the dogs to attack they'll do just that,' she added.

Pop went his fantasy bubble. He choked. He turned to stare down at the mutts who were draped decoratively over the cushions. 'I don't believe it.'

'Believe it,' she said seriously. 'Daniel did that for me the last time Charles came home.'

'Did what?'

'He trained the dogs. They're great with cattle and they're highly intelligent. Charles... Well, Charles gave me a hard time one night and Daniel decided if I was to stay here alone I needed protection. So now there's just one word I have to say and they turn into a pack of snarling savages. Want to see?'

'No!'

He was getting accustomed to the moonlight now and he could see her grin.

He wasn't getting accustomed to the situation, though. This woman had stood beside him two days ago and promised to be his wife. She'd stood for press photographers, her hand in his, his lovely bride. She'd slept beside him in the plane, she'd tucked her hand in his as they'd gone through customs, she'd let him take control, manage things, do what he was good at.

What had he expected here?

Not this. An invitation to share her veranda with a pack of killer dogs between them.

But...

He stared out at the night. It was...perfect.

He could sleep here. He could sleep with Peta. Or he could go back to the pink puffy concoction that was Hattie's bed, or to the horror-fantasy-poster-covered room that had been the creation of an adolescent Charles before he left home.

Three options.

'It's a very generous offer,' Peta said cheerfully, following his line of thought. 'I don't make it to anyone. But now, if you don't mind, I'm going to sleep.'

She turned over on to her side; the covers came right up, and her body language said that whatever he did was up to him. She'd made her offer and the rest was his business.

He should go home.

Home? Who was he kidding? Home was Hattie's pink palace.

It wasn't so different to his place in Manhattan, he thought. Both seemed suddenly indescribably bleak. He stared down at Peta for a long moment and then slowly walked the length of the veranda.

The bed was made up. It was three times the size of hers. The boys had slept in it, Peta had said. All the boys?

Maybe.

And maybe it wasn't such a bad childhood. He stared down at the mound of bedclothes and thought of four little boys tumbled among the pillows. With Peta sleeping close by.

Not so bad. Not so bad at all.

He hesitated, but not for long. He turned and stared at the mound of bedclothes that was Peta.

No choice.

He slipped off his outer clothes and slid under the bedclothes, feeling like a kid on a camping trip. And here was another surprise. There were no burst bedsprings. No threadbare blankets. The bed enfolded him. The smells and the sounds enfolded him and one of the dogs came up and put his nose above the side of the bed, nosing a hopeful enquiry.

'Let me see. I'm guessing you must be Tip. You're one of the killer pack?'

A wag of the tail and a low woof. A quiver of the backside. Hopefulness personified.

'If you have fleas you're out of here.'

'He has no such thing!' It was an indignant squeak from the other end of the veranda.

'I thought you were asleep?' Then Marcus gasped as the big dog accepted the flea enquiry as a welcome and wriggled right in. Right across his chest.

'Tip likes it there,' Peta said in satisfaction. 'I've never slept with a husband. Doesn't it feel odd?'

Odd? That was the understatement of the century, Marcus thought. He lay and stared outward at the stars while Peta settled again and the big dog started to snore gently beside him.

He'd never sleep. How could he sleep?

He'd never sleep.

He slept.

CHAPTER NINE

MARCUS BENSON hadn't slept for more than four hours straight since he was fourteen years old. He hadn't needed to. Hadn't wanted to. If he slept then he dreamed, and now it was easier to wake and log on to the world's financial markets and exercise his brain by making money rather than letting his thoughts dwell on the demons in his past.

Until this night.

He slept. The sun crept over the horizon. Peta rose and took herself off to the dairy. The dogs bounded off after her, jubilant at having their mistress back in her proper place, and still Marcus slept.

He woke as Harry tore round the side of the house, hauling a school bag over his shoulder while he manoeuvred a piece of toast with half his mouth.

He glanced sideways at the veranda and stopped short.

'You!'

It was hard to say who was more surprised—Harry or Marcus. They stared at each other. Marcus stared down at his watch. Then stared back at Harry.

'You slept with Peta.' It wasn't an accusation. There was no aversion in Harry's tone—just surprise.

'I slept on this end of the veranda,' Marcus said hurriedly. 'Peta slept on the other.'

'Yeah, she'd never share with us,' Harry said, taking another mouthful of toast. 'We told her it was warmer in bed with us but she preferred the dogs. Guess she preferred the dogs to you, too, huh?'

'I guess so,' Marcus said weakly. 'Um... Are you off to school?'

'Yeah. Yikes.' Harry looked round to where a faint cloud

of dust in the distance heralded an arriving school bus. 'Gotta go. What's for tea tonight? Something good? Ace. See ya.' And he was off in a tangle of toast, school bag and undone shoelaces.

Marcus watched him run, saw him catch the bus by the skin of his teeth, grinned, and then turned back to the enigma of his watch.

His grin faded. How on earth had he slept so long?

No matter. He had.

From the dairy there was the gentle hum of the milking machine and the occasional moo of an indignant cow. Peta was up? Peta was working?

Before him?

The thought was almost unbelievable. So, too, was the thought that she was working and he was sleeping.

He was supposed to be rescuing her, he thought. Great Prince Charming he was. Marry the girl and send her back to her cinders.

But helping her wasn't as simple as it had seemed. Two minutes later he walked in the dairy door—only to have the nearest cow start back in alarm and Peta call, 'Stop right there.'

He stopped.

This was a different Peta yet, he thought. She was a woman at work. In faded jeans, a checked overshirt with rolled up sleeves, her hair caught back with a couple of serviceable combs and her knee-high rubber boots liberally coated with mud, she looked every inch at home in her environment.

As opposed to Marcus. The cows stared at him as if he'd landed from outer space and that was exactly how he felt.

'I've come to help,' he told her.

'Thanks, but you'll scare the cows.'

'Why will I scare the cows?'

'They're not used to seeing New York billionaires in their dairy.'

'You didn't have to tell them I was a billionaire,' he said cautiously and she smiled.

'They might have guessed by the shoes. Soft suede shoes don't cut it here.'

'I guess they don't.' He looked down at his footwear. 'Um... Would your brothers have any rain boots I can borrow?'

'There's another giveaway.' She adjusted the cups on a sleek, fat cow and then rose to bring the next cow into the bail. 'We—the cows and I—call them gumboots.'

'Why?'

'Because the cows and I are Australian.' The cow pulled back from her and she sighed. 'Yeah, the boys all have gumboots you can borrow but it won't help. You're making it hard for me.'

'Just by being here?'

'Cows don't like strangers.'

'I have to do something,' he told her. 'If you think I'm just going to sit round being ornamental for two weeks...'

'Don't you like being ornamental?'

'I've never really thought about it,' he admitted. 'I don't think so.'

'So you really want to work?'

Hmm. A little voice was telling him to be cautious. 'I might.'

'Well, then. You could get rid of the pink.'

'Pardon?'

'You could paint Hattie's house.'

'So that you can live in it?'

'I'm staying on my veranda. But the boys bring friends home from university and a non-pink guest house would be nice.' She gave him her very nicest smile. 'That is, if you really do want to be useful. But I'm happy if you're not. You deserve to be ornamental if you feel like it.'

'Is there anything in between?' he asked, thinking it

through. 'Say, if I don't want to be ornamental and I don't want to paint houses.'

Her answer to that was immediate. 'You could make me breakfast.'

'You've decreed that I'm cook?'

'I thought you decreed that yourself. I do a mean bowl of cornflakes and I'm willing to share.' She glanced across at the yard to where only ten more cows patiently queued. 'I'll be back at the house in half an hour.'

'For cornflakes?'

'For cornflakes or whatever variation you care to dream up.'

He'd had enough of pink. He made pancakes in Peta's house. He felt really, really strange.

While he cooked he watched Peta through the window. He saw her finish in the dairy, sluicing it down ready for evening milking. She took herself to the outside shower—a primitive arrangement that he'd already inspected and found wanting—and he watched as she emerged dressed the same way as she'd been in the dairy, only cleaner.

Peta's house had a lean-to kitchen—not a patch on Hattie's bright beauty, but it had the huge advantage of being homely. The kitchen was obviously the place where Peta and the boys spent most of their lives. There was an ancient fire-stove, a vast wooden table, rickety chairs, battered linoleum, and windows looking out over the farmland to the beach beyond. It was a great room.

It was better when Peta walked in. Somehow.

She stopped in the doorway and sniffed in delight, and her smile lit the room.

'Pancakes. Coffee. There. I knew there was a reason I married you.'

'I wish you wouldn't keep referring to our marriage as if I'm some sort of acquired toy,' he complained and she paused from kicking off her gumboots.

'It's the only way I can think of it,' she told him. Her eyes turned suddenly serious. 'Not that you're a toy boy. I didn't mean that. But that it's a sort of game. I can't believe we did it. That I wore that dress. That I made those vows.'

He watched her face, and he shared her confusion. She was right. This was a far cry from white, lacy and bridal in New York. But underneath she was just the same Peta. The reason he married her still held. She needed help and she deserved it. 'It's not a game,' he told her.

'But it's not for real.'

'For two weeks it has to be real.'

'When I think about it superficially,' she said slowly, walking into the kitchen in her socks and lifting the flipper for the pancakes, 'then it's fine. But then all of a sudden it hits me. Wham. A complete stranger married me so I can stay here. So Harry can live here if he wants. So we can have a permanent home. But... To marry a stranger... How on earth did it happen?'

'Fantasy,' he told her. 'Everyone likes a fairy story. I've already flipped the pancakes. They're ready to eat. Sit.'

So she moved to the table and sat. He couldn't object to her reaction to the pancakes—she ate as if she was ravenous—but as the pile dwindled she pushed back her plate and the look of trouble settled on her face again.

'I'm sorry I wouldn't let you help in the dairy.'

'It's fine.'

'It's not. I owe you so much. I should let you do whatever you want.'

'But not sleep on your end of the veranda?'

Now where had that come from? The moment he said it he regretted it. She flinched. And then she faced him. Head on.

'Do you want to?'

Did he want to? Hell!

But as he gazed at her across the table, as he let the sensation of her flinch settle, he knew there was only one answer.

'No, Peta,' he told her. 'I don't want to. I'm not here to take advantage of you. It was a stupid thing to say and I'm sorry.'

'You'd be within your rights.'

'I don't think you've met very nice men,' he told her. 'If that's what you think of marriage. That it comes with automatic rights.'

She stared at him. The moment stretched on. And on.

Ridiculous.

'Tell me what you're intending to do now,' he said at last, and if his voice didn't come out as he'd intended he couldn't help it.

'You mean...marriage-wise?'

'You already got married,' he reminded her. 'What's next?'

'You mean, in life?'

'I was thinking more how you intended spending the morning,' he told her. 'Sort of between here and lunch. There's not a lot of hatches, matches and dispatches we can fit in until then.'

'Oh.' She sounded flummoxed. 'You mean...like shopping?'

'Is shopping on the agenda?'

'We're living out of the freezer. It'd be good to get something fresh.'

'I'm good with shopping.'

'You want to come into town and push a supermarket trolley in Yooralaa?' Her smile, irrepressible, came flooding back. 'There's no cans of caviar for miles.'

'Peta?'

'Yes?'

'Cut it out.'

She peeped him a smile. 'Okay. I'm sorry. But I'm sure you don't want to come.'

'I'm sure I do.'

'You—'

'Peta, I refuse to stay locked in Hattie's house for two weeks while the world decrees our marriage is valid. I'm coming with you.'

'But people will think...'

'That we're married? That's what they're supposed to think.' He hesitated. 'That is—there aren't suitors waiting in the wings who'll be put off if they see me at your side?'

'Um...no.'

'No suitors?'

'I find suitors are an awful pest,' she told him. 'They mess up the house something awful and object to gumboots.'

'Which is why you just cut straight to the chase and got married. Okay.' He rose and smiled down at her. She looked great, he decided. He might even enjoy walking side by side through the supermarket with her holding his trolley.

'Don't get any funny ideas,' she said and he blinked. Peta, the mind reader.

'Look, separate ends of the veranda is a concept I can deal with,' he told her. 'But separate supermarket trolleys is maybe taking independence too far.'

'You can never have too much independence. I thought that was your motto.'

He'd thought so, too. He stared after her as she disappeared to find some shoes respectable enough to wear to town and he thought, yeah, independence. What had happened to his ideal now?

It was a very satisfactory day—the sort of day Marcus had never had in his life.

First there was the trip to the supermarket. He'd expected that she might be embarrassed but instead she introduced him to all and sundry and he was conscious of suppressed laughter.

'Hi, Mrs Michaels. This is my husband, Marcus.'

It was Marcus who was flustered.

'They need to know you're here,' Peta told him. 'Charles knows any number of locals and I'm sure he'll be contacting them to make sure you're here. You don't mind, do you?'

'No, I...'

'After all, you don't have to see any of these people after two weeks. It'll be me who'll be playing the deserted bride.'

'I'm sure you'll play a beautifully pathetic divorcee,' he managed and she chuckled.

'You'd better believe it. How many cans of spaghetti do we want?'

'None,' he told her. 'Canned when you can have fresh?'

'Sure. I'm a canned girl.'

'If you don't want to be a divorcee by tomorrow then you put the cans back.'

There were locals watching them. Whispering. News was spreading.

'There's not a lot of friendliness,' he said as they proceeded through their shopping list.

'My dad lied and cheated and my cousin did the same,' she told him. 'Our family are still pretty much outcasts.'

'Even you?'

'I learned early to keep myself to myself.'

'But you pay your debts?'

'I don't have debts. The O'Shannassy credit dried up a long time ago. I pay cash or I get nothing and that's the way it's always been. Now... Baked beans?'

'Not baked beans.'

'But...'

'And not processed cheese, either. Honestly, woman, do you have no soul?'

'I eat to live,' she said with a certain amount of pride.

'You're proud of that?'

'Yes.'

He shook his head. 'It's a culture thing,' he told her. 'It must be. You come from convict stock?'

'I surely do,' she told him. 'I have baked beans in the blood.'

'It's a whole life I never knew existed,' he said faintly. 'And I'm not sure I want to.'

But he did want to know.

As the day wore on, the more fascinated he became. They took their shopping home, and then Peta took him on a tour of the fences. 'They need to be checked once a week,' she told him. 'The cows damage them and if stock gets out I'm in real trouble.' So they hiked along the fence line with Peta's fencing tools slung over her shoulder. For the first two minutes.

'You're not carrying them,' she told him. 'They're dirty. You'll get your nice shirt soiled.'

'Peta...' He lifted the tools from her grasp. 'Your ankle still hurts and you're married, remember? Isn't the husband supposed to be hunter gatherer?'

'Only in families when the little woman stays home and cooks. And you wouldn't let me buy baked beans.'

'So I wouldn't,' he said, and grinned. He handed one of the six tools back. 'Okay. You get to carry one spade and you get to cook cornflakes and toast. But for the rest, you have a husband. Use him.'

They fenced. They found a cow in the bottom paddock caught up in a hedge of gorse and a gully caused by erosion. They dug her free and watched her make her way back to the herd, with nary a thankful glance. They ate sandwiches that Peta had stuck in a backpack before they'd come out and they sat on the cliff and watched the sea. A dolphin pod appeared on cue, surfing through the breakers and cruising along the coast line. Marcus could see why Charles fought for development rights to this place. As a holiday resort it'd be fabulous.

As a farm it was better.

'Is the beach safe for swimming?' Marcus asked.

'It sure is.'

'Can we?'

'Nope. I have to milk.'

'What, already?'

'Harry will be home any minute. Take him swimming.'

'Doesn't anyone help you milk?'

'I like milking. I don't need help.'

'Peta, you have me. Use me.'

'No.'

'You need—'

'I don't need a husband in any more than name,' she interrupted, her face closed. 'You know that. Thank you for my day.' She rose and gave what seemed to him to be a regretful glance at the ocean. 'Stay here and rest. I'm off to play milkmaid.'

'Peta, I want to come. Your foot must be hurting.'

'My foot's fine. It has to be. And I told you, you'll scare the cows. Keep Harry company.'

But Harry didn't want company. Harry had homework. 'I'm way behind and there's a cool project I have to do on volcanoes.'

'Would you like some help?'

'Nah,' Harry told him. 'Thanks anyway but I'm used to doing stuff on my own.'

So was Marcus. Wasn't he? Dismissed and not enjoying the sensation as much as he might expect, Marcus made his way back to the beach.

At least here was pleasure. The water was gorgeous. He swam with the strength of a champion swimmer—not for nothing had he purchased an apartment with rights to an indoor lap pool—but he swam alone.

He was so unsettled. What was he doing?

Nothing. He was doing nothing. He wasn't needed.

It should make him contented. Two weeks holiday with nothing to do and no demands on him.

It made him... He didn't know what. He'd never had nothing to do in his life.

And he'd never wanted to be needed—by someone who didn't want him.

She watched him.

Peta milked her cows and all the time she was achingly aware of the man on the beach below the dairy. She could see him stroking back and forth across the bay. He looked superbly fit and at home in the surf, a far cry from the tailored New York businessman she'd fallen for five days ago.

Fallen for?

Uh-oh. The words settled. Then they settled some more. Had she fallen for Marcus Benson?

Of course she had.

'And I've fallen hard.'

She said it out loud and the cow whose teats she was cleaning swivelled round and stared down at her. Bemused.

'Do you guys fall inappropriately in love?' she demanded and the cow kept on staring.

She stared back, and then sat back on the wet cobbles and stared some more. What had she said?

The truth. She'd said the truth.

'How can I fall in love with Marcus Benson?' she asked herself. 'How can I possibly do that?'

She'd done it.

She turned and stared down at the sea. He was still stroking back and forth in steady, even strokes.

'We have absolutely nothing in common,' she told her cows. 'He's like some modern-day Prince Charming, Marcus the Magnificent, rushing round rescuing damsels in distress. It's all very well being a damsel in distress but it doesn't make for any sort of equal relationship.'

'Do you want an equal relationship?'

'I don't want to feel rescued for the rest of my life.'

'Yes, you do.'

'No.' She was talking to herself, to the cows, to anyone who'd listen. She had two sides of her brain competing. Or maybe it was her head and her heart.

'He'd come up my end of the veranda,' she told her cow. 'If I pressed.'

'You wouldn't have to press. You know darn well what it feels like whenever we touch. He feels it, too. I know he does. And he's a male.'

'Are you suggesting a spot of seduction?'

'You're married to him. It's hardly illegal.'

'Are you out of your mind? In two weeks he'll go away and…'

'And break your heart.'

Head and heart converged right there. The truth was unpalatable but it was unescapable.

'You've really fallen for him, haven't you?' she whispered.

'Maybe I have,' she whispered back. 'But it's not the knight in shining armour I want. Or…not very much. It's the man who makes Harry laugh. The man who cares for his assistant. Who makes Ruby smile. Who makes my heart twist…'

Stupid, stupid, stupid.

'So keep on with what you're doing,' she told herself. 'Keep it light. Keep it distant. And above all, keep your heart intact.'

'Your heart hasn't been intact for five days.'

'It has to be.'

Peta finished milking and returned to the house to find Harry packing sausages into a picnic basket.

'Beach night,' he said as she paused in the kitchen door.

Beach night. It was a custom they'd had for years. On a warm, still night like this they'd take their dinner to the beach, light a fire and cook it there. They'd swim and eat and return to the house at dusk.

It was a great idea. But... Was it a great idea when Marcus was around?

'He's still down there,' Harry told her. 'I went to see and he's gone for a run. He's just a dot on the horizon. I reckon we could get the campfire burning before he comes back.'

'I thought... Won't he want to cook? He bought lots of ingredients this morning.'

'It's our turn to cook—and we make great sausages,' Harry retorted. 'I'll watch them so you don't even get to burn them.'

'Gee, thanks.'

'Go get your swimsuit,' he told her. 'Hurry up.'

'But...'

'But what?'

But... She just knew it wasn't wise. Help.

They'd done this often. They were expert. By the time Marcus returned from his run, they had the fire burning and there was already a bed of hot coals. They'd scooped the flame from the centre and the sausages were sizzling in their pan. Marcus had seen the smoke in the distance and, as his jogging slowed to a walk, he realised they were here and waiting for him. The smell of sausages reached him and he had no need of Harry's shouted announcement.

'We're having a barbecue. Come and get it.'

Peta looked up from turning the sausages. She had on a swimming costume, but she'd thrown an oversized T-shirt over it. A pity...

'Hey, great pecs,' Harry called and he suddenly thought an oversized T-shirt was a really good idea. Peta was smiling at him and heck, he felt like blushing.

'Cut it out,' he growled.

'Are you brave enough to eat one of my sausages?' Peta

was saying, taking pity on him but still smiling. Harry hastened to reassure him.

'I've done most of the cooking and the cake for afterwards is one you guys bought at the bakers today.'

'So I needn't worry about being poisoned?' he asked and watched Peta's smile widen. She had the loveliest smile...

'My cooking's not that bad.'

'Yes, it is,' Harry said cheerfully. 'How many sausages, Marc? Three or four?'

'Six.' He sank down on the picnic rug. Sausages were something he normally wouldn't consider but they looked great. He'd been outside all day. He was starving, he realised. Even if Peta had burned them...

'If you're hungry enough you'll eat anything,' she said, as if reading his thoughts. 'Cooking classes are a waste of time.'

'And cooks are a waste of time?'

'I'm sure whatever's important to you is your own business,' she said primly and he grinned at the twinkle behind her green eyes. She had the capacity to tease. To make him smile inside. To make him feel...

Heck, to make him feel as if he did want to save her. To take her as his Cinderella and turn her into his companion for life. If she could always be here. Laughing at him. Gently mocking. Making his life light from within...

Stupid thought. Brought on by hunger and by sausages. He made a frantic attempt to haul his senses—all his senses—back to what was most important.

'Did you bring ketchup?' he asked.

'Ketchup?' Harry looked nonplussed.

'He means sauce,' Peta told him. 'He talks American.'

'You should learn Australian,' Harry said, handing over the sauce bottle. 'It's not really even sauce. It's dead horse. You say pass the dead horse and every Australian knows what you mean. So I guess dead horse is Australian for ketchup.'

'I have a lot to learn,' Marcus said faintly.

'You do,' Harry agreed. 'You're going to have to hurry up to fit it all into two weeks.'

They ate their sausages and their chocolate cake and then Peta went for a swim. Harry disappeared back to the house—to finish his volcanoes. Maybe Marcus should have gone, too, but how could he leave Peta swimming alone? The fact that he knew for sure she swam alone nearly every day didn't cut it. She was swimming alone now and he was staying.

In truth, he wanted to go back into the water as well, but he couldn't. Something stopped him.

Being in the water with her... Somehow it seemed like taking a step to her end of the veranda.

So he watched from a distance that was safe enough to almost seem detached. Almost.

She didn't swim as he had. She must be tired, he thought, as he watched her float on her back and gaze up into the flame-filled sunset. She'd been up since five this morning and for most of that time she'd been working hard. Her ankle *must* be hurting. She had no need to stretch her muscles as he had. She was content just to float.

She was content.

There was the difference, he thought. That was why he was so attracted to her. She was...peaceful. She'd settled back into her lot with joy. All she wanted was her farm and a future for her brothers. She had no need of anything else.

Problems that would fester and sour in others were nothing to her. The locals seemed to have sent her family to purgatory. She had little money and even less in the way of material possessions. Her future was bound by this tiny farm.

She wouldn't want what he had to offer, he thought, and the thought jarred.

Was he offering?

He didn't know.

But... Was he offering? The thought stayed. Like an insidious fleck of some matter he'd never heard of, it nestled in his brain and grew.

She was lovely. She made him smile. If he could take her back with him to the US... Turn her into his real happy ever after...

She wouldn't leave Harry.

She could bring him, too.

They'd never desert this farm.

He could put a farm manager in, he thought. Keep it safe for them. For their future.

What the hell was he thinking?

Nothing, he decided fiercely, or nothing that made sense. He'd decided early that he was a loner. What had changed now?

Peta had changed. Peta had changed him.

He watched her float on, desperate to join her but forcing himself to stay. Forcing himself to be sensible. By the time she emerged from the water he almost had himself convinced that his thoughts were a nonsense.

She came up the beach towards him, smiling, shaking her head with the water from the curls forming a glistening arc around her head. The dogs went flying down the beach to meet her and then wheeled away to chase gulls, to chase their tails, to simply soak up the warmth of the gathering dusk. Marcus sat back on the sand and watched Peta towel her hair, smile down at him, simply...simply be.

This was a sensation he'd never experienced before. For the last half hour he'd sat and done nothing, simply let the night soak into him. The place. The time.

Peta.

'You're lovely,' he said softly and his words hung in the night with a promise of something that was as yet undisclosed.

She stopped towelling and stared down at him. She'd giggle, he thought, or disclaim. Or arch her brows... He'd seen it all.

Instead she smiled, a gentle smile that was almost sympathetic.

'You're not bad yourself.'

'Gee, thanks.' It was inane but it was all he could manage. He swung himself to his feet and took her towel. 'Let me do that?'

She pulled away, ducking under the towel and backing.

'You don't want to.'

'Towel your hair? I do. Very much.'

'You know what I mean.' Her smile had died. 'The up close and personal bit isn't going to work.'

'Why not?'

'Neither of us are in a position to take it further.'

'We have two weeks...'

Wrong thing to say. Her face shuttered and the barriers went up. He could see it.

'Keep to your own end of the veranda, Marcus,' she told him. 'Or maybe it'd be better if you went back to Aunt Hattie's.'

'No!' Keep it light, he told himself desperately. Keep it light. 'Anything but that. Please don't condemn me to drown in pink.'

'Then don't touch me.'

'Why don't you want to be touched?'

'Who said I didn't want to be touched?'

'I assumed...'

'You assume all over the place,' she said crossly. 'You assume and assume and assume. I needed to accept your very generous offer to marry me and save my farm but that doesn't make me inclined to see you as Mr Wonderful for the rest of my life.'

'I didn't—'

'Want to be Mr Wonderful? No. Of course you didn't. You don't want to be up on a pedestal, and I don't want to keep you there. But when you come down...' She took a deep breath. 'You see, the problem is that when you come down from your pedestal, Marcus, then I see you just as a person. Or, not just as a person. As Marcus. Marc. Someone who's as needful as me. Someone who's even more lonely. And who's lovely and generous and who smiles and makes me feel crinkly inside and... Marcus, no, I didn't mean... I don't mean...'

He didn't get to hear what she didn't mean. How could he? Standing there with her hair dripping and her green eyes luminous and her face earnest, she was so obviously trying, trying to sort it in her mind, to tell the truth, and he'd have to be inhuman not to react.

She was so lovely. She gazed up at him and he reached forward and took her hands in his and their eyes locked and held.

Afterwards he couldn't remember who had moved first. Whether she'd stood on tiptoe and tilted her chin so her face met his, or if it had been he who'd drawn her into him and who'd cupped her face and tilted those lips...

No matter. Nothing mattered. Nothing mattered but that her body was being drawn into his and all he could feel was the warmth of her, the feel, the softness of the curves of her body against him. Dear heaven. The way her still damp body curved into his, her breasts moulding to his chest, her body melting, her lips tasting of sea and salt and warmth and desire and...

Peta.

He didn't know whether he said the word. Whether he said her name. He couldn't. How could he kiss and speak at the same time?

But it was as if he shouted it. It was as if his whole being was an exultant cry. Peta!

She was his. His! His hands held her, linking around the small of her back, tugging her closer, loving her, wanting her.

Loving her.

The world stopped right there. Or maybe it started. It was

as if his heart had stopped and then started afresh, anew, and he was someone else. The wonder. The joy.

He'd never known he could feel like this. All his life... The barrenness of his childhood. The awfulness of his time in the army. The knowledge that he could never let anyone close. That people disappeared all the time. The dreadful time in the Gulf, learning for the first time about friendship only to have it blasted to bits before his eyes. The years of business where all that mattered was money; where employees were people you treated with consideration because that way they worked best but you never, ever got involved...

He was involved now. He was involved right up to his heart.

And this woman was his wife. His wife! What miracle was this?

The kiss deepened. She was surrendering to him. Her lips had parted and he was plundering her mouth, taking the kiss deep, deeper...

Dear heaven, he wanted her. Her wanted her more than life itself. More than he'd ever dreamed he could want a woman.

'Peta...'

The kiss lasted for ever. The waves rolled in and out; the dogs wheeled back to them, vaguely worried at their immobility but fast bored. They wheeled away again. All except Ted-dog, who lay at his mistress's feet and softly whined, as if in warning.

She was heeding no warning. She'd given herself up to this moment, to the taste of him, to the feel of him. To the sensation he was feeling and that he knew she must feel, too. Here was her man and here was his woman. Man and woman. One.

It had to end. Somehow it had to end. The dusk was turning to night. The next move had to come and it had to come from him.

He pulled back somehow, and he stared down into her

face. She looked up at him, her eyes confused, tender, but there was still that wonderful smile. The laughter that had been there the first time he'd seen her. The laughter that caught and held...

'It seems... Peta, it seems that indeed you are my wife,' he said in a voice he hardly recognised. 'My wife.'

Her smile faded. 'What do you mean by that? "Indeed you are my wife..."'

'We made vows.'

'No.' She backed away, a trace of fear washing over her face. 'No, we didn't mean them.'

'We didn't mean them but they're coming true.'

'To have and to hold?'

'That's the one.'

'In sickness and in health. Until death us do part. To love and to cherish. To be one. I don't think so, Marcus.'

'Maybe not,' he said slowly. Not that. Not a complete joining. She was beautiful, he thought. She was the most desirable thing. But... Somehow he forced his confused mind to think. Somehow.

He was a loner. He'd been raised to be a loner; it had been instilled in him since birth and how could he change that now?

But... She was a loner, too. She was independent. She wasn't a clinging vine. She'd take what he could give.

'No,' she said and he stared.

'No?'

'I know what you're about to suggest and I want no part of it.'

'Peta, we're married.'

'We're not married.'

'Are you denying you want me?'

'Of course I want you,' she said shortly. 'Of course I do. You can feel it. Like I can feel you want me. But it's not enough. Not nearly enough.'

'Why not?'

'Because I want it all,' she said abruptly, her fingers going to her lips as if they were bruised. As they well might be. 'All or nothing. I won't do less.'

'What on earth do you mean by that?'

'I've fallen in love with you, Marcus.'

Just like that. He couldn't believe she'd said it. He stood back, stunned.

'I don't know what you mean.'

'I know you don't,' she whispered. 'But oh, Marcus, I want you to know. I want you to learn.'

'What the...'

But her face had closed. 'I'm being stupid,' she whispered. 'I'm looking for the fairytale. Stupid, stupid, stupid. And it's time for us to go home.' She stooped and lifted the picnic basket, breaking eye contact. He felt it. It hurt. It was a withdrawal and it hurt more than he could have imagined it would have. 'I'm sorry. I should never have kissed...have let you kiss....'

'We both wanted it.'

'I know. But not...to take it further.'

'We could,' he said urgently. 'Peta, listen. This love thing. I don't know it. I've never—never dreamed... But you, what I feel for you... I'm prepared to take a chance.'

'That's big of you.'

'No.' He tried to grasp her hands but she stepped back again. 'Don't. Peta, listen. We're married. You're my wife. We could do this. You could have this place as your base while Harry needs you but I'd rebuild. I'd make it fit for you. You'd visit me in New York when I had time to spare...'

'You'd make this place fit for me?' Her voice was suddenly dangerous.

'It's a dump, but it could be fabulous. The house site—could you imagine what we could build here?'

'And you'd visit...how often?'

'My work's in New York. But I'll have spent two weeks here now. I'll come when I can.'

'This is sounding more and more romantic.' Her voice said it wasn't romantic at all.

'You say you love me.'

'I don't love you like that.'

'Like what?'

'Like I'll give in to you because I love you. Like I'll take the crumbs because I love you. I've fallen hard for you, Marcus. Stupidly hard. But I have the sense to see it's never going to work.'

'It will work.' He reached out again. This time he caught her hands and she froze.

'Let go of me.'

'Peta—'

'I said let go. I've told you. The dogs are trained.'

'You're saying you'll set the dogs on me?' His voice rose incredulously.

'I surely will.'

His own anger rose then. What sort of a game was she playing? 'Hell, Peta, if I leave, if I go back to the States tomorrow you're sunk.'

'You're saying you'll call this whole thing off because I won't sleep with you?' she demanded. 'Because I won't fit in with your crazy plans for a mock marriage then you'll let Charles have the farm?'

He froze. What the hell...? 'Of course not. I'm not into blackmailing.'

She stared at him for a long moment, her anger turning icy. 'That's good then,' she said at last. 'So you're not blackmailing me and I'm not doing anything else. Good night, Marcus. It'd be better if you didn't come near my veranda tonight.'

'But...'

'Good night.'

CHAPTER TEN

WHAT followed were five very strained days.

'Don't you guys like each other any more?' Harry demanded.

'We like each other,' Marcus told him. He was cooking—a beef casserole with red wine and mushrooms. Harry would eat with him and take home a plateful for Peta to eat when she came in from the dairy.

For she'd refused to eat with him again. She'd put herself to work. She'd thrown herself into the farm and Marcus had been free to fend for himself.

It hurt—but in a sense he accepted it was right. They couldn't come near each other without sparks flying. He'd asked her to be his wife and she'd refused. That was her right and in a way it was nothing less than he'd expected. To love a woman was impossible.

To love anyone was impossible.

But he'd become attached to Harry—more attached than he cared to admit. While Peta spent her time with her cows, avoiding him, Harry hauled his homework to the pink house each night. He gossiped while Marcus cooked or worked on his laptop. He was inquisitive and friendly and bubbly with twelve-year-old enthusiasm, and Marcus knew that when this two weeks was up it wouldn't just be Peta he'd miss.

So why didn't he do something about it?

What could he do? He'd already asked her to take it further. He'd offered...

He hadn't offered enough. He hadn't offered himself.

'I'm a loner,' he told Harry now as they chopped onions over companionable tears. 'Peta's a loner, too. That's why she eats her dinner by herself.'

'She never eats dinner by herself when my brothers are at home. It's just 'cos she's avoiding you.'

'So she doesn't like me.'

'Of course she likes you.'

Maybe she likes me too much. The words were there, unsaid. The thought…

It made him feel…

Scared. He sliced his last onion and turned to get the steak from the fridge. Giving him time to get his voice in order.

'Peta and I are very different,' he told Harry. 'My life's in New York and Peta's is here. If we get…attached…'

'You're saying if you eat together you guys might fall in love?'

'No!'

'You might.' Harry was an intelligent and perceptive twelve-year-old, and now his face creased into a smile of pleasure. 'That'd be ace.'

'Why would it be ace?'

'You could stay here all the time. We could keep your cool little Morgan. You might even drive me to school in it.'

Some plans had to be scotched, and scotched fast. 'My life's in New York.'

'Why? You're working here. You work on the telephone and the computer. You don't have to milk cows for a living.'

'No, but there are other things.'

'Like what?'

'Harry, you don't have a clue what my life entails.'

'I bet this life is better,' he said solidly.

'I have a Porsche in New York,' Marcus told him, trying to put his decision in terms Harry could understand. But could he understand it himself? He slammed the cleaver through the steak as if it had personally offended him.

'But you've got your Morgan here already, and we've got an ace tractor. Our tractor's practically veteran.'

'Wouldn't you rather have a Porsche?'

'Why?'

'All twelve-year-old boys like Porsches,' he said with an air of near desperation.

'I know what Porsches are, of course,' Harry told him. 'My mate Rodney's got a bunch of posters up on his wall. And if you brought it out here I'd love to have a ride. But I don't reckon they're as good as Morgans. Is that what you want?' He cocked his head to one side, questioning. 'For Peta to go back to New York and drive your Porsche?'

'Peta is staying here,' Marcus told him and sliced the steak again. Hard. 'And I'm going back to New York. I'm sticking with my Porsche and Peta's sticking with her tractor.'

'Yeah, but Peta's got more than the tractor,' Harry said wisely. 'She's got the cows and the dogs and the house and me.' He grinned up at Marcus, confiding. 'You're going to have to come up with something better than a Porsche to compete with us.'

'I don't want to compete.'

'Peta's saying she isn't going to fall in love with you, too,' Harry told him, veering off at a tangent that was as stunning as it was perceptive. 'I think the two of you are nuts.'

Harry and Marcus were down at Hattie's house making dinner. Peta sat in her dairy longer than she needed. Much longer.

Soon she'd have to go home. There'd be a plate of something delicious in her oven, made by Marcus, brought home by Harry and left for her to eat by herself. Harry thought she was a dope.

He was right. She was a dope.

No. What was happening was dangerous. She knew enough about her own heart to realise how vulnerable she was.

She'd fallen so hard. Well, why wouldn't she? she asked herself bitterly. He'd saved her world. He'd dressed her as a princess. He'd swept her off her feet and now he was offering her...

He was offering her his world.

So she should take it.

Be contented with crumbs?

That's what he was offering, she thought. There was no way Marcus was offering his heart. He was holding himself separate, still playing the hero whose life didn't change with the redemption of his heroine.

Yeah, great.

How did Cinderella cope? she thought. Being grateful for the rest of her life. Knowing you owed the whole of your life to one man.

But she could sleep at night in his arms...

Marcus was hardly even offering that, she thought. Yeah, sleep in his arms when it was convenient. And the rest of the time... Sleeping here in a great house built with his money, being grateful, being endlessly grateful, or sleeping in that dreadful, cold apartment in New York, being more grateful still.

Stupid.

'The whole thing is stupid,' she told Ted-dog when his greying head nuzzled her hand in concern. 'He's dreaming. He's playing fairytales and one of us has to be sensible.'

I don't want to be sensible. I want to go down there and eat with them, and laugh with Marcus and enjoy the work he's helping Harry with, and walk home with him to my veranda and...

'Cut it out.'

She had to cut it out. There was no choice.

She gave her dog one final pat and rose to fetch the hose. She'd sluice out the dairy. Slowly.

And then she'd go home to dinner. To bed. Alone.

It was mid-morning when they came.

Peta was down the paddock, cleaning out a water trough. She saw the car turn into the driveway. Marcus was home, she thought. At nine in the morning it was five at night back in New York so he'd be in mid-conference with someone important. Maybe she'd better go back to the house and intercept the visitors before they interrupted him.

Maybe if he was interrupted he'd come out...

No. It had only been that first day that he'd spent time with her. He wouldn't come out. She'd told him to keep his distance and he obviously agreed.

Who would blame him? That night on the beach had been an aberration. She looked down at herself with a rueful smile. She was coated in mud. The trough had been overflowing and the ground around it was knee-deep mud. The float had blocked—the float that cut off the water flow when the trough was full—so she'd had to wade through mud and realign the float regardless of mess.

Urk.

She wiped her face with the back of her hand and then wished she hadn't. Yuk.

So who were the visitors?

No one important, she thought. Please.

Marcus was staring at his computer screen and seeing nothing. His razor-sharp mind seemed to have become fluff. Instead of the fierce concentration he applied to his work, his attention kept wandering to the window. Sometimes he'd see her, in her overalls and her gumboots, her hair pulled back from her face but wisping in escaping curls. Sometimes her face would be smudged with dirt. Usually her face would be smudged with dirt. She'd be doing something heavy and filthy, like carting buckets or driving the tractor or...

Or any of the things he'd offered to save her from. She shouldn't have to do it. She shouldn't want to!

And there was the rub. He'd envisaged his happy ever after and she wanted no part of it.

'Are you there, Mr Benson?' The online teleconferencing was in full swing and he should be concentrating. But Peta...

He could see her. She was down the paddock, delving in a trough of some sort. He could see the mud from here.

It looked…fun?

'I'm here.' It took a huge effort to haul his eyes from the window and back to the screen.

And then he heard a car turn into the driveway.

Great. He'd have to wrap it up now. Peta was too far away to welcome visitors.

'I need to leave this, gentlemen,' he told the screen, not even caring that the corporate problem they were discussing wasn't near to being resolved.

He had his own problems and they were nothing to do with New York.

Or maybe they were. He walked outside and a car was pulling up before the main house. As he stared in astonishment, out stepped Darrell. Darrell gave him a wave, then walked around the car and opened the passenger door.

Ruby.

'It was too complex to do from New York.'

They were all seated on the edge of Peta's veranda. Peta had brought out lemonade and handed it out like a good hostess. She'd ditched her gumboots. Now she sat and swung her feet. One sock had a hole in it. Her toe peeped out.

Marcus was trying to concentrate on two things—what Ruby was saying and Peta's toe. If anyone had ever told him he'd find a woman's toe erotic he would have said they were crazy.

Her toe was driving him wild!

'What was too complex to do from New York?' he managed and Ruby beamed. She looked thoroughly pleased with herself. Darrell sat by her side and he, too, looked like the cat that had just got the canary.

What had got into the pair of them?

'It's about your will,' Ruby said.

'My will?'

'Peta's aunt's will,' Ruby told him, as if humouring a child. 'For heaven's sake, Marcus, focus here.'

Ruby—telling *him* to focus? 'Okay.' He put up his hands as if in surrender. 'Hattie's will. What about it?'

'You asked me to find out about it before you left. There wasn't time for any investigations before you needed to be married, but we've done it now.' She turned to Peta. 'You told Marcus that your aunt had high calcium levels and was confused in the last weeks of life?'

'I... Yes.' Peta frowned. 'She *was* a bit confused. She wasn't all that clear when she left here. I was really worried.'

'Did you know that your doctor here took blood samples two weeks before she left Australia?'

'She was having blood tests all the time.'

'That's right.' Ruby pulled a form from her capacious bag. 'One of the forms Marcus had you sign before you left gave us the power to check medical records. We put in a request for the information on the grounds that she's now deceased and you stand to lose.'

'How do I stand to lose?'

'You stand to lose by her change of will. There's an earlier will leaving you the farm.'

Peta's frown deepened. 'I remember. She always said she wrote one. But that was well before she went back to the States.'

'Of course it was,' Ruby told her. 'And we found it. Our lawyers discovered that Hattie wrote a will two years before she died—long before she got sick—and she lodged it with a Yooralaa solicitor.'

'What's that got to do with me?' Peta asked.

'That's why we've come,' Ruby said triumphantly. 'I knew you two couldn't do the investigations. You had to stay on the farm and be happily married. I was planning on sending one of Marcus's solicitors but then I thought, maybe I could do it. And Darrell decided to come, too.' For the first time she looked a little disconcerted. Embarrassed, Marcus thought, stunned.

But she was moving on.

'And guess what we've found?' she told them. 'Hattie's medical records. Marcus was right. The tests here said her calcium levels were through the roof before she left Australia. Once she had medical attention in the States, her records there confirm it. The calcium levels would force any judge to concede that her judgement was significantly impaired for at least six weeks before her death. Darrell and I have been here for two days and we've been working hard. We've had legal opinions from Australian lawyers and we've had legal opinions from US lawyers. They concur. The new will doesn't stand, Peta. The farm is yours. Married or not, Charles can't touch you.'

Peta stared, not immediately comprehending. 'It's... The farm's mine?'

'It's yours.' Ruby was still smiling. She cast a sideways glance at Marcus, expecting him to be pleased. 'Marcus told me to do everything to get the will overturned. He suspected this.'

'He suspected...'

'He wasn't sure, of course, or he'd never have married you.'

'No.' Peta looked blankly at Marcus. 'No. Of course he wouldn't.'

'So now all you have to do is get the marriage annulled,' Darrell told them. And then he, too, smiled. Teasing. 'You can use the old non-consummation line. Unless, of course, you have...'

'No,' Marcus snapped. 'We haven't.'

'That's good,' Ruby told them, her smile fading. She looked from Peta to Marcus and back again, for the first time seeming to sense the deep undercurrents running between them. 'I'm glad you've had that much sense.'

'Ruby...'

'Well, that's what we came to tell you,' she said, setting

down her lemonade glass with a definite clink. 'Adam and Gloria presented Charles with the legal evidence invalidating the will last night our time. The evidence is indisputable. Peta, the farm is yours and no conditions apply. So... There's no need to keep on with the marriage. I've brought the annulment forms. If you both sign them you can go on with your lives as if this had never happened. Marcus, there's no need for you to stay.'

'No.'

'Unless you want to,' she added. 'You really could do with a holiday.'

'This isn't much of a holiday,' Marcus told her and Peta flushed.

'Our accommodation isn't quite five-star,' Peta muttered. She, too, lay down her glass and turned to Marcus. 'So you can go home?'

'Yes.' There was nothing else to say.

'I need to thank you. So much...'

'There's no need.'

'There is.' It was an absurdly formal little tableau but there seemed no right way to go forward from here. 'I can't... I don't know how to repay you. If I could think of anything...'

'My offer still stands,' Marcus told her while Ruby and Darrell watched in silence.

'What—to make our marriage last?'

There was an audible intake of breath from Ruby but Marcus didn't move his gaze from Peta.

'That's right.'

'Marriage when you can fit me around the edges.'

'Don't be ridiculous,' he told her. 'We could do this. If you'd be prepared to give it a chance...'

'It doesn't have a chance.'

'What doesn't have a chance?' Ruby demanded and Peta turned to her, despairing.

'He wants to build me a mansion, right here, instead of my veranda. He wants to visit for a couple of weeks a year and for the rest of the time he wants to install me in his black marble apartment and keep his bed warm for the twenty minutes a day he can spare for me.'

'That's not fair,' Marcus snapped.

'What else are you offering?'

'I run a financial empire, Peta,' Marcus told her. 'I've never asked anyone else to marry me…'

'And I should be really grateful,' Peta told him. 'I'm sure Cinderella did it really well. But not me.'

'What else do you want?' They were almost unaware that Ruby and Darrell were staring, agog. This was too important to be distracted.

'You.'

'I don't know what you mean.'

'Then figure it out,' Peta told him. She sighed and her shoulders slumped as the rest of the world appeared to enter her consciousness again. She turned and faced Ruby and Darrell. 'I'm sorry. You've been so good. Do you have to go back to the States immediately or can I put you up here for a night or so? My accommodation's pretty basic.'

'It looks great to me,' Darrell told her. He looked sideways at Marcus. 'I've spent months on a battlefield. Marcus has, too. I've no need for marble tiles.'

'Will you go straight home?' Ruby asked Marcus and Marcus tried to get his addled brain to think. He might as well. This was stupid. What was Peta expecting? That he share her gumboots? He hadn't worked so hard all his life for this.

'Yeah,' he told them. 'I will.'

'I haven't had a holiday for years,' Ruby told him, still eyeing him with a dubious look that said her mind was running at a tangent. 'Do you mind if I stay on?'

'Go for it. Just as long as you like pink.'

'There's nothing wrong with pink,' Peta flashed. 'If you're happy you don't notice.'

'Of course you notice.'

'Get a life, Marcus,' she told him.

'It's you who's refusing—just because you don't like black marble.'

'If you think that's the reason I'm refusing then you have rocks in your head,' she told him. 'I'm refusing because you can't see that it's not important. That I've offered the only thing that's important and you haven't a clue how to return it. And I'm not even sure that you want to. Ever.'

He left half an hour after Harry returned from school. He could have left earlier but the thought of leaving before saying goodbye to the kid was almost impossible.

And saying goodbye even then was incredibly hard.

'I sort of hoped you guys might have made it long term,' Harry told him, trying not to let his almost-manly chin wobble. 'I sort of liked cooking. And you helping with projects and stuff.'

'Your brothers will be home soon.'

'Yeah, but they don't stay and they're not the same. And you made Peta smile...'

'Only at the start.'

'Yeah, but you could again if you wanted to,' Harry said with perspicacity. 'Couldn't you?'

There was no answer to that. 'I have to go.'

'Did you say goodbye to Peta?'

'She's milking.'

'You're mean,' Harry said. His jaw set a little and he moved around Marcus's car and gave a kick to the tyre. 'I thought you were a friend.'

'Harry...'

'See you.' He picked up his school bag and sloped off into the house.

Darrell and Ruby were nowhere to be seen. Peta was in the dairy.

There was no one to watch him drive away.

He went.

* * *

Peta was putting cups on one of her favourite cows when she heard his engine start. She turned and watched as his lovely little Morgan turned out of the driveway and headed out towards the highway.

Terrific. He was gone.

She put her head on the cow's warm flank and wept.

'Are you going to tell me what that was all about?'

It was late that night. Darrell and Harry had both gone to bed, Harry reluctantly but Darrell because his head was still halfway between New York and Australia. Peta and Ruby were left alone. They gravitated towards the veranda and sat, watching the moon out over the ocean.

'Are you saying he really asked you to stay married to him?' Ruby demanded and Peta nodded.

'You heard him. Sort of.'

'Are you intending to explain?'

'He didn't say he loved me. He just said... He figured it could work. He kissed me and he liked it. He enjoyed playing fairy godfather, genie, whatever. He'd give us more. Build this place up to be a mansion and come and visit for a few weeks each year so he could see how benevolent he was. And I could visit him in New York—I think he actually used that word, visit—and stay in his horrible mausoleum of an apartment and be there waiting for him in between corporate necessity.'

'It...it doesn't sound like a romantic kind of proposal,' Ruby said a trifle unsteadily and Peta eyed her with suspicion.

'Are you laughing at me?'

'Oh, my dear, I'd never laugh.' Ruby hesitated and then placed a large hand on Peta's. 'You did the right thing. He has to see...'

'He'll never see.'

'Sometimes miracles happen,' Ruby said gently. There was a moment's silence and then she continued. 'For instance, me and Darrell...'

'Now that's something I don't understand.'

'Darrell needs me,' she said simply. She closed her eyes. The sound of the sea intensified in the stillness and when Ruby opened her eyes again there was a peace about her that Peta had never seen. 'Life's been bleak,' she said. 'I couldn't put my pain behind me. But with you...playing brides, seeing what was happening to Marcus while he thought you needed him... I don't know. I let my guard down for a moment, I guess. And then Darrell took me home after your wedding and we got to talking. His body... He's so scarred and he's closed off as well. We talked and we talked and we've been together ever since.' She smiled, a slow soft smile that contained all the joy in the world. 'I guess we'll be together for ever. It's that simple.'

It's that simple.

The words wafted around them. There was joy here, but also...

Sadness. Despair.

'He can't see it,' Peta said.

'You mean... You love him?'

'Of course I love him.'

'You told him?'

'Mmm.'

'And he ran.'

'No. He offered me marriage. On terms.'

'For a billionaire, he really is a dope,' Ruby told her.

Silence. The silence went on and on. And on.

'Well,' Ruby said at last. 'Well. What we need here, girl, is a plan.'

'A plan?'

'It's what Marcus is principally good at. Corporate plans. Takeovers. Strategies. He's spent eight years teaching me how to do it. So let's get to work.'

'Ruby...'

'You telling me to butt out, girl?'

'No,' Peta told her, half laughing. 'No, Ruby, I need all the help I can get.'

'Spoken like a true Benson,' Ruby told her. 'We haven't annulled that marriage yet!'

'So what's the plan?'

'Silence.'

'Is that all?'

'He's had a taste of something he didn't know existed,' Ruby told her. 'Let's leave him alone to think about it.'

CHAPTER ELEVEN

THE telephone service was out of order.

'Out of order?' Marcus had his people contact the telecommunications authorities in Australia, only to be told that the fault had been reported as non-urgent. The people concerned had cellphones. And no, he couldn't obtain those numbers, no matter how much he paid.

He knew Ruby's cellphone number. She had it turned off. She'd sent a fax from the local post office saying she'd decided to take a month off and learn how to milk cows.

Ruby was milking cows while Marcus was...

Marcus was earning money. Launching a new range of Internet software. Ruling his empire.

Doing what he always did.

'How long can silence last?' Peta asked and Ruby paused from her first attempt at milking a cow.

'As long as it takes. Be patient.'

'I can't.'

'You can.'

Two weeks. Three.

Marcus took a lunchtime stroll down to Tiffany's. He spent a long time staring at the jewel cases and in the end chose a single diamond. Perfect. Flawless. Worth a king's ransom.

He insured it for another king's ransom and sent it courier.

'To my Cinderella,' the card read. 'Please reconsider.'

By return courier came a small box containing the diamond and something else. A withered daisy chain.

'I'm not Cinderella. I'm just me. I love you, Marcus. But I don't want your diamonds.'

Nothing else.

He stared at the note for a long time. So long that his temporary assistant grew nervous.

'Are you okay, Mr Benson?'

'I'm fine,' he told her, his face grim. He handed over the diamond. 'Can you arrange to have this returned?'

'Oh, Mr Benson...' The girl looked down at the diamond and let out her breath on an ecstatic sigh. 'Oh, Mr Benson, any woman would die for a diamond like this.'

'Not my woman,' he said before he could stop himself. 'Not the woman I love.'

'Are you sure?'

It was the end of three long weeks and Peta was still staring out at the moon every night. Somewhere under this moon was Marcus. Alone.

'He has to see,' Ruby told her. 'He has to have time to realise what he's missing.' She gave a rueful smile. 'It took me more than twenty years to learn to love again. Let's hope Marcus can do it faster.'

'And if he doesn't?'

'Then we panic,' Ruby told her. 'But not yet. There's things we can do.'

Marcus was in a meeting when the next delivery arrived. His secretary interrupted him with apologies. 'But you did ask me to let you know if anything came from Australia.'

Two boxes were waiting.

The first box contained Peta's wedding dress. Satin, lace, matching shoes, ribbons from her hair. Regardless of the curious eyes of his office staff, Marcus lifted it out. He could smell the perfume she'd worn that day. There was a small note.

'Thank you for the fairytale.'

'There's another box,' his secretary told him, obviously agog to see what it held.

He took a grip—sort of—and opened the second box.

It was a pair of gumboots. His size. And another note.

'Reality is more fun.'

He set the gumboots down on the gleaming mahogany desk. Ridiculous.

Fun?

Ridiculous.

The time dragged. He put the gumboots and the wedding dress in the top of his closet and left them there. The concept of him ever needing either again was crazy!

He dated again. Or he tried to date again. The women seemed shallow, pointless, cold.

Peta…

Peta was on the other side of the world.

She'd said she loved him. If she loved him why wouldn't she take him? he asked himself. On his terms.

Because, a small voice whispered behind his heart, because his terms were…cruel?

What he'd offered was all he was prepared to concede, he thought grimly. To promise more was to promise something that he couldn't deliver.

Coward, he told himself.

But to take the next step…

To take another step was impossible.

Ruby contacted him at the end of the month. For a moment he couldn't believe he was hearing right, and then he excused himself from his meeting and locked himself in his office to take the call where he could concentrate.

'Ruby. Where the hell are you?'

'Where you should be,' she informed him cheerfully. 'Here. In Australia. Having a really good time.'

'You're my employee.'

'Not any more. I quit. Darrell's asked me to marry him.'

Silence. He thought of his clinical, efficient assistant who in the years he'd employed her had never let her personal life interfere with her work. She'd never had a personal life!

She was marrying his dour, scarred sergeant?

'He's lovely,' Ruby said in a voice he hardly recognised. 'You know he is. And we've decided to stay on and help Peta for a while. This farm really needs more than just Peta to run it. Marcus, I can milk!'

'Peta's never let you near her cows!' He couldn't believe it.

'It took time to gain their trust,' Ruby conceded. 'A month. Darrell and I have been helping to bring the cows in, getting them used to us, learning each one's name. And now I can put the cups on. I can clean the vats. I know all about mastitis and bacteria counts and swishing down the dairy's my favourite. Oh, Marcus, it's so much fun.'

'But...you belong here.'

'No. I belong here. Darrell's here. No one stares at his scarred face here. He's much better at milking than me. Peta says we can redecorate the pink house and live in it for as long as we want. We've both got savings and Darrell's got his veteran's pension. We can be really comfortable. We don't need much here. There's so much already. We can be really rich—with nothing. Nothing but each other.'

Silence. Marcus sank down on to the desk behind him, aware suddenly that he needed its support.

'You know that I asked Peta to be married to me?' he said at last. 'Properly, I mean.'

'Are you talking about sending her that darned fool diamond?'

'It cost a fortune,' he snapped and from the other side of the world he could hear the smile crossing Ruby's face.

'Why would Peta need a ring that cost a fortune?'

'She said she loves me.'

'She told me that, too.'

'So why won't she marry me?'

'You didn't ask her to stay married to you,' Ruby said softly, her voice growing serious. 'You know you didn't.'

'How the hell...'

'You asked her to visit you in New York. Visit! You implied she'd be your society hostess. Your wife in the short periods you had time for her. You told her you'd stay here for a couple of weeks a year. What sort of marriage is that?'

'If she loved me...'

'She'd give up her life for you. Is that what you want? Well, maybe she would. Maybe she's breaking her heart because she can't.'

'She can.'

'You know, the real Cinderella didn't have commitments,' Ruby said gently. 'Stepping out of rags into riches is all very well if you have nothing to leave behind. Nothing to lose. As I remember, Cinderella had no alternative. But there's Harry.'

'Harry could come with her.'

'And her three other brothers? They're still really close. She'd never leave them. She has an old dog, Ted-dog. You met him. Ted-dog went off his feed last time Peta was in New York. He'd pine. So... Peta has a life here. And what are you offering? Diamonds? Diamonds don't make very good bedtime companions.'

'Ruby...'

'It's your fear,' Ruby told him. 'I've never said this before because I've been just the same as you. Dead scared of life. But you know very well that Peta could never accept your offer of riches and position. She loves you.'

'How can she?'

'Of course she does,' Ruby snapped. 'But you, you don't love her. You love what she could be if she forgot her responsibilities—her family, her farm—yet it's that very loyalty that's made you want her. You're deceiving yourself, Marcus. You're telling yourself you'd like a wife but you're making it impossible for her to be just that. You're a loner. Your offer of marriage to Peta is nothing more than a taunt.'

'Ruby...'

'I know, I know,' she said and her tone was suddenly almost cheerful. 'This is no way to speak to my employer. Isn't it lucky I quit?'

He was left alone. With his corporation. His fortune. His position in society. With the black marble in his bathroom.

Hell!

It took three months. Three months when every morning Peta sat in her dairy and thought of what she'd left in New York. Three months when the annulment papers weren't served. She should do something about it herself, she thought, but each time she raised it Ruby said, leave it.

'He won't...'

'He must,' Ruby told her.

And then one morning she could bear it no longer. She woke and found Darrell and Ruby were already bringing in the cows. Harry was preparing his own breakfast, interspersing cornflakes with wedges of chocolate cake Ruby had made the night before. Peta walked into the kitchen: the warmth of the old wood stove reached out to meet her and her ancient dog wuffled around her feet.

And she couldn't bear it.

'Harry, would you mind if I went back to New York for a bit?' she asked, and Harry gave it his careful consideration while he attacked his cornflakes.

'To fetch Marcus?'

She took a deep breath. 'Someone has to.'

'Ruby says we have to wait for him to be sensible.'

'I think I've waited long enough.'

Harry thought about it some more. And nodded. 'Okay. Ace by me.'

'You'll be all right here by yourself?'

'Darrell and Ruby will look after me. Will Marcus come, do you think?'

'I hope so.'

'Tell him Ruby cooks now. He doesn't have to eat your sausages.'

'If he loves me he'd eat my sausages.'

'Even Ted-dog doesn't like your sausages,' Harry told her. 'But good luck.'

Marcus emerged from a meeting and his chauffeur was waiting for him. Which was unusual. Robert usually met him at street level. What was even more unusual was his message.

'There's someone waiting for you on the fire-escape.'

'What do you mean, there's someone on the fire-escape?' he demanded.

'Just what I said. Someone with lunch.' Robert smiled and Marcus's heart gave a lurch.

'Is it…'

'See for yourself, sir,' Robert told him.

Peta.

Of course it was Peta.

She was sitting on the fire-escape where he'd first met her, only this time she was seated on a step out of range of the swinging door. She was wearing tattered shorts, a faded T-shirt and sandals. She was holding a bag of bagels and a couple of drink containers were by her side.

'Hi,' she said and held out her bag. 'You want a bagel?'

'Peta,' he said cautiously and she smiled.

'Yep. You remember me?'

Remember her? It was all he could do not to lunge forward and take her in his arms—right now. But her expression forbade it. She was smiling but she was formal. Holding him at arm's length.

'What are you doing here?' he managed.

'I thought we could start again.' She bit into a bagel.

'You thought we could start again?'

'We could share.' She wiggled over on the step so there was room beside her. 'I've brought enough for two.'

'But why…'

'I figured out we started all wrong,' she said. 'You saved me and I'm very grateful. By the way, I see Charles's plate has disappeared from your list of occupants. That makes me even more grateful. But no relationship can exist on gratitude. Ruby says I should leave you a bit longer but I got lonely. So I figured… If I was lonely you might be worse. I thought I should come across and see if we can be friends.'

'Friends.' She was still sitting on her step, holding out her bag of bagels. She was taking his breath away. 'I don't know whether I can be a…a friend.'

'Everyone needs a friend,' she said, biting into her bagel as if the bagel and not the words were the most important thing. There was a moment's pause while she chewed and swallowed. Then she stared down at the bitten bagel, considering where to bite next. Not looking at him. Chatting as if they were casual acquaintances. Nothing more. 'According to Ruby, you think you can live in isolated splendour for ever,' she told him. 'But black marble's not all it's cut out to be.'

'No?'

'Sit. Eat your bagel.' She held out her bag again and he sat and took one without thinking. The last thing he wanted at this minute was a jelly-filled bagel.

'We get to share,' she said and the seriousness in her voice was unmistakeable.

'Share what?'

'What friends share. Bagels. Fire-escape steps. Life.'

'Peta…'

'I love you, you know,' she said conversationally. 'You might have rescued me, but now it's my turn to try to rescue you. To save you from a lifetime of black marble. If you want saving. But you have to decide. Now... Tell me if I'm intruding. Robert says you're busy.'

'I'm always busy.'

'See, that's the thing I don't understand,' she said, licking a jelly-smeared finger with concentration. 'You're a billionaire already. You're busy making money. Why? So you can buy more black marble?'

'No.'

'So what else do you want to buy?'

He stared at her. They were seated side by side but she'd pulled back as he'd sat so she was two feet away from him. Too far.

What did he want to buy?

'A new bed for your veranda?' he said cautiously. 'A big one.'

'Now you're talking.' She beamed. 'What else?'

'Maybe a jet. So I can commute.'

'What, come home at weekends?'

'Home?'

'Home's where I am, Marcus,' she said softly. 'I love you. Ruby says I should stop saying it, and let you figure it out for yourself, but I can't. I love you so much that I can't bear it a minute longer. I love you, I love you, I love you. And I love you so much that there's no way I can accept your offer of a couple of weeks a year and a few weekends thrown in for good measure. I'd go crazy. That's the life for someone who wants your position. But I don't want the position, Marcus. I just want you.'

'I can't...'

'I know. You can't take it in. That's why I'm here. Now don't panic. I'm not here for ever. I'm just here for a little while to see... To see if there's any possibility that it can work.' She rose, crumpling her empty carrier bag and looking at it ruefully. 'That's lunch. Finished. But you've got things to do, places to go. I'll meet you tomorrow.'

To say he was bewildered would be an understatement. He reached out to grasp her but she backed off fast.

'Same time, same place?' she said. 'Bagels okay with you?'

'No!'

'I'm not eating caviar.'

'You don't have to eat caviar.' He made a lunge but she was fast, dancing down to the next landing and laughing up at him.

'See you tomorrow. Bye.'

It was a really long day.

Marcus went to his afternoon meeting but he had to excuse himself. He could think of nothing but Peta. Peta of the ragged clothes, the dancing eyes, the lovely voice...

I love you, I love you, I love you.

People had said it before.

No one had meant it. No one like Peta.

All he had to do was step forward. Risk everything?

Risk what? His independence? His money? His black marble?

Halfway through the afternoon he left the building and made his way to Central Park. And walked. Never before had he walked as he walked that afternoon. He walked and he walked, unaware of where he was going, unaware of the people around him, unaware of anything but Peta's lovely face and her dancing eyes and her words...

I love you, I love you, I love you.

Such a simple thing. To take this step...

Fairytale heroes had never had it this hard, he thought ruefully. Find your Cinderella, marry her in all honour, install her in your palace and get on with your life.

His Cinderella had had the happy ending. The white lace and wedding vows. His Cinderella wanted more.

A friend? A friend as well as a hero?

And finally he found he was smiling. The longer he walked the more he smiled.

She was no Cinderella. She was his own lovely Peta. She'd sent back the white lace and offered him gumboots instead. He'd ignored her offer. So she'd followed him. She was doing her own rescuing. She was offering him...

He knew what she was offering him. The world.

The world his mother had taught him to believe in was a world where the white lace was everything. He'd rejected that, but he hadn't seen that there was an alternative.

A lovely, lovely alternative called Peta.

Where was she?

She wouldn't be staying at the same dangerous place she'd stayed at last time, he thought. No! Almost as soon at the thought entered his head he was in a cab heading across town.

She wasn't there.

At least she wasn't staying somewhere dangerous. The thought was a little comforting but not very.

Where the heck was she?

She'd meet him same place, same time tomorrow? Could he wait that long? Short of phoning every hotel in New York it seemed he had no choice.

Dammit, what was money for? He headed back to his offices, put his staff on to the job and together they phoned every hotel in New York.

No Peta. Where...?

He travelled across town to Ruby's and then to Darrell's apartments. Both of them were locked and deserted.

There was nothing else he could do. He just had to wait.

Or... Maybe there was something he could do. Maybe there were a few things...

CHAPTER TWELVE

SHE sat on the fire-escape and waited. To say she felt ridiculous would be an understatement. What was she doing? Sitting on a fire-escape with a bag of bagels, waiting for a New York billionaire to come and share them with her?

Waiting for him to figure out what she was trying to do. Waiting for him to see that it was important.

Twelve. Twelve-thirty. He was running late.

Running late? What, was she crazy? Late for what? Late for his bagel?

The door swung open. And it was Marcus. He'd obviously just come from a meeting of some sort—he was wearing the lovely Armani suit she'd seen the first time she met him.

He was carrying his briefcase. And a shopping bag.

'Good afternoon,' he said gravely and she gave him a tiny, faltering smile.

'H...hi.'

'Bagels again?'

'I like bagels.' She knew she sounded defensive but she couldn't help it.

'Can I sit down?'

'Sure.' She edged along on her step and eyed him sideways. 'Be my guest.'

He sat. He propped his shopping bag against the railings, set his briefcase between the two of them and flipped it open.

'I brought my contribution. I hope to heaven it hasn't spilled. Sam assured me the container was safe.'

'Your contribution?'

'Clam chowder and corn flapjacks. I remembered that you like them.'

'I do,' she said cautiously and watched as he hauled two

bowls, two spoons, two plates from his case. 'You want to share my bagels?'

'That's the plan. If you share my chowder.'

'Deal.'

He didn't say anything more. He served his chowder, they split the flapjacks and they ate. The silence between them was strange but not strained. The sun was warm on their faces. For now, they were content to eat and let what was passing between them hold sway.

It was a really strange meal, Peta thought, but there was such a warmth running between them. Such a force of...love? They were a foot apart but she could feel his strength as if he was holding her. He was smiling. He looked as if he was smiling inside.

Somewhere inside her, something started to sing.

'Too bad if someone wants to use the fire-escape,' she murmured and Marcus attempted to look grave.

'They can find their own. This one's taken. For however long we need it.'

'It's a shame we can't settle here for ever,' she said softly. 'On neutral territory.'

'I've been meaning to talk to you about that.'

'You have?'

'This love thing...' He set down his plate and turned to her. And waited while she set down her plate. 'I'm not very good at it,' he confessed.

'You have the basic ingredients.'

'Yeah, but not the recipe.'

'I'm sure we could teach you. Me and Harry and Ruby and Darrell and Ted-dog...'

'I think you already have,' he said softly.

There was definitely a singing thing going on inside her. Marcus was smiling at her. Smiling with her. He wasn't moving towards her, but he didn't need to. This big, smiling man with the eyes that had seen far too much but had finally found their home.

With her.

She smiled back at him, and somehow... Somehow right at that moment she knew that it would be okay.

There'd be a place for them. There'd be some way they could do this.

'I have a couple of gifts,' he told her and her joy faltered a little.

'Marcus, I don't want diamonds.'

'No jewels at all?' His face fell. He felt in his jacket pocket and brought out a jeweller's box.

Nestled on white velvet was indeed a jewel but this was no diamond. It was a twist—a knot of strung silver, breathtakingly simple and breathtakingly lovely. Embedded in the web of silver strands were three tiny sapphires. Tiny but perfect. They glistened in the sunlight, and in their depths was the colour of Peta's eyes, the colour of the sea.

'It's a ring made specially for you,' Marcus told her. 'Because of who you are. Because of what you are. I know you don't want tiaras and ball-gowns but I needed to do something to express my love for you.' Then, as she opened her mouth to speak, he placed his finger on her lips. 'And there's more. I might as well get it over and done with. Show you the full catastrophe.'

He flipped up the shopping bag. Out tumbled...gumboots?

They weren't just gumboots, though. They were gumboots with attitude. They were amazing—as if Frida Kahlo had used each as a blank canvas for the most amazing artwork Peta had ever seen.

There were four gumboots. Four stunning pieces of art. Two Peta's size. Two Marcus's size.

'I had to move heaven and earth to have a friend do these for us,' Marcus said. 'He's sealed them so we can use them in the dairy. Together.'

She gasped. She held a gumboot up and turned it around, awed. 'You think the cows will let us milk with these on?'

'I think the cows will love them. When they get used to them.'

'How can they get used to them,' Peta whispered, 'in two weeks a year...?'

'Well, there's another thing we need to discuss,' Marcus said. 'Now I know you love your veranda. And I know you won't let the boys sleep at your end. But would you look at this?'

From the depths of his briefcase he hauled out a set of plans and, while she sat in stunned silence, he spread them out for her perusal. The wind was starting to rise, so he spread them over the landing and weighed each corner down with a gumboot.

'Plans,' he said in satisfaction.

'Plans?'

'Here's your veranda. It's turned into a master bedroom in the plans but it's still very much a veranda.'

'Marcus...' She shook her head in bewilderment. 'I told you. I don't want a mansion.'

'Will you cut it out?' He was grinning at her. 'Peta, there's a huge gap between your veranda and what the rest of the world calls a mansion. I think we're pretty safe adding extravagances like, say, a hot shower.'

'A shower...'

'I know. Sheer luxury,' he retorted. 'A friend—Max—has made these plans up. He's worked from my memory and he worked in a rush but it's a start. Your veranda, although I hope we can rename it *our* veranda, stays intact—almost—though the holes in the floorboards will have to go. The kitchen, I love—and so do you—so that stays as well. Just restored as it should be. He's added a big living room out the back for when the boys come home—somewhere they can entertain their friends. A bedroom for each of them. Two bathrooms. Now I know two bathrooms sounds a lot but hey, I swear it still doesn't rank as a mansion. I bet your everyday run-of-the-mill mansion has at least four.'

'Marcus...'

'And this bit out here is the office,' he told her, and she heard, for the first time, a hint of real anxiety in his voice. 'I thought...seeing Ruby's staying there anyway we could set up a base. I could delegate a lot of the responsibility to our top people here, and Ruby and I could work with teleconferencing, faxes, the Internet. I mean, we are an Internet company. It does seem reasonable. Mind, I'd probably need to visit New York—twice a year, maybe, but for not more than ten days or so. If I promised faithfully not to use first-class travel and put my knees under my chin... What do you think, Peta?'

What did she think? Her world was exploding around her, shards of joy bursting in all directions. He was looking at her with such a look of anxiety. Her Marcus.

Her love.

'You'd sit in economy class for me?'

'I'd sit anywhere for you.'

'Even on a fire-escape?'

'If you were there.'

'Marcus, I'd stay in a black marble apartment if you were there,' she admitted and the look of anxiety faded.

'Really?'

'Really.'

'Will you wear my ring?'

Once again, that absurd anxiety. She looked down at the tiny velvet box and there was no choice. She lifted the ring and slipped it on her finger. It glistened in the sunlight; she held it out and she fell in love all over again.

'Oh, Marcus. It's lovely.'

'Really?'

'Really.' She faltered. 'I should have something for you.'

'You have you. You have your love.'

'Will...will you wear gumboots for me?' she said in a voice that wasn't quite steady.

He kicked off his shoes and his spectacular gumboots were

on his feet in an instant. She looked down at them and she managed a shaky chuckle. 'They're wonderful.'

'Did you know that I fell in love with your bare toe?' he asked and she looked at him with wonder in her eyes.

'How can that be?'

'Sexiest toe I've ever seen. Just like Cinderella.'

'Marcus…'

'Mmm.'

'Do you intend to kiss me or will I kiss you?'

'Well, there's a problem.'

'A problem?' Her heart felt as if it must surely burst. Her Marcus. Her love…

'I'm a bit worried about this fairytale thing we appear to be stuck in,' he admitted and stared down at his gaudy feet. 'My feet are already transformed. If you kiss me, will I turn into a frog?'

'Let's try, shall we?' she whispered. 'Let's try really hard. And if you turn into a frog—I promise to keep right on loving you. Marcus Frog. Marcus Anything. I'm yours for ever.'

EPILOGUE

A WEEK later they were heading home—home to another wedding ceremony that was even simpler than the first but far, far more important. Marcus ushered her on board his jet; he took her into his arms and, as the jet soared to cruise altitude, he silenced her protests with a kiss.

But he couldn't silence her for ever.

'Marcus, this is obscene! You promised me that you wouldn't fly first class. And this…'

'Why? What's wrong with it?' He was inclined to be indignant.

'This is so… First class has nothing on this!'

'I know,' he said smugly. 'This is nothing like first class. First class, by definition, is the set of seats for those with more money than the normal passenger. The seat you're sitting on is the seat for the normal passenger. Therefore, it's economy. Cattle class.'

'It's your own private jet.'

'Yep. And you're in the economy section. Get used to it.'

But still she was stunned, torn between indignation and laughter.

'Marcus, how much did it cost to get those gumboots painted?'

'Do you care?'

'Yes!'

But he was smiling. 'My love, we'll do good things with our money,' he told her. 'Wise things for the needy. Sensible things for our family and for our farm. For the good of our cows and our dogs and our kids. And we'll do fun things. Fun things just for us. I've worked too hard for my fortune not to derive some pleasure from it.' His smile deepened.

'Like the money I spent to pay out Charles's lease so that neither you, nor I, nor any of our employees have to see the man again.'

'Marcus...' Once again he'd left her speechless.

'Mind, I can't help feeling almost sorry for the man,' Marcus told her gently. 'He's just so...stupid. He can't see that all he's hurting is himself.' He smiled softly into her hair. 'Maybe he needs to find his own Cinderella,' he whispered. 'But he's not having mine. Mine's taken. Now... What do we do in economy seats? Do we put our knees under our chins? I think I promised to do that, and I'm prepared to do whatever it takes to make you happy. Or will you kiss me instead, my love? What do you think? Take your pick.'

Take your pick. He was incorrigible. Peta tried to glare but it didn't come off. Instead she chuckled but her chuckle was drowned as his lips met hers and she was kissed as he'd never stopped kissing her and he never would.

Their seats inched back to reclining. Man and woman, loving each other. For ever.

Heading homeward, for a life together—in the world's most extraordinary gumboots!

THE BRIDE ASSIGNMENT

by

Leigh Michaels

Leigh Michaels wrote her first book when she was fourteen and thought she knew everything. Now she's a good bit older and wise enough to realise that she'll never know everything. She has written more than seventy-five romances, teaches writing in person and online, and enjoys long walks, miniatures, and watching wild deer and turkey from her living room.

E-mail: leigh@leighmichaels.com

Mail: PO Box 935, Ottumwa, IA 52501-0935, USA

CHAPTER ONE

THE woman sitting across the desk from Macey looked nervous. No, Macey thought, worse than nervous. She looked terrified.

"I've tried everything," the woman said. "Though I don't suppose I should tell you that. If you knew how many places I've applied for a job and been turned down, you wouldn't want to hire me either." She bit her lip.

Macey smiled. "Well, I'm looking for a little different sort of person than many personnel managers are," she said, deliberately keeping her voice low and soothing. "As a matter of fact, Ellen, we find that women like you are our best workers."

"Really?" Ellen's voice was little more than a squeak.

"Oh, yes. We love hiring women who are returning to the job market after taking a few years off to raise children. As a rule, women like you are highly motivated, you're realistic, and you have excellent time management skills."

Ellen sighed. "Looking for a job has certainly made me realistic. And the divorce has given me all kinds of motivation. I don't know about time management."

"Any woman who's raising a couple of kids has learned how to balance at least six tasks at the same time."

Ellen smiled faintly. "I guess you're right about that. Do you have kids? You sound as if you know."

Macey kept her voice light. "Only observation, not personal experience."

"Sorry," Ellen said under her breath. "I guess I shouldn't have asked that."

"There's nothing wrong with asking questions. We encourage it around here. When we send you out on a temporary job, it will be important for you to know what questions to ask so you can get the work done."

"I see." Ellen sounded doubtful.

Macey didn't push the point. "Of course, there's also a downside for women in your position—your skills are a bit rusty and you're not really sure what you want to do with the rest of your working years."

Ellen relaxed. "Yes. That's it exactly. And some of those jobs sounded so complicated—"

"That you were afraid of getting in over your head, and so perhaps you didn't interview very well. That's why I think you'll find temporary work is a good choice, for now. You won't have to face any more interviews after today, and you'll be able to try out all sorts of different jobs."

"But if I can't do the work—"

"We won't send you out until you've had some refresher courses and practice, and we'll choose your first jobs very carefully. Trust me, Ellen—our biggest problem here at Peterson Temps is that just when we get an employee completely trained and comfortable so she can handle anything a new office throws at her, she finds a niche she really likes, the company hires her full-time, and we're left shorthanded again."

Ellen smiled. "I guess that's lucky for me. At least you have an opening."

"Let's get you started with the official paperwork." Macey pushed back her chair and led the way to the reception room. "Louise, please review the personnel handbook with Ellen and then take her over to the skills lab for an evaluation."

Ellen said, "You mean like a test."

"Not really. Just a checkup so we can see where you'll need practice and extra training."

The receptionist pulled a booklet from a drawer. "Macey, Mr. Peterson left word for you to see him as soon as you're free."

"Thanks, Louise." Macey held out a hand to her newest employee. "Don't hesitate to come and talk to me at any time, Ellen." She crossed the waiting room, tapped on the closed door of her boss's office, and pushed it open without waiting for an answer. "Robert? You wanted me?"

Too late to retreat, she saw that there was a second man in the office, sitting across the desk from Robert Peterson. He turned halfway around at the sound of her voice, as if he was annoyed by the interruption.

Why hadn't Louise warned her? "I'm sorry," Macey said. "I didn't realize you weren't alone." She started to back out of the room.

But Robert beckoned her in. "My visitor is the reason I asked for you. Come and sit down, Macey. This is Derek McConnell. Derek, my office manager, Macey Phillips."

McConnell...the name didn't ring bells. Was he a new client, perhaps? Though it was a bit unusual for someone who wanted to hire temporary help to actually come to the office; most of their business was developed through word of mouth as one employer told another about everything Peterson Temps could do. And in most cases, the actual requests came not in person but by phone, often with no time to spare for the niceties. *We need a receptionist for a week while the regular one is out with the flu. We need an executive secretary so ours can go on vacation. We need a financial analyst to handle a one-time project.*

Or perhaps Derek McConnell was on the other end of the equation—he, like Ellen, might be a worker seeking a job. Though he didn't seem to fit the part, Macey thought as he stood up to greet her. There was something about him which spoke of power—and he was giving her an appraising look, almost as if she was being subjected to some sort of test. Not at all the sort of survey she was used to getting from people who were applying for work.

She returned the look, studying him just as closely. He was tall and broad-shouldered, obviously an athlete despite the perfectly tailored navy pinstriped suit he wore. His hair was brown but liberally threaded with gold, which glimmered in the sunlight falling through the office window and made him look like a wayward angel. His eyes were brown as well, framed with lashes which in Macey's opinion were far too long, dark, and curly to be wasted on any man. She'd gotten only a glimpse of his profile, when she'd first walked in and he'd turned halfway 'round, but even a glance had been enough to show that it, too, was flawless.

In short, in all the obvious ways in which the world judged men, he was Mr. Perfection.

And there's not the least doubt that he knows it, she thought. She stretched out her hand. ''My pleasure, Mr. McConnell. What can I do for you?''

Derek McConnell didn't answer right away. He waited for her to take her chair before he sat down. Then he propped his elbows on the arms of his chair, tented his hands together, and said, ''Ms. Phillips, I want you to find me a wife.''

* * *

For an instant, Macey Phillips looked as startled as if he'd kicked her in the kneecap. Then she gave a little gurgle of a laugh that Derek thought sounded almost like a low-pitched set of wind chimes.

"Well, that's one we don't hear too often," she said. She looked toward Robert, obviously expecting him to share the joke. Derek watched a small line form between her brows as she realized that Robert apparently didn't see the same humor in the situation that she had. She looked back at Derek. "I'm afraid I don't quite understand. You must realize that Peterson Temps isn't a matchmaker, or a dating service."

"I'm perfectly aware of that. If I wanted a dating service, I'd consult one. I very deliberately chose to come here instead."

She frowned. "You want to hire a temp?"

"Not exactly. Perhaps it would be easiest if I started from the beginning, Ms. Phillips. If you have time, that is."

"Oh, yes, please." She leaned forward. "And of course I have time—I couldn't turn my back on this story right now any more than I can walk out of a movie halfway through."

She was laughing at him. Irritating as that was, it was also comforting in an odd sort of way. At least it appeared that Robert was right about her—this woman wouldn't take any crazy notions of trying to marry him herself. Now if she'd just get serious enough about his problem to actually help him...

"My father is George McConnell," he began. "You would probably be more likely to recognize his nickname—"

"You mean the founder of the Kingdom of Kid? The one who made it possible for a child to turn thirteen in this country without ever having slept in, crawled over, climbed on, eaten, or played with anything that wasn't produced by a McConnell company? That George McConnell?"

He was startled. "As a matter of fact, yes."

"So if he's the king, that's why they call you the crown prince of the Kingdom of Kid."

Robert cleared his throat reprovingly. "That's nothing more than a tasteless reference by a popular magazine which is only trying to increase its circulation."

Macey glanced at him and then back at Derek. "Sorry," she said. "I'm all ears. Really."

Derek's gaze wandered for just an instant, coming to rest on the small, almost pointed ear that peeked out from under the gleam of her dark brown hair. It would have been a nice ear, if she'd been wearing a tasteful single pearl in the lobe instead of a chunk of something that looked like broken pottery. And there was only one piece of pottery, he noted. The other earlobe, tiny and elegantly shaped, was bare. "My official title is vice president of operations."

"Same thing," she said, almost under her breath.

"Not quite. My father has reached the age when he'd like to—" He caught himself in the nick of time; he'd almost said *abdicate*. Damn her royal references, anyway. "He's planning to retire. But the members of the board of directors, he tells me, are a little itchy at the idea of making me the new CEO."

"They probably still think of you as the kid whose picture is on the baby food jars and toy packages."

"That doesn't help matters, but it isn't the crux of the problem."

Her eyes widened. "I was joking. You mean it really *is* you on all those labels and boxes?"

"An updated version of an old photograph," Derek said stiffly. How absolutely stupid it was to feel defensive about it.

"I see. That explains why you need a wife—so they'll take you seriously."

"Not exactly. They're quite aware I've grown up."

"Yes—partly because of that magazine we were talking about. You know, your directors have a point. You're not only thirtyish and unmarried, but you have quite a reputation as a man about town. Naming a single and childless playboy as the CEO of a company specializing in kids would be something like hiring a guy who's violently allergic to cats and dogs to manufacture pet food."

Robert said, "Or a vegetarian to run the sausage factory."

Derek jumped. He'd almost forgotten the man was still there. "I can understand that it might cause some consternation on Wall Street, yes. That's why I'm here."

Macey said, "Because you want to hire someone to pretend to be your wife, just until you're established in your new job? That shouldn't be too—"

"No."

She frowned. "You've lost me, Mr. McConnell. Which part of that did I get wrong?"

"Most of it." He held up one hand and ticked off his points on his fingertips. "No hiring. No pretending. No temporary arrangement."

Her jaw dropped. He had to restrain himself from reaching over and nudging her chin back into place. She had a cute mouth, actually, but it was distracting when it was hanging open that way. Almost as distracting as that single kooky earring. Where had she found it, anyway? On some archaeological dig?

Derek forced himself to look at her eyes instead. "It's

not as if I have any objections to the idea of marriage. As a matter of fact, intellectually I agree with the board of directors that image is important and a married man would make a better CEO for a company like this one.''

''So what's the problem?''

''The problem is, my father's sudden wish to retire has caught me unprepared. I have to act soon, but right now, I don't have the kind of time it would take to find the right woman. And you see, I have to be certain she is the right woman.''

Macey nodded slowly. ''Because a *divorced* childless playboy as CEO of a company specializing in kids would be even worse than a never-married one.'' She rubbed her temples. She looked as if her head hurt.

Derek shrugged. ''If I'm going to do this at all, I might as well do it right. It's time for a new picture on the baby food jars, anyway.''

She stared at him, her eyes widening as she took in what he'd said. ''You're not serious. You expect this wife to have your kids?''

''It's just part of the deal. As long as we agree to the details up front, I don't see any reason for her to object—and I certainly don't understand why you should get your toenails twisted, Ms. Phillips. Considering what I'm offering, there will be no shortage of interested women.''

He watched as her dainty white teeth closed hard on her lower lip. There was no doubt in his mind about what she would have liked to say—he could almost see the words she was trying so hard to swallow.

He conceded that the statement had probably sounded a bit egotistical. But that didn't make what he'd said any less true. And since when was it conceited for a man to recognize and admit that he was considered to be a prize?

He watched her gaze flicker; she was apparently ticking

through a card file in her brain, considering possibilities. Finally she shook her head. "I can't think of anyone in our agency who would even consider the idea, Mr. McConnell. I think a dating service might well be a more logical—"

"I didn't seriously expect you to have a list of workers categorized under the heading *Prospective Wife*. The kind of woman I intend to marry isn't going to be working for a temp agency anyway."

"All kinds of people work for temp agencies," she said coolly. "For all kinds of reasons."

"Sorry. I didn't mean that the way it sounded."

She looked as if she doubted it. "Never mind. The point is, I'm afraid you've lost me, Mr. McConnell. You said you wanted us to find you a wife. Now you're saying you don't think we can. What exactly are you looking for?"

"Someone who will consider all the possible candidates, winnow through them, and select a few finalists for me to choose from."

She was still looking at him as if he were two blocks short of an alphabet, but the professional calm was back in her voice. "Well, that makes a little more sense. You want to employ a personal assistant who has human resources experience and familiarity with hiring. Maybe someone with a little psychological training thrown in. Do you prefer to work with a male or female?"

Robert leaned forward. "We've already concluded that a woman would be better for the job. Making this kind of judgment seems to require a feminine eye."

Macey didn't miss a beat. "Well, let me think about the people who are on our employment rolls right now. We have a number of good personal assistant types, but I'll have to check on the details. Can I get back to you in a day or two?"

Robert said, "Macey will take care of you, Derek."

She shook her head. "Don't make promises lightly, Robert—it won't be easy to find someone to fit the bill. Are there any other restrictions, Mr. McConnell? Would you prefer a motherly sort to choose your bride, or a younger woman who would have more direct experience with the sorts of concerns you have?"

"Macey," Robert repeated, enunciating each word carefully, "will take care of you, Derek. She'll get your problem solved—*personally.*"

Macey had bit her bottom lip so often and so hard during this conversation that it was starting to feel permanently indented. But the idea that Robert wanted to stick *her* with this job was the ultimate; she simply couldn't swallow any more. She took a deep breath and stood up. "Mr. McConnell, if you'll excuse us for a moment, Robert and I need to have a short conference. Alone."

Was that amusement she saw flickering in those big brown eyes? But he politely said, "Of course. I'll just wait outside."

She held her tongue until the door had closed behind him and then spun around to face her boss. "Robert, you can't saddle me with this!"

"It's an opportunity we can't turn down, Macey. Think of the business that young man will be able to throw our way. We could open another branch office. Just think of the goodwill we'll earn when you succeed."

"Think of the disaster when I don't!"

"Macey, stop and think. How hard can it be? Honestly, my dear—how difficult can it possibly be to find a woman who wants to marry young Mr. McConnell?"

Considering what I'm offering, there will be no shortage of interested women, Derek McConnell had boasted.

The damnable thing was that he was probably right. That mix of arrogance and power acted as an aphrodisiac for a lot of women. Even if he hadn't been the crown prince of the Kingdom of Kid, even if he hadn't had a dollar to his name, there would still be women swooning over Derek McConnell.

The fools.

No, finding willing women wouldn't be the problem. But Robert was missing the point. Derek McConnell had said *the right woman*—and that was the part that wasn't going to be easy. A man who was Mr. Perfection himself wouldn't settle for less in the woman he married.

"Robert, the man's delusional." Macey knew she sounded desperate, but she didn't care. "If he thinks he can just buy himself a crate of happily-ever-after—"

Robert shook his head. "Oh, I don't think that's what he believes at all. You know, Macey, it's really the wild-eyed romantics who are the delusional ones, believing in love at first sight and all that sort of garbage. Derek feels that the odds of having a successful marriage are a lot better if one chooses carefully—uses one's good sense instead of relying on instinct and hormones and luck."

"So let him use his own good sense instead of trying to hire someone else's!"

"Under the circumstances, it seems to me to be smart to seek an outside opinion. Derek seems to me to be a very levelheaded young man. He just doesn't have time for—"

"And you think I do have time? Come on, Robert—you know how busy I am. Why don't you hire some sensible grandmotherly type? Somebody who would make it her top priority to find someone who can make him happy?" *Instead of someone like me, who doesn't care who he marries as long as the choice doesn't come back to haunt me?*

"Because you're all those things you rattled off a little while ago, Macey. You have human resource and personnel experience and a psychology background. And you're a young woman who can understand the additional stresses on a marriage today."

"Because I've been married," she said slowly.

"And—forgive me—because you're so obviously not interested in being married again," Robert said. "That fact will give you a certain perspective, an extra measure of distance so you can see the situation clearly. Most people would get caught up in the romance of the whole thing. Your grandmotherly type—even if she existed—certainly would."

"You're quite right that you don't need to worry about me getting romantic over this," Macey said dryly.

"Exactly my point." He made a shooing motion toward the door. "Now, run along before Derek gets impatient and thinks we're not interested anymore."

"I couldn't be so lucky," Macey muttered.

She was right; Derek McConnell hadn't given up. He was sitting next to Louise's desk, paging through a magazine. He was apparently oblivious to the admiring looks he was getting from Ellen, who was eyeing him over the edge of the personnel handbook she was supposed to be reviewing.

He stood when Macey came out of Robert's office. "Who won the argument?" he asked with obvious interest.

Macey looked through him. "It wasn't an argument. It was a professional discussion. And can we please continue this in my office instead of in public?"

"That means you lost."

"No, that means I don't have a great deal of time free today."

"Robert warned me about that." He consulted his wristwatch. "I've got a busy schedule too, you know, but I blocked out two hours to deal with this, and you've already used up one of them."

"That's certainly efficient. You're devoting two whole hours to settle a matter that you'll be living with for a lifetime."

"No, I'm devoting two hours to bring you up to speed so *you* can settle it. Though I admit to having second thoughts about turning over my future to a woman who can't hang on to both of her earrings."

Macey's hand went automatically to her earlobe. "Oh. I pulled one off this morning because the phone was making my ear hurt, and then I forgot to put it back on."

"The dinner plate you were wearing is what made your ear hurt. It's hardly fair to blame it on the phone." He paused just inside her office door and looked back at her, one eyebrow raised. "You did invite me in, I recall. I presume you have some questions?"

Macey gritted her teeth. She closed the door on Ellen's avid interest and Louise's more tactful but no less eager curiosity, sat down at her desk, and pulled out a fresh notepad and a new pencil. "Perhaps you'll give me some parameters that will help narrow the search. Of course, I'll start by noting that anyone wearing funky earrings need not apply. Obviously you would interpret a difference of opinion regarding her jewelry as indicating a serious character flaw in a woman, and we certainly can't have that."

"Since I'm the one who'd have to actually look at the jewelry, I think I'm allowed to have a say in it," he pointed out. "You can't see your own earrings, so that's why you're not even sure if you're wearing both of them. It's everyone else in the room who gets an eyeful. Though the size those things are, I don't understand how you can walk around and not notice that you're lopsided."

Macey looked for her second earring, found it stashed in the pen tray of her desk drawer, and very deliberately threaded the post through her earlobe. "There. Perhaps you'll be less cranky now that I'm not lopsided anymore." *But I'm not counting on it.* "What else?"

"I haven't exactly made a list."

"You amaze me. She doesn't have to be a natural blonde, five-feet-ten, size four, big blue eyes, with a doctoral degree?"

Derek settled back in his chair and looked thoughtfully past Macey and out the window. "I hadn't thought about it, but that sounds like a good start."

She considered stabbing him with the pencil. *No, it's not deadly enough.* "I'm serious here."

"All right—you can skip the doctorate. A degree of some sort would be nice, but—"

"By all means," she said, and wrote it down. "For the sake of the future children's genetic heritage, she should not only be eye candy but brilliant too. Would you prefer that degree to be in math or science?"

His eyes narrowed. "Do you get paid extra for sarcasm?"

Macey looked at him blandly. "No, it's a fringe benefit and available only on rare jobs. Consider yourself one of the lucky few. What about hobbies? Do you want a woman who shares all your interests, or one you can escape from on the golf course?"

"It would be nice if she played golf. Maybe a little tennis, too."

"All the comforts of the country club. And she should

be a gourmet cook, I suppose, so she can entertain all your important guests? At least, I don't imagine the board of directors eats baby food when they all get together.''

His eyes sparkled. "You might be surprised. A few of them are old enough that's about all they can manage anymore.''

The flash of humor came and went so quickly that Macey tried to convince herself that she'd imagined it. But the gleam of laughter in those big brown eyes had left her feeling a little breathless, almost light-headed—and she certainly hadn't fantasized that.

"She doesn't need to cook," Derek said. "She can hire caterers.''

Macey had to pull her attention back to the subject. *Caterers? Oh, yes, we were talking about entertaining.* "Still, if she knows her way around a kitchen, the caterers can't take advantage of her. Do you have any pet peeves I should know about?''

"Well—I detest frivolous names. You know the kind of stupid monikers I mean—Bunny and Muffy and Taffy and Honey and—" He paused, looking at her thoughtfully.

"Oh, don't spare my feelings," Macey reassured him. "I have a very frivolous name—I've always thought so. All right. Anyone named Elizabeth, Sara, or Rachel may apply, but all others will have to legally change their names first.''

"You're right," he said. "Your name does sound pretty funny. How did you come to be named Macey, anyway?''

"I was born there.''

"What?"

"In the department store. There was a big white sale going on, one day only, and my mother thought she had enough time to pick up an extra set of sheets and a few towels before she went to the hospital. She was wrong."

He looked as if he was too stunned to speak. Macey decided she liked him better that way.

"Mom always said at least I had the good taste to be born in linens instead of pots and pans," she mused. "Anyway, that's why she named me after the store, because they ended up giving her the sheets and towels. She just spelled it a little differently."

"Good thing the white sale wasn't going on at Wal-Mart," he said faintly.

"Thanks—I'll add that to my list of things to be grateful for." Macey doodled on the notepad. "You do realize that with this thing about names you're eliminating two-thirds of all former sorority girls? Unfortunately, that's the very place I was going to start looking."

"You won't have to look. Just select."

Macey stopped doodling. "I'm not sure I know what you mean."

"It's not a matter of finding this woman. I've already found her."

She blinked twice and shook her head, trying to clear it. "What are you talking about? If you already have a woman in mind, what do you need me for?"

"Crowd control. I know at least a hundred women who on the surface appear to be possibilities. The trick is to pick the half dozen out of those hundred who could actually make the cut, so I don't have to waste my time with the other ninety-four or so."

"And how do you suggest I do that? Ask them to fill out applications?"

Derek shook his head. "Too obvious. Interviews, I think."

"Oh, I can see them lining up on the sidewalk, waiting

their turn in my office. And what would that prove, anyway? Anyone can look good on a job interview, when they know they're on trial.''

Derek frowned. ''You have a point there.''

''To judge whether they'd be right for you, I'd almost have to study them in their natural habitat. And that—''

''—is an excellent idea. Brilliant, in fact. No wonder Robert was so certain you were the woman for the job.'' He leaned back in his chair and smiled.

Macey tapped her pencil on the notepad in an attempt to buy herself a little time to figure out what was going on. Not that it mattered; she wasn't likely to understand Derek McConnell if she had an eon or two to study him.

Perish the thought.

''We'll start tonight,'' Derek said. ''There's a cocktail party before the symphony concert. At least a dozen of my possibles should be there. I'll point them out and you can start observing.''

''I don't—''

He frowned. ''Now's where it gets tricky,'' he said. ''What's the proper etiquette, since you're working for me? Do I pick you up, or just meet you there?''

CHAPTER TWO

MACEY stared at him, trying not to believe what she'd heard. But she couldn't avoid the facts. It was quite clear to her that Mr. Perfection not only assumed she'd be attending the party, he actually thought she'd be eager to go.

"Hold it right there," she said. "I am not going out with you."

Derek looked as if she'd picked up the industrial-size stapler from her desk and slammed it over his head. "Of course you're not. Get a grip, Ms. Phillips. Going somewhere together is not the same thing as going out. This is not anywhere close to being a date."

Fury roared through Macey's veins, but she kept her voice icy calm. "For your information, Mr. McConnell, I hadn't made that mistake. I didn't assume you were inviting me to be half of a cozy little romantic duo."

"Well, I'm glad we have that all cleared up."

"But my evenings are already reserved."

From the way he suddenly sat up a little straighter, it was plain that she had gotten his attention. *Probably only because he doesn't believe I could have anything worth doing after work,* Macey thought. But at least he was taking her seriously.

"*Every* evening?"

She nodded. It was only a small exaggeration, after all.

"Then I see just one alternative."

You need to get someone else. Relief surged through her. Finding the right matchmaker was still going to be a pain, but at least she'd be rid of the major portion of this nightmare. And if Derek was to request a change, Robert could hardly argue. He might be annoyed. He might even be a bit suspicious—but he couldn't very well blame Macey simply because the client had changed his mind.

She was drawing a breath to tell him that she would buzz Robert and arrange another conference right away when Derek spoke.

"I'll tell my father that I've hired a personal assistant, and you'll run this operation right out of my office."

Macey choked.

"It won't be as efficient, I'm afraid," Derek said thoughtfully, "and I expect it'll take longer for you to meet all the women on my list, because I don't encourage them to hang around me at work."

Macey could almost feel herself turning blue from lack of air.

"Of course, in that case I couldn't pay you directly—it would look very fishy if I didn't put my personal assistant on the company payroll. So to convince my father that you're worth a paycheck, you'll have to look like a real employee, which means you'll have to do some bona fide work as well as your undercover assignment. Just to maintain appearances, you understand. But from what Robert told me about what a great worker you are, I'm sure you can handle whatever I need."

Macey finally managed to get a single wheezing breath, but the only difference it made was that she started to cough.

"And it might cause some problems around here, too," Derek mused. "Of course, since this is a temp agency, surely it won't be any trouble for Robert to find someone to fill in for you as office manager for a few weeks."

"A few *weeks?*"

"I suppose you'd be taking a risk that Robert would like the new person better and you'd come back to find your job gone—but then you might also decide you like working for me. If we got along well enough, I might even keep you on."

Talk about a fate worse than death.

Derek looked very directly at her. "Unless you'd rather rethink the matter from the beginning, of course."

If she'd built the box herself, Macey admitted, she couldn't have made it fit any tighter.

He lounged back in his chair. "You're absolutely certain that every single one of your evenings is spoken for?"

"Perhaps not *every* one." Macey felt a little hoarse.

"Good. Then let me ask you again. Shall I pick you up tonight, or meet you at Symphony Hall?"

The moment Macey stepped into the town house, the scent of roasted garlic greeted her, and she knew Clara had had a better-than-usual day. With a sigh of mingled relief and gratitude, Macey hung up her coat and went into the kitchen.

Clara was stirring a big pot on the stove. Her gray hair was askew, looking almost as if it hadn't been combed today. But she was wearing a burgundy slacks set instead of the sweatsuits she favored on her off days, and she had even put on a dash of makeup.

Macey gave her a hug. "Something smells wonderful."

"Potato soup. It's a new recipe—I got it from one of the ladies at ceramics. There's lemonade in the refrigerator if you'd like some."

Macey poured herself a glass and leaned against the counter. "You went to class today?"

Clara nodded. "I got the second coat of glaze on the

wise men so they can be fired again, and I cleaned the shepherds and a couple of the animals. I think the whole nativity set will be done in time for Christmas."

"That's great, Clara." Not that Macey really cared when—or even if—it was finished. But having a project gave Clara a reason to get up in the morning and to get out of the house. "I'm glad you went." Macey sipped her lemonade. "Clara—I have to go out for a bit tonight."

For a moment, she thought Clara wasn't going to answer at all, and her heart sank. It took so little sometimes, even on a good day, to throw Clara into the depths again.

But finally the woman said, "Where are you going?"

Just my luck, Macey thought. *The one time I wish she wouldn't take an interest in the outside world, she's going to want the details.* "It's something to do with the city orchestra. I'm afraid I have to hurry—I need to be at Symphony Hall by seven."

"Then it's a good thing the soup is ready." Clara gave the pot a final stir and reached for a ladle, frowning a little. "Why so early? The concert doesn't start till eight-thirty."

Macey winced. How on earth did Clara happen to know that?

Clara glanced at her and answered the unasked question. "There was a story in the newspaper this morning, all about the soloist. It sounds like it'll be a very good program. You'll have to tell me all about it."

"Well, I'm not sure I'll actually be going to the concert, just this thing beforehand."

"What thing? You mean the fund-raising cocktail party?" Clara put the ladle down. "Macey, that's what the story was mainly about. That party costs two hundred dollars a ticket. I didn't know you were so fond of the symphony."

Trust Derek McConnell to leave out a few minor details.

"Actually," Macey admitted, "I'm...well, I'm meeting someone there."

"Meeting someone?" Clara said slowly. "You mean like a date?"

Macey's heart dropped. *Now we're in for it.*

"Macey, you've actually got a date? With a man?"

"Honey, this is so far from being a date it isn't even on the same continent."

Clara looked at her more closely. "You're blushing as if it's a date."

"It's not a date, all right?" Macey heard the sharpness in her voice and took a deep breath, trying to calm herself. "It's work."

"I thought you had an ironclad agreement with Robert that you don't work nights or weekends."

Macey bit her lip.

"You thought I didn't know about that," Clara mused as she dished up a second bowl of soup. "It's not that I don't appreciate it, you staying at home to keep me company, to help keep the black clouds away. But with this new medicine, I really am getting better, Macey. And in any case it's well past time for you to come back to life."

"You are my life, Clara."

"And I've been selfish enough and sick enough to let you think that, and act as if it were true. But it's three years now since Jack died. You're a young woman. He wouldn't have wanted you to mourn him forever."

Just what I don't need tonight, Macey thought. *Reverse guilt—my husband's aunt giving me a hard time for* not *leaving him in the past.*

"We'll talk about it later," she said hastily.

Clara didn't bring it up again, but the subject hung in

the air between them. With relief Macey finished her soup and went to get dressed.

Perhaps it was fortunate, she thought, that she didn't have many choices, so she couldn't drive herself crazy wondering what was appropriate to wear to an upper-crust cocktail party. The only disadvantage was that she had absolutely no excuse for being fashionably late, because it took no time at all to select her forest-green business suit. It was the dressiest thing she owned, it was almost new, and it fit well. It was even stylishly cut, compared to most of her wardrobe—which fit solidly into the business-basics category.

Nevertheless, when she was dressed, she looked into the full-length mirror in her bathroom and surveyed the suit and the coordinating pinstriped blouse with a flicker of distaste.

She sighed and started to dig in her closet, emerging finally with an ivory silk camisole, all but strapless and covered with delicate embroidery, to substitute for her tailored blouse. She couldn't even remember where it had come from. A long-forgotten lingerie party given by a friend, perhaps.

Now if she could just get out of the town house without Clara commenting about her running around in something that looked like underwear... She put the long jacket back on and buttoned it all the way up.

Clara inspected her without a word and said a calm good-night. But as Macey pulled the front door shut behind her, she thought she heard Clara mutter, "It sure *looks* like it's a date."

Macey paid off her cab outside Symphony Hall and got a receipt to add to her expense account. Tucking it into her tiny evening bag, she stopped just inside the main entrance. There were people all over, and they—unlike her—obviously knew where they were going.

A man spoke behind her. "Excuse me."

Macey felt herself flush. "Oh, I'm sorry. I didn't realize I was blocking traffic. It's just that I'm not sure where the cocktail party's being held."

"Then I'm your man." He held out an arm with a ceremonial flourish. "My name's Ira Branson. And you are—?"

By the time Macey had introduced herself, they were nearing a wide arched doorway which led into what looked like a ballroom. A man who resembled a cartoon caricature of a butler was standing at the door, his posture so stiff that for a moment Macey wasn't certain whether he was real or a wooden statue wearing white tie and tails.

Ira pulled a strip of red paper from his pocket and the butler-figure looked disdainfully at it before he took it carefully between two fingertips. Then he turned a narrowed gaze on Macey.

Macey said, "I'm sorry, I don't actually have a ticket, I—"

The doorman put his head back so he could look down his nose at an even more precipitous angle. "Madam, this is not the sort of occasion where we sell tickets at the door to anyone who happens to have the price of admission."

Fine with me, Macey wanted to say. *Because—as a matter of fact—I don't have an extra two hundred bucks on me this week.*

"Now come on, Wilson," Ira protested.

The doorman ignored him. "This event is open only to those who have been specifically invited."

From somewhere inside the room, Derek McConnell materialized beside the butler. "Wilson, my dear jerk, you can knock off the grandiose act and stop insulting my guest.'' He pulled a ticket from his breast pocket and flourished it under the man's nose. ''She doesn't have a ticket because I'm holding it.''

The doorman's gaze flickered. ''Your guest? Very well, sir. If you say so.'' Doubt dripped from his voice.

''I'm *so* pleased to meet you, Wilson,'' Macey murmured. She was tempted to give the man a friendly punch in the arm, or maybe offer a high-five, but she didn't want to be responsible for causing him to have a stroke.

The doorman ignored her and managed to look even more like a stone-faced statue.

Ira stuck out his hand to Derek. ''McConnell—good to see you again. I didn't mean to barge in on your territory, buddy, but Marcie here was a bit lost—''

''Macey,'' Derek corrected. ''Her name's Macey.''

''Oh. Sorry. As I was saying—''

''Thanks for bringing her in,'' Derek said, and drew Macey away from the entrance. ''It's about time you got here.''

She headed automatically for a secluded corner. ''Was it really necessary to be rude to Ira?''

''You're worried about his feelings? He couldn't even get your name right.''

''At least he made sure I got to the right place.''

''Hey, it's not my fault you were late. I waited around out in the hall for you till people started looking at me oddly.''

''Including the guard at the door, I imagine. I'll bet if you had greased his palm with an extra hundred he might have found me slightly more palatable.''

''Well, you have only yourself to blame for the reception you got. I offered to pick you up.''

''And you think walking in beside you would have

made him any more impressed with my style? You know, Derek—'' Though they'd agreed to use first names, it was the first time she'd actually done it. His name felt funny on her tongue, as if she'd taken a bite from the jelly dish expecting it to be sweet, only to taste jalapeno peppers instead. "That's the man who should be vetting your choices."

"Wilson? You're joking."

"Dead serious. He obviously already knows everybody who's anybody—to say nothing of who isn't. I'll bet by the end of the evening he'd have a short list all ready for you. And after all, why should choosing you a wife take any longer than selecting a new Miss America? The requirements are so similar. I'll go ask him to take over, if you like."

"Have a drink instead—you'll feel better. I'd recommend you stick with the wine. It's not the best vintage, but at least it's not watered down like the Scotch is."

"Two hundred bucks a ticket and they water the booze?"

Derek shrugged. "It leaves a little extra for the symphony that way." He waved down a waiter. "White or red?"

"White, please." Macey took the glass he handed her and looked across the room.

It was swarming with people, young and old, all of whom obviously knew each other. She watched a matched set of blondes air-kissing near the hors d'oeuvre table. Derek had said something about a dozen possibilities attending tonight, but it looked to Macey as if the crowd included more like fifty women of the right age and pedigree.

She smothered a sigh. "Anyway, now that I'm actually

in, you don't have to hover over me. Just point out the most likely candidates and I'll get to work.''

"I'll take you around and introduce you to them."

She eyed him over the rim of her glass. "You're not serious. Bad enough they may have already seen you talking to me."

"How? We're standing in a corner behind a pillar."

"Trust me. If they're interested in you at all, they know exactly where you're standing and who you're with."

"If that's the case, I can't see that it'll hurt anything if I introduce you."

"You can't really think these women will show their true colors with you standing right there. Are you completely illiterate about the way women think, or what?"

"They're sure as heck not going to confide in a total stranger."

"You might be surprised at what they'd do. But in fact I don't expect them to. I'm not going to sidle up to each one and ask her to whisper in my ear what she really, truly thinks of you. Even if I didn't die of boredom from listening to the platitudes, it would be completely useless."

"So what are you going to do?"

Excellent question. But in fact, Macey reminded herself, she didn't have to become best friends with every woman in the place, she only needed to get a feel for the sort of people they were. And she didn't have to make the final choice. All she really had to do was eliminate the obviously impossible—like the bottle redhead who was standing next to the bar, almost wrapped around a man in an effort to keep herself upright.

The woman must have had a head start to be drunk already, Macey thought. Especially if Derek was right about the purposely weak drinks being served at the party.

Macey didn't doubt it a bit, because he'd certainly been correct about the wine. She couldn't imagine forcing enough of it down to even get a buzz, much less lose her inhibitions.

Which was something of a shame, actually, for this job would be a whole lot more fun if her mind was just fuzzy enough around the edges not to remember tomorrow exactly what she'd done in the name of finding Derek McConnell a bride.

At any rate, the redhead was definitely out. It might be a slow beginning, but at least she was on the road.

One down. Forty-nine—give or take—to go. And that's just tonight's crop.

"Hold this," she said, handing Derek her wine. She unbuttoned her suit jacket and slipped it off, folding it over her arm. "See you later."

"Don't you want your—" He held out the stemmed glass.

She shook her head. "Just pretend you don't know me, all right?" she said, and plunged into the crowd.

Derek swore under his breath. *Pretend you don't know me.* Well, that was just great. What was he supposed to do now? Prop himself against the pillar with a wineglass in each hand and wait while Macey made her rounds?

He'd sooner go home. He wasn't used to being treated like a coaster—nothing more than a handy place to park her drink until she decided whether she wanted it again—and he was damned sure he didn't like it. It would serve her right if she came back to report and found him gone.

Not that he dared leave, with her out there acting like a loose cannon.

Bringing her to the party at all had been a calculated risk, of course. But if she was going to check out all the women he knew, she would have to go where they congregated. He'd considered the odds and decided he could live with them, but that had been before she'd ditched him and gone off on her own.

What had happened to the woman he'd hired—the one Robert had sworn was capable, levelheaded, and completely trustworthy?

He heard a low wolf whistle nearby and looked around in surprise. Ira Branson was holding up the pillar from the opposite side and staring across the room. "If I'd had any idea what was under that jacket," he said, "I wouldn't have been so willing to let you cut me out at the door, McConnell."

Derek eyed him with distaste. "If you think it'll do you any good, go ahead and give it a shot."

"You mean you don't mind?"

Pretend you don't know me. Fine—if that was what she wanted, he could play along. "Hell, no. Just holding her ticket doesn't give me any claim."

"You mean it really was her ticket? I thought you were just picking her up. Thanks, buddy." Ira ducked between a bald guy with a paunch and a matron in maroon.

Just as well, Derek thought. With both hands full, he couldn't have given Ira the punch in the nose he deserved, anyway.

Idly, Derek watched him cross the room in the direction Macey had gone. It might be amusing to watch Ira get his comeuppance. If Macey ran true to form, the guy would probably end up standing in the opposite corner from Derek, acting like a hat stand and holding the jacket he'd been so pleased to see her shed.

A waiter came by with an empty tray so he ditched the pair of wineglasses, then turned back to survey the room. Near the hors d'oeuvre table he saw Ira on the outskirts of a group of young women. The group shifted, and Derek's jaw dropped.

He'd been too preoccupied when Macey took off her jacket to notice what was underneath, and in any case, barely a moment later she'd disappeared into the crowd. Just a couple of minutes ago, he'd been too irritated at Ira's juvenile reaction to stop to wonder why he'd been so impressed.

Now he understood.

She turned as he watched, and the overhead lights shimmered on the almost-sheer fabric, and on the fancy stitched design, and on the equally silky, nearly bare shoulders.

No wonder Ira had shot across the room like a bird dog who'd spotted a quail.

Derek caught a flash of movement from the corner of his eye just as a low feminine voice said, "The male of the species truly is a disgusting animal. Shall I get you a napkin to mop up the drool?"

He deliberately turned his back toward Macey and resumed his place against the pillar, folding his arms across his chest as he looked down at a blond woman in a yellow cocktail dress. "Hello, Dinah. How are you tonight?"

"Fine. Who's the babe?"

"How should I know?"

Dinah's big blue eyes narrowed. "Because until a few minutes ago the two of you were huddled in this corner whispering."

Huddled? That was a point for Macey, Derek admitted. *They know exactly where you're standing and who you're with,* she'd said. Apparently she'd been right.

His gaze drifted back across the room. It took him a moment to find Macey, because she wasn't where he'd expected she'd be. Instead of standing with the group of women by the hors d'oeuvre table, she was strolling across the room. With her hand on Ira Branson's arm.

"Now just a darn minute," he said.

Dinah shook her head sadly. "You really do have it bad," she murmured.

Not even close, Derek wanted to say. But if he opened his mouth, of course, it would lead to all sorts of questions he didn't want to answer.

With a careless wave, Dinah moved off toward the bar.

Dammit, Derek thought. Macey was supposed to be cozying up to the women in the room, not to Ira Branson. What in the hell did she think she was doing, anyway?

Not what you're paying her for, he told himself. But Dinah's reaction had made it clear that he could hardly go break up that twosome without causing an earthquake.

So what was he supposed to do instead? Hover in the corner watching in frustration?

It would serve her right if he took matters into his own hands. Went over her head. Made his own decision after all.

Because it was a sure bet he couldn't make a worse choice than she was likely to. If Macey Phillips's taste in men ran to a loser like Ira Branson, what kind of woman would she pick out for him?

He was damned if he'd sit around and wait to find out.

It had taken Macey less than five minutes to wipe the names of every woman in the group off her mental blackboard. Figuratively speaking, of course, since she didn't actually know any of their names—and that, she could see, was going to prove a major handicap.

Still, the elimination process had been easy enough. Of the six women standing by the hors d'oeuvre table, two were wearing wedding rings, one was sporting an enormous solitaire diamond, one waved her hands nervously whenever she spoke, one had a laugh that sounded like a tortured cat, and the last was at least ten years older than she was pretending to be.

Six women down. Sort of.

Because there were two problems. Not only did she not know exactly who she'd eliminated, but she had no idea whether they'd been on Derek's list in the first place. If he'd just been reasonable about pointing out who he wanted her to check out...

Of course she hadn't exactly helped matters by shooting off on her own, she admitted. Perhaps if she'd stuck around, explained, made her case...

She looked over her shoulder toward the pillar. All she could see beyond it was part of Derek's coat sleeve and the woman he was talking to. A very pretty blonde wearing soft creamy yellow.

No point in walking back over there as long as he was occupied with Princess Buttercup.

You're on your own, Macey.

She noticed Ira Branson hanging around the fringes of the group. He perked up the instant he saw her glance at him, and he came straight to her. "I actually thought there for a while that you were with McConnell," he confided. "Till he straightened me out."

And you're going to be on your own for a while longer, Macey. Well, she'd asked for it—telling Derek to pretend he didn't know her.

So what was she going to do? At her current rate of progress, Derek McConnell would have checked himself and his walker into a nursing home before she'd found him a wife.

But maybe Ira could help...

She laid her hand on his arm and drew him a little way from the group of women.

"You know," she said earnestly, "I was hoping you'd come over. It's so hard to meet people in a group. For one thing, they always mumble, and in a noisy crowd like this I have trouble hearing. It would make me much more comfortable if I knew people's names before I was actually introduced to them. Like that group I was just with. I think there was a Betsy and a Susan, but I wouldn't dare actually use the names for fear of being wrong."

Ira looked puzzled. "Betsy?" he said. "Susan? I don't think I know them."

Okay, Plan B flopped too—what's next?

Macey tried to be philosophical about it, but it wasn't easy—not only wasn't she making any progress, but now she'd saddled herself with Ira.

Talk about shooting yourself in the foot, Phillips.

A woman in burgundy chiffon came up to her. "I don't believe I know you," she said. "I'm with the Friends of the Symphony. Most of the people here tonight are. If you'd like to join, our membership chairman is right over there." She pointed to a woman in blue lace who was standing by the piano. "I'll introduce you, if you like."

Macey gave a casual glance to the woman in blue lace, and then looked again, longer and more thoughtfully, at the patrician face, touched with a few lines left by time and laughter.

Membership chairman, she thought. The woman would know everybody. And probably everything *about* everybody.

Macey felt as if the sun had just broken through a mass of storm clouds. "I'd love to meet her. That's a wonderful—"

Derek's hand came to rest on Macey's arm. "That's a

wonderful idea you should think very carefully about," he said. "Because it's not just a matter of paying dues and carrying a membership card. Belonging to the Friends demands lots of time and energy."

The woman in burgundy looked confused. "What are you talking about? You know perfectly well—"

Derek had pulled Macey out of range.

She protested, "I was just starting to make progress!"

"What the hell do you think you're doing?"

"What you should have done in the beginning. I ought to have realized right away that it's a waste of time to talk to the young women. The matrons are always the ones who really know what's going on. But just as I'm about to meet the person in charge of membership, you come barging in and make me look like some kind of nut. Now if you want to make up for this blunder, take me over there and introduce me to the woman in blue lace by the piano."

"Not on your life."

Macey wanted to stamp her foot. "Why on earth not? I'll bet you she has some pretty definite ideas who would make a good wife for you."

"I'm not taking that bet."

"See? You've just proved my point, if you think she…" Macey paused, suspicious. "And exactly why not?"

"Because," Derek said grimly, "the woman in blue lace by the piano happens to be my mother."

CHAPTER THREE

DEREK had seen the flash of temper in Macey's eyes before. A couple of times, in fact—once that afternoon in her office and again soon after she'd arrived at the party. But compared to the way she was looking at him now, those occasions had reflected nothing more than minor irritation. He braced himself for the hurricane that was about to hit.

But her voice was low and almost sweet. "And you were seriously going to stroll me 'round the room making introductions and hoping she wouldn't notice me?"

"Could we discuss this in a corner somewhere?" *Like maybe a corner of Asia—that might be far enough away.*

"Oh, it's way too late to hide behind a pillar."

"Of course, if you hadn't decided to call attention to yourself tonight by dressing up like a—" Derek caught himself a millimeter from the edge of the chasm.

"You were saying?" Macey's eyebrows arched inquisitively. "Like a...?"

"Never mind. It's done now. Fortunately the symphony's tuning up and the party's over. So let's just consider this a trial run, assess what we've learned, and start from scratch."

"I have a better idea. Let's consider it an unmitigated disaster and quit while we're ahead. Don't let me keep you from the concert." Macey turned on her heel and was gone.

Beside Derek, Ira Branson cleared his throat. "I could

have told you that would happen. You had your chance with her, McConnell, and you blew it."

Derek had had enough. "So now it's your turn? I notice she didn't ask you to drive her home."

Ira frowned, working it out, and then his brow cleared. "Probably has her own car."

"Otherwise she'd have been begging you for a ride—I know." A flicker of yellow caught his eye and he turned toward Dinah, feeling irritable. "What is it now?"

The blonde said, "Goodness, we're touchy tonight. Your mother went on into the hall, Derek, since she'll be introducing the guest conductor. But she asked me to give you a message—she's saved a couple of seats next to hers in the front row. Shall I go let her know that since your little friend has walked out on you, one will be enough? Or are you too broken up over your spat to sit through the concert at all?"

McConnell Enterprises—informally known as the Kingdom of Kid—owned offices, warehouses, and factories scattered across the country, but the headquarters were located in a sprawling new building on the outskirts of St. Louis. In large part, it had been Derek's ideas and Derek's plans which had shaped the new building, and since the day they'd moved in, he had never approached the place without feeling a sense of accomplishment and pride.

Until this morning.

They'd built the structure solidly enough to withstand a direct hit from a tornado, but today it looked a little fuzzy to Derek, as if he was looking at it through a fog. It wasn't the weather outside that concerned him, however, but the climate inside the executive wing—and the threat it presented to his future.

His plans had all been laid out since he'd joined the firm right out of college. But even before that, when he'd worked each summer at one of the McConnell factories, it had been in the back of his mind that someday he would succeed his father. And he suspected George McConnell had been thinking about the matter earlier yet—like clear back when he'd brought home each new toy for a toddler Derek to try out.

But now it was all at risk because the directors wanted a married CEO. Their point of view might be prehistoric, shortsighted and just plain wrong, but convincing them otherwise would be no easy matter. And though the requirement was probably discriminatory in a legal sense, what was the point in filing a lawsuit? Even if he succeeded in forcing his way into the job, the working conditions would be impossible for him and threatening for the company's survival.

It wasn't as if he had any real objection to going along with the requirement, anyway. So he got married—big deal. He'd always intended to get around to it sometime.

It had been a perfectly decent plan, his sensible search for a wife—and there was no reason it should have fallen apart. If Macey just hadn't gone off like a rocket last night...

But the fact was she had, and now his plan was shot to smithereens. The trouble was the full board of directors had scheduled a formal meeting to take place in exactly two weeks, and one of the items on the agenda would be his father's planned retirement. Derek had hoped—had even expected—to use that meeting to announce his wedding date.

Now he was going to have to pick himself up and start over again, from scratch.

Well, almost from scratch. The symphony party had

accomplished one thing, at least—it had marked Dinah off his list. He supposed he had Macey to thank for that much, because she was certainly the reason Dinah had let the corrosive acid seep into her usually sweet voice. He wondered if Macey would appreciate it if he called her to express his gratitude.

His father was already in the office, leaning against the desk of their mutual secretary and reading a letter. When Derek came in, George McConnell pushed his reading glasses up on top of his head, making his thinning reddish hair stand up in a sort of rooster's comb. "Late night, son?"

Derek resisted the urge to check his wristwatch, because he knew perfectly well he was on time to the minute. "Not particularly."

George grunted. "Well, I'm glad you're here. The chairman of the board is stopping by this morning. Perhaps you'd like to sit in on the meeting? I've asked for a presentation and taste test on the new line of organic baby foods."

Macey's voice echoed in his mind. *I don't imagine the board of directors eats baby food when they all get together...* He could picture the appreciative gleam that would spring to life in her big hazel eyes when she heard this story.

But of course she wouldn't be hearing it.

"Derek?" his father said, his voice a little sharper. "Do you want to join us?"

"I—uh..."

"He said he'd like to see you.... That must be him coming down the hall now. Half an hour early, too." George McConnell let his voice sink to a whisper. "Keep him occupied for a minute, will you? I have a couple of things to finish before I can spend all day dancing attendance on him.''

The chairman of the board advanced on Derek with a toothy smile and outstretched hand, his voice booming. ''Hello, Derek! I was hoping you'd be able to sit in today. Truth is, I wondered if you'll be free this weekend. My daughter's home right now—from Stanford, you know. She's almost finished with her degree. I think the two of you will have a lot in common.''

Derek didn't let his smile slip. ''Not this weekend, I'm afraid.''

''Then just name the day. She'll be here for a while. She'll be doing an internship downtown, so she's taking advantage of the free rent at home.'' His grin grew even wider.

''I...uh...'' Derek took a deep breath. ''Well, this is a little embarrassing, sir. I can't very well....it would be a little awkward....you see, I'm...''

Okay, McConnell, make up your mind where you're going with this. I'm dying of a mysterious disease... I'm hearing the call to become a monk... I'm running off to join the Foreign Legion...

''I'm engaged to be married,'' he said.

The chairman's grin disappeared. ''First I've heard about that.''

And you're not the only one. ''I can't go into detail just now.'' Derek shot a look over his shoulder at the door of his father's office, trying his best to look like an anxious son. ''You see, I haven't had a chance to inform my parents yet, so I really shouldn't be telling anyone at all. Actually we haven't even talked to *her* parents, and you know how it is with etiquette, sir. Women insist on taking all these things in what they think is proper order.''

George McConnell came out of his office, rubbing his

hands together. "Well, now we can get on with business. Derek, are you all right? You look pale and sweaty."

No fooling, Dad. You should feel it from this side.

"Your mother tells me you were restless last night—not acting at all like yourself."

"Well, you know how that goes. It was the symphony, after all—"

George frowned. "But you *like* the symphony, Derek. She thought you weren't feeling up to par, and she wondered if you were coming down with something."

"You know," Derek said heartily, "I think she's right. And I'm awfully afraid I might be contagious. Maybe I should just go home."

Normally, Macey liked going to work. There were days, of course, when her level of enthusiasm wasn't exactly stratospheric, but on the average she loved her job. Loved the unexpectedness of each new day. Loved the people. Loved the puzzle of putting the right worker together with each new job. Loved hearing the stories of how Peterson Temps had once more saved the day.

Not this morning. Today, she was going to have to face Robert Peterson and explain the unexplainable.

She wasn't even going to have the advantage of confessing that she'd messed up. Not that she was exactly proud of the way she'd blown last night, because she wasn't—but she wasn't about to take the blame for something that wasn't her fault. She'd tried to tell Robert that the plan was unworkable. She'd tried to tell Derek that he was nuts. She'd tried in every way she could think of to stop the train wreck from happening.

But it wasn't much satisfaction to know that she'd been absolutely right.

And she *really* wasn't looking forward to telling Robert

about how all the goodwill, along with the future business he'd hoped to win from Derek McConnell, had flown south like a flock of butterflies—because it wasn't going to migrate back again.

She dressed with extra care—though she didn't wear her best suit, the forest green one. After last night, she thought, it might be years before she could bear to put it on again. Though she often left her hair loose around her shoulders, today she put it up in a professional-looking French twist. She added a pair of chunky earrings that Clara had made in ceramics class and painted to compliment the apricot and teal tweed of her suit. And she stepped into her highest heels. She was going to need every inch of self-assurance when she faced Robert.

She'd been at her desk for an hour, shifting paper and trying to be productive, when Robert came in. She gave him a few minutes to get settled and then tapped on his door. "If I can have a minute, Robert..."

He was just picking up the telephone. "Yes, this is Peterson." He waved Macey to a chair and mouthed, "I'll be right with you."

She sat down, folding her hands primly in her lap and trying to come up with an opening line that wouldn't simply make things worse.

"Yes," Robert said and turned his chair to face the window, so his back to was to Macey. "Yes, I think.... I understand. Yes, we can do that." He wheeled around and put the telephone down.

She took a breath to begin, but Robert spoke first. "That was Derek McConnell."

Macey was stunned. The last thing she'd have expected from Derek was that he'd be a tattletale.

Oh, do grow up, Phillips, she told herself. *You sound like a second-grader.*

"I can explain, Robert. At least, I'll try to explain—though since you weren't there, you can't possibly picture what it was like last night—"

"Explain what?" Robert sounded only mildly interested. "Never mind, you can fill in the details another time. I told him you'd be right over."

"Over?" Macey asked uncertainly. "Over where?"

"Derek's apartment. He's taking a day of sick leave, he said, in order to plan what he called Stage Two. Run along, now—you don't want to keep him waiting."

Yes, I do.

"And then," Robert said comfortably, "you can tell me all about how Stage One went when you get back."

Derek didn't live in a sleek glass tower as Macey would have expected, but in a solid old block-square warehouse that had been converted into lofts. Part of a once-bustling complex that overlooked the Mississippi River, it had sat empty for years before being rescued and renovated.

It even had a uniformed doorman, who looked Macey over and said politely, "Who did you wish to see, ma'am?"

"There's no wishing about it," Macey muttered. "Sorry, it's not your fault that I'm a bit steamed. I'm here at Mr. McConnell's request."

He picked up the house phone. "I'll announce you anyway, ma'am. Who shall I say—" He paused. "A lady to see you, sir. Yes, sir, I'll send her right up." He turned back to Macey. "It's the fifth floor. The elevators are right down that hall."

She didn't remember to ask for an apartment number until she was already on the elevator, and then she decided it was too much bother to go back downstairs. As it happened, however, she didn't need a number. Derek's apartment wasn't *on* the fifth floor—it *was* the fifth floor.

He opened the door before she could even ring the bell. "You don't look sick," Macey announced.

In fact, she thought, he looked pretty good all the way around. He was wearing jeans and a dark blue pullover that emphasized the breadth of his shoulders, and he was barefoot. The casual look suited him.

"Maybe not," Derek said. "But I feel pretty sick at the moment."

"Not nearly as sick as you're going to be if you don't leave me alone. I only came today in order to get this settled once and for all. I told you last night I was done, and—"

"Macey, take it easy on me, will you? I really do have a tearing headache."

"You deserve it."

"How about sitting down over a cup of coffee and talking about it?"

"What is there to talk about?"

"Please?" He pointed to a long leather couch. It was the only place she could see to sit, except for the hardwood floor. The spike heels of Macey's shoes clicked firmly against the polished oak as she crossed the room.

Behind the couch, a wall of windows looked out over the river. The stainless steel Gateway Arch gleamed off to one side, and far below a row of barges made slow but steady progress north against the current.

She sat down and looked around. The apartment was almost entirely open, except for a big square brick core placed smack in the center and reaching all the way to the shadowy ceiling far above. From the couch she could see two sides of the core; built into one wall was a huge fireplace and an even larger television screen. Along the other visible wall, indented into the block, was a small but efficient-looking kitchen, set at an angle from the front door and separated from it by a narrow work island. Though the living room soared the full height of the loft, at one corner of the core an openwork iron staircase spiraled upward to what must be a bedroom. It occupied half of the upper reaches of the loft and was blocked off from below only by a wrought-iron railing.

Talk about your basic bachelor pad, Macey thought.

Despite the lack of furnishings, however, it didn't appear that he had recently moved in. The room didn't have the unfinished appearance of a brand-new decorating scheme. It didn't look raw; it just looked empty, as if he didn't want to be bothered with more.

Derek came back with two big mugs. "It's only fake cappuccino," he admitted. "But it's actually not bad stuff."

Macey took a tentative sip, set the cup down, and looked him straight in the eye. "You honestly have no clue how much your life is going to change if you get married," she said. She didn't intend it to be a question.

"You don't like the cappuccino."

"I didn't say that. Anyway, the cappuccino is only a detail. Any woman on that list of yours either already owns a cappuccino machine or she'll get one for a shower gift. She's also going to have a lot of other stuff."

Derek shrugged. "It's not like I've already filled the place up."

"I'm not just talking about physical baggage. The point is, instead of talking about Stage Two—whatever that involves—I think you'd be better off to give some serious thought to whether you want to do this at all."

"Of course I do."

"Of course you *don't*," Macey said flatly. "That's why

you're trying to hire me. So you'll have someone to blame if it doesn't work out.''

"You're just trying to get out of the job."

"Yes, I am. But I still think you shouldn't be in such a rush. Have you even considered how you're going to go about fitting a woman into your life?"

He said dryly, "There have been a few, you know."

"I don't doubt it a bit. That just proves my point. Having an overnight guest now and then is a whole lot different from living with somebody. All right, let's leave emotional adjustment out of it for a minute and just talk about space."

He waved a hand. "There's lots of it."

"Open air, yes. But I'm betting this apartment doesn't have enough extra closet space for a three-year-old, much less the kind of clotheshorse you're contemplating marrying."

He sighed. "You may have a point there. But I don't have a choice about what I do anymore."

Macey put her head back against the soft leather couch and gave an exaggerated sigh. "And I obviously don't have a choice about whether I hear the details. What's happened now?"

"This morning, I was talking to the chairman of the board. And I...sort of...announced that I'm engaged."

She sat up slowly. "Who's the lucky woman?" she asked suspiciously.

"I didn't give him a name."

Slowly, she released the breath she'd held. At least he'd maintained a shard of common sense. It could have been a great deal worse. On the other hand, if he had just blurted out a name off the top of his head, Macey would be off scot-free. It would be Derek's problem to convince the lady in question, and nothing at all to do with Macey.

Unless, of course, it had been *her* name he'd blurted out....

And why, she asked herself, would an idiotic idea like that come into her mind? Even Derek wasn't desperate enough to think of that little twist—and Macey was glad.

Very glad. So glad, in fact, that she wasn't even going to consider the idea for an instant, for fear he might overhear her thoughts and act on the notion before he stopped to think. It would be just like him.

"So the rumors will be flying," she mused.

"I bought myself a little time by telling him I had to talk to my bride's parents before there could be an announcement."

"Talking to the bride might be a nice idea, too. You actually think he'll keep quiet about it?"

"He keeps company secrets all the time."

"That's an entirely different thing. But you know him—I don't. Maybe you'll be lucky. So what are you going to do?" she asked, keeping her voice carefully casual.

"Get engaged, of course."

"Oh, now that's a shocker. It's so original. So unexpected. So inventive... Dammit, Derek, I was talking about your plan. What's Stage Two?"

Derek propped his elbows on his knees and dropped his face into his hands. "I was hoping you'd help me figure that out."

Macey considered pouring the rest of her cappuccino over his head. "You haven't got even the shadow of an idea?"

"I wouldn't have called you if I wasn't desperate, Macey."

She released a long, tired sigh. "Tell me something I

didn't already know,'' she muttered. "Do you realize you have all the tact of a buzzard, McConnell?"

He sat up again and shot a look at her. "Would you rather I use my charm to get you to help me?"

"You *have* charm?"

"Ouch. I'm begging you, Macey."

"Oh, now we might be getting somewhere. Derek McConnell begging..." She considered. "No. Sorry. I thought for a minute there that the idea of Mr. Perfection on his knees might be interesting, but I'm afraid it doesn't move me after all."

"Then what does move you, Macey? What will it take to persuade you?" His voice was low and husky.

That's what he sounds like in bed. She didn't quite understand how she knew, but she was certain of it. The sudden, incredibly vivid image that came into her mind was almost more than Macey could handle. The idea of Derek begging had left her cold. But the vision of Derek persuading...convincing...seducing...

Her mouth went dry. With distaste, she told herself— but she knew better. "I'll see what I can do," Macey said. Her voice felt shaky.

Derek smiled. "That's my girl." He leaned a little closer. His hand moved along the back of the couch toward her shoulder, caressing the leather as if he were caressing skin... The nape of her neck prickled with anticipation.

A buzzer sounded, harsh in the empty air. Without hurry, Derek withdrew his hand and stood up. "Sorry, but that's the house phone and since the doorman knows quite well I'm here, I'd better answer. He wouldn't call unless..." He frowned.

Unless it's important, Macey finished. *Because he knows there's a woman up here.*

Derek crossed the expanse of gleaming oak floor toward the kitchen and picked up the phone. "What is it this time, Ted?" He winced. "All right. Thanks."

"Let me guess," Macey said. "Ten eligible women are downstairs negotiating to see who gets to audition first."

"No. It's my mother. She's on her way up carrying a bucket of chicken soup."

"That's what you get for pretending to be sick. Though it could be worse—she might have talked to the chairman of the board and be coming to grill you. I'll just..." Macey paused. "Wait a minute. It hasn't occurred to you to bribe the doorman to keep your female guests from running into each other?"

"Of course I pay him extra. Only it's called a tip, not a bribe."

"That's a matter of opinion. So why didn't he stop her in the lobby?"

"Because there's never been a doorman on the planet who could stop my mother if she wanted to go through, that's why. The best he could have done was slow her down. That's why he called—to warn me."

"He wouldn't have told her I'm here?"

"Of course not. It's a sizable tip."

"Probably not sizable enough, considering the trouble you must put him to. What now? How do I get out of here?"

"You don't. If you leave, there's no way you can miss running into her."

"The fire stairs?"

"They're right beside the elevator door, which will be opening just about—" He glanced at his watch. "Now."

The doorbell buzzed.

"Oh, this should be fun," Macey muttered.

"Upstairs," Derek ordered. "And be quiet, because sound bounces in here."

"It's never occurred to you that echoes may be an inhibiting factor for some women?" She climbed the stairs on tiptoe so the spike heels of her shoes wouldn't catch in the openwork iron steps.

The room at the top of the stairs was only half the size of the lower floor, but it was just as spare and open as the living room below. In the center of the room was a king-size bed swathed in a muted plaid bedspread in harvest colors. On either side stood a small table; each held a lamp. Atop one of the tables was a book, open and facedown as if he'd been interrupted while reading—the autobiography of a Wall Street mogul, she noted.

Near the top of the stairs, in the brick core, was a door which must lead to either a closet or a bathroom—there must be enough room in that core for both. Perhaps she'd been wrong about the amount of closet space, Macey thought idly.

The rest of the room was empty. From the railing, if she dared, she could look down onto the living room. But of course she didn't dare.

She sat down on the end of the bed and tried not to listen. But Derek had said himself that sound echoed. He had to know that she couldn't help but hear.

The door opened, and a warm, low, cultured voice said, "What's wrong, darling? You haven't been sick enough to take a day off work in at least a year."

Macey took off her shoes, setting them as quietly as she could on the hardwood floor, and lay down across the bedspread, on her back with her elbows out so she could press her fingertips against her ears to block the sound of the conversation from below.

But if listening had felt immoral, not listening felt stupid—how was she supposed to know when it was safe? When Derek came upstairs and found her lying in his bed?

Talk about asking for trouble.

She tried not to remember the way his hand had moved over the leather couch, tried not to imagine how it would feel against her skin.

She told herself it was no big deal. He'd touched her last night, after all. But that had been little more than a brush of his hand against her arm. And it had been in a crowd.

Here...alone...in his bed...

She muttered a curse and sat up.

From downstairs there was an instant's silence. "It's only from the deli," Mrs. McConnell said. "You know I don't do homemade. I hope it helps you feel better. I'm afraid I can't stay longer, but then you don't look as if you need your mommy to nurse you anyway."

"You're not going to spoon-feed me?" Derek asked lazily.

Macey thought she could hear relief in his voice. No surprise there.

"No, I have a lunch date. You don't mind if I freshen up before I go, do you?"

"Of course not, Mom."

"I'll just run upstairs for a moment then."

Macey heard footsteps crossing the room. It must be her imagination, she thought, but it sounded like the threatening tread of an army battalion.

"Uh—Mom—"

"What's the matter, Derek? I promise not to scold if your bed's not made. It's just that I much prefer a bathroom with a mirror that's actually large enough to see my whole face. I've never understood why, with all this space to work with, the builders made your downstairs powder room smaller than the lavatory on an airplane."

She was halfway up the stairs when Macey regained control of her muscles. She twisted off the mattress, stifling a groan when her hip bumped against the hard floor, and squirmed underneath the bed just as Mrs. McConnell reached the top of the stairs.

The woman walked without hurry across the room, and Macey felt the vibration of each footstep. A moment later a door opened and closed.

Macey tried not to breathe for fear the dust under the bed would make her sneeze.

The door opened again. Footsteps once more crossed the room.

Another minute and she'll be gone. You can do it, Macey. You can hold your breath for one more minute…

But the footsteps didn't go down the stairs. A soft voice said, "Excuse me for intruding, dear. But perhaps you'll let me give you some advice, as one woman to another. Next time you're hiding under a man's bed…" Her voice dropped to a whisper. "Don't forget to take your shoes."

CHAPTER FOUR

FROM her shallow, dimly lighted niche, Macey could hear only the murmur of voices downstairs; she couldn't pick out words. But at least neither of them was yelling. That was a good sign....wasn't it?

Though she honestly couldn't imagine Derek's mother losing it enough to scream under any circumstances. Judging by her reaction to finding a woman under her son's bed, Macey thought it was fair to conclude that all of Mrs. McConnell's reprimands would be delivered with similar style and grace, plus a calm that would be absolutely deadly.

Macey lay still until she heard the click of the door closing before she cautiously started to maneuver herself out from under the bed. It was more difficult to move than she'd expected because the space was so confined.

How, she wondered, had she been able to get under there so fast when it took such concentrated effort to wiggle her way back out?

As soon as she was back on her feet, though she was still feeling a little light-headed, she walked around the end of the bed. The bedspread was rumpled where she'd been lying. And sure enough, there were her teal-colored heels in plain sight, one standing upright, the other lying on its side, precisely where she had so carefully taken them off. They looked almost like a department store display. She kicked one of them, and tried in vain to bite back a yell when the end of her toenail collided with the metal-capped spike heel.

Derek's bare feet made little sound on the iron stairs, but she heard him coming anyway. "Is she really gone?" Macey asked, suddenly suspicious. She'd heard the door close, but...

He crossed the room without a word and flung himself on the bed, face up, eyes closed, and arms outstretched. "She's gone."

"What did she say to you?" Macey asked warily.

"The usual sweet nothings. Not a word about the live dust bunny under my bed."

"So what did you say to her?"

"Nothing. You can't explain something to someone who's pretending it didn't happen."

Macey tried to brush the smudges off her jacket. "Speaking of dust bunnies, I wasn't the only one. Don't you ever mop the floor up here?"

Derek opened his eyes. "You're worried about the floor?"

"Oh, damn— Look, I snagged my jacket. There must be a loose spring under there or something."

He didn't seem to hear her. "Under the bed. You had to go hide *under the bed*. Of all the childish, shortsighted, idiotic stunts—"

"Hey, Einstein, look around and you may notice there aren't a lot of options up here. What else was I supposed to do?"

"It didn't occur to you to sit still and say, 'Hello, Mrs. McConnell'?"

"What?" Macey's voice was little short of a shriek. "You're the one who shoved me up and told me not to make a sound!"

"There's a point of diminishing returns, Macey. When you're inevitably going to get caught, you're better off to admit to it and take your punishment."

"Oh, that's rich. At least now I understand your philosophy on marriage—if it's inevitable, admit it and take your punishment." She tugged at the broken thread. Before it had snapped, it had pulled at the loose weave of the tweed, and the sleeve was now twisted so awkwardly it was beyond repair. "You owe me an outfit, McConnell."

He didn't move. "Send the bill to my mother."

"Oh sure. And I'll just include a note explaining that I'm the woman who was under her son's bed and I want compensation for damages to my clothes."

"She'd probably be amazed to find out that you had any on."

Macey sighed. "The only blessing in this whole thing is that she doesn't know exactly who was under the bed. If I'm really lucky, she might even assume it was Princess Buttercup."

"Princess—*who?*"

"The blonde in the yellow dress you were talking to at the party last night."

"Oh, you mean Dinah. No, I don't think Mom would believe it was her. Dinah wouldn't have gone under the bed, she'd have stripped down and hopped into it."

"Does that disqualify her from your list, or move her up higher?" Macey didn't wait for an answer. "Gee, why didn't I think of that? I wonder if I could have managed to get my clothes off fast enough to be convincing."

Derek held up his wrist. "I've got a stopwatch. Want me to time you while you practice?"

"I was being sarcastic, Derek."

"Imagine that. Macey Phillips—sarcastic!"

"I was trying to make the point that things could have been worse."

"I don't know—if she'd actually seen you between the

sheets, Mom couldn't have ignored the subject. Anyway, you might have been being sarcastic, but I wasn't.'' He propped himself up on one elbow. ''We could have a race, if you'd like. See who can get naked first.''

She turned 'round to give him a cold and disbelieving stare—one that would put him in his place. But as she looked at him lounging across the bed, she was stunned to find just how little imagination it took to picture him without jeans and shirt. To visualize him reaching up to pull her down beside him. Beneath him...

All right, she admitted. The man did absolutely drip sex appeal. A woman would have to be blind not to notice that.

And deaf, too, whispered a voice at the back of her mind. *And probably also suffering from a head cold that wiped out her sense of smell.*

But being aware of his magnetic power didn't mean that she, personally, found him irresistible. Far from it.

The best way to handle this, she told herself, was to ignore him.

''I want handicap points for the race, though,'' Derek went on.

Macey's good intentions went straight out the window. ''For what? Why? You're wearing less than I am to start with!''

''But I'm lying down, so it would be harder for me to get out of my clothes. To say nothing of how distracting it would be to watch you.''

Macey tried not to gulp at the idea of him lying there watching her undress. ''This is not getting us any farther toward developing Stage Two.''

''Spoilsport.'' He rolled off the bed and landed on his feet within inches of her, so close she could almost taste him.

She stepped back and the arch of her bare foot came down hard on the spike heel of the shoe she'd kicked in frustration. Off balance, she grabbed for the nearest support, which happened to be Derek's wrist. But she couldn't get a good enough grip to save herself, just enough to pull him down with her as she tumbled sideways onto the bed.

"You didn't have to attack me, sweetheart," he murmured. "All you had to do was ask." He shifted his weight so he wasn't quite pinning her down, and his fingertips grazed her temple, her cheek, her throat. "But now we're both going to have trouble getting out of our clothes."

Macey wasn't worried about that challenge. Another few minutes of this and her suit would have turned to ash anyway.

His lips brushed the line of her jaw, leaving a scorched trail. She watched his eyes darken.

"Don't bother trying to figure out the logistics." She planted a hand in the center of his chest and shoved, and when he pulled back she rolled out from under him and onto her feet. Picking up her stray shoes, she headed for the stairs.

By the time he followed, she was already perched on a high stool at the kitchen island, and the planning calendar she always carried was open on the counter in front of her. She didn't look up. "You have thirty seconds to get serious about Stage Two, or I'm leaving."

"You know, Macey," he murmured, "it's a good thing for you I'm not a suspicious sort of guy. Because if I was, I'd be wondering if the reason you were in such a hurry to get out of my bed was because you didn't trust yourself to stop at a kiss. Another cappuccino?"

"Not unless you mean a real one this time."

He put a large spoonful of brownish powder into a mug and filled it from an extra faucet in the kitchen sink, then sat down beside her, stirring the brew. Macey watched the steam rise from the mug. The water from that tap must be almost at the boiling point.

Just like your skin still is where he touched you.

"Your thirty seconds are almost up," she reminded. "And you can start by convincing me why I should hang around and help you work out a plan at all."

"Because your boss won't be happy with you if you don't."

She planted her elbows on the counter. "Do you realize that Robert fully expects you to throw enough temp work our way to justify opening another office?"

"Another office?" Derek sounded as if he'd suddenly had the breath knocked out of him.

"Another complete branch of Peterson Temps," she clarified. "So besides whatever fee he's charging you for this, you may as well know that he's expecting you to be paying forever."

He didn't answer.

"That's what I thought," Macey said with satisfaction. "I'll just be running along—you can stop in sometime and give Robert some story about why it didn't work out."

"How many temps does an office handle?"

"You don't seriously want to know."

"I'll see what I can manage. Robert can't ask any more than for me to try."

Macey sighed. "Well, first you'll have to manage getting married and getting named CEO. And after last night, I don't see how I could be much help."

"The problem last night was our being there together." He took the spoon out of the mug and licked it.

Macey tried not to watch the way his lips caressed the stainless steel. Tried not to think about how he might approach something which was softer and more flexible.

"We were unprepared," Derek said, "and we drew attention to ourselves."

"And whose fault is that? I asked you to quietly point out the possibilities, but no, you wanted to introduce me personally."

"My mistake. I admit it. From now on we can't let it be known that you're connected with me."

"Don't you think it's a little late for that?"

"It was only one evening. People will dismiss it as a coincidence, as long as we're not seen together again."

That means no more parties, she thought. *And I'm glad.*

"So what do we do instead?" Macey asked. "If you can get me all the information about these women, I can do a sort of statistical analysis, but I'm not sure how much good that will do."

"None. The whole reason I need you is the personal approach. Your feminine judgment. So you'll simply have to start hanging out in the same places these women do and getting to know them."

"You think they're just going to take a stranger under their wing and make we welcome? Get real, Derek. I don't belong in those places."

"You'll have to make yourself belong. You can't buy an Armani suit if you only shop at discount stores."

"Armani," she mused, and brushed a hand over the broken thread, still dangling from her sleeve. "That would make a nice replacement for my ruined tweed."

He didn't seem to be listening. "I'll make you a list. Two lists, in fact. Places to go, and people to look for. Mind if I grab some paper?" He reached for the planner.

"Not that page, it's got my grocery list on it." Macey pulled a sheet from the back and handed it to him. "So where am I shopping?"

"You can start with lunch at Arcadia, though unfortunately it's too late to go today. It's the in spot at the moment among the young women in this town, and on any given day there are going to be a dozen of them there. Then you'll be in, and you won't need me."

Macey stared at him. The man actually sounded as if he were serious. "I'm supposed to just drop in for lunch and end up best friends," she said. "Would you suggest I simply sit there and look forlorn until someone invites me over? Or shall I be direct and ask straight out if I can come and join the play group?"

"Well, I don't suggest that you sit there and read a book. Take someone with you. Hire somebody if you have to."

"Did I say you had as much tact as a buzzard does?" Macey asked sweetly. "Forget it—you're not even close to reaching the buzzard's level."

"Okay, I'm sorry. I didn't mean to imply that you don't have friends. There must be somebody you want to take to lunch." He winced. "That wasn't much better, was it?"

"No, you pretty much just recycled the insult. As a matter of fact, there is someone I'd like to invite. I'll let you know how it goes." Macey shut her planner with a snap. It would probably be smart, she told herself, to leave before she told him exactly what she thought of his plan. But she couldn't quite suppress the urge to have the last word. "Amazing," she murmured. "I'd have sworn you said just a little while ago that you didn't have any ideas at all about how to approach Stage Two."

Derek opened the door with a flourish. "I didn't, a few minutes ago. Isn't it incredible how sharing a bed with you inspired me?"

Macey had read the food critic's column about Arcadia when the restaurant first opened, and she'd concluded that the review was probably the closest she'd ever get to the trendy new bistro. Not that she wouldn't like to see the place. What attracted her, however, was neither the food nor the upscale clientele. She just wanted to see what a professionally run con game looked like, and she thought Arcadia was the best anywhere around.

"People don't eat at Arcadia," she told Clara as they walked from the parking ramp across the street to the sprawling building which housed the restaurant. "They *graze.*"

Clara frowned. "Like cows?"

"Something like that. There's no menu, so you don't order. You choose from a selection of food laid out on a big horseshoe-shaped table."

Clara shrugged. "Sounds like a buffet to me. Or a smorgasbord. What's so original about that? For that matter, what's so wrong with it?"

"Nothing at all. That's what makes it ingenious. You promise an unlimited choice and quantity of food, but you promote it to a clientele who survives on diet colas and lettuce. The women come to be seen, they pay an incredible price for lunch, and then they eat two carrots and a slice of cucumber. The rest is profit. It's like counterfeiting money, only it's completely legal."

Clara balked at the door. "So if it's ruinously expensive, why are we here?"

A young woman in a very tight sweater bumped into Clara's capacious handbag, almost knocking her off balance. Instead of apologizing, she rolled her eyes and ostentatiously walked around them.

Well, honey, Macey thought, *if it were my list we were checking out, you'd be off it right now.*

"Lunch is like getting a bonus," she said vaguely.

Clara's eyes widened. "You're kidding. *Robert's* paying for this?"

"No. A client I'm working for." Macey approached the maître d's stand. "Reservation for Phillips, please."

The maître d' looked pained at the idea of a diner so anonymous that she had to give her name, but he led them to a table. "Would you like to look at a wine list, madame?"

"Certainly," Macey said.

"Is this the same client you met for the symphony party?" Clara asked.

Macey nodded curtly and pretended to read the wine list. If she didn't volunteer anything, maybe Clara would let the matter drop.

"He likes your work that much?"

Macey looked over the edge of the burgundy leather folder. "Clara, I don't believe I ever said whether this client was male or female."

"You didn't," Clara said, and smiled. "But you have now, because if it was a woman you'd have answered the question instead of dodging it." She sat back in her chair with an air of contentment and looked across at the array of food. "So those are the choices of the day? Well, they won't make much money on me, because I plan to taste everything."

Macey put the wine list down and surveyed the buffet table. Though it was enormous, it was dwarfed by the sheer size of the room. There was only one dining room at Arcadia, and the tables were arranged so each one had maximum visibility. As the reviewer had said, what point was there in paying a fortune to be seen at the trendiest place in town if you ended up sitting in a spot so isolated that no one knew you were there?

"I doubt it tastes as good as it looks," Macey warned. "For all I know, the chocolate cheesecake is really made of plastic. If my suspicions are right, nobody's ever actually tried a slice, so it might as well be fake."

Not that Macey particularly cared whether the food was good. She hoped it was, for Clara's sake. But Macey hadn't come to eat, only to observe. If Derek wanted to pay the price of admission, she'd happily people-watch at Arcadia.

Because that was all she could accomplish, really. His notion that all she had to do was show up in order to be taken to the collective bosom of the young women of his social set fell somewhere on the scale between peculiar and ludicrous. What she could do was watch and listen, try to put names with faces, and get an idea of how the women on his list behaved when there wasn't a man around to impress.

Or at least, when the man in question wasn't Derek—because there were a few men in the crowd. She watched one crossing the room with a plate so fully loaded that he couldn't actually walk; he was shuffling along like a snail in an effort to keep everything level. Maybe Arcadia didn't turn quite such a marvelous profit as she'd thought....

And though Derek had been right about the number of young women milling around the buffet, table-hopping, and striking poses to impress the onlookers, there were plenty of people who didn't fit into that category too.

Clara nudged her and pointed to a table, just two rows away, where four matrons were already at the dessert stage. "It looks like you're wrong about the chocolate cheesecake. I have an idea—let's start with dessert and work our way backward through the main courses and appetizers."

Macey wasn't listening. One of the matrons at the table was the woman who had approached her at the symphony cocktail party—the one who had offered to introduce her to Derek's mother.

And right across the table from her was Mrs. McConnell. Right where she could hardly avoid staring straight in Macey's direction. And, possibly, wondering where she might have encountered her before...

That's only your guilty conscience talking, Macey told herself. There was no reason Derek's mother should recognize her. If she'd gotten a look at the symphony party, it could only have been a brief one. And there was no reason for her to notice one young woman more or less in Arcadia's dining room.

So why, every time Macey darted a look in her direction, did Mrs. McConnell seem to be watching her?

Macey chose only a few samples from the main courses to nibble on, more to keep up appearances than because she felt like eating. With Mrs. McConnell just across the room, the last thing she needed was to drip tomato sauce down the front of her dress.

But Clara made good on her threat to focus on dessert. "It's actually very nice, the way they've cut everything into bite-size pieces," she said as she finished a square inch of carrot cake and moved on to the black forest torte. "You can try them all. It's so disappointing to get a whole slab of something and then discover it doesn't taste as good as it looks. Raspberry mousse—this looks good. So tell me, Macey. You're obviously not here to eat, so I'd like to know what kind of secret operation I'm providing the cover for."

Macey was startled.

"I know—the old, depressed Clara wouldn't have noticed," Clara said. "Of course, the old, depressed Clara would have stayed home altogether. I told you I'm feeling better on this new medicine." She shook her head at the rest of the raspberry mousse and moved on to the key lime pie.

"It's a sort of research project," Macey said. "Observing the young women. It would help if I knew their names, but I suppose even a description will help him figure out which is which."

"You don't seem to be doing much looking."

"Well, I can't exactly stare. It's rude—and it draws attention."

Clara's fork was suspended over her dessert plate. "What exactly are you observing?"

"Their behavior, their attitudes. Why?"

"Because I can stare all I like. Nobody pays attention to one old lady more or less—we're almost expected to be rude. The blonde by the buffet table, for instance…"

Macey took a quick look. "Oh, that's just Buttercup. She doesn't count—at least, she's not on the list. But what do you think of the two women she's with?"

Clara looked for a long moment. "Not much to distinguish them—from each other or anyone else."

Macey sighed. "That's the problem. They all run together, somehow."

A shadow fell across the table. "I don't mean to intrude," said Mrs. McConnell. "But I'm almost certain I recognize you."

Macey's breath froze in her throat. Very slowly, she turned to face Derek's mother.

However, the woman wasn't looking at Macey, but at Clara. "You're very familiar," she mused. "And yet..."

"Oh, that's because unlike some of our contemporaries I haven't gone in for face-lifts and skin peels and hair dye," Clara said comfortably. "And I see you haven't much either, Enid—but a bit of age looks good on you."

"Clara! I thought—"

"That I was long dead? Lots of people got that idea. This is my niece, by the way."

"Your sister's daughter?" Enid McConnell offered her hand. "Or your brother's?"

Macey tried to will herself not to tremble as she took it. She shook her head, but her voice didn't seem to work anymore.

"Macey is my brother's son's wife, actually," Clara explained. "It sounds pretty complicated, I'm afraid."

"Oh, yes. I'd forgotten for a moment, Clara, that you had just the one brother. How nice to meet you, Mrs. Phillips. I love your earrings."

Macey's hand went automatically to her earlobe as she tried to remember what she'd put on this morning. Oh yes—the ones Derek had called dinner plates.

"I made them in my ceramics class," Clara said. "But I'm getting a bit bored with it. I think when I'm finished making Macey's nativity set I'm going to try porcelain painting."

"Do sit down," Macey managed to say finally.

"Go spend some time with your friends, dear," Clara said placidly. "Enid will keep me company for a few minutes—won't you?"

Run along and play, Clara might as well have said. What was she thinking? Worse, what was she likely to say? But Macey was in no position to argue about it. All she could do was hope that since Clara didn't know her client's name, and Mrs. McConnell hadn't seemed to recognize her, that they would have no reason to compare notes.

It wasn't much comfort. Still in shock, she managed to get herself to the buffet table.

Buttercup—no, the woman's name was Dinah, Macey reminded herself—and her two friends were hovering over the salad bar as if their selections were as important as partitioning a nation. Dinah moved aside barely an inch and said, "Well, if it isn't the mystery woman. You're turning up everywhere these days. Tell me, are you new in town or just an upstart?"

One of the young women squeaked as if in protest. The other tried to hide a smile.

"Oh, I wouldn't want to ruin all the fun you're having speculating," Macey said gently. She put a strawberry on her plate and moved toward the dessert section—as far as she could get from the trio.

Well, Phillips, that wasn't a very successful investigative move.

She glanced back at the table. Clara and Enid McConnell were practically nose to nose. Macey sighed and decided to wander around the room as if she were admiring the art on the walls. If she dawdled beside each table, maybe she could overhear enough of a conversation to pick up some names, at least.

When she looked back a few minutes later, she was stunned to see that their table was empty. A busboy was gathering up the wineglasses and Clara's dessert plate.

"The ladies who were here," Macey said. "Did you see where they went?"

The busboy shrugged. "Sorry, ma'am."

Macey hurried toward the door. Even the maître d' was gone. Perhaps they'd stepped outside for some air, because it was feeling stuffy in the building—or was that only because she felt so flustered?

She paused just outside the door. As a cool breeze lifted the tendrils of hair around her face, a hand closed on her arm and pulled her aside, behind a huge concrete planter full of decorative grasses.

"Derek," she gasped. "What are you doing here? And why are you acting like a spy?"

"Because I just saw my mother come out of there."

"So you hung around to see what would happen next? That's brilliant. Was she with anyone?"

"No. Why? What happened?"

So wherever Clara was, she was alone. "Nothing much. This is impossible, Derek. They're all interchangeable anyway. Why don't you just tack all the names up on a wall and start tossing darts? If the first one you hit isn't gullible enough to take you, you can just keep on throwing till you get lucky. Look, I'll tell you the details later—the little there is to report—but right now I've lost track of my...someone...and I really need to go." She didn't wait for an answer but headed back into the restaurant.

Clara was standing just inside the foyer, swinging her handbag. "Ladies' room," she explained. "I thought you saw me leave. That was incredible, Macey."

"The ladies' room, or lunch in general?"

"No, dear. You're a smart girl, wandering around that way—giving me the excuse to ask Enid about everyone you strolled past." She unclasped her handbag and pulled out the wine list from their table. Her voice dropped to a conspiratorial whisper. "I've got the scoop on every one of them, right here."

Enid McConnell was unusually solicitous, which was enough to send Derek's suspicion meter well into the danger zone. "I'm so glad you're feeling enough better to come to dinner," she cooed as he fixed her a drink from the cart in the McConnells' living room. "I hope you're up to eating spicy things—your father's bringing home Mexican."

"I'll risk it. What's the occasion, anyway?"

"No occasion. Can't I invite my son to dinner without having an excuse? Thank you, dear." She took a long sip of her Scotch and soda. "So much better than the stuff we served at the symphony party, don't you think? I wonder if that's what gave you the funny bug yesterday... Why didn't you introduce me to that young woman, by the way?"

Well, it hadn't taken long for her to come to the point. "Which young woman?"

"You know perfectly well which one I'm talking about. The only young woman there that I didn't already know."

That was a distinction he hadn't considered before.

"I saw her again at Arcadia today," Enid said. "She was having lunch."

Treat it casually. "I didn't realize you hung out there." He dropped a couple of ice cubes in a glass for himself and put in a splash of Scotch.

"It turns out," Enid said without looking at him, "that she's the niece of an old friend of mine."

No wonder Macey had been so distracted when he'd showed up outside Arcadia. But why hadn't she told him she'd actually been introduced to his mother? Unless she hadn't. *I've lost track of my...someone...* Her words came back to him.

And he'd thought she'd been nervous because she didn't want to tell him that the person she'd taken to lunch was a guy. As if he'd have cared!

But maybe she hadn't been part of the old friends'

meeting. Maybe there hadn't been an official introduction after all. Or maybe she'd known all along that there was a relationship between his mother and this relative of Macey's....

"Whose niece?" he asked, trying to sound casual. "Anybody I know?"

"I doubt it. An old school friend. And to be absolutely accurate, she's not the niece."

Derek's head was throbbing again. "I thought you said—"

Enid shrugged. "Oh, it ends up being the same thing. She's my friend's nephew's wife."

Married? Macey was *married?*

Derek's glass slipped out of his fingers and shattered on the flagstone floor.

CHAPTER FIVE

DEREK looked down at the wreckage of the cocktail glass, but he didn't see it. He was picturing Macey.

As a long-confirmed single man, it had become second nature to him to glance at the left hand of every woman he met. It was such an ingrained habit, in fact, that he couldn't even recall for certain whether or not he'd checked Macey's. Surely he had—and yet under the circumstances in which he'd met her, perhaps for once he hadn't paid any attention.

Focused on his own marital status, it might not have occurred to him to check hers. There was no reason to, after all—he had simply accepted Robert's assurance that Macey was safe, that she was not at all the sort of woman who would get carried away by the romantic notion of marrying him herself...

No wonder Robert was so certain, dummy.

But he could see her in his mind as clearly as if they were still sitting together in Robert's office, with Derek explaining his situation and Macey listening intently—and wearing only one earring. He'd certainly noticed that. How could he have missed a wedding band?

He hadn't missed it because she didn't wear one. That was the only explanation.

Lots of professional women don't, McConnell.

Not that it mattered, of course. Ring or no ring, married or not—it didn't make any difference.

He didn't quite see why Robert hadn't told him exactly why Macey was no risk. It wasn't as if being married was a sin, for heaven's sake. But he supposed that was Robert's business, and maybe Derek just hadn't given him the chance to go into detail.

He also didn't quite understand why Macey hadn't ever mentioned it. But then perhaps he'd been so focused on his own plans that he hadn't given her an opening.

Or maybe he just hadn't been listening closely enough. All that rigmarole she'd gone through yesterday about how much his life would change if he got married... He'd thought it was just the usual feminine diatribe, but he supposed it could have originated in personal experience.

No wonder she'd said at first that her evenings weren't free....

Still, the whole question wasn't important. It was only the unexpectedness of the announcement that had shocked him, and the fact that the information had come from his mother, of all people.

He'd been startled. That was all.

Enid's voice was wistful. "That is a Waterford crystal glass, Derek."

Derek looked ruefully down at the mess. "I think you mean it used to be, Mom." He stooped to begin picking up the shards.

The wine list Clara had lifted from Arcadia was covered with her small, cramped writing. It took a couple of long and patient hours for Macey to decipher all the names and cryptic references, and then more time for Clara to recall and expand on what she'd meant by each of the notes.

"There's one where you just wrote *self*," Macey pointed out. "Does that mean self-centered, self-conscious... What else could it be? Self-possessed? Maybe selfless?"

Clara looked thoughtful. "I'm trying to remember. But

it wasn't *selfless,* that's for sure. None of those young ladies got that sort of rating. Of course, the selfless sort is more likely to be working in a soup kitchen than having lunch at Arcadia, so the deck was stacked from the beginning."

You can't buy an Armani suit if you only shop at discount stores, Derek had said. There was some truth to that philosophy, Macey thought. A marriage was much more likely to be successful if the partners had similar backgrounds and similar expectations. And since there was no doubt whatsoever that Derek was an Armani suit kind of guy, of course he was looking for the same sort of woman.

And Macey supposed that working from his original list made sense, too. If he was going to get married in a hurry, it was more reasonable to select one of the women he was already acquainted with than to court disaster by choosing someone he knew absolutely nothing about. The odds were better—or at least they looked better.

It was just that in Macey's opinion, the women on his list were beginning to look as if they'd come from a flea market instead of a designer's workshop.

But that wasn't her problem, she reminded herself. All she had to do was cut his list down to manageable proportions. She would eliminate the obviously ineligible and leave the rest to him.

It was not part of her job to suggest that he might be wise to at least window-shop before he actually made a purchase.

"Now I remember," Clara said triumphantly. "*Self-aware.* That was what Enid called her."

"Is that good or bad?"

"The kind who can't walk past a mirror without checking herself out."

"Bad." Macey crossed off the name. "That's the very last one you got the scoop on."

They'd made a considerable dent in the list Derek had given her. In fact, Macey noted, there were only six names left on it—and wasn't that the goal he'd set originally? Her mission, he had said, was to pare his list of a hundred or so down to the half dozen most likely possibilities, and he would take it from there.

Thanks to Clara's talent for picking Enid McConnell's brain, Macey was done. Finished. It was almost like magic—all she had to do now was hand over the list and she could wrap up the entire problem of Derek McConnell.

That conclusion called for a big wave of relief, and Macey was surprised when she didn't feel it surge over her immediately. Of course, she still had to deliver the list, and probably Derek would want her to explain— maybe even justify—why each of those particular women was still in the running while the others were not. That wouldn't be fun. But when that discussion was over, she would feel light as a feather.

So the sooner she got it over with the better. She'd already wasted the better part of three days on this job, and her work was stacking up at the office. If she presented her conclusions to Derek tonight, her life would be back to normal in the morning.

And *normal* couldn't come soon enough for her.

The last thing Derek expected to see, when he strolled into the lobby of the converted warehouse, was Macey sitting on the high desk at the doorman's station, a slice of pizza in her hand and the box open beside her, flirting with Ted the doorman.

Though perhaps it wasn't quite fair to say she was flirting, just listening with ultra-flattering attention while Ted talked. He was saying something about the classes he was taking, and Macey didn't even look over her shoulder as Derek came in. He was standing beside her before she noticed him at all, and even then it was probably only because Ted stopped talking in midsentence and jumped up to greet him.

Finally she turned 'round and smiled. "How was dinner?"

"Very spicy. What are you doing here?"

"Waiting for you. Ted thought you'd be home early, so I decided to hang around for a while in the hope he was right. I have a list for you."

List? Oh, the finalists. "I thought you said you didn't find out much."

"I hadn't checked all my other resources yet when I talked to you this afternoon."

"Resources like my mother? What the devil were you thinking of?"

"Mostly," Macey said crisply, "I was thinking about how I could escape. Do you want this list or not?"

Ted was looking interested, Derek noted. "Come on upstairs."

She wriggled a bit. He wasn't sure if she was trying to get down off the desk or she was just uncomfortable at the idea of being alone with him again. But he'd already said more in front of the doorman than he'd intended to.

Unceremoniously Derek put both hands on her waist and swung her down. She was so little and light that he could have thrown her over his shoulder and carried her...but he'd already done the caveman act yesterday, he reminded himself. She hadn't made a fuss, but she'd very efficiently freed herself. If he tried it again, she'd probably slug him.

"Enjoy the rest of the pizza, Ted," she called as they reached the elevator.

"Thanks for bringing it, Ms. Phillips."

"You brought a pizza for Ted?"

"Not exactly. I was hungry and I thought you might be too."

"Sorry I wasn't home. Pizza sounds good." Derek unlocked the door of the loft and turned the lights on.

"You can relax about your mother, by the way," Macey said. "Clara—my aunt—doesn't know it's you I'm working for. And your mother didn't recognize me."

"Don't bet on it. She knows you were at the symphony party."

"She does?" She sounded as if she was short of breath.

Derek nodded. "She just doesn't know it was you under the bed. Want a brandy? Or would you like some leftover chicken soup?"

"No, thanks. Here." She held out a sheet of paper.

He glanced at it. There were six names—and one of them, he supposed, would turn out to be the future Mrs. Derek McConnell. Well, he'd deal with that a little later. He set the page on the kitchen counter and anchored it with the salt shaker. "I'm sorry about earlier."

Macey said slowly, "What are you talking about?"

Women always made themselves out to be so damned subtle, he thought, and yet they insisted on having every single detail spelled out. They seemed to especially like dwelling on the ones that were most embarrassing for the guy they were talking to. "Wrestling you around on the bed. Things like that."

"Oh. Of course."

She sounded wary. No, Derek thought in disbelief, she sounded like she'd honestly had no idea what he was referring to. As if the incident had been so unimportant to her it had been instantly dismissed from her mind. But one thing was sure—he was in too deep now to back out without finishing. "I shouldn't have done that."

"That's right—you shouldn't have," she said crisply. "Thanks for the apology. Do you want me to go over the list with you?"

"Dammit, Macey, why didn't you tell me you're married?"

"Why on earth should I?" Her voice was sharp. "Is that why you apologized? Because you're afraid of finding an irate husband on your doorstep wanting satisfaction? I thought better of you than that, Derek."

If she thought he had apologized just to save himself from a punch in the jaw... Derek gritted his teeth. He'd like to see the guy try—but he didn't suppose it would be too smart to tell Macey that. "Throw that little fact in, and it's no wonder you didn't want my mother to find you under my bed."

Her eyes narrowed. "That was low."

"So was calling me a coward."

She knew it, too—that was obvious from the way she looked away. She said, more softly, "I wasn't aware that my marital status had any bearing on the job."

"Well, of course it doesn't," he said, feeling awkward. "It just... Well, it would have been better if I'd known."

"Better how?"

"Because it would have been a perfect setup. A married woman whose husband is too busy to accompany her needs an escort sometimes—like to the symphony party. I'd have just been doing you a little favor. Heck, we could have gone anywhere together without causing comment."

Her eyes widened. She was looking at him as if he were one mattress short of a bunk bed—for no reason that he could see. What had he said that she thought was so far off track, anyway? "Are you really that naive, Derek?"

"It happens all the time. There are a couple of guys who are always taking my mother to the places that my father doesn't want to go."

"That's a little different."

"Doesn't matter. It's too late for that now anyway. But we can still make the most of the situation. We'll double date."

"We'll—*what?*"

"Now that you've got the list pared down, I need to make a final decision. So I'll have to spend a little time with each of these women—"

"Might not be a bad idea," she muttered.

He decided to be charitable and ignore the sarcasm. "—without making it seem that I'm devoting myself to her and excluding all the others. So if we make it a foursome—you, me, your husband, and the woman of the moment—it will all be more casual, and—"

"And not very practical, I'm afraid." Macey took a deep breath. "Look, I'm only going to say this once, so pay attention for a change, all right? I used to be married."

"Used to be?" Derek said slowly.

"He died three years ago."

Derek felt as if she'd slugged him right under the breastbone.

Her voice was soft and low and sad. "The doctors said that Jack was far too young to have the kind of cancer that killed him. That's why they didn't find it in time. I'm sorry if that interferes with your plans, Derek—but you're on your own now. Good night."

He was still reeling when she very gently closed the door behind her.

* * *

The flowers arrived at the office only a few minutes after Macey did. Ellen signed for them and carried the vase into Macey's office.

The arrangement was so huge that the combination of the vase and Ellen looked like a flowering shrub which had grown legs. Macey stared in astonishment as Ellen maneuvered the flowers through the doorway.

Roses, lilies, daisies, carnations—it looked as if someone had jammed the entire contents of a sizable floral shop into a five-gallon bucket without regard to color, style, or shape. The stems stuck out every which way. Though Ellen set the vase on the far corner of the desk, a branch of something white stretched out so far it was almost tickling Macey's nose, while on the opposite side of the arrangement, a stem of lilies actually brushed the office wall.

She was blocked in behind her desk by a bouquet.

"There's a card here somewhere," Ellen said breathlessly. "I got a glimpse of it when the delivery man set the vase down. But it's sort of like hunting buried treasure now."

Macey finally found the envelope hiding under a droopy yellow mum. Inside was a plain white card on which had been sketched a small black animal with a raised tail and a white stripe down its back, and the words, *So I'm a skunk. I admit it. I hope the flowers will smell better to you than I do.* It was not signed.

She leaned back in her chair and laughed till she had to wipe tears from her eyes. Hardly the reaction Derek would have hoped for, she supposed, but it seemed pretty much par for the course to her.

Robert came out of his office to see what all the noise was about. Macey slid the card smoothly into the pocket of her suit jacket and said, nodding toward the vase, "A thank-you from Derek McConnell."

His eyes brightened. "You got the problem solved, then?"

Beats me, but I guess we'll find out sooner or later.

But that was hardly an answer that Robert would find acceptable, so Macey opted to dodge the question. "I did everything I could."

"Fantastic. I must start watching the papers for an announcement."

Macey tried to hide her smile. "That'll be a new experience for you, Robert—reading the society pages for engagements."

"Society? I meant the business pages—looking for when he's named CEO."

Oh. I'd almost forgotten that part. "Of course."

Robert rubbed his hands together. "This is going to be terrific, Macey. If he says thank-you with temp jobs on the same scale he does with flowers, we'll need two new offices."

He was gone before Macey could suggest that it might not be smart to go looking for real estate just yet.

As for Macey herself, she decided that she wouldn't be reading the business pages—or the society section, either. Though in fact, whenever it happened, she would hardly be able to escape the news. Now that Clara was back in touch with the world, reading the newspapers and talking to her friend Enid, she would certainly hear about the announcement. And just as certainly, she'd tell Macey. Clara might even go to the wedding, and if she was invited to bring a companion she'd no doubt ask Macey to accompany her.

And I suppose as the matchmaker, you'll to be asked

to give a toast, she mocked herself. *Knock it off, Phillips. It's not your business anymore.*

She pulled the card with the little skunk on it out of her pocket and put it safely under the pen tray in her desk drawer. "Ellen? Go find some more containers and we'll try out your flower-arranging skills."

She was still with Ellen several hours later, going over the results of the woman's performance review and role-playing her first job assignment, when the receptionist tapped on Macey's door.

"Lunchtime," Louise said briskly.

Macey felt a trickle of exasperation. Louise knew better than to interrupt when she was in a training session. Besides, Macey had never before thought her receptionist was a clock-watcher. What had gotten into her? "I know what time it is, Louise. Just give me a couple of minutes to finish with Ellen, and then I'll cover up front while you go to lunch."

"No, I mean it's *your* lunchtime. Ellen can cover for me—she's been doing it for a couple of days anyway, while you've been gone."

"Fine," Macey said levelly. "Thank you very much for the reminder, Louise, but I'll go when I'm ready." *I'm not hungry, anyway.*

Ellen took one look over Louise's shoulder and muttered, "If you're not ready this minute, Macey, you're crazy."

Macey maneuvered past the vase on the corner of her desk and went to see what was going on.

Derek was leaning against the end of Louise's desk, his ankles crossed, facing Macey's office door. Draped over his shoulder was a blanket, and in one arm he held a brown paper bag that was stuffed to the bursting point and had a loaf of French bread protruding from the top.

"Thanks for the flowers," she said. "Of course now my office smells like a toxic spill at the perfume factory, but I appreciate the sentiment."

"That's why I thought we'd have lunch at the park instead."

"Self-defense?"

"In the open air, you might be able to stand being around the aroma of skunk."

He sounded serious, but she didn't miss the smile lurking in his eyes. And to think she'd once wondered whether he possessed any charm at all.... "I'll get my jacket."

She waited till they were out of the office, and then she said, without looking at him, "It's okay, Derek. Really. It was a natural mistake. You don't have to go to such trouble to make it up to me."

"I don't?" He stopped abruptly in the middle of the sidewalk. "Well, in that case, lunch is off. Back to work with you."

Macey kept right on walking. "On the other hand, I'm sure you'll feel a thousand percent better once you've made amends, so who am I to deny you the opportunity to abase yourself? What's for lunch?"

The park was just a block from Peterson Temps. It wasn't much of a park, actually, just a tiny green space intended to break the monotony of the storefronts, with a few benches and a couple of flower beds that were beginning to look bedraggled with autumn coming on.

Derek had obviously scoped the place out ahead of time, for he didn't hesitate at the edge of the park but led her across to the far corner, where a row of honeysuckle bushes, heavy with red fruit, protected a patch of sunlit grass. The breeze rustled through the leaves, but the dense bushes broke its force and kept it from chilling them. High above in an oak tree a cardinal sang.

Macey helped spread out the blanket and sank down on a corner of it. "Nice," she said. "Solar heat, live background music, even a nice log to serve as a backrest."

"And a simple picnic lunch." Derek began to unpack the bag.

In one sense, Macey concluded, it was a very simple lunch. He'd brought bread and butter, cheese, olives, and fruit. But the bread was so fresh it was still warm; the butter was rich, and there were four varieties of cheese and two of olives. She hadn't seen so many kinds of fruit lined up anywhere but a supermarket. And from the bottom of the bag he pulled out a thermal mug full of the best cappuccino she'd ever tasted.

He had, however, forgotten to bring anything to slice the bread with. So they tore chunks off the loaf, and he reduced the cheese and fruit to irregular slices with his Swiss army knife.

The tiny blade slipped as he cut up an apple, and Derek swore. "I knew I should have sharpened this thing after I used it to cut duct tape the other day."

"Doesn't it have more than one blade?"

"Yes, but I broke the tip off the other one when I used it to pry the lid off a paint can."

"Well, be careful," Macey warned. "You don't want to slice a finger so badly you can't draw anymore."

"Did you like the little skunk? That's just a sketch—it's more cartooning than art. But it comes in handy sometimes when we're designing packaging, labels, stuff like that. It's easier to draw an idea than to put it into words."

"Maybe it's easier for you." She reached for a bunch of grapes. "Not for everybody."

"I've always drawn a little. Just like I've always known

I wanted to run my father's company." He folded up the knife. "What got you into the temp business?"

She hesitated.

"You don't have to tell me, if you don't want."

"No, it's all right. It was after Jack died. I had to take some time off work, and the bills were pretty steep."

"No life insurance?" His voice was gentle.

"We never got around to buying any. When you're twenty-five, you don't think you need it, and there are a lot of other things you want more. I went back to work as soon as I could, of course, and I moved in with Jack's aunt to cut expenses. But my regular paycheck still wasn't enough to make a dent in the debts, so I started to take some temp jobs for a little extra income."

"And you liked the work?"

Macey nodded. "I liked the constant change, and the pay was good. By the time Robert offered to make me office manager, I'd finally gotten my head above water, and I gave up my other job so I could be at home with Clara more."

"Her idea, or yours? You staying home, I mean."

"A little of both. She took it pretty hard when Jack died." Macey leaned back against the log, savoring her cappuccino. "Thanks for lunch. You can apologize to me anytime you want."

Derek ate the last crumb of cheddar. "I'm not exactly apologizing," he admitted. "At least not entirely. I thought maybe I could take you up on your offer from last night."

To discuss the six women she'd left on the list. Macey knew she should have expected something of the sort, once he'd had a chance to consider the names she'd handed him.

And it was probably just as well, she thought, for her

to be reminded that he'd only gone to all the trouble of arranging a picnic in the park because he couldn't take her somewhere like Arcadia—at least, not without raising every eyebrow in St. Louis so high that baldness wouldn't be a problem anymore.

"Finally got around to looking at the list, did you?" She tried to keep her voice light.

"Yeah. Why those six, and not some of the others?"

She slid down a little and turned so she was at more of an angle to him, rather than sitting side by side against the log. "I wondered if that would happen." She was talking more to herself than to him.

"If what would happen?"

"Whether you'd be surprised when you looked at the list. If you might be startled—maybe even disappointed—because one particular name wasn't on it."

"I still don't understand what you mean."

Macey pulled her knees up and wrapped her arms around them. "Have you ever had so much trouble making up your mind between two options that you ended up flipping a coin?"

"Sure. Everybody has."

"But then did you go along with what the coin toss told you? Or did you find yourself wanting to flip it again—maybe go two out of three? Because either way, whether you were satisfied with the coin's advice or not, after you made that flip you knew what you really wanted to do. Tossing a coin just cuts through all the intellectual stuff and tells you how you really feel deep down inside."

"So what does flipping a quarter have to do with this?" He reached into his shirt pocket and dangled the list under her nose.

"Because if there's one name that you really want to ask me about, Derek, and you feel a need to know why it's not there, then that's the woman you ought to marry—not one of the six on the list.''

Derek frowned. ''So you're telling me this piece of paper is nothing more than a psychological trick you made up.''

She was annoyed. ''No, it's not. At least, I didn't set it up that way—and if I had, I sure wouldn't tell you about it. But if that's how it works, at least you'll know what you want. *Who* you want.''

The silence grew. Macey took another sip of her cappuccino. All of a sudden, it wasn't so good anymore. The brew had gone cold, and it tasted almost bitter.

''Well?'' she said finally. ''Who is she, Derek?''

He shook his head. ''I wasn't thinking about anybody in particular.''

Macey wasn't sure whether to believe him or not. He sounded sincere, but if he was telling the truth, why had it taken him so long to answer?

He laid the paper down on the blanket between them and tapped a finger squarely in the middle of the list of names. ''I just wondered what was so special about these six. What made them stand out to you?''

''You want to know what I saw so you can look for the same qualities to admire? I'm honored by the faith you're putting in me, Derek, but I'm not the one who's going to have to live with this woman. Don't you think it's time *you*—''

''I just want to know what you based this list on.''

''All right,'' she said slowly. ''I guess it's fair to ask what standards I measured by. But you see, the deciding factor was actually more what *wasn't* special about these six.''

''Now you've really lost me, Macey.''

She sighed. ''The others—the ones I took off the list—

all stood out from the crowd, all right, but for reasons that were less than pleasant."

"For instance?"

"One of them nearly knocked Clara over at the door of Arcadia."

"Accidents—"

"—happen, yes. And I'm not saying it wasn't accidental. But she could have stopped to make sure Clara was all right—it wasn't like she was rushing inside to stop somebody from hemorrhaging. She didn't bother."

"Which one of them did that?"

Macey gave him the name.

Derek's eyebrows shot up. "I have never seen her being anything but perfectly polite."

"Of course you haven't," Macey said. She was beginning to feel a little cross. "And you won't until after you've married someone else and she's convinced you're completely out of range. Or until you've married *her,* and she feels she doesn't have to put on a show anymore." She set her cup down. "I really have to get back to work—and you probably do too. I'll help gather up the mess."

"Don't bother. I'll get it."

"Are you sure?"

He smiled. "It's my favorite kind of kitchen cleanup—everything goes in the garbage can except the blanket." He stood up and offered a hand to pull Macey to her feet.

"Thanks again." It felt awkward just to turn around and walk away. "Derek—let me know how it goes."

"Sure," he said.

She forced herself to smile. "If it all works out, will you write me a recommendation? I just might be looking for a job someday—and maybe there's a future in matchmaking."

He laughed.

Macey walked back toward Peterson Temps with her head bowed. The breeze had sharpened, and outside the sheltered little corner of the park it felt positively cold.

Would he actually keep her informed?

And—the even bigger question—did she really, truly want him to?

CHAPTER SIX

WHEN Macey came into the town house carrying two bags of groceries, Clara was sitting at the small kitchen table contemplating a bare, plain white china plate which sat in front of her.

"Have you started dieting?" Macey asked lightly. "Because if you have, you'll simply have to give it up right now. I just picked up everything we need for beef stroganoff."

Clara didn't look up. "It'll keep till tomorrow."

Macey stopped in the middle of the room and stared at Clara. "You love beef stroganoff as much as I do. Why would you want to put it off?"

Clara shrugged. "I'm guessing that you might. Don't start cooking till you've returned your phone calls."

Macey tried to set the bags down carefully. "Okay— explain. Who called?"

"A man. Fairly young by the sound of his voice. He left a number." Clara picked up a ruler and a felt-tipped marker and began to make small dots at regular intervals around the rim of the plate.

Macey picked up a slip of paper from beside the phone. "No name?"

"Don't blame me. I asked, but he seemed to want to be the mystery man."

Derek. Macey's heart beat just a little faster. No doubt he would rather have seemed rude than to tell Clara who he was—it would invite too many questions about why her old friend Enid's son was calling Clara's niece.

The number didn't look familiar, but then it wouldn't—Macey hadn't ever called him at home. Hadn't been able to, in fact, because his number wasn't in the phone book. That was one of the reasons she'd actually gone over to his loft that night to deliver the list, taking the pizza that she'd ended up sharing with Ted because Derek hadn't been at home.

Two days had passed since their picnic in the park, and she hadn't heard a word from him. Had he called to tell her he'd made his selection? If so, no wonder he hadn't left a message with Clara. *"Tell her Derek McConnell called and I've decided to marry Rebecca."* Or Emily. Or Constance...

No—a message like that would stir up way too much curiosity.

But it hardly seemed possible that he'd decided already, anyway. In the span of just over forty-eight hours—and spread across a couple of workdays, at that—how could he have possibly fit in enough time with six different women to choose one of them over the others? Because somehow Macey didn't think he would have settled for the first one on the list without taking a closer look at the rest, even if that woman had managed to impress him. Just because Macey had the sneaking suspicion that all of them were pretty much interchangeable didn't mean that Derek saw them in the same light.

In fact, she thought, in a weird sort of way the man was actually kind of a romantic...

Stop dithering around about it and ask him, Macey. Call him back.

She dialed the phone and held it against her ear with one shoulder while she unpacked the groceries.

A male voice answered. But it wasn't Derek's voice.

Macey frowned. Surely no one else would answer

Derek's phone in that casual way—and why would anyone but Derek be answering it at all?

They wouldn't. Which must mean her guess was wrong, and it hadn't been Derek who had left that message in the first place. She told herself it was ridiculous to be disappointed, but it didn't help much.

"Hello?" the voice said again.

Long training kicked in. "This is Macey Phillips. I had a message to call this number."

"Macey! I was afraid you weren't going to call me back."

She still didn't recognize the voice. "Excuse me, but do I know you?"

"Oh, that's right—I always forget that people sound so much different in person. It's Ira."

Ira. Macey rummaged through her brain. Was he a business acquaintance? Surely not, because he'd called her at home, and that was something she would never have encouraged a client to do.

It must be personal, then. And it was obviously someone she'd actually met, not just spoken to on the phone. But who—?

"Ira Branson," he said, sounding just a little impatient. "From the symphony party. Derek McConnell's friend."

Well, at least he got my name right this time.

"Look, I don't blame you for being peeved at me for taking so long to call."

He thought she was only pretending not to remember him? Macey wondered if he actually thought she'd been sitting by the phone day after day, waiting for it to ring. "Heavens, no. I've been so busy I hadn't given it a thought."

He laughed as if that was the funniest story he'd ever heard. "I wanted to call you right away, but I couldn't.

I've been trying for days now to get your phone number. You forgot to give it to me at the party.''

No, Ira, that's not the kind of thing I forget. If I'd wanted you to have the number...

"Do you have any idea how many women named Marcie Phillips live in St. Louis?"

So much for giving him credit. "It's Macey," she said. Of course, she told herself wryly, she was hardly in a position to complain no matter what he called her, since she hadn't remembered him—or his name—at all.

"Yeah, I finally figured that out. Anyway, I wondered if you'd like to go out with me."

"It's very kind of you, Ira, but I'm afraid I can't."

"Wait, I haven't even told you yet what the invitation is."

Noticed that, did you? Very perceptive.

"There's a party tonight and I thought you'd like to go with me. It's another fund-raiser, but this one's for the zoo. You know, cute fuzzy animals all over the place, that sort of thing. I know women love that kind of thing." He paused. "Look, you're not angry with me for asking so late, are you? I know it's not much notice, but I just got your number today."

"I'm sorry, Ira, but I've already made plans for this evening." *Put together a beef stroganoff, check all my silk flower arrangements to be certain they're not getting root-bound, rearrange the words in the dictionary from shortest to longest instead of alphabetically...*

"What about tomorrow night? There's a Halloween thing I thought you might like."

"I have plans." She put a skillet on the range and reached for the olive oil. Couldn't the man take a hint?

Clara looked up from the china plate. "You don't have to stay home for my sake."

Macey shook her head, hoping Clara would get the message. She didn't think Ira would have been able to overhear her since Clara was all the way across the kitchen, but the last thing she needed was for him to feel encouraged.

"Sunday?" Ira asked.

She was actually starting to feel sorry for him. *Careful, Macey—that's dangerous.* "Ira, it's very kind of you, but I'm not dating at all right now."

He made a sound that resembled a snort. "If you're sitting at home waiting for McConnell, you might as well get over it."

"My plans have nothing to do with…" Macey turned to reach for a spatula, noticed that Clara was watching her, and swallowed the name just in time. "I think you've misunderstood the situation, Ira."

"What else am I supposed to think?"

You might consider the idea that I'm simply not attracted to you.

"Anyway, if you're trying to give him the silent treatment by staying home," Ira went on, "you should know it's not working. I've seen him several times lately, and never twice with the same woman. Pretty soon people will be taking bets about who he'll turn up with next."

"That's very interesting. Not that it has anything to do with me, but—"

"I'm just telling you, there's no point in moping around waiting for him to come back to you. You might as well get out there and play the field yourself."

"I'll certainly keep that advice in mind," Macey said dryly.

"Good. Now how about Sunday? You didn't give me a chance to really ask you. There's a nice brunch at my country club."

"I've already—"

"You've made plans for the entire weekend—I get it. A lady never accepts the first invitation. Well, you think it over. I might check back with you in a day or two, though you shouldn't count on it."

I'll be holding my breath in anxious anticipation. "Good night, Ira."

She put the phone down and dumped beef chunks into the skillet. The angry sizzle of the hot oil mimicked her mood.

Though she supposed Ira had meant well. At least, she'd try to give him the benefit of the doubt. Surely nobody could be that annoying on purpose.

Clara held up the plate at arm's length, inspecting it. "You shouldn't turn down a date to stay home on my account, Macey."

"I didn't."

"But you did turn him down, and pretty definitely. Saying you weren't dating at all is about the firmest excuse I've ever heard."

"It's not an excuse. It's the truth, Clara." Macey stirred the beef. "I'm just not interested in dating."

"Nobody's saying you have to get married. But what's the problem with you going out with a man now and then? Just having some fun? Who would that hurt?"

"People like Ira," Macey said. "All I did was go to a fund-raiser. It wasn't even really a party, and it certainly wasn't a date. Now he's got the idea that I'm available, and worse yet, that I'm interested in him and only pretending to be coy."

"Ira? Is that the man you've been working for?"

"No. Why?"

"That's too bad. I thought maybe that was going to turn into something. You were going somewhere with him pretty regularly for a while, and then *pffft*. It turns to dust.''

''Well, that's the nature of my business, Clara. Temporary.''

''Don't get tart with me, young lady.''

''I'm sorry. But I wasn't dating him, so please don't get confused.'' Macey looked over the older woman's shoulder. ''What are you doing to that poor plate?''

''Trying to decide how to paint it. I started my porcelain-painting class this morning, and this is my first project.''

Macey eyed the cryptic squiggles and dots which almost covered the plate. ''It's...very modern.''

''That's just the guide marks so I'll get the design on straight. I'm going to paint a wreath of violets on this one.''

''Sounds pretty.''

''After I do a few practice pieces to learn the techniques and get my hands steady, maybe I'll make you a whole set of china.'' Clara's voice took on a wistful note. ''I've always felt bad about you having to sell your wedding dishes after Jack died.''

''I needed the money at the time. And though I'd love to have you make me something, I really don't need china. I'll probably never entertain in that style.''

''You never know what you might need,'' Clara said vaguely. ''Do you really like the idea of violets? Or would you rather have a different flower? Or just a pattern? Because I should practice painting what you want.''

''You should paint whatever you like, Clara. If it ends up being an entire set, that's lovely, but I'd think it would be very dull to paint the same thing over and over till you had a service for twelve.''

The phone rang and Macey picked it up. She half expected it was Ira calling back, now that he'd given her a few minutes to regret the magnificent opportunity she'd turned down.

But this time the caller was Derek. "Macey? I was hoping it would be you who answered."

She tried to fight off the sudden breathless feeling that had hit her at the sound of his voice. "I'll bet you were," she said, shooting a sideways look at Clara—who was obviously listening. "I hear via the grapevine that you've been busy."

"Has my mother been talking to your aunt again?"

"No—another source entirely." Macey stirred the cubes of meat so they'd brown more evenly. "How are things going?"

"These are actually the best six names you could come up with? You didn't accidentally give me the list of rejects instead?"

"No, that's the only list. You've already run through all of them?"

"In two days? I'm not Casanova, Macey."

All appearances to the contrary. "Then why are you giving up already?"

"I didn't say I was giving up. In fact I have another date tonight, and—damn, I'm running late. I just wanted you to know that so far I'm not excited by your choices."

"Then it's probably just as well I haven't sent you a bill for my time yet," Macey said gently. "Now run along and get dressed up so you'll make the best possible impression on the lady of the evening."

He was swearing—and she was smiling—when Macey put the phone down.

On Saturday morning Derek left a message on the answering machine while Macey and Clara were having breakfast at the neighborhood café. "I'm looking for you, Macey," was all he said. He left no name and no number.

Clara looked a little concerned. "He sounds like a nutcase."

"It's not some sort of threat," Macey said, and frowned. "At least, I don't think it is."

The phone rang just a couple of minutes later. When Macey answered, Derek said, "Come for a ride with me."

"I'm busy." She noticed a picture frame which had gotten knocked askew on the wall above the phone. The light reflecting from the front window turned the glass almost mirror-like, but when she reached up to shift it back into place the light changed and the picture inside, a snapshot of Jack at a barbecue, reappeared.

"You can't be busy yet," Derek argued. "You just got home."

"How would you know that? Have you been calling all morning to check?"

"No—I've been keeping an eye on your front door for the last hour. I'm parked across the street."

Macey checked her watch. "You've been out there for an hour already? The only conclusion I can draw is that it must have been a very long date last night and you're just on your way home now. Otherwise you wouldn't be out running around so early. Oh, I know what that means! We struck pay dirt last night, so you decided to swing by here on your way home just to thank me. That's such a sweet thought, Derek. Who's the lucky woman going to be?"

"You wish. Are you coming out or shall I come in and get you?"

"Oh, by all means come in," Macey said sweetly. "You can meet Clara. She's very curious about you." And a good thing it was, she thought, that Clara had gone up to her room and wasn't within hearing distance at the moment. "Just think, the two of you can drink coffee and talk about all of your mutual acquaintances."

He muttered something under his breath.

Macey smiled. "Does that mean you've changed your mind about coming in?" She didn't wait for an answer, because she was honestly curious. "The date was really that bad? Which one was this?"

"Rebecca."

"Really? I thought she was a serious contender."

"So far you're zero for three, Macey. If this were a baseball game, you'd have been called out on strikes."

"Unfortunately, I was never very good at baseball. Wait a minute—did you say you've eliminated *three?* When have you had time?"

"It didn't take much time to throw Constance off the list. I ran into her last night, and by the time she'd giggled her way through a five-minute conversation I was ready to commit murder."

"In that case, it was probably a good idea not to actually marry her," Macey said solemnly. "But maybe she was just nervous. Are you quite certain you're approaching these women properly? I mean, take last night for an example. If you were actually supposed to be out with Rebecca but in fact you were carrying on with Constance—"

"*Carrying on?* That can't really be what you just said. My battery must be going dead. Hold on, I'm coming in."

The phone went silent in her hand. Macey swore, punched the off button, and called up the stairs, "Clara! I'll be back in a little while!" She opened the front door just as Derek was raising his hand to the bell.

He had definitely been home since his date last night—

or else it had been a very casual date, because he was wearing jeans and a leather jacket.

He looked from her face to the windbreaker she was carrying over her arm, and raised his eyebrows.

"I changed my mind," she said. "Some fresh air sounds like a great idea." She slid her hand around his elbow and tried to urge him off the front steps.

Derek didn't budge. "I wonder why you don't want me to meet Clara."

"Because the first thing she'll do is tell your mother and then you'll really be in the chicken soup. Isn't that reason enough?"

"It should be—but somehow I don't think it's *my* welfare you're concerned about. Now what were you saying about my approach?" He led her down the sidewalk to a candy-apple-red convertible and opened the passenger door.

Macey stopped short, eying the folded-down top. "I don't think I'm up for this much fresh air."

"It blows the cobwebs out of your brain."

Macey didn't doubt it. The little car looked as if it was capable of mach speed, and considering the mood he was in... "Can I drive?"

"Over my dead body."

"Then I'm not going for a ride. I have more important things to do today, anyway." She leaned against the car. "That attitude of yours is exactly the kind of thing I'm talking about. *Over my dead body,*" she mimicked. "I suspect you're coming on too strong. Being too intense."

"Being focused is a good thing."

"Perhaps it is—but the word I was thinking of wasn't *focused.* It was *inflexible.*"

He closed the door and braced a hand on the top of the windshield, tapping his fingertips against the glass. "I have to give you credit, Macey. It takes a lot of nerve to critique my methods when you're not even there to see what's going on.''

''Well, that much is only common sense, Derek. It's tough enough to get through a first date when it's just dinner. When the stakes include a whole lifetime—''

''You surely don't think I'm fool enough to tell these women what I'm contemplating.''

''Heavens, no,'' Macey said airily. ''Why would you give your prospective bride any say in the matter? There will be plenty of time to let the one you choose know what you're thinking after you've made up your mind. Because how could she possibly be anything but thrilled to win the honor of playing your wife—even if she didn't know ahead of time that she was auditioning for the role?''

His eyes narrowed. ''Don't let concern for my feelings keep you from expressing your opinions clearly, Macey.'' His voice was dry.

''Thanks, I won't. But even if they didn't have the details, they were probably feeling the pressure anyway, just because you're under so much stress. Give everybody a break, Derek.''

''I don't have time. Besides, you seem to have misunderstood what's going on here. I'm not exactly taking these women out on dates, so the pressure on them isn't nearly as intense as you seem to think.''

''What do you mean, you're not taking them out on dates?''

''I can't,'' he said bluntly. ''Having already informed the chairman of the board that I'm engaged, I can hardly be seen having an intimate supper with Rita and then dancing the night away with Lou.''

That was a problem. "If you went to a movie," Macey mused, "you could at least hold hands in the dark."

"And exactly what would going to a movie tell me about a woman, beyond whether or not she likes butter on her popcorn?"

"You've got a good point there," Macey conceded. "Especially because I can already tell you that they don't—none of them. Butter has far too many calories. So if dates are out, what are you doing?"

"Trying to check them out in situations that are public enough not to leave the wrong impression—with them or with anyone else."

"I don't think you're succeeding," she said frankly. "At least, Ira told me that people were going to start betting on who you'd be seeing next."

"Ira Branson?" He folded his arms across his chest and looked her over. "When did you talk to him?"

"Yesterday. He invited me to some fund-raiser last night."

"The one for the zoo? You turned him down? Macey, that would have been perfect. You could have been right there to lend me a hand, and nobody would even have wondered why, as long as you were with Ira."

"Don't you think that would be a shabby way to treat Ira?" Macey held up both hands, palms out. "I take it back. Don't even try to answer that. What am I thinking? A man who carries on a serious courtship at a fund-raiser for the zoo, without letting the women he's courting know what he's got in mind, couldn't possibly understand the finer points of dating etiquette. Anyway, now that I've answered your question, I'll be going back inside."

"What's so important today that you can't come for a ride?"

"Lots of things," Macey said crisply. "I didn't sign

on to work around the clock. What's so important about the ride?''

"I was hoping you'd do me a favor. I broke one of my mother's glasses, but when I called the store to have them send her a replacement, they said the company doesn't make that exact thing anymore.''

"And you don't know what to give her instead—but you think I'm supposed to? Are you listening to yourself, Derek?''

He shrugged. "Women think differently about these things.''

"You can say that again.'' If he hadn't looked at her like a three-year-old who had just been scolded, she might have walked away. Instead she sighed. "I can give you an hour, tops. Agreed?''

"You got it.'' Almost ostentatiously, he looked at his wristwatch, then helped her into the car and walked around to slide behind the wheel. The engine roared to life and the convertible shot into the street at a speed that pressed Macey deep into the leather seat.

"Can you take it a little easier?'' she asked breathlessly. "If I had a hat, it would be three blocks behind us by now—and I feel like my hair's about to follow.''

The traffic light changed ahead of them and Derek shifted gears and roared through the intersection. "I'm not the one who's in a hurry,'' he pointed out. "Besides, we're not going as fast as it seems. It only feels that way because of the wind and the way the car's engineered to sit so close to the street.''

"Thanks for the physics lesson, but I'd just as soon not have a tooth jarred out if you hit a speed bump unexpectedly.''

He looked injured. "Jarred? In this car?'' But he slowed down.

Fast or not, he was an excellent driver, and once she got used to the sensation of the wind whipping her hair, Macey enjoyed the drive. He was right about the cobwebs, she thought. The fresh air was definitely clearing out her brain. She practically didn't have a sensible thought left to her name.

That phenomenon might have explained why she actually asked him how he planned to check out the last three remaining names on the list—because, she told herself as soon as the question was out, it was dead sure that she didn't really want to know.

"There's a Halloween party tonight, so with any luck I should be able to catch at least two of them there." He shot a sideways look at her. "Did Ira invite you to the Halloween party?"

"If it's the same party, yes. And no, I'm not going to call him back and beg him to renew the invitation so I can come and help you out. At a costume party, you don't need help anyway—nobody will know who you are, so you can circulate freely."

"I'd rather go to a movie," he grumbled. "Alone."

"Brace up, it's almost over. Three down, three to go. And you know what they say, Derek—the item you're searching for is always in the last place you check."

"That's because when you find it, you quit looking."

"Of course. But the saying's still true."

"So are you suggesting I just cancel Liz and Rita and skip straight to Emily?"

"Oh, no—because then Emily *wouldn't* be last, and you'd have to go looking for Liz and Rita again."

"You're a whole lot of help," he grumbled.

Macey gave him her most tranquil smile. "All I can do is try."

* * *

She was trying all right, Derek thought. Trying his patience.

At least on Saturday downtown traffic wasn't as heavy, though parking outside the main branch of the city's largest department store was atrocious. Half the city seemed to have gone shopping this morning.

He noticed Macey eyeing him with interest while he maneuvered the convertible into the last available spot within blocks.

"I thought we'd be going to one of the mall stores," she said.

"But this one has the best inventory."

"As a matter of fact, it does. I'm just surprised you know that."

"Rebecca told me," he admitted. "So I guess I'd have to say last night was only ninety-five percent wasted instead of being a complete loss."

"I'm glad you got something out of it," Macey murmured. "At least this store used to be the best. I haven't been inside in years. I don't suppose it was just a basic water goblet you broke."

"I'm afraid not." Derek held the main door for her and wondered if it would be prying to ask why she hadn't been shopping for so long. Though that wasn't exactly what she'd said, he reminded himself.

Macey stopped a clerk to ask for directions and led the way to the elevator.

When they stepped off on the housewares floor, he almost collided with a lighted display case full of glass pieces that looked as if they had been left out in the cold until frost formed over the designs. "These are pretty," he said.

"They're gorgeous," Macey said. "I've always adored Lalique."

"Maybe I could get her a nice vase."

"You certainly could. How much is that one?"

He bent to look at the price tag and choked.

She turned around, eyebrows raised, to inspect him. "What's the matter, Derek? You sound as if you've been hit with an ax."

"There's a comma in that price."

"Yes, my friend," Macey said. "Isn't your mother worth it?"

He looked at her sharply. She looked innocent, but there had been a malicious note in her voice. "I dropped a glass, Macey—I didn't systematically shatter every single one she owns."

"So the answer is no?" Macey relented. "Fortunately for you, she wouldn't want a vase, anyway. She's got a thousand of them already."

Suspicion chewed at him. "And exactly how would you know that?"

"You can trust me on this, Derek. Vases, like coat hangers, multiply when left in dark cupboards—particularly when the cupboard belongs to a woman like your mother." She paused beside a long polished dining table. It was fully set, complete down to the last napkin, wineglass, and knife rest, but each place displayed a different kind of china. "Now that's an idea. Why not an assortment of patterns?"

"Are you talking to me?"

"No, to myself. Clara's threatening to paint a set of china for me. I was just wondering what it would look like if she did each piece with a different flower."

"Like a garden that's badly in need of weeding."

"You're probably right. What kind of a glass was it you broke?"

He looked around, feeling helpless. "Something like those over there, I guess."

But Macey wasn't listening. One of the china patterns, the one at the head of the table, had obviously caught her eye. "This is my china. The pattern I had when I was married." She picked up the dinner plate and turned it over to look more closely. "Ouch—it's even more expensive now. Clara's right—I should have held on to it."

"Why didn't you?"

"Between the hospital bills and the funeral costs, I needed the money." She set the plate down with a firm click and turned away. "Now, which glass was it?"

Derek stared at the plate. It was pure white, with a thin black rim, a red block in the center and a silver triangle off to one side.

Interesting, he thought. If she'd asked him to guess which pattern she liked best, that would have been the last one on the table that he'd have chosen.

On the other hand, he reminded himself, she was still turning up with ghastly new earrings just about every time he saw her, so what did he know about her taste?

He turned to follow Macey over to the cabinet he'd pointed out and came face-to-face with his mother.

"Hello, dear," Enid McConnell murmured. "And what might you be doing here on a nice day like this? Thinking about choosing a china pattern?"

CHAPTER SEVEN

WHAT playful trick of fate had inspired his mother to go shopping on this very day and in this very store? Because, much as Derek would have liked to blame someone, it couldn't be anything but fate.

Replacing a broken cocktail glass hadn't been the top item on his agenda when he'd left home this morning, though he'd had every intention of doing something about it sooner or later. But since he hadn't even known himself where he'd be, there was no point in looking for a hidden meaning in his mother's presence. Nobody could have tipped her off. It was sheer, stupid coincidence that she'd turned up.

It had to be, he told himself. Because the only other explanation was that his mother was learning to tune in on his thoughts like a radio receiver—and that would be a whole lot worse.

But of course she wasn't reading his mind, or she wouldn't have asked that particular question. *Thinking about choosing a china pattern?*

In fact, there was nothing further from his mind than china. But that didn't make the question any easier to answer, because the entire subject was a minefield. He opened his mouth, but the only sound that came out was halfway between a gulp and a hiccup.

Macey came up beside him.

Derek wished she'd had enough sense to keep her distance and pretend to be looking at something else. His mother might not have seen them together, but now there would be no doubt in her mind.

"He'll be all right in a minute, Mrs. McConnell," Macey patted his arm comfortingly and smiled at his mother. "To answer your question, though—no, we're not shopping for china."

Now why couldn't he have said that? Straightforward, calm, to the point. Macey really was a treasure. No wonder Robert thought so highly of his office manager.

Of course it was fairly easy to be composed and candid when dealing with someone else's mother. It was just like being frank and composed when talking to an employee.

Macey went on, "Actually, we're looking for the perfect crystal."

If the entire eight-story department store had fallen on his head, Derek couldn't have been more stunned. What was she going to do next? Formally invite his mother to the wedding?

So much for Robert's assurance that Macey Phillips wouldn't try to snag him for herself. Instead, this female shark had been circling for nearly a week, waiting for him to be off guard. Waiting for the moment when he'd be easy prey.

It was no particular comfort to realize that he'd handed her the opportunity. Asking her advice on a gift for his mother—what the hell had he been thinking?

Macey waved a hand in front of his nose. "Breathe, Derek," she ordered. "You're getting cross-eyed from lack of oxygen. Come on, you can do it." She held out a hand to Enid. "We met at Arcadia, if you remember."

"Of course. You were with your husband's Aunt Clara."

Derek managed a gasp of air. There was his salvation, he thought. It was his mother who had told him that

Macey was married. As long as Enid McConnell believed that, she couldn't possibly take the shopping-for-crystal story seriously. Now he just had to get Macey away from his mother before Enid figured out the truth...

"Please accept my sympathies, Macey," Enid said. "I didn't realize the day we met that you'd lost your husband."

Too late.

"Thank you," Macey said quietly. "I'm very glad to run into you, Mrs. McConnell."

I'll bet, Derek thought grimly. *It makes your scheme much easier to pull off.*

"Derek felt so badly about breaking your glass and not being able to find a replacement that he asked my advice on how to make it up to you." Macey made it sound as if it was no big deal after all.

Derek shot a look at his mother and noted that she looked neither surprised nor shocked. Maybe—just maybe—he'd misjudged Macey. Jumped to conclusions about what she was trying to accomplish.

Very carefully, he forced himself to relax. This up and down stuff was wearing him out in a hurry.

His mother was surveying him. "That's sweet of you, dear, but I know perfectly well it was an accident. It could have happened to anyone. The shock of the moment caused you to be distracted for an instant, that's all."

Macey frowned. "What was the shock of the moment?" she said under her breath.

Derek ignored her, and as he'd hoped, she gave it up.

"I thought," Macey went on, "that we'd be able to find a pattern which would at least be compatible with yours. Foolish of me to think that Derek could remember it well enough to compare. So this is even better—you can make a choice yourself."

"That's lovely of you, Derek, to let me choose a replacement." Enid McConnell looked around. "Let's see—what might I like?"

"Derek was admiring the case of Lalique," Macey murmured. "He thought perhaps the vase."

There was a note of mischief in her voice that made him want to smack her.

"But somehow I didn't think that would be quite right for you," she went on.

The expression on his mother's face was unreadable, but Derek could guess what it meant. Whether Enid McConnell wanted that vase or not, she wouldn't allow a snip of a young woman—one she didn't even know—to interpret and dictate her tastes.

The net result was that any minute now, because Macey had let herself run off at the mouth like that, he was going to be paying for a vase. And paying. And paying.

"At any rate, since you're here, Mrs. McConnell, you and Derek can make a choice and perhaps you'll excuse me."

Macey patted his arm again—just about the same way she'd say goodbye to a dog, Derek thought—and stepped away.

"Oh, no, dear." Enid McConnell linked her arm into Macey's. "You're quite right about the vase, by the way. How did you know I prefer clear glass to the decorated sort?"

In the midst of his own surprise, he derived a tiny bit of satisfaction from the fact that Macey seemed taken aback. And a little more, he admitted, because he wasn't going to find that vase on his credit card statement next month after all.

"I'd love to have your opinion," Enid went on, "because what I really came for today was to choose a new pattern. The glass Derek broke was older than he is, and so much of my wedding crystal is gone now that it's time for an entirely new set. It's just that I'm not sure what I want."

The two of them moved off toward a lighted case lined with goblets and wineglasses. Macey cast a desperate-looking glance over her shoulder at him. Derek pretended to ignore it. She'd dug herself into this mess; let her work her own way out.

"Styles have changed so much," Enid McConnell went on, "since I chose my patterns. And of course my tastes have changed as well, so I'm—"

Derek leaned one hip against a railing to make himself comfortable for what he could see might be a very long wait. Then, abruptly, he realized that letting the two of them get out of earshot was a very dumb move. He wasn't sure which one of them he distrusted more—though it didn't make much difference; either of them was clearly capable of causing trouble.

And not that he could actually do much in the way of damage control, either, because his tongue still felt as useless as if it were made of recycled chewing gum. But at least if he knew what they were discussing, he'd have a shot at defending himself.

He almost bumped into Macey as he came around the corner of a rack that held nothing but glass lamps and clocks.

His mother was pointing at a wineglass and saying something about the softly rounded lines, but she paused in midsentence and looked thoughtfully at him. "Derek, I'm sure you're bored silly by all this. Don't let us keep you from the other important things you must need to do."

"I hadn't planned anything else for this morning."

Enid pursed her lips. "You're only going to make this take longer, you realize, if you can't bear to be away from Macey's side."

Now there's a scary thought. However, Derek realized, she'd given him the excuse he needed. He almost snapped his fingers in relief. "Macey, you told me you only had an hour to spare this morning, and that's more than up. I'll take you home—"

"I'll be happy to take her home," Enid said. "I can choose crystal anytime, and I'd like to see Clara again, anyway."

"Why don't the two of you stay here and look," Macey murmured, "and I'll take a cab."

If she thought she was going to abandon him and run away, she could think again. Derek took her firmly by the arm. "See you later, Mom."

Macey resisted for an instant and then gave in with a smile and a shrug of the shoulders—no doubt both intended for Enid's benefit.

Back on the street, in the relative safety and anonymity of the crowd, Derek stopped in the middle of the sidewalk and scowled at her. *"We're looking for the perfect crystal,"* he mimicked. "Were you *trying* to cause trouble?"

"I certainly didn't give her any ideas that weren't already in her mind," Macey said defensively. "What I said was absolutely true. Besides, it's the last thing we'd have said if we were actually trying to hide something—so by saying it I made it clear we weren't hiding anything."

"Right. The next time I want to be entertained by twisted logic, I'll remember to ask you."

"And you can stop putting the blame on me, anyway," Macey went on. "You're the one who was raising red flags all over the place. You must have been grounded till you were twenty-one."

"What's that got to do with anything?"

"Because back when you were a kid and you actually pulled off a stunt, if you looked half as guilty as you did today, your parents would have locked you up."

"You're saying I looked guilty?"

"You should have seen yourself," Macey said flatly. She crossed the street to the car.

Derek closed her door and walked around to slide under the wheel. But he didn't start the engine. "That wasn't guilt you saw, Macey. That was pure horror. You have to understand that from where I was standing—"

"I know guilt when I see it. And I think the sentence you're looking for begins with *I'm sorry,* Derek."

He was incensed. "You actually expect *me* to apologize?"

Macey turned 'round in the seat to stare at him. "And why exactly wouldn't you feel it necessary? To all appearances, you don't have a general policy of never saying you're sorry, so your objection must be to apologizing for this specific incident."

"Damn right. I don't say I'm sorry unless I'm responsible, and in this case I'm not the one who caused the trouble. You, on the contrary, were scary in there."

She tipped her head back and her eyes narrowed. She looked at him for so long that Derek was beginning to think she'd faded into some kind of coma. Then, suddenly she laughed—but there wasn't much humor in the sound. "I've got it. You were actually afraid I was going to stand there in front of God and your mother and claim you—like planting a flag at the North Pole or on the top of Mount Everest."

"Well, you just came straight out with that bit about—"

"Oh, for heaven's sake. As if I'd want you. Let's get

two things straight here, Derek. There is nothing in the world that would make me consider getting married again. *Nothing.* Do you want that written in blood? Not that I'd actually do it, because I can't stand having my finger stuck. And if I ever did change my mind about that—"

He frowned. "The finger-sticking?"

"No, the getting-married part. If I ever did change my mind about that, which I won't, the last man I'd consider marrying would be you. You're arrogant and spoiled and self-centered and conceited. If you married all six of those women, you'd have enough ego to make every last one of them regret it. I've had enough trouble just having you hanging around for the last week, so why on earth would I want to sign up for a lifetime of it?"

Her voice had risen. People on the sidewalk were veering off in a semicircle, Derek noted from the corner of his eye. They were going out of their way to avoid the car.

He didn't blame them.

Finally Macey paused for a breath, and after the silence had gone on for a few seconds, Derek said, "Is there anything else you'd like to tell me?"

"No, I think that about covers it." Her voice was suddenly calm, almost friendly, fresh as the air after a sudden thunderstorm. "Do you feel better? Because I sure do, now that we've talked this over."

Macey caught the phone on the first ring Sunday morning, hoping that it wouldn't disturb Clara. "Hello, Derek," she said as she put it to her ear.

"How did you know it was me?"

"Because no one else would be rude enough to call at this unearthly hour."

"Did I wake you up?" His voice dripped pseudo sympathy.

She wouldn't have admitted it even if he had. Nor, for that matter, would she confess that unlike the usual Sunday morning, she'd been awake and restless for a couple of hours. "So sorry to disappoint you, but no, you didn't." She deliberately rattled the newspaper as she pushed it aside to settle down against the pile of pillows at the head of her bed with her coffee mug in her hand. "How was the Halloween party?"

"I do not understand why supposedly intelligent grownups insist on dressing up and acting like fools just because it's autumn."

"Uh-oh. Which one's off the list now?"

"Rita and Liz."

"Another two-for-one sale? You do run through them, McConnell. What happened?"

"You don't really want to know, do you?"

"Not particularly, but I thought I'd be polite and ask. In that case, I'll just cut to explaining why this is actually a positive thing and why you should be in a really good mood this morning instead of acting like the grump of the week."

"You can try explaining it to me. I'm not sure I'll believe you."

"It's because you have one name left. Only one."

"That's what you call a positive thing?"

"Of course it is. The search is over. Emily is it."

"She's the only survivor from a list that included five bad choices. That's hardly a recommendation."

"Derek, you are such a pessimist."

"After the last five, I have good reason to be edgy."

"Come on. The best part of everything always comes last. I bet she turns out to be like a tasty chocolate mousse that's served up after the overcooked pot roast and lumpy mashed potatoes are gone.''

He admitted, ''Even a watery chocolate mousse would look good about now.''

''There's only one way to find out,'' Macey said cheerfully. ''Go look for her. At this hour of the morning, you might even find her in a Sunday school class, teaching a bunch of little kiddies—and what better recommendation could you ask for than that?''

Derek said something under his breath and hung up on her.

Macey put the phone down. So it was going to be Emily.

Emily McConnell—it would be a nice name. Macey hoped, for Derek's sake, that Emily would turn out to be a pleasant young woman. She hoped they'd be happy together—in whatever ways each of them defined happiness.

But as for Macey herself, she mostly just felt tired. And, of course, very glad that it was over.

Macey half expected that on Monday morning Derek would be waiting for her at the office. Considering everything he'd put her through for this engagement, it seemed to her that the least he could do would be to announce it in person.

But he didn't appear, and he didn't phone. Which no doubt meant that Emily had turned out to be perfection, and Derek—in a fit of delirious relief—had entirely forgotten about Macey.

Which was just fine with her. She'd use the time to think up an appropriate gift for him and his bride.

A cappuccino machine, perhaps? The idea should have

felt funny, but it didn't. A gift certificate from a company that reorganized closets so they could hold more stuff?

Or perhaps she'd just wait a few months. There was no doubt in her mind that if Derek was cynical enough to marry to get the job he wanted, he wouldn't stop there. So sometime in the next year, there would probably be another important event to celebrate—the birth of an heir to the Kingdom of Kid. In that case, she could just combine the gifts. A lead crystal baby bottle should do the trick nicely...

Louise tapped on Macey's office door and came in. "We just got a very weird phone call," she said. Almost automatically she leaned over the one vase which was still on Macey's desk, filled with the longest-lived of all the flowers Derek had sent, and breathed deeply. "An executive secretary at McConnell Enterprises."

Macey was puzzled. "A secretary? That's odd. I wonder what Derek wants now, and why he didn't call for himself."

Louise shook her head. "It was George McConnell's secretary. She requested that we send over a temp worker for a few hours today."

Derek was already starting to pay Robert back, Macey thought. Emily must have truly turned out to be a prize. *You're glad, remember?* "What's the job? Do you think Ellen's ready to take it on?"

"She didn't give any details about the job requirements. But Ellen won't do."

"If she wasn't specific about the duties, Louise, how do you know Ellen isn't qualified? She can run just about any—"

"Oh, the secretary was specific all right, just not about the duties." Louise straightened a lily in the vase. "She wants you, Macey. Said you were the only one who'd do." She handed over a slip of paper. "Here's the address. And she wants you there right away."

By the time Derek had escaped from Emily it was after midnight, and much as he'd like to have called Macey right then, he figured that waking her up in the middle of the night to tell her exactly what he thought of the last of her six finalists wouldn't be the brightest move he'd ever made. It would be much smarter to restrain himself until Monday morning.

Of course, even if Macey yelled at him for interrupting her sleep and told him never to speak to her again, he wouldn't be much worse off.

He should have listened to his instincts, that first night at the symphony party when he'd suspected that her choice for him might be the feminine equivalent of Ira Branson. But instead he'd dismissed the feeling, telling himself that surely—with half a dozen shots at the target—she'd hit one candidate who was acceptable. After all, it only took *one*—he wasn't some kind of sheikh trying to set himself up with a harem.

Instead, a full week later he was still sitting exactly where he'd started. And Macey was going to hear about it.

His determination to catch her first thing in the morning made him restless all night, which was no doubt why he ended up oversleeping. Instead of confronting Macey at her office, he found himself rushing madly to get to his own. He was miserably late, he'd forgotten his briefcase, and he had a headache. He was also nursing a resentment the size of Boulder Dam, because he'd tried to call Macey while he was driving to work, only to be told by the receptionist at Peterson Temps that she was on the phone with an important client.

An *important* client. Implying, he supposed, that he wasn't. He didn't even leave a message, just slapped his cell phone closed.

He wasn't being fair and he knew it. He could hardly expect that she'd be reachable every instant of the day. But no matter how unreasonable it was of him, her being unavailable at the moment he wanted her only increased his aggravation level.

So he was already on a roll when he walked into the waiting room outside the executive offices to find the chairman of the board sitting there. He barely remembered to say "Good morning" to him before asking the secretary if she had an aspirin handy.

"You're having headaches fairly often these days, aren't you?" the chairman asked. "No surprise, I'd say."

"Excuse me?"

The chairman slapped his magazine shut and laid it aside. "Look, Derek, I've done as you asked and kept your confidence."

"I'm not sure I—"

"About your engagement," the chairman said impatiently.

"Oh, yes. Thank you, sir. I really appreciate your sensitivity to the—"

"But exactly who are you trying to fool here?"

Derek's blood turned to cold chunks that rattled through his veins. "Sir?"

"Friday evening when I saw you out with the blonde, I thought she must be your fiancée. So when my daughter said she'd seen you at the Halloween party with a redhead, I thought she must be mistaken. Then I thought back to what a friend said about seeing you with a brunette at the symphony party. Three different women in less than a week."

And that's not even the half of it. Derek swallowed hard.

The chairman's voice dropped, but though it was quiet it was no less chilly. "The full board meeting is coming up next week. Unless I'm satisfied with your explanation of what's going on, I will have no choice but to share this information with them. And I must warn you that not all of the directors take a worldly view of this sort of behavior."

I'm toast, Derek thought.

"And please don't expect me to believe that they were all the same woman, but she was wearing different wigs."

"I wouldn't dream of doing that, sir." *But only because I didn't think of it first—so thanks for the warning.*

The door of his father's office opened and George McConnell came out, handing a tape cassette to the secretary. "Type this letter up and get it out first thing, please. Thanks for waiting," he told the chairman. "Come on in."

The chairman stood up. "We'll finish this conversation later," he told Derek, under his breath. "I see no need for your father to be subjected to it."

At least he had a reprieve. He had a few minutes to think—if only his head wasn't pounding so badly that he couldn't.

George McConnell finally seemed to see him standing there. "You come, too, Derek—this discussion affects you as well."

There went his reprieve. Now he couldn't even call for help. And had there really been an edge to his father's voice, or was that just his guilty conscience speaking?

"Sure, Dad," he managed to say. "Just let me grab a cup of coffee and I'll be in."

* * *

But just how, Macey asked herself, did George McConnell's secretary even know her name, much less have developed the burning desire to want to work with her? Who had told her about Macey, and why had she called?

Wrong question, Macey concluded. In fact, a whole string of wrong questions. Or, to be painfully accurate, the questions themselves were sensible ones, but the person they involved was wrong. The secretary wouldn't be acting independently; she was only following orders.

Which meant it must be George McConnell who was checking out Macey.

She was still just as much in the dark about the *why*, but at least the *who* was making sense. She didn't quite see why Enid should have mentioned Macey to her husband, and why George should take the whole thing one step farther. But that must be what had happened.

Enid had seemed to accept the blithe explanation of a replacement for the crystal Derek had broken as an adequate explanation for them being seen together smack in the middle of the biggest bridal registry in town. But obviously Macey had once more underestimated Enid McConnell. Derek's mother had gone home and told Derek's father. What she'd said was anybody's guess, but it had obviously inspired George to get into the act...

Don't assume the worst, Macey told herself. *Maybe this conspiracy stuff is all in your imagination and it really is a straight temp job.*

But she couldn't make herself believe it.

She signed in at McConnell Enterprises' front desk, clipped on the visitor's badge, and followed the receptionist's directions to the corner office suite on the top floor. There another receptionist took her name and consulted someone on the phone before passing her on to the secretary whose name Louise had written down.

Macey stood before the secretary's desk, feeling very much like a student who'd just been sent to see the principal.

"Thank you for coming, Ms. Phillips," the secretary said.

"Perhaps I should explain that there's been a bit of a misunderstanding," Macey said. "I'm actually the office manager at Peterson Temps, not one of the staff. I used to go out on jobs from time to time but I don't anymore."

"I know." The secretary's voice was crisp. "Your telephone person told me."

"But then why—"

"Why are you here? I have no idea. I'm just following orders." She picked up her telephone and pressed a button. "Mr. McConnell? Ms. Phillips is here."

Macey took a deep breath and tried to brace herself.

The office door opened, and Derek came out. "Thanks for coming, Macey."

"What the—" she said.

He looked around and beckoned her across the room. "Not right now, okay? There isn't much time."

"*You* arranged this? You let me think—"

His gaze flicked toward the secretary.

Macey caught herself. "I could kick you," she muttered.

He didn't take her into the office he'd come from, but to the room next door. It was a large conference room with a long walnut table, a dozen leather chairs, and a wall full of shelves which contained enough toys to equip a day-care center, from infant rattles to tricycles, puzzles to pretend-doctor kits.

Macey took it all in at a glance as she wheeled to face

him. "What's this all about, Derek? Is it just some kooky way to announce that you got the job? Because you scared me half to death."

He shook his head. "No. Believe me, you couldn't be more wrong. You have to help me here, Macey."

"You haven't heard of *please?* What's with all the drama, anyway? Why didn't you just call me? Why haul me over here on some obviously made-up temp job?"

"I was stuck in a meeting with my father and the chairman of the board. I could hardly say, 'Excuse me, but I need to go phone the woman who's helping me pull the wool over the chairman's eyes and ask for her advice.' So I had Miranda call you. And if you need an explanation of why I didn't give her all the details…"

Macey shook her head. "No, I can see why you didn't want to explain it to the secretary. But I thought the whole thing was settled. You and Emily made an agreement, you came to work and told everybody, and now you've got the job."

"Far from it."

"Emily wasn't the answer to your prayers?"

"Please. She— Oh, never mind, it doesn't matter. There's no time for that. The chairman will be free any minute—and he wants an explanation of why I've been seen with a number of different women lately when I'm supposed to be engaged to be married."

Macey gave a low whistle. "That's not good. Though I can't say I'm surprised, because even Ira was onto that. I warned you—"

"Such a comfort you are."

"However, I'm a little lost as to what you expect me to do about it. If you think I should just start over, Derek—"

"No time for that. I need an explanation, Macey, and

I need it right now. And it wouldn't hurt if I had a name, too. Just one name—not another list.''

A name? He expected her to reach into her memory and pull out a single name? And not just any name, but the name of a woman who would meet all his criteria for a wife *and* be willing to marry him? Her mind had gone blank. Even if she'd wanted to give him a name, she couldn't have remembered one.

''I—'' she began. Her voice felt wobbly.

The door opened and a big, white-haired man came in. ''Well, Derek? I'll listen to your explanation now.''

Derek was still looking at Macey. ''That's brilliant,'' he whispered. He turned to face the chairman. ''Sir, I didn't think a simple explanation would be enough. So I'd like to introduce you to my fiancée. This is Macey Phillips.''

The blood started to roar in Macey's ears.

''She can tell you about the other women I've been seen with, too,'' Derek went on. ''Because she's the reason I've been seeing them—she wanted me to.''

CHAPTER EIGHT

DEREK thought the chairman seemed thoughtful, as if he was giving the whole idea due consideration. Macey, on the other hand, appeared to be about two inches short of murderous—and the distance was closing fast.

Uncomfortably aware that he had gambled his entire future on Macey's ability to pull herself together, Derek watched her from the corner of his eye and concluded that his best move would be to distract the chairman for a while.

He cleared his throat and said, "You see, sir, there have been at least half a dozen women in my life."

He could actually feel the vibrations of Macey's thoughts, could almost hear her saying to herself, *And that's only in the last week. Heaven knows what the real total is.*

"Of course," he went on, "Macey knows all this. We've talked about it, and I've tried to reassure her that they are entirely in the past. But the matter of these other women has continued to concern her a little."

The chairman gave a grunt. "From what I've heard about you flitting from one to another like a butterfly, I'd say she has reason for concern."

"Macey wanted to be certain—so she suggested that I see each of them one more time, keeping an open mind about their attractions and my feelings. That's why I've been flitting, as you put it—because I was anxious to satisfy her request and get back to my real choice." He smiled fondly down at her.

The chairman looked as if he'd bitten into a lemon. "Is this true, young lady? Did you actually suggest that Derek go out with women other than yourself?"

Macey swallowed hard.

Just tell the truth, sweetheart. The exact truth.

"Yes, sir." Her voice was barely audible. "I did."

Derek tried not to let his relief show.

"You actually wanted your fiancé to go out with other women? Well, that seems a mighty strange thing to me."

Macey wet her lips. "I wanted to be certain that Derek was making a decision he could live with forever. For a man who's been something of a playboy to settle down with one woman—"

"It just takes the right woman," Derek murmured.

"Marriage requires total commitment, and complete confidence between the partners." Macey's voice was gaining a little strength as she went on. "And it's much better to find out if there's a problem with that commitment before there's a wedding instead of after."

"You have nothing to worry about, darling. None of them could hold my attention for a whole evening, much less a lifetime."

She didn't seem to be listening. "Since our...engagement..."

She sounded as if she was trying not to choke on the word, Derek thought.

"...was very sudden, I thought it would be wise to take some precautions. To stop and look around before we leaped."

The chairman nodded. "I understand now, and I commend you, my dear. I hope my daughter will be as wise, when she makes her choice." He shook hands. "I'm sure I'll be seeing a great deal more of you, Miss—Phillips, was it?"

Derek held his breath, but Macey didn't correct him about the title. The last thing he needed right now was to explain why his fiancée was known as *Mrs.* Phillips.

After the chairman had gone, the silence was deafening. Macey was standing in the middle of the conference room as if she were a fashion-store mannequin who had been placed there, carefully posed, and then left to gather dust.

She was still stunned, Derek diagnosed. Well, he could sympathize with that.

Prudently, he planted himself between her and the door. "That was very good," he said. "Excellent, in fact."

She didn't answer, but at least she finally moved. Rather than trying to get around him to escape, however, she walked across the room to survey the shelves of toys and activity equipment.

"You're even better on the uptake than I hoped you would be," Derek went on. "It must be all your experience with temp jobs, but you can really roll with the punches."

Macey strolled up and down in silence, studying the shelves. Finally she stopped in front of a junior carpentry set—a workbench equipped with small scale but real tools—and picked up a hammer.

Derek eyed her warily. "Macey, that really isn't a toy. You could hurt somebody with it."

"I know." She sounded as if her teeth were gritted together. "I'm planning on it."

"Uh—Macey...."

"The only reason I rolled with the punches, as you put it, was because watching the chairman turn you into road-kill wouldn't have been nearly as much fun as doing it myself. What were you thinking of? No, let me rephrase that—because you obviously weren't thinking at all."

"When I asked you for a name, Macey, you said, 'I—' and that made me think—"

"You assumed I was volunteering?" She advanced on him.

Derek backed up a step and held both hands up, palms out. "All right—you've made your point. No, I realized you weren't talking about yourself. But still, it put the idea in my head—"

"So you're shifting the blame onto me?"

"Blame? I thought it was a great idea."

"And I suppose you also think I should fall on my knees in gratitude because I've won you as the prize in a lottery—even though I didn't have a clue I was holding a ticket. Didn't you hear me when I told you I had no intention of ever getting married again?"

"Of course I heard you," Derek said dryly. "Everybody within two blocks of that store heard you. You don't want to marry me—fine. I don't want to marry you, either."

"Then excuse me, but I don't understand what that little exercise gained you—besides a fiancée you don't want."

"That's the beauty of it, Macey. I don't know why I didn't think of it before. Now that I have a real fiancée to show off, all the pressure's gone."

"Off *you*, maybe," she muttered.

"The board's going to make their decision next week."

"And you think this pseudo engagement will satisfy them?"

"Sure, it will. They can hardly expect me to be officially married by then, since weddings do take a little time, I understand. And I'm sure you're insisting on doing the thing up right, with satin and lace and all the trimmings. No," he said heartily, "my Macey wouldn't settle for a rush job in a courtroom."

"I certainly wouldn't. As it happens, I wouldn't settle for a church ceremony either, but—"

"But as long as they don't know that, we're in great shape. Macey, they don't really want to go outside the company for the next CEO. They'd much rather give me the job, so they'll seize the excuse. And once that's settled—"

"Then the engagement's over?" There was an eager note in her voice.

He hated to squash the hope, but it wouldn't be fair to lead her on. "I'm afraid not. If a temporary engagement would have fixed the problem, I wouldn't have spent the last week trying so desperately to find someone I could marry. No, I'll still have to go through with it—but now I can take my time, look around, observe."

"It's the part about *taking your time* that I don't like."

"It'll go a lot faster when we're working together," Derek promised. "We'll make the social rounds, I'll tell you who interests me, and you can check her out. When you find someone with promise, you'll be right there beside me, so there can't be any gossip about me seeing other women behind your back."

"And when you find the right one, you'll shed me and turn up with her instead? I'm only a place-holder in the meantime?" She sounded wary.

"Well, an active place-holder—but yes."

"And when you pull off this little switch, you expect the chairman of the board not to notice?"

"Oh, he'll know it, all right, but he won't blame me. In fact, he'll probably feel sorry for me, because he already thinks you're the flighty one. With this business of wanting me to date others, it won't be any surprise at all to him when you back out. Beautiful, isn't it?''

She was looking at him with something akin to admiration in her eyes. ''And you think *I'm* the expert in twisted logic? Derek, of all the incredibly insane plans—''

''Of course there's always the alternative.''

''Which is?''

''We could go through with it.''

She didn't even hesitate. ''I'd rather be tied to a nest of fire ants and eaten alive.''

Derek shrugged. ''Then I guess you'll just have to play the game and help me find your replacement.''

She sighed. ''Let me think about it. Because in the long run it might be easier if I'd go looking for the fire ants.''

Derek suggested she come along to help break the news to his father. Macey declined as politely as she could manage, reluctantly put the hammer back in place on the junior carpentry workbench, and got herself out of the building before Derek's announcement could set off some sort of fireball.

Macey thought it was quite likely. She'd tried to convince Derek to tell his father the truth about the scheme, but though he'd listened patiently to all her arguments, in the end he shook his head and said that the fewer people who knew the details, the better. Which meant, he said, that only the two of them would ever know what had really happened.

''Three,'' Macey corrected. ''You'll tell your wife, surely.''

Derek frowned.

Macey was horrified. ''You can't mean you're thinking of not telling her.''

"The only thing I'm thinking about is exactly why we're having this pointless conversation."

"Because if you can't tell her the truth about something like that— Oh, never mind. It's none of my business. I have to go find Clara right away, because if she finds out from your mother instead of from me, it won't be pretty."

"I hadn't thought about her," Derek admitted. "You told me she's actually your husband's aunt, right? Is she going to give you trouble about the whole idea of getting married again?"

"Probably." *Just not the sort you'd ordinarily expect.* "Derek, if I can just tell her the truth—"

But even as she said the words, Macey knew the idea would never work. Clara was a dear, but she was no conspirator. If Enid McConnell asked the right question, Clara would spill everything she knew. And no doubt Enid would have lots of questions.

So the only safe way was for Clara not to know that the engagement was only a sham until the whole thing was over. And when she found out it wasn't true after all...

"It'll break her heart," Macey said.

"I'm sorry about that."

"Not as sorry as I am," Macey muttered. "Give me a chance to find her before you start broadcasting the news, all right?"

But Clara wasn't at home. Macey waited around for a bit, but the town house felt uncomfortably empty. No— worse than empty. Most of the time, she simply didn't look at Clara's collection of photographs, but today it felt as if Jack was watching her from every wall. After a while, when Clara still hadn't appeared, Macey went back to work.

It was probably just as well if she didn't talk to Clara

for a little while, Macey tried to convince herself. She needed some time to sort this out in her own mind first. And if she couldn't find Clara, neither could Enid McConnell—so surely the news would stay under wraps for an hour or two longer.

Louise had gone out for a late lunch and Ellen was manning the reception desk when Macey came in. Macey could almost see Ellen's curiosity bubbling in her eyes.

But she wasn't about to start explaining. "I need to get hold of my aunt," Macey told her, "but I don't want to leave a message and risk alarming her. Just keep calling every fifteen minutes or so, and when she answers, buzz me."

She went on into her office and closed the door. Not that she accomplished much except to shuffle paper, for she was still too stunned by the sudden turn of events to concentrate.

As if in a nightmare, she replayed the moment when Derek had made his announcement to the chairman of the board—and worse yet, the instant when she'd actually opened her mouth and confirmed what he'd said.

Temporary insanity, she told herself with a groan. She'd been overwhelmed by the sheer force of Derek's personality, and her own good sense had cracked under the strain.

She'd fallen into a pit full of molasses—and now she was thoroughly stuck.

Clara was in the kitchen when Macey got home, humming as she put together a stir-fry. "Nothing fancy tonight," she warned. "I'd planned a pot roast, but I was busy all afternoon."

"I know you were out."

Clara gave her a sideways look. "Anyway, I didn't get

the roast started on time, so I'll fix it tomorrow. Would you chop up that onion, please?"

Almost mechanically, Macey picked up a knife.

"And how do you know I wasn't home?"

"I stopped by to talk to you. Clara—you know how I said I wasn't dating?"

"I seem to remember a conversation along those lines," Clara said dryly.

"Well, it wasn't quite true." *It wasn't false, either, but that's beside the point at the moment.* "I've been seeing someone, and....well, somehow we ended up engaged."

Clara's wooden spoon hung suspended for a moment that seemed to stretch into eons. "Oh."

"That's all you have to say about it?" Macey said finally.

"I was waiting for you to finish. *Somehow we ended up engaged* doesn't seem like a good place for the story to stop." She began to stir again. "Frankly, it sounds as if you're already having doubts about whether you've made the right choice."

No doubts at all, Clara. I'm absolutely certain I'm doing the wrong thing.

But it was a warning for Macey to be very careful about what she said. She wasn't used to Clara reading between the lines like that. Just a few months ago, when she'd still been in the depths of her depression, she wouldn't have noticed.

"You're wondering if it will upset me all over again if you move out," Clara deduced. "I'll miss you, that's sure, but—"

The front doorbell rang, and Clara put down her spoon and went to answer it. Macey pushed the chopped onion into the wok and methodically set to work reducing a green pepper to chunks.

Clara was gone for five minutes, and when she came back, she wasn't alone. "Macey, why haven't I met this young man before?"

Macey looked up in dread, but she already knew who she would see. Perhaps it was only because Clara was so tiny, but Derek looked impossibly large, looming behind her in the doorway. As if he were taking over the town house as easily as he'd commandeered her life.

"Because," Derek murmured, "Macey was afraid you'd steal my heart away from her if she let you come near me."

Clara laughed.

"What are you doing here?" Macey asked him.

"I came to meet Clara, and—now that our secret is no longer a secret—to take you to choose a ring."

"Oh, no." Macey's protest was both automatic and heartfelt, and only after it was out and she saw Derek's frown and Clara's narrowed eyes did Macey realize how it must have sounded. She scrambled for an excuse. "I mean, I think it would be much more romantic if you were to surprise me."

Clara relaxed. "That's true, you know. In my day, women never had a hand in choosing their engagement rings."

No wonder so many antique rings looked like circus jewelry, Macey thought. If the women who wore them had no say in what they looked like...

Since Derek hadn't a clue about Macey's taste, it was probably dangerous to turn him loose in a jewelry store to choose a ring for her. But it was too late to change her tactics now. Fortunately, no matter what sort of abomination he bought, she wouldn't have to wear it for long. A couple of weeks, perhaps—because surely in that length of time they could run through the entire social register.

If they went to a party or a fund-raiser or a restaurant every night...

"Dinner tomorrow," Derek was saying. For a moment, Macey thought he'd read her mind. "At my parents' house, to officially introduce the families. That includes you, Clara."

"We'd be delighted," Clara said firmly.

Macey managed to nod. So much for tomorrow's hunt for potential brides. Of course, one day more or less didn't make much difference.

"You'll stay for dinner tonight, won't you?" Clara asked.

"Thank you, but no—I have a very important purchase to make, and the jeweler is staying late to help me."

Relieved, Macey said, "Some other time, then. See you tomorrow."

Derek didn't move. "Aren't you going to walk me to the door?"

Belatedly, Macey put down her knife and led the way out of the kitchen.

"My father thinks we should entertain the board of directors, by the way."

"We?" Macey said. "Entertain? I don't suppose you're talking about a tap dance routine."

"More like dinner."

"That's what I was afraid you meant."

"The whole board only assembles about four times a year, and they travel from all over—so when they get together, they generally stay a couple of days. Dad thinks they'll want to meet you. But it doesn't have to be an elaborate thing. We could just take them to a restaurant."

Clara's head appeared in the doorway between kitchen and living room. "No, no, no. Do it yourselves. That's the only way to impress someone. It's far better to serve a very simple dish that's home-cooked than the most elaborate menu a restaurant chef can devise." She turned pink. "Sorry. I didn't mean to eavesdrop." She vanished around the corner.

"The heck she didn't," Macey said under her breath.

Derek lowered his voice. "Hey—she's not nearly the dragon I was expecting, from what you said."

Macey had no intention of explaining. "Good night. See you tomorrow." She started to open the door.

Derek put a hand on the panel and pushed it shut. "Stop and think. If she's eavesdropping, don't you think she's going to expect to hear...other sounds?"

"Oh, please." But Macey had to admit he'd pegged Clara perfectly. She was capable not only of listening but of peeking around corners. Which meant that if Macey didn't kiss Derek good-night, Clara was likely to know it. Macey sighed. "I suppose I'd better get used to it."

The corner of Derek's mouth twitched. He put his arms around her as carefully as if she were made of wax, and obediently Macey stepped closer, laid her hands on his shoulders, and turned her face up to his.

Just a kiss, she was thinking. How many times, on how many dates, had she gone through this ritual? Certainly enough that it no longer seemed important, or even meaningful. Just a good-night kiss.

And then with Jack—

Don't think about Jack right now.

She felt small and delicate, in contrast to Derek's size and solidity. She could feel the strength in his arms, and she knew that he could crush her. But she also knew that he wouldn't.

The first brush of his lips against hers was cool, almost cautious. "Oh, for heaven's sake, at least try to make it look good," she muttered.

Too late she saw mischief spring to life in his eyes. His arms tightened until she was pressed against him from shoulder to knee, and his kiss became the brand of a lover, teasing and tasting at first, then hot and hungry.

Involuntarily, she tensed, and he mimicked her own words, whispering against her lips. "At least try to make it look good."

Macey forced herself to relax. *It's only a kiss,* she told herself, but the words rang hollow. She might be vertical and fully clothed, but he was making love to her as surely as if they'd been lying together between black satin sheets...

When he finally raised his head, Macey was thinking that if she actually had been made of wax there would be no more left of her than the burned-out stub of a candle.

"We'll have to do that again," Derek said. His voice had a rough edge.

"I suppose so," Macey managed. "I'm a bit out of practice."

"Really? I just meant it was enough fun to be well worth repeating. But if that's what you're like when you're out of practice, I want to see what happens when you get back on the team." He kissed her once more, a long and lingering caress, and said, "So what kind of ring do you want?"

Macey was having trouble breathing. "What do I care? Choose something you can recycle."

"That's a thought. Maybe I'll ask if I can rent one for a while. What did you have before?"

"A solitaire diamond set in yellow gold."

"I suppose that went the way of the china."

"You suppose right."

He flicked a fingertip against her earlobe. "Too bad

everybody's expecting a traditional ring, or I'd get you a pair of diamond earrings instead."

"Too easy to lose."

"You sure can't say that about these."

"I like my earrings. Clara makes them for me."

"In that case," Derek said, "you can tell her I like them too."

And there was as much truth in that, Macey thought as she watched him cross the lawn to his car, as there was in anything else he'd said that day.

Which added up to precisely none.

The menu was the ultimate in simplicity, though it was far from easy to execute. But by late Sunday afternoon, the prime rib was roasting in the oven, the twice-baked potatoes were ready to go under the broiler for just long enough to melt the cheese on top, and the salads were already arranged on individual plates in the refrigerator. The freshly baked dinner rolls were giving off an aroma fit for the gods, and Macey was arranging a tray of appetizers while Derek finished setting up a makeshift bar on a cart just around the corner from the kitchen.

Macey set the appetizers in the refrigerator and went to give a last inspection to the dinner table. The furniture had been pushed back in the living room of the loft to accommodate the rented table, which had space enough to seat the twelve diners they were expecting. Macey thought the whole loft looked better that way—less cavernous and more homey, and in a strange way more spacious than it had before.

Derek obviously hadn't agreed, but beyond suggesting once more that they make a reservation at a restaurant instead of going to all the bother, he hadn't argued the point. And even he had admitted, once the battered surface of the table had disappeared beneath white linen and Enid's china, crystal, and silver, that it looked pretty good.

Was that a smudge on a wineglass? No, Macey decided. Just a stray reflection from the track lights above the fireplace.

"Tell me again why you think I should take a second look at Natalie," Derek said. He pushed the cart to one side and opened the glass doors to put another log on the fire.

Natalie, Macey thought absently. Now which young woman was Natalie? There had been so many.

For the last week—except for the night she and Clara had gone to the McConnells' house for dinner—Macey and Derek had partied their way across St. Louis, shopping for a suitable wife, and Macey was feeling the strain. Even tonight's dinner for the board of McConnell Enterprises looked peaceful in comparison.

Oh, yes, she remembered. Natalie was the little blonde they'd run into the night before last at the chamber orchestra. And what had been special about her? Macey tried to remember. "Because she seems nice."

Derek made a noise somewhere between a grunt and a snort.

"Come on, Derek. *Nice* might not look glamorous right now, but it would be a lot easier to live with than some other qualities I could name."

"There's such a thing as too nice."

"You don't think she was for real?" Macey straightened a salad fork and pushed a napkin back into line. "What would she have to gain from faking it?"

"I don't know. It's just a feeling."

"Well, I guess the only way to find out for sure is to marry her. You can call me in ten years and let me know which one of us was right."

"Your concern for my welfare is charming, Macey."

"That's what you're paying me for. Did I remember to tell you that my per-hour fees are triple on Sundays?"

"You remembered. I'm afraid to add it up, but I suspect your hourly rates rank right up there with the world's most exclusive courtesans."

"Really? That's quite flattering, Derek."

"But all I've gotten for it is the occasional smooch in the shadows, and then only because someone might be watching."

"Does that bother you? Here I thought the possibility of being observed just added a little illicit excitement to the whole thing," Macey murmured. "Besides, if I slept with you and you were disappointed, it would just be too awful."

"So I'm better off this way, with my idealistic dreams intact? Yeah, right. I had breakfast with my mother today."

Macey asked idly, "Your idea or hers?"

"Hers. Why?"

"Just that it's about time for her to start trying to talk you out of this. She's given you almost a whole week for the novelty to wear off, so now—"

"On the contrary. I should warn you that she's planning an engagement party."

"That's cunning of her. Can you get her to put it off?"

"Not for long. Besides, it'll be a great way for you to meet everyone on my list that we've missed so far, because they'll all be there."

"That's true," Macey said dispassionately. "I can take note of which ones are sobbing in the ladies' room at the idea of losing you."

"Mom offered to come early tonight to help."

Macey felt a jolt in the region of her solar plexus. "You didn't accept—did you?"

"No. But I wouldn't bet any money on whether she'll stay away."

"Then I'd better get changed." Macey reached for the garment bag she'd hung on a cabinet door in the kitchen and started on around the center cube to the powder room.

"You can use my bedroom," Derek said.

"I thought you—" Macey paused. "No, thanks. I'm not sharing."

"You're always looking for ulterior motives."

"That's because you generally have a few."

"Not this time. My mother's right about the size of the powder room—you couldn't maneuver yourself into a dress in there without help. Which wouldn't be a bad idea, actually, and I'd be happy to volunteer, except that there isn't room for me in there too."

"No ulterior motives, huh? If I go upstairs, I'm locking myself in the bathroom."

He held up a hand. "On my honor, Macey. I won't follow you."

She hadn't been upstairs since the day she'd rolled under his bed to escape his mother. Such a desperate and useless move that had been—though as far as Macey was aware, Enid still didn't know it had been her. Macey couldn't help but wonder who Enid thought it might have been.

She stopped halfway across the room, her breath catching in her throat. Across the muted plaid of the bedspread lay a dress.

Now I know how Enid felt when she saw the shoes, Macey thought.

But the cases couldn't be the same. No woman would have accidentally left this little number behind. It must have been deliberately left there for her to see. And Macey couldn't resist taking a closer look.

The dress was the same rich orange-red as bittersweet berries. It was long for a cocktail dress, but the modest hemline was more than balanced by the narrow straps and the deep-plunging back.

A perfect dress for the occasion. A perfect color for her, to bring out the auburn highlights in her dark brown hair. The perfect size.

And there was a note tucked into the folds of the skirt. *You told me I owed you an outfit,* it said.

She wondered who had helped him buy it.

When she came downstairs, cautious of her heels on the open ironwork of the steps, Derek was waiting. He didn't say a word, but the appreciative gleam in his eyes gave Macey goose bumps.

"Cold?" he asked.

"Just the air currents. I'll be fine."

"I can keep my arm around you all evening."

"Oh, that would be handy, trying to serve food." She looked at the clock instead of at him. "It's almost time."

"How about a kiss for luck?"

She could hardly say no. "Careful of the makeup."

"Haven't I been careful all week?" His arms were gentle, his hands soothingly warm against her bare back.

She should be used to it by now—being in his arms, being kissed. By now she should have been able to detect a pattern. But each time was new, different, unpredictable.

"You taste good," Derek whispered.

"I've been sampling the dip."

"Let me see..." He kissed her again. "Definitely not the dip. That's you."

The doorbell rang. Macey freed herself and took a quick look at her reflection in the polished brass trim on the glass doors of the fireplace. Careful or not, she looked as if she'd just been thoroughly kissed—which was no doubt exactly what Derek had had in mind. "Oh, wait," she said. "My ring—I took it off in the kitchen when I was shaping the rolls."

The ring was lying exactly where she'd left it. As she was each time she picked it up, Macey was taken aback by the sheer beauty of the enormous pear-shaped diamond and the silvery glow of the titanium band. She slipped it onto her finger, held her hand out to admire it—and only then did she actually hear what she'd said.

My ring.

But it wasn't her ring. It was only on loan to her. For all she knew, Derek might have actually talked the jeweler into letting him rent it for a while. She wouldn't blame him; though it was a ring any woman should be proud to wear, Macey couldn't see any of the beauties on his list being willing to settle for a ring that had adorned another hand, no matter how temporarily.

My ring.

How easily the words had slipped out. How easily the thought flowed through her mind.

No wonder, she mused almost dispassionately, that though she had made him lists of possible brides, she hadn't been able to feel enthusiastic about a single one of them. No wonder she hadn't been able to find one who was suitable. One whom she thought was good enough for him.

Because the fact was she wanted him for herself.

CHAPTER NINE

OF ALL the stupid moves a woman could make, Macey told herself, this one was right at the top of the heap. Falling in love with Mr. Perfection, the crown prince of the Kingdom of Kid, the guy who'd cold-bloodedly hired her to find him a wife...it had to be the most naive mistake in the history of the world.

Because, no matter how much she'd like to deny it, that was exactly what she'd done. She'd had so much fun fighting with Derek—teasing him, opposing him and annoying him—that she hadn't even noticed when fondness had sneaked into the picture, or when it had turned to affection, and then to attraction, and then to love.

Not for her the breathless adoration, the idolization, the blind devotion that was so commonly thought of as being in love. She knew Derek's every flaw, and she loved him in spite of them. Even, perhaps, because of them.

It was no wonder, she realized now, that she'd been unable to summon anything more than faint praise for a single one of the women on his list. No wonder that she'd felt so sad the day of their picnic, when she'd thought the adventure was over and she might never see him again. No wonder that she got all wobbly whenever he kissed her, no matter what the circumstances.

It was no wonder that she'd gone all domestic in wanting to have the dinner party at his loft. When she'd decided to show off her skills in the kitchen, she hadn't been thinking of impressing the members of the board—she'd been performing for Derek.

And it was no wonder she'd found herself thinking just a short while ago that this dinner party was surprisingly lacking in stress, considering the stakes. Compared to going to parties with him night after night, dinner with the board was nothing. Tonight she was not only where she wanted to be—beside him—but she would be the only woman he was watching. Tonight she could pretend that it was all real.

Or at least, that was what she would have done if this uncomfortable revelation hadn't sneaked up and kicked her in the head.

She'd believed she was safe. She had thought that her resolution never to marry again would protect her against falling in love. But somehow she'd forgotten that the two things were completely separate. She had let down her guard, and now she would pay the price.

Because when it came right down to it, nothing about the entire situation had really changed. Derek was still looking for a wife—and Macey wasn't what he was looking for. The only difference was that now she knew exactly how foolish she had been.

Derek opened the door, and George and Enid McConnell came in.

Just get through the evening, Macey ordered herself. *You can think about it all later.*

George took over the bar, and Enid ran a practiced eye over the kitchen. "I don't see how you've done it, Macey," she said. "This kitchen was obviously designed by a man who'd never cooked anything more complicated than a TV dinner."

"It's been a bit of a juggling act," Macey admitted.

The doorbell rang again.

"You've made my china look quite lovely," Enid said. "Perhaps I should just leave it here, and buy new china and silver as well as crystal. Oh, dear—how tasteless of me. Of course you'd prefer to choose your own. Perhaps we could go together sometime this week, Macey. We really need to get your patterns registered.''

Macey smiled and hoped Enid wouldn't notice that she had said neither yes nor no.

"We could take Clara and go out to lunch," Enid went on.

The loft began to fill. A couple of the wives joined Enid at the kitchen island. One of them cast a look around the big, sparsely furnished living room, and said, "Well, considering it's bachelor's quarters, it's not bad. Of course you'll want a house right away—but at least we know what to get you for a wedding gift. Chairs."

The chairman of the board was the last to arrive, well after everyone else. On his arm was a very young and very stunning blonde.

Trophy wife, Macey thought.

But the chairman introduced her as his daughter. "Jennifer, take a lesson from this young woman," he said as he presented her to Macey. "She's got some uncommonly good sense when it comes to husband-hunting."

If you only knew, Macey thought.

"When I get ready to stalk my prey, I'll certainly call you for instruction." Jennifer gave a little rippling laugh.

Her warmth was infectious, and Macey couldn't help smiling back. An instant later, however, she looked past Jennifer and realized that Derek was still standing just inside the door, as if he'd closed it almost mechanically and then forgotten what to do next. His entire mind was obviously focused on watching Jennifer.

Macey felt ice start to form in her heart.

The woman was lovely. She was warm. She had a sense

of humor. And she was the chairman's daughter. How much more perfect could she be?

How odd, Macey thought, that he'd searched so desperately and so widely, only to find the woman of his dreams right at his own front door.

All evening, Macey tried not to even look in Derek's direction, for fear of what she might see in his eyes as he watched Jennifer. The young woman was the life of the party, that was sure—everyone seemed entranced with her. The men vied to draw her attention, but even the women indulged her.

In comparison, Macey felt like a lifeless frump. She toyed with her prime rib and tried not to listen to the ringing laugh coming at regular intervals from the far end of the table, almost next to Derek. Was Jennifer laughing at something he'd said?

It was hardly the most formal of dinner parties, for the layout of the loft wouldn't allow it. Macey had fleetingly considered hiring a waitress or two to serve and clear, before she realized how silly it would look to attempt such formality. In such an open space, the staff wouldn't even be able to scrape the used dishes, because every sound from the kitchen would echo.

But by the time the entrée was finished, the last trace of formality had broken down. Derek paused as he removed the plates, slung a napkin over his arm, and began to improvise a role as an uppity butler waiting table at a picnic as he finished clearing the table.

He was funny, Macey admitted, but hardly as hilarious as Jennifer seemed to find him, judging by her almost-continuous rippling laugh.

In truth, however, no one else seemed to think Jennifer was overdoing it—only Macey seemed to be disturbed.

There's nothing wrong with the girl, she told herself. *You're just upset because he's performing for her instead of for you.*

Her hands trembled a little as she served up the cheesecake for dessert. The evening was drawing to a successful close, but instead of congratulating herself she was wishing it could go on longer.

"More wine, madam?" the pseudo butler asked Jennifer with a bow.

The blonde laughed. "I'd love some. Careful what you call me, though—my daddy might not like you calling a nice girl like me a madam."

Macey gritted her teeth to keep from muttering that a truly nice girl wouldn't have drawn the connection between a term of respect and the operator of a whorehouse.

The guests lingered over coffee, but when Macey offered to refill the cups again, one of the wives laughed and said, "No, I think it's time to call the evening to a halt. I've been feeling like a voyeur for long enough."

Macey's hand slipped and she barely caught herself in time to keep hot coffee from splashing over the linen tablecloth—or far worse, over the chairman of the board. If others had noticed the intimate byplay between Derek and Jennifer…

Well, at least then they won't be surprised at the change in brides, she told herself, trying to take it philosophically.

The woman smiled at Macey. "Don't look so embarrassed, dear. You haven't done anything tasteless—in fact you and Derek haven't done anything at all to make me feel like a Peeping Tom. It's purely the way you *haven't* touched each other, or even looked at each other, that gave you away."

Macey's head was swimming.

"It's just very apparent that the two of you can't wait for all of us to disappear so you can enjoy your privacy." She set her cup down and pushed her chair back. "So though I hate to break up the party—"

Only the chairman of the board seemed to take his time in departing, but Macey admitted that perhaps Jennifer wasn't really dawdling—maybe it just seemed that way because Macey was so anxious to be rid of her.

As soon as they were gone, Macey began to transfer china from the stacks on the counter to the dishwasher, while Derek finished clearing the table. He brought the last few coffee cups out just as Macey was adding detergent.

"This thing probably hasn't worked so hard before today." She pushed the button to turn it on.

Her thoughts seemed to slosh in rhythm with the running water. *Don't even try to dodge the problem,* she thought. It would be better to bring up a painful subject herself—and try to make the mention look casual—than to have it hit her when she was even less prepared to face the question.

She wet a paper towel and began to wipe the counter. "What did you think of Jennifer?"

Derek moved the basket of rolls so she could wipe under it. "You don't ever quit, do you? I thought I told you she's the reason we're in this mess in the first place."

"You've met her before?" *And she wasn't on your list?* A trickle of relief seeped through Macey. Perhaps she'd been seeing things that weren't there. It would be no surprise if she had been feeling a twinge of jealousy, considering the shock that she had absorbed only a few minutes before Jennifer arrived.

But then why were you looking at her as if you'd been hit by lightning?

"No, I don't know her. But I had sort of had a knee-jerk reaction when her father offered to introduce me."

"And that was when you told him you were engaged—for fear his daughter would be less than compatible."

"That's the polite way to put it."

"So now that you know what he was offering, are your knees still jerking?" Macey kept her voice casual, but the effort cost her.

Derek picked up a chunk of cheesecake that had fallen onto the countertop and ate it. "You must not have heard her political views."

"No." *I was trying not to hear anything she said to you.*

"I can't even remember being that young," Derek mused. "Or that liberal, either. She's so broad-minded the wind whistles through."

"You probably never were that liberal, and you haven't been accused of being broad-minded lately, either. But being young isn't such a bad thing. You could raise her to suit you." Her conscience prodded her. *Just couldn't resist that one, could you, Phillips?*

Derek snorted. "Train her right? Not likely, with her father overseeing every move."

Macey shrugged, trying to hide her pleasure. "Well, I was just trying to do my job."

Derek stared at her. "You mean you actually would have put Jennifer on the list? Good Lord, Macey, that cheesecake must have clogged up your brain. Whoever marries her will get mighty tired of hearing about what her daddy might not like."

You should not be feeling happy about this, Macey lectured herself. *The longer it takes to find someone to suit Derek, the more painful it's going to be for you.*

And yet...in the meantime...

As long as she could keep her guilty secret hidden, she could simply enjoy being beside him. She could pretend that she belonged at his side. She could soak up the joy of being with him.

"I think that's everything." Macey tossed the paper towel away. "At least until the dishwasher finishes the first load."

"It was a knockout of an evening, Macey." He reached out, lazily, and put an arm around her shoulders. "Everybody was impressed. Including me. So, now that I don't have to be careful of the makeup anymore, I'm going to destroy it."

He was as good as his word, but he didn't stop with her makeup. He was cautious not to hurt her as he systematically ruined her upswept hairstyle, pulling out pins and dropping them at random on the floor until he could run his fingers freely through the wavy mass. Then with one hand cupped around the back of her head, he drew her close and settled to the serious business of kissing her senseless.

It took all of Macey's concentration to remember that this was more a kiss of celebration and of gratitude—and opportunity—than one of real passion. Though as it went on and the heat between them grew to nuclear proportions, she found that more and more difficult to recall.

With the last of her self-control, she put both hands against his chest. "It's late."

He sighed, and his hold loosened. "I'll take you home. Though I'd much rather not."

"You don't have to go out. I can call a cab."

"You know perfectly well that wasn't what I meant." He cupped both hands around her face and made her look at him. "Stay with me."

His voice was low and sultry, and yet there was a catch

in it. Like half-melted chocolate, Macey thought—mostly rich and creamy, but still with a lump here and there. Somehow it was even more appealing that way than if it had been entirely smooth.

"I want to make love to you, Macey." He was whispering, almost pleading.

She had expected that it might come to this, sooner or later. Pretending to be a loving couple was no big deal for a while, but if one put on a show for long enough, it was hard to escape the role. It was difficult to remember what was real and what was mere performance.

Put any normal, virile man in the situation and she suspected it wouldn't be long before he was paying more attention to physical urges than to common sense. And Derek was a perfectly normal, virile man—there was no doubt about that.

What Macey hadn't expected was that the strongest persuasion would come not from him, but from inside herself.

She had enjoyed his kisses, had even—if she was honest with herself—looked forward to them. But she had not anticipated having any difficulty in stopping the situation from going farther than kisses and caresses. She had not expected to have trouble remembering that his reaction was more to the situation than to the precise woman in his arms.

Of course, all that had been before she'd fallen in love—or at least before she'd recognized it.

That, she thought, should have made it easier to refuse—knowing that he didn't care about her at anywhere close to the same depth that she cared about him. Knowing that if it had happened to be Rita, or Liz, or Emily, or Constance—or Jennifer—in his arms, he'd have felt much the same urges.

He was kissing her again, and she suspected he was

using every seductive wile he knew. The sensual assault was taking a toll; she could feel the last ounce of objectivity beginning to slip away.

It's only one night, the little voice at the back of her brain was whispering. *What's so bad about that? Why shouldn't you have one night to remember?*

Because it was only one night, she told herself. And because one night would not satisfy—it would only feed the flames of desire.

So it's a week or two, the little voice said with a shrug. *Until he finds someone else.*

Which pretty much summarized the entire problem. Macey pulled herself together and tried to keep her voice sounding casual. "This celibacy business is killing you, isn't it?"

"It doesn't appear to be doing you any good, either," Derek pointed out. "Your skin is so hot you're practically steaming."

"Oh, you're good—no doubt about that. But that wasn't part of the deal, Derek."

His voice was rough. "So let's make it part of the deal."

If he'd slugged her she couldn't have been more taken aback. "What?"

"Let's make it real. Just leave things the way they are."

Real? Macey felt every muscle in her body contract as if it was about to go into spasm. "You mean..." Her voice cracked and she had to start over. "Surely you don't mean to suggest we get married."

Just saying the words made her ache—because asking him to deny it was too close to admitting what she wanted.

"Why not?" Derek kissed her temple, her eyelid, her cheekbone. "We've done all right together so far."

And, she could almost hear him thinking, *if we're anywhere near as good in bed as it feels like we could be...*

"Look," he said, and brushed her hair back from her forehead with his lips. "I understand that you have this thing about getting married again. But this wouldn't really be like being married."

"It wouldn't?" Macey asked carefully.

"It's just a nice little affair, really. Yes, we'd have to go through the legal paperwork to satisfy everybody, but when it came right down to it—"

When it came right down to it, Macey thought, it was like being dunked in ice water.

Still....

All she had to do was say yes—and she would have what she wanted most. She would have Derek—forever. Everybody would be happy...at least more or less. Enid seemed to have warmed to the idea. Clara would be thrilled. The board of directors would be appeased. Derek would be pleased to have the whole thing settled. Even her boss would be delighted at how things had turned out and the effect it could potentially have on the temp agency.

And Macey would be ecstatic....

No, she admitted. She wouldn't be ecstatic. She wouldn't even be content for long. Unless he loved her in return, there would always be a basic inequality between them, and it would ultimately lead to insecurity, and unhappiness, and resentment.

She couldn't be satisfied with half a loaf, but that was all she would have if she married Derek. A halfway husband. A halfway marriage.

She didn't move. "So you're thinking what the hell, you have to marry somebody," she said. "Why shouldn't it be me?"

It was apparent that Derek heard the irony in her voice, for he drew a deep breath that was almost a gasp and abruptly let go of her. "I didn't say—"

"No, you didn't say it quite that way," Macey agreed. She moved away and leaned against the counter next to the dishwasher. "But it's pretty obvious what you were thinking. What happened to the idea of a new picture for the baby food jars? Had you given up that notion, or were you thinking this nice little affair would actually produce a baby?"

Derek's jaw tightened.

"And if that's the case, then exactly what is the difference between a nice little affair and a marriage? Do you intend to define it according to what's convenient for you at the moment?" She folded her arms across her chest. "No, Derek. I'm not interested."

The expression in his eyes, she thought, was a strange mixture of fascination and consternation. Too late Macey wondered if the tone of her voice had roused him to suspicion about exactly why she'd sounded sharp, almost strident.

Distract him. Try to make a joke of it.

The dishwasher went suddenly silent and then just as abruptly roared to life again, almost scaring the life out of her. But after Macey had absorbed the jolt, she welcomed the diversion. She forced a laugh. "Admit it, Derek. You're only asking me to stay because you don't want to be left with the rest of the dishes to take care of in the morning." It was lame, and she conceded the point. But perhaps it would be enough to convince him that she meant what she'd said—and absolutely nothing more.

He was very quiet for a moment. "I'll drive you home."

"I think I'd rather take a cab."

"Don't be absurd, Macey. You've made yourself clear, and I'm not about to lose my self-control. Get your coat."

She was glad he wasn't going to make a fuss about it. Very glad.

Though she thought she might have to keep on telling herself that for a while before she actually believed it.

The directors' meetings alternated between McConnell Enterprises' many locations, so it had been well over a year since all the directors had been gathered at headquarters. On Monday morning, Derek gave them all a tour of the newest production line, which was currently building bright-colored, kid-size bookcases and bins from pellets of recycled plastic, and he patiently answered questions about new products and marketing and sales for more than an hour.

Then they had a buffet lunch at the country club followed by eighteen holes of golf, and Derek had no sooner hit a long drive off the first tee than he found himself wishing he was back in the plant. At least there, the questions had been clear and direct—and he'd known the answers.

On the golf course everything was less explicit. Nobody came straight out and asked when his wedding would take place, but there were hints and allusions and references aplenty.

He hadn't anticipated that the subject would be of such overwhelming interest to a bunch of middle-aged men. And though he'd been perfectly prepared to deal with generalities, he was completely taken off guard by the jokes. Jokes about weddings, jokes about newlyweds, jokes about babies. Funny stories, foolish stories, tasteless stories.

But all of them had one thing in common—an undercurrent of approval. They liked Macey. And tomorrow, when they voted to make him CEO, and asked exactly when he planned to marry Macey...

Derek shot his worst round in a year, made excuses that sounded lame even to him in order to escape the shot-by-shot postmortem in the bar, and sat in his car stalled in rush-hour traffic trying to figure out what to do. All his options seemed to circle around and around and come inevitably back to the center, like water swirling 'round a basin before it trickled down the drain.

Which—at the moment—was a pretty apt description of the situation he was caught in.

It was Clara who answered the door, and Derek, unsure of what Macey might have told her, braced himself, because he half expected to be told to go away. But Clara merely eyed the long white box he carried and said, in the same friendly manner she'd always used toward him, that Macey wasn't home from work yet.

"I thought she made it a point not to work evenings and weekends," Derek said, before he stopped to think.

"She did—until she met you," Clara said crisply. "Now she's having some trouble keeping up. Come on in and I'll make you a cup of tea."

A stiff Scotch on the rocks sounded more inviting, but Derek wasn't about to turn Clara down. At least he was inside the door, and he suspected that was farther than he'd have gotten if Macey had been at home to greet him.

He started to follow Clara to the kitchen, but she waved him to a seat on the couch. "I'm cleaning out cupboards," she said. "There's no place even to lean."

He was too restless to sit, so he wandered around the living room instead.

He hadn't spent much time in Macey's living room.

Mostly he'd just walked through it to get to the kitchen—except for the night he'd first kissed her, and on that occasion the only part of the decor he'd been interested in had been Macey herself.

The room was comfortable rather than elegant, with an odd mixture of furniture—ranging from a Mission-style sofa table to a Victorian velvet side chair—that somehow managed to look as if it belonged together. On the sofa table and above it on the wall was a lineup of picture frames. Idly, he glanced at them, and then took a closer look.

There were a few pictures of Macey—one a formal pose in a wedding gown, another a snapshot which included a thin, sickly looking young man.

The husband, he deduced. What was his name? He knew he'd heard it, but he couldn't remember.

The rest of the photos were of the young man alone, but there was another difference as well—he was lively, healthy, smiling. With a tennis racquet, in a business suit, leaning against a classic Corvette. It was too bad that Macey had no doubt had to sell the car, too, since it was probably worth twice as much now.

Clara came in quietly, carrying a tray. "That's Jack," she said. "Though I don't guess I need to tell you that."

Derek cleared a spot on the coffee table for the tray she carried. Clara filled a teacup for him, then settled back in the velvet chair with her own cup and looked at him expectantly. "You have a problem," she said finally.

Was it that obvious? *As a matter of fact,* he wanted to say. *I need to convince Macey to marry me. Can you help?*

But of course he couldn't say anything of the sort. Clara thought the engagement was real, so if he admitted it wasn't, he might as well go stand in the middle of the freeway and wait for a truck to hit him.

"Have you and Macey had a quarrel?"

At least that he could answer—though it would still be wise to weigh his words carefully. "Not a quarrel, exactly. More like a disagreement."

"And you've brought flowers." She pointed at the long white box. "That's a good start. I'll excuse myself, of course, as soon as she comes home. Unless there's something else I can do to help—"

"You're not unhappy? About Macey and me, I mean." *You liar,* his conscience whispered. *There is no Macey-and-me.*

"On the contrary. I'm relieved that Macey has finally stopped mourning Jack and picked up her life again." She sipped her tea. "I helped my brother raise Jack. He was like a son to me—the only family I had after his father died—and when I lost Jack too, I took it very hard. But Macey thought her life was over, and that has worried me a great deal. She's far too young to be so solemn about never wanting to marry again."

But Clara didn't know the truth, Derek reminded himself. All the changes she was celebrating existed only because of the part Macey was playing.

"Of course, that was all before she met you." She smiled. "It would take a pretty special guy to convince Macey she'd been wrong."

Yeah, Derek thought. *Trying to change Macey's mind is like requesting the faces on Mt. Rushmore to look the other direction for a while.*

"She's been very brave, through everything," Clara went on. "That's why I'm so happy that she's finally moved on."

But the truth was Macey hadn't moved on, Derek

thought. From his seat on the couch he could see at least twenty photos of Jack. And how many reminders of her marriage—symbols of her vanished happiness—didn't he recognize? The sofa table, perhaps? Or the pillow he was leaning against?

And he had blithely—foolishly—lightly suggested that she marry him. He had made it sound like some kind of prank.

You should be locked up for your own protection, McConnell.

The back door banged, and Derek winced at the sound. "I think she must have seen my car."

Clara nodded and set her cup down. "I'll just go up to my bedroom."

Macey appeared in the doorway between kitchen and living room, her coat still on, her hands dug deep into the pockets.

Derek stood up. "I came to tell you I'm sorry about last night. I didn't handle that very well." He held out the long white box.

Macey didn't take it. She didn't even move from the doorway. "You're on your own tonight, Derek. I have a pile of paperwork to get through."

"You think I came to talk you into going to another party?"

"Isn't that why you're here? You still need a wife."

"Yes," he said very quietly. "I do. Macey—please listen. I made a mess of it last night."

"You certainly did."

Somehow, that quiet statement gave him hope. He'd messed it up, yes—but surely he could still fix it. "Will you think about what I asked you? I don't want to push you—but I really need you to consider it."

"I suppose that means the board is pressuring you for a wedding date."

He tried to smile. "The trouble is, you did too good a job with that dinner party last night."

She moved finally, but only to take off her coat and drape it across Clara's chair. "So your being stuck is *my* fault?"

"No. Of course not. Please, Macey—I've got myself in a hole."

"What's new about that? Anyone with half a brain could have seen it coming. You deserve it."

"The formal vote is tomorrow. But before they offer me the job, they're going to want to know my plans."

"So what are your plans, Derek?"

He said, very quietly, "I want you to marry me."

The words seemed to echo around her. For a moment, Macey let herself feel, and think, and hope, that it was real. That he meant what he'd said. That he truly wanted not just to get married, but to marry her.

Then she sighed and said, "Give me one reason why I should find that proposition any more inviting than I did last night."

Please, a little voice deep inside her whispered. *If you can't tell me you love me, that's all right. If you can just tell me you care a little…*

"I know you had a difficult time, with Jack's illness and the bills and everything," he said softly.

"You have no idea."

"It wouldn't be like that again. I can make it easy for you."

She said slowly, "So this is about money? That's what you're offering?"

"You're twisting things, Macey. I desperately need you."

She half turned toward him, afraid to believe what she'd heard.

"Last night I was cocky and rude, and I made you angry. It wasn't very respectful of me to joke about making it an affair. So—you set the rules, Macey. Our marriage will be whatever you want. Any conditions you set, I'll agree to."

She let the silence stretch out, waiting and hoping. But there was nothing more.

"Why so flexible all of a sudden?" she asked finally. "Because now that the board's actually met me, only I will satisfy them?" She saw the answer flicker in his eyes, and if he'd stabbed her it couldn't have hurt worse. "Well, you're just going to have to deal with that—without my help."

"Macey, please—"

She wheeled to face him. "No. I will not marry you. So what's your next plan? Because if you're thinking of asking me to pick up where we left off and keep looking for some willing guinea pig, you can think of something else. I should have called a halt to this childish stunt a long time ago. In fact, I should never have agreed to get involved in the first place. But no more, Derek. I am not going to be a part of it anymore, watching you cheat and lie and manipulate the system to get what you want, no matter what it costs other people. I'm done with this—and I'm done with you."

The sudden attack had shocked him into silence, that was obvious. The color had drained from his face, but he wasn't just pale—his skin actually seemed to have turned a sickly shade of gray.

Good, Macey thought. At least she'd managed to stun

him back to reality. Obviously he was so used to getting his way that he seemed to think it was his right—but she'd managed to clear up that misapprehension, and none too soon. He looked as if he'd never been told *no* so sternly in his life.

"If you're quite finished with your analysis of my character," he said, "then consider yourself relieved of duty."

Macey hadn't thought it was possible for her to feel angrier, but that did it. "You can't fire me, because I've already quit!"

"Call it whatever you wish." Derek's voice was quiet. "I'll take it from here." He closed the door behind him with a soft click which was brutally final.

Macey stood in the center of the room for a couple of minutes, listening to the silence. Then she picked up the long white box and carried it to the kitchen to put it in the garbage.

CHAPTER TEN

MACEY dumped the box on top of a cantaloupe rind and a heap of coffee grounds and squashed it down so the wastebasket would still fit under the sink. Clara walked in just as Macey was pushing it back into place.

"What kind of flowers did Derek bring you?" she asked brightly.

"I don't know."

Clara's forehead wrinkled. "But you just put the box in the garbage."

"Yes—I did. I have a headache, Clara. If you'll excuse me, I'm going to spend the evening in my room." Macey thought Clara might argue, or ask for explanations. But the old woman didn't say another word.

Macey carried her stack of folders upstairs with her, but she didn't turn the lights on in her bedroom. She hadn't been exaggerating the headache, and the very idea of bright light and fine print made the pain throb even worse. She lay down on the bed and stared at the ceiling.

She had done the only thing she could.

Looking back on the discussion, she thought that it might perhaps have been wiser not to go into quite so much detail about what she saw as Derek's shortcomings. But at that moment it had appeared that nothing less would have convinced him that she meant what she said. In any case, it was done now.

It was all done. Over. Finished.

Until tonight, she had still felt a glimmer of hope. Even though she had told herself it was impossible Derek could care about her the way she cared about him, somewhere deep inside she had still cherished the possibility. Even while she denied it, she had dreamed. But tonight that illusion had flickered like a guttering candle and finally gone out.

She felt empty.

For so long, she had been only half alive. Then, despite herself, Derek had awakened her once more—only to end up by proving she'd been right in the first place. Right to depend only on herself. Right not to trust. Right not to take the chance of being abandoned again.

She didn't blame him exactly, for heaven knew he hadn't done it on purpose. He hadn't led her on, or made promises. In fact, he'd been brutally honest from the start about his intentions. It was Macey's own fault that she had dismissed the facts and looked instead at the fantasy figure she'd created.

Despite everything he'd said and done, she had believed that deep down inside he was a romantic. She had concluded that he was unable to settle on a logical choice for a wife because the emotional side of him longed to find the one special woman who could make his life complete. And she'd foolishly allowed herself to hope that she might be that woman.

She'd been wrong. Instead of being a starry-eyed dreamer in search of love, he was a perfectionist and a fussbudget. No wonder he'd been finding fault with every woman who crossed his path—he was impossible to please.

She wondered what he'd do now. Draw a name out of a hat? Pity the poor woman who came up the loser in that lottery.

Not that it would make any difference to Macey. Most

likely, she'd never even know whether it was Liz he married, or Emily, or Rita, or Constance...

As her eyes grew accustomed to the dim glow which filtered through the curtains from the streetlights outside, Macey noticed the dress she had worn for the dinner party. It was hanging on the back of the closet door, waiting to go to the cleaner's.

What a perfectly apt, melancholy, heart-breaking shade of red it was, the color they called bittersweet....

It hurt too much to think about, but she didn't have the energy to get up and put the dress out of sight. She looked around her bedroom instead, seeking something else to concentrate on.

When she'd first moved into Clara's guest room, she'd been too numb to think about redecorating it as her own. Then she'd been too busy, too concerned with her job and with Clara's illness. But now, with her finances finally straightened out and Clara feeling better, she might consider finding an apartment for herself. Somewhere she could make into a home just for her.

For it was darned sure she was going to be on her own.

Derek had turned his desk chair to the window and was staring out. In the distance, under a gloomy October sky that promised rain later in the day, he could see the stainless-steel Gateway Arch looming over downtown St. Louis. Today, with no brilliant sunshine to reflect, it looked as dull as a worn-out mirror. Just about the same way he felt, now that he'd finished sorting through all his options and he'd come to a decision.

He turned his head at a tap on the office door, and George McConnell came in. "The board's all here," he said. "They're in the conference room chowing down doughnuts and coffee."

"I'll be there when the meeting starts."

"You'd better come in now and do a little last-minute politicking."

"In a minute."

"Derek, don't count on having this thing won." George laid a hand on Derek's shoulder. "I get the feeling there are still some doubts—they just haven't been expressed openly. If you're acting aloof, you'll just give those guys a reason to wonder about you."

He was right, Derek knew. He reached up and put his hand on top of his father's. "I understand, Dad. Thanks."

George wrinkled his brows as if he'd like to ask for an explanation, but he didn't press. He closed the door behind him.

Derek sat still a little longer, thinking. Then he stood up, took a deep breath and let it out, and put on the suit jacket he'd discarded earlier. He stopped beside his secretary's desk to sign a couple of letters, knowing full well that he was purposely dawdling. But finally there were no more excuses for delaying.

The board members were settling themselves at the long conference table when he came in. There were still trays of doughnuts, but he shook his head when his father gestured him in that direction. Instead he took his regular seat near the foot of the table, where he could see the row of shelves full of their products—including the junior carpentry set which contained the hammer Macey had used to threaten him.

The chairman called the meeting to order, and Derek let his mind wander while they proceeded through the usual formalities. Then the chairman said, "The next order of business is to decide the procedure the board will follow in hiring a new chief executive officer." He looked over his half-glasses at Derek. "You're an *ex officio* member of this board, so we can't require you to excuse yourself from this discussion. However—''

Derek stood up. ''In order to allow a frank and open discussion, I will of course leave the room. But first, gentlemen, I have an announcement to make.''

Macey usually enjoyed talking to Peterson Temp's workers when they came back to the office after completing a job, especially when it had been the worker's first assignment. The debriefing process was usually enlightening, frequently making it easier in the future to match workers with the company. And most of the time, it was just plain fun to listen to a worker who had successfully completed an assignment—especially one like Ellen, who had gone out with so many doubts about herself and returned with so much more confidence that she hardly seemed like the same person.

Nevertheless, today Macey was having trouble concentrating. It had been just thirty-six hours since Derek had walked out of the town house, and Macey had been suffering pangs of regret for at least thirty-five of them.

She knew she had made the only decision she could. She knew that accepting his proposal would have taken a horrible toll on her self-esteem, and that it was a price she could not afford to pay.

Nevertheless, part of her wished that she had said yes instead of no.

Perhaps, whispered a wistful little voice in the back of her mind, *just perhaps he would have learned to love you, if you had only given him—and yourself—the opportunity.*

''Not a chance,'' she said firmly. That was only wishful thinking, and it would lead her precisely nowhere.

Ellen looked startled. ''Excuse me? But—why won't you let me try a longer assignment next time?''

Macey tried to pull herself together. "Ellen, I'm sorry. I was...my mind had drifted. You were saying...?"

She had awakened at dawn that morning to the sound of the garbage truck pulling away from the house, and that was when the twinges of regret had become sharp, shooting anguish—for the garbage collectors were taking away the last thing Derek had given her.

Until the moment when the garbage truck roared away down the street, she'd almost made herself forget about the long white box. She'd kept herself too busy to think. It was only when it was too late to retrieve it that she realized what she'd done.

She didn't even know for sure what the box had contained. Flowers, Clara had said—and she had probably guessed right.

Of course, Macey reminded herself, even if she had kept them, flowers would be gone in a matter of days, wilted and faded and musty. Perhaps it was better to cherish the idea of a dozen roses than to have tried to hold on to the reality.

And perhaps it hadn't been a dozen roses at all, but something more along the lines of stinkweed....

No, that was what he'd be likely to send her now—if he felt some overwhelming need to send her anything at all. Which he wouldn't, of course. There was no reason for him to be in contact ever again.

And no reason for her to feel as if the world had jolted to a halt because Derek McConnell wasn't coming around anymore.

Mechanically, she finished Ellen's assessment. "You can check with Louise about another assignment," Macey told her. "After two or three—or whenever you're comfortable—you won't need to come in to the office to report each time. Then you'll just phone in on the last day of a job, and Louise will tell you about the next one.''

When Ellen opened Macey's office door, Robert was just raising his hand to knock. ''Oh, good, you're free,'' he told Macey. ''Terrific news—but why hadn't you told me?''

''News?'' she asked warily. ''I'm not sure what you mean.''

''Oh, come on, Macey. About Derek.''

It would be just her luck, Macey thought, if after she'd spent an entire week doing a mental balancing act every minute of every day, Robert was just now hearing the rumor of her engagement. For a solid week it seemed she'd thought of nothing else—trying to keep straight who knew, who had yet to be convinced, and who was to be kept in the dark.

She had deliberately not mentioned it to anyone at Peterson Temps. She had deliberately not worn Derek's ring anywhere near the office, just so she wouldn't have to answer questions. But now—two days after her fake engagement was over—her boss had finally heard about it.

It was enough to make a woman shriek.

And even if that wasn't enough to cause hysteria, she realized, the very thought of the ring was.

She hadn't been wearing the ring on the night Derek had actually proposed—the night she'd turned him down for the final time. She had just come from work when she'd found him waiting for her, and the ring had been safely tucked away in the bottom of an old purse in her closet.

Where it was still lying, forgotten—until this moment—in the dark.

* * *

Louise returned from her lunch break with a sandwich for Macey, who took it into the computer lab just for a change of scenery. While she ate, she idly paged through a newspaper that someone had left lying there, and in the business section she saw what Robert had been talking about this morning. It hadn't been her pseudo engagement he'd been reacting to, she realized. It was the announcement that the board of directors of McConnell Enterprises had named their next CEO.

Derek had gotten the job.

It seemed he was a magician of note after all, Macey thought, if he could pull that rabbit out of the hat. She wondered how he'd managed to make her vanish so neatly that the board seemed to have entirely forgotten her existence. Smoke and mirrors? Or had he used the old saw-the-girl-in-half trick?

And who had he put in her place?

As if it ever was your place, she mocked herself.

The news complicated matters for Macey, however, because she still had to return his ring. It wasn't the kind of thing she felt like trusting to a messenger, yet she certainly didn't want to do it herself. Not only didn't she want to face him, but having her turn up in person was probably the last thing Derek wanted, too.

Since she had no idea what he'd told the board—or even his parents—about the breakup of his supposed engagement, she could hardly pay a call at his office. If, for instance, he'd told them that she'd abruptly moved to Paris, or that she'd broken both legs and landed in the hospital in traction, or that she'd been arrested and thrown in jail because she'd been blackmailing him into pretending they were engaged....

No. No matter how he'd explained the sudden breakup,

she didn't want to face him in public. But she *really* didn't want to seek him out in private.

Her entire body hurt at the very idea.

Ted the doorman looked from Macey to the pizza box and back. "Mr. McConnell didn't say anything about you coming by."

"I'm not surprised. He wasn't expecting me." She thought she saw him sniff, and she tried to unobtrusively waft the scent of pepperoni in his direction. "Is he at home?"

Ted shook his head. "He went out a little while ago. Didn't say where he was going. Maybe to his mother's for dinner, because she was here earlier."

A family dinner with the new fiancée, no doubt. I wish the poor woman good luck.

"Oh." Macey tried to look disappointed. "Then he won't be back for hours, I suppose." She set the pizza box down on the doorman's stand, next to Ted's elbow.

There was no doubt about it this time; he inhaled deeply.

"Look," she said, lowering her voice. "I just wanted to drop off something for him. A silly little thing."

"Leave it with me and I'll give it to him the minute he comes in."

Oops. This wasn't going at all the direction she'd hoped. "It wouldn't be the same, Ted. Exactly where I leave it is as much a part of the message as the thing itself. It's silly, but you know how it goes. You have a key to his loft, don't you? You must have. Look, you can stand right outside the door. One minute, that's all it'll take."

"Yeah," he muttered, "like any woman on earth actually knows how long one minute is. Twenty would probably be more like it. This thing you're leaving isn't full of explosives, is it?"

He was weakening. "Do I have reason to want to blow him up?" Macey opened the small bag she was carrying. "Look. It's completely innocent."

Ted took the small stuffed skunk she handed him, turned it upside down, squeezed it, sniffed it, and handed it back. "Okay," he said finally. "I'll let you in, and you lock the door on your way out. I'm not standing there waiting for you."

Even better than I hoped. "Deal," Macey said. "You don't mind if I leave this pizza with you, do you? I'm not nearly as hungry as I thought I was."

Ted rolled his eyes and didn't answer.

He let her into the loft and pulled the door closed behind her. As the latch clicked, Macey stood just inside the door for a long moment and looked around.

The table and chairs they'd rented for the dinner party were gone. Enid's china was either stashed away in a closet, or she'd taken it home. The couch had been pulled back into place in solitary splendor. The kitchen once more looked as if it had never been used. The quiet was intense.

She reached into her pocket and pulled out the engagement ring and a length of white ribbon. She tied the ribbon in a floppy bow around the neck of the stuffed skunk, tied the ring to the ribbon, and tried to decide where to leave it so he'd be sure to see it. The kitchen counter? The mantel? Not so good if he brought the fiancée home with him.

On his pillow?

Macey had to bite back a smile at the idea of the new fiancée discovering a stuffed skunk wearing an engagement ring on Derek's pillow. Now that was truly an inspired idea.

Still, even though she strongly disapproved of what he was doing, Macey was determined not to deliberately cause trouble. It was going to be difficult enough for this couple to make things work without any help from outside to make things worse.

The coffee table, she decided, was the least personal, least intrusive spot, and yet—since the couch was the only spot to sit—he'd be bound to see it almost as soon as he came home.

She walked across the room and stopped dead in the center of the room. On the coffee table, as if it had been carelessly tossed there, was a long white box.

A long white box, still taped shut, stained brown and orange all along one end. Stained by coffee and cantaloupe from when she'd shoved it into the wastebasket in Clara's town house.

She reached out a hand and then drew it back as if the box might burn her.

It's yours, part of her whispered. *He gave it to you.*

But you threw it away, her conscience replied. *So even if it did belong to you once, it doesn't anymore.*

A key clicked in the lock. Macey's heart jolted violently and then settled back into place. *It's Ted,* she thought. He must have come upstairs to remind her that her one minute was long gone.

The door swung open and Derek came in. He tossed his car keys on the kitchen island, stripped off his leather jacket, and crossed the living room toward her.

He looked very tall, very strong, very powerful—and not at all startled to see her.

"Ted told me you went out for the evening," she said, feeling as foolish as she must sound.

"I did go out. He called to tell me I had a visitor, so of course like a good host I came straight home."

She was incensed. "He called you? That no-good little—"

"You of all people shouldn't be surprised, Macey. I took your advice after my mother walked in on us that day."

She should have expected it. "You increased his bribe?"

Derek nodded. "When it comes to buying loyalty, a pepperoni pizza isn't even in the same galaxy. So what brings you here?"

She picked up the little skunk and held it out.

His eyebrows raised. "Another comment on my character?"

"No! I meant... I felt bad about forgetting to return your ring. It's..." She fumbled with the ribbon, loosened the knot, and released the ring. "Here. I meant it to say that I felt like a skunk for not giving it back. I just forgot." She was babbling, but she couldn't stop herself.

"You forgot?"

"Well, it wasn't like I meant to keep it," she said defensively. "The skunk was supposed to be funny."

He didn't smile. And he didn't seem to notice that she was holding the ring out to him.

The metal band felt so hot she couldn't hold it any longer. She reached for his hand, turned it, and dropped the ring into his palm. "I'm sorry. I only meant to return the ring in a way that wouldn't hurt either of us. I'll go away now."

His fingers tightened on hers for an instant—or was it only her imagination?—and then let her hand slip away.

Slowly she walked across the room. But she couldn't just leave; she had to know. "Derek? What's in the box?"

For a moment she thought he wasn't going to answer at all. "You had your chance to find out, Macey."

"Yeah," she said softly. "I really blew it, didn't I?" She was putting her hand on the doorknob when he turned to face her.

"I got the job," he said abruptly.

"I know. I saw it in the newspaper." She tried to put a little liveliness into her voice. "Sorry I forgot to congratulate you—I was a little preoccupied when you first came in."

"You were wondering how the box got here," he said. "Because the last time you saw it, it was in a wastebasket."

There was no point in trying to hide the facts. "Well—yes. I did wonder. Not that it's any of my business."

"Clara rescued it from the garbage and gave it to my mother today at their porcelain painting class."

"Your mother's taking porcelain painting too?"

"And Mom brought it by on her way home."

"But neither of them opened it? That's next door to superhuman."

He moved a little closer. "You didn't open it, either."

"That was different." Uneasily, she fumbled for a change of subject. "When's the wedding, Derek? And who's the lucky woman? Jennifer? She's the only one I can think of who could have won such quick approval from—"

"There isn't going to be a wedding."

Macey frowned. "But—you got the job. How— You're not still trying to convince them that *I'm*—"

"No." His voice was unusually deep. "I thought over what you'd said, and what I was trying to do. And in the end I told them the truth—that there isn't going to be a wedding."

"You confessed to the board that you'd made it all up? And they hired you anyway?" Macey shook her head in disbelief. "Well, if that isn't a kick in the pants. All that work, all that effort, all those damned parties we went to, for nothing?"

"It wasn't quite that smooth or easy. I admitted that I had tried to fix the odds, that I had every intention of marrying just to get the job and that I didn't much care who I married." His voice had softened until she had to lean closer to hear clearly. "And I told them that when it came right down to it, I couldn't go through with the plan."

She had thought she'd rooted out every last fragment of hope, but a few leftovers must have been crouching in the back corners of her mind, for now they crept forward into the light. "Why?" She could manage nothing more than a whisper.

"Because it would have been cheating—and in the end nobody would have been happy. Not the board, not the company, not me, and certainly not the woman I had married for all the wrong reasons."

But not because of you, Macey. The feeble fragment of hope retreated into the darkness.

"I told them they had to make a choice," Derek went on.

"To give you the job anyway, or—" She couldn't think of an alternative. "What?"

He shook his head. "No. I told them I would stay on at McConnell Enterprises if they wanted to keep me in my current job. Or if they'd rather, I would leave when the new CEO came on board, so he'd have a free hand."

Macey was aghast. "Derek, that's got to be the world's biggest bluff. What if they hadn't taken you seriously?"

"I wasn't bluffing, Macey." He put a fingertip under her chin and nudged her jaw back into place.

"You'd have given up your job? Left your father's company?"

"Yes—I would have." He looked down at the ring, still gleaming in his palm, and set it carefully on the kitchen island next to his car keys.

He was treating it with such care because it was valuable, Macey told herself. Not because it was important to him in any other way. He probably couldn't wait to take it back to the jeweler so he could be rid of it—and the bill.

She had to get away. But her feet seemed to be glued to the floor.

"You can open the box if you want, Macey."

She was afraid to open it. Afraid to see what was inside. But if she refused, then she had no excuse to stay longer. And though part of her yearned to go, the other part couldn't bear to leave.

She worked a fingernail under the edge of the tape to loosen it, and the top of the box tore as the flap finally came loose.

Inside, nested in layers of tissue paper, was the Lalique vase he had considered buying for his mother, until Macey had told him it wouldn't be the right gift for Enid. The one Macey had admired for herself.

"It's beautiful," she whispered. But he had said she could open the box, not that it was hers. Her fingertips seemed to cling to the cool glass, and it took effort to let it slide back into the box. "Thank you for letting me see it." She held the box out to him.

He didn't move to take it. "But you already have a thousand vases, right?"

"Not like this one," she said softly. *Nothing could be like this one—because you chose it for me.*

"When Mom brought it back, I went out to find you. That's what I was doing when Ted phoned."

Macey frowned. "You were looking for me? Why?"

"To make you accept the vase. Only I was in such a hurry I forgot to take the vase with me."

"That doesn't make any sense."

"Neither does anything else I've done lately." He sounded almost sad. "What you said to me that night made me think, Macey."

"It was intended to," she said dryly.

"You were right. I was trying to manipulate the system. I thought I'd figured out a way to play the game without following the rules. And it wasn't until that night, when you made me step back and look at the mess I'd created, that I realized I'd gotten myself caught in a snare, and you were the only answer."

She took a step toward the door. "There's really no point in going over this ground again, Derek. Now that you have your job settled—"

"This has nothing to do with my job. And I'm not finished. It was only when you turned me down that I realized what was happening. Though I suppose I should have known the day you told me your husband had died."

"You should have known what?" she asked carefully.

"Because when you said that, it was like you'd hit me right in the gut with a baseball bat. I thought at the time that I felt bad because of what I'd just been saying to you—giving you a hard time about not telling me, stuff like that."

"It *was* pretty tasteless of you."

"Don't rub it in. It was only later—a long time later—

when I realized that the reason I felt so bad was that I felt guilty about feeling good.''

Macey put her fingertips to her temples. ''I don't begin to understand what you're talking about.''

''I wasn't happy that he was dead. But I sure was pleased to find out that you were free after all.''

''So I could still lend you a hand. What's new about—''

''No,'' he said. ''Though that's what I thought at the time. The whole idea of double dating wasn't to provide cover while I got to know those six women you'd chosen. It was only an excuse to see you.''

She was suddenly breathless with hope—and with fear that the sudden stirring of optimism would once more be crushed into dust.

''You'd done what I asked—you'd given me the list of finalists. Your job was finished. But I didn't want to let go of you. That's why I leaped on the excuse to announce that you were my fiancée—because I wanted you to be. And that's why I told the board that there won't be a wedding. Because only you will do.'' He glanced at her and then looked away again. ''Macey, I know you said you'd never get married again. And I know I could never be what Jack was to you. But—''

Macey said quietly, ''I wouldn't want you to try.''

He took a deep breath, and released it slowly. It sounded harsh in the quiet loft. ''Well, that's pretty plain. I won't bring it up again.'' He moved to open the door for her.

Macey stayed rooted to the spot. ''When Jack first got sick—before we knew how serious it was—I was almost glad. It explained so much, you see. If he was ill, that's why he'd been so tired and so short-tempered. That was why he didn't seem to want to go anywhere or to do anything with me. That was why he didn't seem to find me attractive anymore."

Derek stopped with his hand on the doorknob. "He had a brain tumor, right? And it messed up his thinking?"

She smiled a little. "No brain tumor. He had a girlfriend—but she had pretty much the same effect on the thinking. I found out about her the first time he was in the hospital. I'd gone home to rest, couldn't sleep, went back to his room. And there she was."

Derek swore under his breath.

"It was the next day the doctors told us that he had only a few months to live."

"And then he swore he'd give her up and begged you not to leave him?"

"No, he didn't," Macey said coolly. "He made it quite clear that we were both welcome at his bedside, and if either of us objected to sharing, that was our problem, not his. And since the girlfriend—"

"You mean The Tumor?"

"That's a good name for her. Since The Tumor had known about me all along, she was quite content to share. Especially the parts that weren't much fun."

"You actually stayed with him after that?"

"You're thinking I should have created a scene and walked out? Maybe I should have. But I was too shocked to do anything. One week I was reasonably happy, just bumping along, telling myself that every marriage has its problems from time to time. And then the next week my husband was dying and my marriage was dead. Besides, there was Clara. She was losing her favorite nephew—the only family she had left."

"She told me once that she helped raise him."

Macey nodded. "I couldn't bring myself to destroy her image of him."

"It wouldn't have been your fault. It was his."

"Yes—and perhaps I would have told her sooner or later. But the few months the doctors expected him to have, turned out to be only a couple of weeks instead. So I thought, why tear Clara up? He was gone. Why not let her keep her vision of him as this wonderful young man?"

"The pictures," Derek said suddenly. "Why are the pictures all over your house?"

"They're Clara's. It's her town house—I moved in after he died."

"Oh, yes—you told me that once. So that's why you sold your engagement ring, and the china. You didn't want the reminders."

"They weren't exactly sentimental souvenirs—but I truly did need the money."

"And his Corvette—"

She shook her head. "I didn't sell the car. I didn't find out till after he died that he'd signed it over to The Tumor just a few days before."

"She got the car, and you got the bills?"

"Sharing is such a wonderful thing," she said lightly.

"No wonder you said there's nothing on earth that could make you want to get married again."

Except you—if you want me, Derek. But she couldn't say it.

"I don't blame you," he said. "After something like that…" His fist clenched. "But dammit, Macey, I'm not Jack."

She managed to say, "I think you've made that abundantly clear."

"Good. We've got that much settled. I can't quit now. I *won't* quit now. I am not going away, and I'm not taking no for an answer."

"Wait a minute. Are you proposing again?"

"Yes. Well, not exactly."

Macey's head was spinning.

"I won't push you, Macey. But there's one thing we need to get straight. Last time I told you that you could set the terms—that I would agree to any conditions you wanted to put on our marriage. But now..." He took a deep breath. "I'm willing to wait till you're ready. I'm willing to prove myself, however you think I can do that. But when you marry me, it needs to be with your whole heart. No games. No conditions."

She felt as if she was melting inside. "*When* I marry you? Not *if?*"

"When," he said firmly. "Because I won't let myself believe anything else."

She put her hands against his chest, as tentatively as if she'd never touched him before. As if he might fade away under her touch. "There's nothing you need to prove, Derek."

He looked at her for a long moment, and then pulled her close and kissed her as if he would never stop. There was nothing teasing about this caress, nothing playful. He was almost solemn, and every fiber of Macey's body responded in trust.

"I couldn't marry you then," she said finally, breathlessly. "Not when it was only for show. I was a surplus wife once, Derek—handy to have, convenient, but not exactly necessary. I couldn't live like that again. I couldn't bear it."

"You are anything but convenient," he said, punctuating his words with kisses. "You're not handy, you're a nuisance. You're a thorn in my side. You're the voice of conscience and reason and doom. And you're absolutely necessary, if I'm ever going to be happy. You'll marry me?"

"I don't play golf," she pointed out. "I wear funky earrings. And I have a frivolous name that I'm not about to change."

"Macey McConnell," he said thoughtfully. "It has a nice ring to it. I'll get used to the earrings, and I'm not all that wild about golf myself. Answer me, Macey."

"Maybe I'd better flip a coin," she said, "just to test how I feel."

He held her a few inches away. "I haven't got a quarter on me. But I have a better idea. If you want to know how you feel, I'll kiss you till you figure it out."

"Just try it and see what happens," she threatened—and then she laughed and threw her arms around his neck, and surrendered all control.

**On sale
2nd November 2007**

MILLS & BOON
BY REQUEST
3
NOVELS ONLY
£4.99

In November 2007 Mills & Boon present two bestselling collections, each featuring three wonderful romances by three of your favourite authors...

Pregnant Proposals

Featuring

His Pregnancy Ultimatum by Helen Bianchin
Finn's Pregnant Bride by Sharon Kendrick
Pregnancy of Convenience by Sandra Field

Available at WHSmith, Tesco, ASDA, and all good bookshops
www.millsandboon.co.uk

MILLS & BOON
Romance

Pure romance, pure emotion

Needed: Her Mr Right
Barbara Hannay

Outback Boss, City Bride
Jessica Hart

4 brand-new titles each month

Available on the first Friday of every month
from WHSmith, ASDA, Tesco
and all good bookshops
www.millsandboon.co.uk

GEN/02/RTL11

New York Times bestselling author

DIANA PALMER

is coming to

MILLS & BOON
Romance

Pure romance, pure emotion

Curl up and relax with her brand new *Long, Tall Texans* story

Winter Roses

Watch the sparks fly in this vibrant, compelling romance as gorgeous, irresistible rancher Stuart York meets his match in innocent but feisty Ivy Conley…

"Nobody tops Diana Palmer when it comes to delivering pure, undiluted romance. I love her stories."
—*New York Times* bestselling author Jayne Ann Krentz

On sale 2nd November 2007

Available at WHSmith, Tesco, ASDA, and all good bookshops

www.millsandboon.co.uk

MILLS & BOON
Special Edition

Life, love and family

6 brand-new titles each month

Available on the third Friday of every month
from WHSmith, ASDA, Tesco
and all good bookshops
www.millsandboon.co.uk

GEN/23/RTL11

MILLS & BOON
Super ROMANCE

Enjoy the drama, explore the emotions, experience the relationships

4 brand-new titles each month

Available on the third Friday of every month
from WHSmith, ASDA, Tesco
and all good bookshops
www.millsandboon.co.uk

GEN/38/RTL11

MILLS & BOON
Desire™ 2-in-1

2 passionate, dramatic love stories in each book

3 brand-new titles to choose from each month

Available on the third Friday of every month
from WHSmith, ASDA, Tesco
and all good bookshops
www.millsandboon.co.uk

GEN/51/RTL11

MILLS & BOON
MEDICAL™

Proudly presents

Brides of Penhally Bay

Featuring Dr Nick Tremayne

A pulse-raising collection of emotional, tempting romances and heart-warming stories — devoted doctors, single fathers, Mediterranean heroes, a Sheikh and his guarded heart, royal scandals and miracle babies...

Book One

CHRISTMAS EVE BABY
by Caroline Anderson

Starting 7th December 2007

A COLLECTION TO TREASURE FOREVER!
One book available every month

MILLS & BOON
MEDICAL

Proudly presents

Brides of Penhally Bay

A pulse-raising collection of emotional, tempting romances and heart-warming stories by bestselling Mills & Boon Medical™ authors.

January 2008
The Italian's New-Year Marriage Wish
by Sarah Morgan

Enjoy some much-needed winter warmth with gorgeous Italian doctor Marcus Avanti.

February 2008
The Doctor's Bride By Sunrise
by Josie Metcalfe

Then join Adam and Maggie on a 24-hour rescue mission where romance begins to blossom as the sun starts to set.

March 2008
The Surgeon's Fatherhood Surprise
by Jennifer Taylor

Single dad Jack Tremayne finds a mother for his little boy – and a bride for himself.

Let us whisk you away to an idyllic Cornish town – a place where hearts are made whole

COLLECT ALL 12 BOOKS!

Available at WHSmith, Tesco, ASDA, and all good bookshops
www.millsandboon.co.uk

MILLS & BOON
MEDICAL

*Pulse-raising romance –
Heart-racing medical drama*

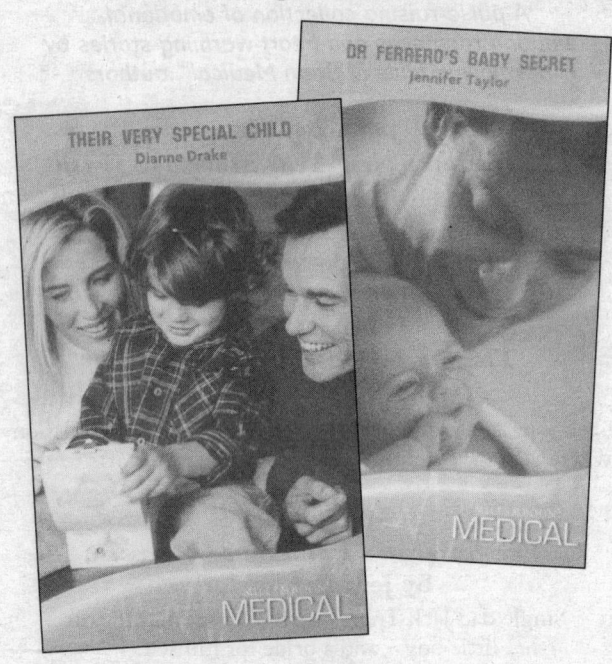

6 brand-new titles each month

Available on the first Friday of every month
from WHSmith, ASDA, Tesco
and all good bookshops
www.millsandboon.co.uk

GEN/03/RTL11